up in the TREEHOUSE

USA TODAY BESTSELLING AUTHOR
K.K. ALLEN

Copyright

K.K. Allen Novels

Up in the Treehouse
Haunted by the past, Chloe and Gavin are forced to come to
terms with all that has transpired to find the peace they deserve.
Except they can't seem to get near each other without combatting
an intense emotional connection that brings them right back to
where it all started... their childhood treehouse.

Under the Bleachers
Fun and flirty Monica Stevens lives for food, fashion, and boys...
in that order. The last thing she wants to take seriously is dating.
When a night of flirty banter with Seattle's hottest NFL quarterback turns passionate, her care-free life could be at risk.

Through the Lens
When Maggie moves to Seattle for a fresh start, she's presented
with an unavoidable obstacle—namely, the cocky chef with a
talent for photography and getting under her skin. Can they learn
to get along for the sake of the ones they love?

Over the Moon

Silver Livingston has spent the past eight years hiding from her past when the NFL God, Kingston Scott, steps off the bus to mentor a football camp for kids. Kingston wants to be anywhere but at Camp Dakota... until he sees her. The intoxicating woman with the silver moon eyes, the reserved smile, and the past she's determined to keep hidden.

Dangerous Hearts (A Stolen Melody, #1)
Lyric Cassidy knows a thing or two about bad boy rock stars with raspy vocals. In fact, her heart was just played by one. So when she takes an assignment as road manager for the world famous rock star, Wolf, she's prepared to take him on, full suit of heart-armor intact.

Destined Hearts (A Stolen Melody, #2)
With stolen dreams, betrayals, and terrifying threats--no one's heart is safe. Not even the ones that may be destined to be together.

British Bachelor
Runaway British Bachelor contestant, Liam Colborn, is on the run from the media. When he gets to Providence to stay with his late brother's best friend, all he wants is a little time to regroup from his time on a failed reality show. That is, until he meets the redheaded bombshell nanny who lives in the pool house.

Waterfall Effect
Lost in the shadows of a tragedy that stripped Aurora of everything she once loved, she's back in the small town of Balsam Grove, ready to face all she's kept locked away for seven years. Or so she thinks.

A Bridge Between Us
With a century-old feud between neighboring families with only a

bridge to separate them, Camila and Ridge find themselves wanting to rewrite the future. It all starts with an innocent friendship and quickly builds to so much more in this epic second chance coming of age romance.

Center of Gravity (Gravity, #1)
Lex was athleticism and grace, precision and passion, and she had a stage presence Theo couldn't tear my eyes from. He wanted her...on his team, in his bed. There was only one problem... He couldn't have both.

Falling From Gravity (Gravity, #1.5)
Amelia was nothing like Tobias had expected. Even after all the years—of living so close to her, of listening to her giggle with his sister in the bedroom next to his—he hadn't given much thought to his sister's best friend, until a secret spring break trip to Big Sur changed everything.

Defying Gravity (Gravity, #2)
The ball is in Amelia's court, but Tobias isn't below stealing—her power, her resolve, her heart. When he wants a second chance to reignite their connection, the answer is simple. They can't. Not unless they defy the rules their dreams were built on and risk everything.

The Trouble With Gravity (Gravity #3)
When Sebastian makes Kai an offer she can't afford to refuse, she learns taking the job will mean facing the tragedy she's worked so hard to shut out. He says she can trust him to keep her safe, but is her heart safe too?

Enchanted Gods
As powerful forces threaten the lives in Apollo Beach, Katrina can't escape the evocative world of mythological enchantment

and evil prophecies that lurk around every corner. If only she wasn't cursed.

Find them all here: www.kkallen.com

up in the TREEHOUSE

Dedicated to the innocence that lives in us all.

PROLOGUE

The best kind of love is one that stems from friendship. One that grows as it's nurtured with patience and kindness, blossoming at just the right time. All it has to do is withstand the forces of nature that threaten to drown it, pluck it, blow it, and burn it until it withers back into its soil. As if it never existed at all.

BRANCH ONE

GRADUATION NIGHT

"SOMEBODY TOLD ME THAT THIS IS THE PLACE WHERE EVERYTHING'S BETTER, EVERYTHING'S SAFE." ~ WALK ON THE OCEAN, TOAD THE WET SPROCKET

Chapter 1

Mistakes (part one)

Chloe

His face twists, resembling an old string of holiday lights most would have given up untangling years ago. It's a messy, broken, and hopeless jumble of old memories . . . one that, for some reason, I can't bring myself to throw out. Just like my relationship with Devon Rhodes.

Devon raises every red flag that exists, yet he could charm the pants off you and make you forget the difference between a red flag and a white one. He's the type of guy who bends and breaks the rules because the rush is more than worth the risk. The one who's always sworn he would never be in a committed relationship because—well, what's the point? The kind of guy—with his million and one problems, his dangerously good looks, and his strength that terrifies me—who somehow chose me. Now he's *my* string of hopeless holiday lights to deal with, but I can't seem to drum up the strength to untangle them again. Or maybe I just don't want to anymore.

Anger rumbles from his chest and his nose flares as he spouts in my direction, "What the hell is this, Chloe?" Yellowed pages of my journal flap through the air with each flick of his wrist, taunting me from across my bedroom.

How did he find that?

Beer sloshes from a blue plastic cup that I know is not his first —or his last. As the liquid splashes on the old wood floors I can already imagine the stale but sour stench I'll be wrinkling my nose to in the morning. It should have been a fun, celebratory night filled with bad dancing, neighbors threatening noise violations, and possibly some skinny-dipping. The drunken mess standing before me is the wrong kind of bad I wanted to experience tonight.

I'm still cloaked in my graduation gown, the rough fabric combing my skin, providing a false sense of security under Devon's heated glare. If only I could tuck my head inside it to avoid another argument. At least the cloth would muffle his words, obscuring his shouts the way tears are threatening to blur my vision. *If only.*

It's no use asking him what he's referring to or why he looks like he wants to throw my journal—and me—across the room. I'm already aware of the passages between the binding he grips with white-tipped knuckles. We've been official for four months, and he somehow feels as if he has the right to invade my thoughts, fears, and dreams. I ignore the fact that his anger might be justified because of what he read and focus on what *he* did wrong.

"You read my journal?" I explode. "Why?" My voice won't stop shaking no matter how hard I try to control it. I know I have to get ahold of myself. Devon can sniff weakness from a mile away, and he will use it to his advantage.

He glowers at me in response, spilling hate with every breath. I might hate myself too for letting it come to this point. His anger has always been a beast, ready to unleash if I make one wrong move, and alcohol only gases his fire. Devon has never hit me, but certain situations have caused me to imagine what a blow would feel like. It wasn't long ago, during one of our bigger arguments, that his fist came close. So close that I felt a rush of air skim my cheek before slamming into the wall. He wasn't aiming for me. I don't think. But I remember squeezing my eyelids together for so long my vision took a terrifying amount of time to return. During my darkened state, I imagined his fist connecting with my jaw, anticipating it like that would somehow lessen the pain when it did come.

Devon is a big guy, an athlete, and six-foot-three—almost a foot taller than me. He steps closer, casting a shadow over me, reminding me of my inferiority. He enjoys this: demonstrating he could hurt me if he wanted to. *I think he wants to.*

The only difference between now and the past is that I've been through this enough, and nothing about him scares me. *Not anymore.* Not even the fact that we're trapped in the same room together. *Alone.* By now, Devon knows I'm not the passive weakling he wants me to be.

Instead of glowering or slamming my lids closed again, I stand taller and meet his furious scowl. If he's going to hit me, I want him to see that I'm undaunted by his threats. "It's a journal, Devon. It's not like I *cheated* on you."

He doesn't know I'm aware of his escapades, but my comment gets his attention. There's a flash of worry in his features before he catches himself and stands taller, puffing out his chest with laughter. I think his laugh hurts more than his fist ever could. He doesn't admit his own deceit—not that I need him to, since I found a pile of empty condom wrappers in the center compartment of his Honda last month. Sure, they could have been from before we dated, but the feeling in my gut told me what my heart didn't want to believe. And honestly, I wouldn't be surprised if he wanted me to find them. Always a hothead, Devon loves a good argument.

He's still steaming when he finally speaks. "Wouldn't that be classic? You won't give it up for me, but you would for *him*."

My face flames with mortification. I've never *given it up* for anyone, which is one of the many reasons we argue. Devon thinks he owns every piece of me because we're dating, always telling me how lucky I should feel to be with him, insisting if I cared for him I should *show* him. No matter the argument, it always ends the same. I say "no" and he casts threats, telling me he'll leave me, cheat on me, anything to get his fill. He hopes these arguments will help me see how badly I want him.

He doesn't know me at all.

"I didn't do anything."

I have no desire to defend myself, not for lack of energy, but because I've run out of reasons to continue trying. It's been a long four months of a relationship that should have never been. The moment romance got involved, everything changed . . . and I mean *everything*. We were better off as friends, but there's no going back to friendship. Not after this. Devon Rhodes can go screw himself and whomever else he wants because he'll never get near me again. He expects me to grovel, to feel as if I'm the one who betrayed him. Not going to happen.

"I think you should leave." My final request does something to him. The fierceness in his eyes loses its flame, and with a flick of his wrist he tosses my journal to the corner of the room. Then he backs away with his hands up, a gesture that releases all tension from my body. He's giving up. Finally.

I don't need to look up to feel the heat escaping his body; it fills my room, creating a humidity we could drown in. Maybe we *have* been drowning, and every moment with Devon is my life flashing before my eyes. That would explain the suffocation I feel every time I'm with him.

He begins to exit my room, undoubtedly heading toward the party next door to relieve his frustrations on the first girl that will spread her legs. Turning, he makes sure to deliver one final blow before crossing the threshold and slamming the door. "Go to hell Chloe, and take my brother with you."

The ball in my throat can't decide whether it wants to sink deep into the pit of my stomach, weighing me down with guilt, or climb out my throat, clearing way for my scream of relief. It's just there, taunting me, reminding me I had the power to end our relationship sooner. Instead, I let it come to this, and I can only take responsibility for my own mistakes. Unfortunately, I've made a lot of them.

In seconds I'm peeling off my gown and throwing myself onto my bed, in no mood to go back to that party. No celebration for me tonight.

Now that Devon's gone, I want to let it all out. Everything my heart has endured in these months of torture. I can't remember the last time I cried, but I have a sense it would feel good to let go right about now. As I smash my face into the flower-stained bedspread and clutch it with all my might, I practically have to force a tear from my eye.

A slow knock on my door jerks me to a sitting position. That's a knock I haven't heard in a while, but I know who owns it. I stand and straighten my dress, then slide a finger across the single tear I was able to muster.

"Come in," I say.

Gavin pokes his head in hesitantly, as if testing the waters, before the rest of his body follows. He shuts the door and leans against it, a look of concern etched into his face. He must have seen Devon. Shame floods me, and I have to tear myself from his gaze.

"He looked pretty pissed this time. Are you okay?"

My swallow overshadows my nod.

"What happened?"

"The usual," I answer dryly. I watch him. He's silent, observing me as he waits for a better response. Gavin has always had the ability to read me, no matter how hard I try to hide the truth. "What?" I demand. "He's drunk."

When Gavin tenses he does this strange thing with his jaw, as if he's clenching his teeth to keep from saying something he might regret. "What happened, Chloe?" he asks again.

Out of the corner of my eye I see the brown leather cover of my journal and sigh. Not wanting to attract attention to it, I turn back to Gavin, who's slowly approaching. "I can't do it anymore. He's impossible to be with. Even when he's not drunk, he's yelling at me or accusing me of cheating on him." I leave out the part where he threatened to leave me if I didn't have sex with him. I'm

9

not sure if Gavin knows this side of his brother, and I don't want to be the one to tell him.

Gavin's face twists, conflicted, and he places his hand on my forearm. "You two were never right for each other, Chloe."

The lump in my throat sinks and latches onto my heart. Fixing my eyes with his, I whisper, "I know."

CHAPTER 2

THE TREEHOUSE, THE BULLY, & BREAKING BENJAMIN

CHLOE

R ain tapped at my window, just a whisper at first, then steadily increased as a roll of thunder chased it. Not at all an odd occurrence for Bonney Lake, Washington, but for some reason it felt different on this particular day. It was like the rain was trying to escape the outside while I wanted the exact opposite. I hated being sick. I was beginning to feel like a zombie, quarantined in solitude while my mind zigzagged around, falling victim to anything that resembled life beyond my four walls.

I sat up, dug my knees into the mattress, and peered through the windowpane toward the community playground. My wide eyes snagged the first moving object they saw: light blue rain boots. As they hopped back and forth, I noticed two more boots, this pair red, stomping through puddles and sending mud flying.

Two boys wearing long, slick jackets matching the color of their footwear were sword fighting, except their swords were made of tree branches. One boy had a playful look about him; he laughed as his brother pretended to jab him under the arm. The other boy held a competitive stance—one that said he wasn't about to be defeated. Despite their physical similarities, it was clear that their differences were many.

As they took turns jabbing each other, I cursed the infection that sent my fever soaring the night before. Dejected, I continued watching long enough to see them eventually drop their weapons and chase after each other into the woods. I'd lived in the same home my entire life and knew everyone in our private neighborhood, but I didn't know these boys. Then I remembered seeing the moving van a couple weeks ago.

"Twin boys your age," my mother told me when I asked about them later that day. "Sad thing about their mom." She turned to my father for this bit, as if I was invisible once again. "Single father raising two boys after a tragedy like that. Such a shame."

Given I was twelve years old with a wild imagination, I convinced myself their mother was a fairy princess who had been captured by garden gnomes. Their father, devastated that he would have to raise his boys alone, traveled the world to seek out his maiden's captors. He was unsuccessful, but along his journey he stumbled upon land next to a section of woods in a town called Bonney Lake and decided to make a new home there for him and his two sons.

It was a few days later. No longer riddled with ache, I wanted nothing more than to escape the confines of my room and create an adventure for myself. I ducked into the woods, traversed the mudded earth, and imagined I was escaping my own captors. All to nature's soundtrack—until a dull hammering began to echo through the woods.

The hammering grew louder and as I closed in on the source, laughter and exclamations filtered through the air. Just a few steps more and there it was: a two-story wood structure snuggled between the branches of a large oak tree. Its height loomed above me in all its impressive glory. Its limbs outstretched, pointing to the sky at odd-shaped angles.

On the deck that wrapped the house sat the twin boys from the other day with a middle-aged version of them planted between their bodies. The man raised his arms in victory. "Well, boys, it's done. Your very own treehouse."

They cheered, and over the course of the next few hours they began setting up their space. I watched from behind the trunk of a tree all day, even when they disappeared from view and played inside it for hours.

This became my post for the next week as I watched and imagined what was going on within those walls. It was either that—spying—or spending time dodging Stacy Berringer, an evil redhead who lived two houses down from me. She could often be found at the community playground with her followers, a clan of mean girls and boys just dying to take direction from the Queen of Popularity. They loved to stake their claim on that spot and terrorize trespassers. Unfortunately for me, the playground was right next to the entrance of the woods.

One night my parents were entertaining guests, four of my father's business partners and their spouses. My mother sent me to bed straight after dinner so they could turn their filters off and their volume up. They must have thought my room was soundproof because they didn't bother to muffle their shrieks of laughter and loud, booming chatter that even earphones wouldn't drown out. I couldn't take it anymore. I threw on a pair of shoes, then slid open my bedroom window and climbed out, allowing the darkness to engulf me.

I ran straight toward the woods, my destination predetermined. What I didn't expect was for Stacy's crew to still be perched up in their nest at the top of the playground. I could smell the booze and smoke upon arrival. Unfortunately, my attempt to sneak past them failed. Their lookout, Blaine, spotted me. "I see Chloe!" he yelled at the top of his lungs.

Their responding silence followed by hushed whispers, told me I was in trouble. I either needed to run or hide. I decided to do both.

"Get her!" Stacy yelled.

It was a witch-hunt. I was sure I'd be stoned if found alive. But they wouldn't find me. I ran this path every day, weaving among the consortia of ferns and rows of vine maples. My journey was an easy one, even in the dark. Stacy and her crew would be lost and petrified the moment they entered the woods.

Breathless, I finally latched onto the bottom rung of the tree trunk's ladder and moved quickly to the landing. Anyone watching would assume I'd done this a million times before. Adrenaline pumped through my body from my escape—and at the thought of trespassing. I was about to step foot inside the tree-house I'd fallen in love with from afar. *The boys will never know.*

It was too dark to make much out of the shadows, but the most delicious smell of freshly chopped wood flooded my nostrils. Mouth closed, I breathed it in with a deep pull until I was sufficiently subdued. When I opened my eyes I spotted a large gas lantern and turned it on.

Every inch of the wide-open space wrote a story I'd only seen the cover of for so long. An old wooden desk was pushed to one side, a stack of comic books scattered atop it. On the other side of the structure sat a small couch beside a workout station. A punching bag hung from the ceiling, and weights were scattered on the floor below it. Another ladder led to a second story, an alcove above the couch. I climbed it to find a mattress against a long window. It called to me as my lids grew heavy.

In no hurry to leave, I rested my head against the pillow and stared out into the darkness. The chatter of woodland creatures and the restless wind that grazed the trees was surprisingly calming. With each breath I fell into a deeper sleep, already loving the little treehouse and the protection it provided.

My entire body ached the moment I tried to move, so I stopped trying. I groaned and peeled an eye open, trying to understand why this morning felt so different from all the others.

When I saw the matching sets of green eyeballs peering over the ladder, one glaring and one questioning, I wanted to scream, but the air in my throat went the other direction. I gasped and propelled myself backward into the furthest corner of the alcove.

"Do you think she's homeless?" asked Eyeballs Number One.

Eyeballs Number Two shook his head as he scanned my body. "Maybe she ran away from home."

"Yeah, or maybe she's a troll that lives in the woods. Are we supposed to feed her?"

"I didn't bring any food. Did you?"

One of the boys threw his eyes around the room, as if afraid to look away from me for long. "No. We should tell dad we need a fridge."

"And how will we keep it cold, moron?"

"Hey! I'm not a moron!"

While the boys fought, I managed to creep forward until I gripped the edge of the bed with every intention to slip down undetected.

But Eyeballs Number One saw me and placed an arm out across the other boy's body. "Shh. She's moving."

My grogginess cleared, replaced by a rush of adrenaline as I stared back at the twin boys—the boys whose treehouse I'd snuck into the night before. At this realization, I straightened with a jolt. "I-I have to get home." Panic seized my chest knowing my parents would be frantic looking for me.

Eyeballs Number Two nudged the other. "She has a home, bro."

I bit my lip to hide my smile, happy they no longer considered me a possible troll. "Sorry. I didn't mean to—" I didn't know why I was about to lie, so I stopped myself. I totally meant to fall asleep there. I just didn't mean to get caught.

"Wait!" one of them called as I headed for the ladder. I turned to see the curious one staring back at me with a sincere expression. "Are you okay?"

All I could do was nod. How could I tell two boys I didn't know the reason for invading their sanctuary—that I had been watching them for weeks, envious of their home in the woods?

Instead of saying another word, I found the ladder and moved down it, missing the last few steps in my haste. The moment I hit the ground, I accepted the impact with a grimace and took off at a sprint through the woods and toward my bedroom window. I climbed inside just as I heard my mom calling me for breakfast.

"Watch it, loser."

For some reason, junior high gave Stacy an excuse to redefine the status quo, and she had something to prove in the bully department. Perhaps it was the fact that she had gone from the most popular sixth grader to a lowly seventh grader, or the fact that she now had a bigger audience so grander antics should ensue. Her behavior troubled me, mostly because I remember the girl I grew up with. The nice girl down the street who was obsessed with dolls and tea parties. Stacy never wanted to leave my house and she rarely did. Our sleepovers were epic; we'd stay up giggling for hours at everything and nothing at the same time. Delirium took over and we'd end up passing out from sugar highs and exhaustion.

She was furious with me when my parents took me away for vacation. We were only gone two weeks, but it was enough time for her to rally together our mutual friends and shun me completely upon my return. But it wasn't Stacy's silent treatment that upset me the most; it was the drastic transformation that happened practically overnight. Like she woke up one day and broke through her cocoon, but what came out was more wasp than butterfly. Yet boys flocked to her like she was the last girl on earth. Girls trailed her, too, afraid to become her next victim, hoping to snag her leftovers as she bounced from boyfriend to boyfriend.

Stacy's hatred toward me started with vitriol spewed at every opportunity. Her words didn't hurt me, though. I think that pissed her off even more. I was smart enough to understand she was a bully with low self-esteem. It was when she began putting her hands on my body that I really started to get upset. Little shoulder nudges here and there in the hallway quickly escalated to shoving the back of my desk during quiet times in English class. She was taller than me. Stronger. When it came to physical attacks, I didn't stand a chance.

Her flock always giggled at her behavior. That's when I would really get embarrassed. It seemed like everyone was in on it. What had I ever done to them to make them want to hurt me?

A few weeks into the school year, Stacy decided to turn things up a notch. I was standing at my locker, pulling out textbooks for math class when a blow to my head propelled me into my locker door, the latch on the side slicing my forehead in the process.

When I turned, I expected to see Stacy and her flock doubled over in laughter. And they were—well, most of them. What I didn't expect to see were the twin boys from the treehouse flanking her with stoic faces.

Stacy pulled the thick leather straps of her weapon—a seemingly innocent backpack—around her shoulders, flipped her red hair, and hooked the straps with her thumbs. That's when she noticed the blood running down the side of my head. "Gross!" she exclaimed before turning on her heel and sauntering off.

I ran my hand across my forehead, trying to find the origin of the wound. I was numb to any pain, frozen in humiliation and confusion. Her groupies followed her down the hall—everyone except for *him*, the curious twin. He lingered behind for a moment, then approached me.

It was the first time we'd been this close since he found me trespassing, but I'd recognized him and his brother on the first day of school. It was obvious from the flustered whispers in the halls that the twins had a following from day one. I learned their names that day—Gavin and Devon—and quickly determined which name belonged to which twin. Gavin was the curious one. Devon, the competitive one.

For a moment Gavin continued to silently observe me, just as he did that day I woke up to his gaze in the treehouse. Then . . . "Are you just going to stand there?"

"What should I be doing?"

Gavin's questioning look turned to disappointment, then he grabbed my hand and tugged me down the hall to the bathroom just as the bell for third period rang. He checked to ensure the girl's bathroom was clear before pulling me in. Then he wet a paper towel and dabbed my forehead clean. We didn't say a word to each other the entire time, and when he was done, we went our separate ways—until lunch.

I sat in my usual corner spot, alone on the far side of the room. It was as far away from Stacy's table as I could manage. As I opened my lunch bag, I noticed Gavin crossing the room, passing his usual spot next to Stacy and her friends and making a beeline for me. Then, without a word, he sat down across from me. A confused Devon followed, burning a hole in my head wound with his heated stare. I tried to ignore him as I nibbled the crust of my peanut butter and jelly.

"You okay there, girl?"

Girl. That's what Devon chose to call me instead of asking my name. Of course he wouldn't already know it. If anything, he probably thought my name was Loser, Stacy's favorite and unoriginal term of endearment for me.

"Her name is Chloe." Gavin glared at his brother.

Devon stirred in his seat, his eyes quickly darting around the cafeteria before returning to mine. "*Chloe.* Why does Stacy hate you so much?"

Gavin practically growled at his brother, causing Devon to chuckle.

"What? Maybe Chloe stole Stacy's scratch and sniff pencil or something. She can say sorry. Kiss and make up."

Devon's amusement angered me, but I diverted my focus, refusing to exacerbate his antics.

"Why do you let Stacy pick on you?" Devon tried again.

I was stumped, not realizing I had other options. Shaking my head, I found myself contemplating the things I could do when she approached me the next time. "I wouldn't know what else to do," I responded, my voice soft. I didn't talk much, so I was always surprised by the sound that came out of my small body.

"You're not going to let her pick on you anymore," Gavin said without meeting my eyes. "You should learn how to stick up for yourself. Stacy can only be a bully if you let her."

A flash of red hair in my periphery caused me to wince.

"Hey, guys." Stacy approached with wide puppy dog eyes pointed straight at Devon. Her sickeningly sweet smile deepened. "There's room at my table."

Devon made a move to stand, but Gavin placed a hand on his brother's shoulder. I couldn't tell if it was fear or desire that had Devon giving in to Stacy so easily. It could have been a mixture of both. All I knew was that I would love to make a boy react like that without any effort at all.

"Not today, Stacy," Gavin said. "We're going to hang with Chloe."

Gavin's words weren't mean or hurtful; they were matter-of-fact. Regardless, Stacy's puppy dog expression morphed into shock, then anger. Devon looked furious at his brother, too. It was clear which of them cared about fitting in with Stacy's crowd.

"Um. Okay," she said, her confusion evident as she looked between the boys and me. "See ya." She stalked off to her table with a final backward glance.

I wanted to laugh, but I settled for smiling as an unfamiliar sensation rose in my chest, causing a blush to stain my cheeks. "Thank you," I said, meeting Gavin's eyes.

He shrugged it off as if it was no big deal, and we ate the rest of our food in silence.

The twins discovered where I lived that same night. Or maybe they already knew. I was doing the dishes, one of my many afternoon chores, and my arms were covered in soap when I heard the knock at the door. I rushed to open it and my mouth fell open in surprise to find Gavin and Devon standing at my doorstep.

Gavin smiled and peered over my shoulder, scanning the interior of my home. "We're not creepy," he joked. "We live on the other side of the woods."

"That's a little creepy," I said, making a face, trying to seem apprehensive. Internally, I struggled to keep my excitement at bay. The twins had made what could have been the worst day the absolute best.

Devon glared at me from the stairs of my porch. "Not as creepy as sneaking into our tree fort and camping out all night."

My cheeks blazed with embarrassment. He was right. What I'd done *was* a little creepy.

"Don't listen to him. We know our treehouse is pretty awesome."

"Is he always that angry?" I asked, purposely directing my question at Gavin.

Gavin chuckled but ignored my query. Instead, he nodded to his right. "We're one house over, on the other side of the woods."

Gavin seemed nice. Devon, I wasn't so sure about. They were twins, but other than certain features—light green eyes with specks of gold, messy mocha-colored hair, and sun-kissed skin—they were nothing alike. Gavin was slightly taller than his brother, which might have been cause for Devon's overcompensation, but they were both tall. His anger seemed to define him, along with his stockier build. For some reason, Devon didn't intimidate me like I could tell he wanted to. I found him entertaining.

"We're going to the treehouse to listen to my new CD." Gavin held up a square box wrapped in thick plastic. "Wanna come?"

I took the CD from him, scanning the cover art and frowning. "I don't know who Breaking Benjamin is."

Gavin's face lit up. "More the reason to come listen. They will change your world."

I'm not sure if Breaking Benjamin changed my world, but that day did. The three of us became inseparable. Even Devon warmed up to me after some time, and I got used to his grumpy demeanor. With the twins by my side, Stacy stopped picking on me, although her glares became fiercer than ever. I knew I had it coming one day, but by then, I'd be ready for her.

Chapter 3

Mistakes (part two)

CHLOE

The tension in the air is so heavy that it's pulling me under. The last thing I want is for Gavin to drown along with me. "You should go," I say, my voice cracking with emotion.

He tilts his head, concern flooding his face as if he has so much to say. Instead of leaving, he closes the gap between us and wraps his arms around me. My cheek easily falls to his chest. I breathe him in, using his fresh and minty aroma to steady my heart rate, but it only beats faster against the well-formed terrain of his body. This isn't the first time we've embraced, but it somehow seems more intimate now.

That I ended up falling for the wrong twin will never stop haunting me. Gavin has always been it for me; the calm one, the smart one, the respectful one. My best friend. My protector. He was stronger than Devon in ways that are more important than physical. I could always see him for all that he was—for all that he is. *Perfect.* But once I started dating Devon, I broke something in Gavin. I broke something in me. And it's slowly killing me.

Gavin doesn't pull away and I'm grateful for his comfort, but I also know this thing between us—what's always been between us—is wrong. For a moment, though, I allow his embrace to give me a taste of what I so desperately and selfishly want.

A loud, angry snarl of a voice pulls our attention to the window. I jump and throw my hands over my mouth, my heart taking off in a sprint. Devon stares back at us with menacing, bloodshot eyes, an *I-told-you-so* sneer, and a middle finger up in the air—a gesture obviously meant for both of us.

As guilty as I am for having feelings for Gavin, I'm innocent of the things Devon accuses me of. Even after six years of friendship, he wants to believe the worst in me. It's always something. Either I'm too weak, too distant, too smart, or too defiant. The alcohol only intensifies his insults, and I'm done hoping he'll change.

Gavin pulls away and reaches over my bed to get to the window. He slides one pane over to talk to his brother. "Bro, calm down! I was just about to come find you. Let's take a walk."

Devon's eyes blaze with anger. "You've got to be shitting me. I just caught you two red-handed or whatever. I'm done with that bitch. And I'm done with you, bro. You two can have each other and dream of me when you're twisted up, sweaty in those pink sheets of hers. I'm out of here."

"What the—?" Gavin turns to me, wide-eyed. "What is he talking about, Chloe?"

Never in my whole life have I been so mortified. How did everything get so messed up?

I let out a shaky breath. "He thinks—"

"I know!" Gavin yells, catching me off balance. I stumble backward. "Why does he think that, *Chloe*?"

The way he enunciates my name racks my body with chills. I shake my head, not wanting to lie, but there's no way in hell I'm telling him what Devon read in my diary.

Not a moment after the first thought, though, I realize Devon will probably tell him anyway. My insides overheat with embarrassment. I should have hidden my journal in a safer place than my underwear drawer, which Devon apparently frequents.

Gavin charges out of my room, pissed at my silence, I'm sure. In an attempt to shove the tears back into my throat before they escape, I throw myself at my window to get a good look at the twins.

"Stay away from me, man!" Devon yells.

"Bro, nothing happened between Chloe and me. She was upset because you're being a dick. I was just trying to comfort her. That's all."

That's all.

Devon stalks off toward the playground, a fifth of whiskey sloshing in his hand as he moves. His blue plastic cup from earlier must not have gotten the job done. Hell, even I could use a drink right now.

"This is a fucking joke," Devon growls.

"Why won't anyone tell me what's going on?" Gavin shouts after him. "Dev, stop!"

Devon turns around, walking backward through the darkness. I can barely see him as he nears the woods, but I can hear him just fine. "Don't follow me. I don't need you to follow me. I just need you to leave me the hell alone."

Gavin doesn't follow him. Instead, he walks back toward my house and lets himself in again. I hear the door slam and his footsteps approaching. I ready myself for another confrontation, knowing I deserve it. He shuts my door and pierces me with a look that could break my heart.

"Close your window—and curtains," he says.

I try to ignore the huskiness in his voice. I'm not sure what his intentions are, but I know I'm growing weaker every second I'm near him. I do as he asks, afraid to make a single wrong move.

His movements are slow, but even through my haze, I'm certain that he's approaching. When he's hovering above me I sigh in his direction, careful not to touch him, terrified to look up into his eyes.

"He just needs time to cool off and then I'll go talk to him." His breathing is heavy. His arms are still by his sides. I see the flinch of his muscles like he wants to touch me. "I just don't want him climbing through your window tonight."

The heat radiating from Gavin's body is palpable. I'm tempted to reach around and pull him to me—and therein lies the problem.

"How did I let it come to this?" My words are less than a whisper and the question is more for me than him, but my thoughts catch me off guard. I know he's affected too because his entire body tenses, pulling a bundle of emotions from my heart and into my throat. I look up, searching for something to latch onto as I climb higher, beyond the fog of the last four months. "I'm so sorry, Gavin. This is all my fault."

He presses himself against me, his hand cupping my chin, forcing me to meet his eyes. "This isn't all on you, Chloe, but when I found out about you two, I have to admit: it was *you* who hurt me, not my brother. Devon will always be Devon. You . . ." he shakes his head, dismissing the thought.

If a heart could crack, mine has just shattered into a million pieces. There's nothing I want more than to press my lips to his and show him what I should have months ago when I finally realized how much he meant to me.

There's something in his expression that stops me from saying more. It's a darkness I've never seen before. We once told each other everything, every secret, every dream. But now he's closed off. I've been so completely absorbed in the drama of my relationship with Devon that I ignored it, but I can't ignore it anymore. I hurt Gavin by choosing Devon . . . and now it's too late. We've surpassed the point of no return. All I wanted was to follow my heart, but somehow along the way I lost my soul.

Gavin's touch feels like home, and saying goodbye will be torture. Torture because he will never know how I truly feel about him. At least, he won't hear it from me. I want to scream it into the wind so the sound carries to the ends of the earth. *It's you, Gavin. It's always been you.*

"You should go find him. He does stupid things when he gets

drunk," I murmur, stepping away from Gavin's body heat. I don't deserve his comfort, and I definitely can't bear to be around it anymore. Our friendship is completely ruined. Whatever damage I inflicted on the three of us is what it is.

Since I received a partial scholarship at Oregon State to pursue journalism, my time here is limited anyway. That's another secret I've been keeping from the twins out of fear of their objections. I'm afraid if I tell them, they'll manage to convince me to stay and attend Seattle University with them. It's what we always planned, but if I want out of my relationship with Devon, I know I can't stay. It's time to leave this place and my mistakes behind.

Gavin surprises me by stepping forward and wrapping his strong arms around me again. I sigh, taking in his scent. Consuming it. Memorizing it. Until I'm abuzz with sensations that almost make me forget everything else.

"You're right. I need to find him, and I will. But I need to tell you something first." His throaty voice tugs at my heart. "You may have made the wrong decision to date Devon, but you weren't the only one who made mistakes. This is on me, too, Chloe."

He pulls away and turns to leave. The cool air circulating from my fan replaces his embrace, racking me with shivers. Moments later the front door slams behind him, confirming the reality of my loss . . . and it's not the loss of my boyfriend that leaves me devastated. It's the loss of my best friend—of what may have been if we hadn't gone and screwed it all up.

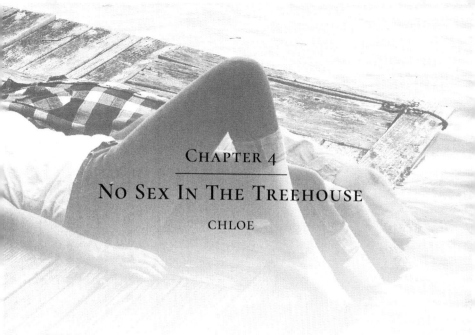

CHAPTER 4

NO SEX IN THE TREEHOUSE

CHLOE

W hen I was fifteen my parents bought a second home in Florida, and that's where we spent the entire summer before my sophomore year of high school. It was my first summer away from the boys and took my mom's insistent prodding to get me to enjoy the sweet Florida summer.

On my first day back at school, I knew everything would be different. I hadn't spotted Devon or Gavin yet, but I made instant friends in my second period art class with a group of girls that had gone to a neighboring junior high. They were a breath of fresh air. They knew nothing about me, about Stacy and her bullying, about the pity the twins took on me.

"I'm going to miss summer. We went out on Justin's boat almost every day," Phoebe gushed. Phoebe and Justin had been an item for two years. That's an eternity in teen years. And it was easy to see how someone could want to hold onto her for that long. Phoebe was a beautiful blonde with model-worthy curls that framed her glowing complexion, and she seemed to carry a positive energy with each step.

"What about you, Chloe? What did you do this summer?"

My response was immediate and just as glowing as Phoebe's.

"My parents have a place in Florida, so we spent the summer there."

Jazz scanned the length of my body, and she grinned. "No wonder. That's an amazing color on you. I was going to ask you which salon you tan at. And if you have one of those sticker tattoos. Like me." She pulled down her jeans a few inches, causing my eyes to widen in surprise. There it was: a tan line in the shape of kissy lips right below her hips.

I laughed, liking her already. Jazz's personality and looks lived up to her name. With a light brown pixie cut that revealed multiple ear piercings and bright blue eyes, she was a stunner with a feisty attitude.

Jazz and I shared fourth period together too, and she tugged me along to lunch the moment the bell rang. She introduced me to more new faces as we sat down. I greeted them and then let my attention wander around the cafeteria. I searched for the twins—realizing how okay I was getting on without them. No longer their shadow.

Gavin spotted me first. I froze at the sight of him. Three months had somehow turned Gavin into a complete hottie. His smile stretched across his entire face as he moved toward me. It was hard not to appreciate his every movement, and it took massive strength to stand and meet his embrace.

The moment I fell into him I finally felt like I was home. It was the first time I felt that way about Gavin Rhodes. He lifted me a few inches off the floor, and I erupted into a fit of giggles. God, I missed him.

Just as he was setting me down, Devon approached with the same wide grin on his face. His muscles had swelled twice the size of Gavin's, and I felt it as he grabbed me and swung me around, telling me how great my boobs looked. I slapped his arm and squeezed a bicep as he set me on the floor.

"You didn't call us. We didn't know if you were coming back." Devon was glaring at me now.

I smiled. "We just got in last night, and I knew I'd see you guys today. I figured we'd have class together or something."

Gavin frowned. "What happened to the electives we chose? Didn't you register for those? I got everything I picked."

"My dad picked my schedule. He thought I'd be better suited for French and Art of the Western World." I made a face. It was no surprise to the twins that my parents didn't know me at all.

After introducing the boys to my new friends, I invited them to join our lunch table. Gavin squeezed in next to me. "Tell me about Florida. Don't tell me your parents are moving there for good. You can't leave me, Chlo. I won't allow it. I'll trap you in the treehouse if I need to."

I blushed and nudged him with my elbow. "No plans to move that I know of—but I hardly think a fifteen-year-old boy is capable of kidnapping."

"Try me."

That fall, things were better than ever. Weekends consisted of hanging out with Devon and Gavin, but we ventured out more, meeting up with our new friends and grilling out on the lake. The twins had all the girls swooning, especially when they were out on the football field.

That was another change. Gavin was suddenly into sports and he was good at them, although Devon was still the more competitive one. Gavin swore he was only participating to have extracurricular activities listed on his college applications, which was probably true—but secretly, I think he also enjoyed his new screaming fan base. And really, who could blame him?

When I returned from Florida the summer before junior year, I didn't expect everything to get so . . . complicated.

This time, my parents brought me home a couple weeks early so I could get some time in with my friends before school started back up. The second we pulled into the driveway I took off running for the treehouse, eager to see the twins.

My scream could probably be heard for miles when a bare ass greeted me from the couch, a moaning Stacy beneath it. Devon flipped around to face me, giving me a complete view of . . . everything. I gasped, unable to peel my eyes from the inches of Devon's skin I never expected to see.

Devon's surprise turned quickly into a confident smirk as he grabbed his length and moved his hand up and down, taunting me. A mortified cry escaped my lips.

"Get the hell out, Chloe!" Stacy screamed as she tried unsuccessfully to cover her body with a throw pillow.

So that's what I did. I got the hell out and ran straight for the twins' home to find Gavin. I fell into his arms the second he opened the door. "Calm down. What's wrong?" He was laughing at me.

"I think I just gave myself nightmares for years." I groaned, burying my head in Gavin's chest.

"What happened?"

"Devon was . . . showing Stacy a good time in the treehouse. I saw everything." I looked up at Gavin, horror evident on my face. "Everything!"

He burst into laughter as I placed my hands on my hips. Obviously Gavin was aware of Devon's antics. Jealousy chose this moment to creep into my chest. "Since when did you two start using the treehouse as your sex pad?"

His eyes widened, his laughter dissipating. "*You two?* Chloe, you didn't find me in our treehouse just now. I've never done that. I wouldn't. I happen to consider that our sacred place."

"Sorry." I frowned. "It's not my treehouse, but—"

"Yes it is," Gavin interrupted. "It's just as much yours as it is ours. Don't say that again. I'll talk to Devon. No more sex in the treehouse."

As I laughed, Gavin winked and pulled me in for another hug. "So, is Devon the first naked dude you've seen? How was it?"

I shoved him, noticing how firm his body had become over the summer. "Shut up. I don't want to think about it anymore."

He threw his head back, laughing. "That disappointing, huh?"

Actually, it wasn't as awful as I once imagined—not that I had imagined the twins naked. Ugh. *What was wrong with me?*

"Come in. I have company, so don't act surprised," he warned.

It all happened so fast. Phoebe rounded the corner from the kitchen and beamed at me. I returned the smile, happy to see her too. I knew Jazz would be furious when she found out I was home and hadn't called her yet.

"Where's Justin?" I asked, expecting him to round the corner behind her.

She looked between Gavin and me. "We broke up." The flush of her cheeks gave her away. Something was going on. "How was Florida? Did you just get back?"

I grinned, trying to ignore the growing gnaw in my stomach, and threw myself onto the couch. "Yup. Back early. I was hoping we could all do something tonight."

"Let's do it," Gavin said.

In the seconds that followed I wanted to swallow my words. Phoebe gave me an apologetic look and glanced at Gavin with moony eyes. "Babe, we have plans tonight. Remember?"

My heart sunk deep into my chest. *Babe?* So now Gavin had a girlfriend, Devon was doing Stacy in *our* treehouse, and I suddenly became the fifth wheel. Hoping to avoid attracting attention to my befuddled heart, I made an excuse to leave and walked home, realizing that once again, another year was gone and everything had changed.

Gavin and Phoebe broke up as soon as school started—but things were still different with Gavin. His focus was mostly on school, and he spent his free time dating other girls casually—though not as casually as Devon. Devon, unsurprisingly, bounced from girl to girl at an impressive rate. It became a struggle handling my emotions. We were all just friends, so the fact that other girls stole their attention shouldn't have bothered me. But it did. I quickly realized that I needed to get a life of my own.

That next summer in Florida changed things for me—for my confidence. I got a part-time job as hostess at a local restaurant and met Shawn, an insanely hot waiter who flirted with me incessantly. When he finally asked me out I realized how much I had been missing out on: dates, casual flings, flirting, and spending time with boys that weren't Gavin and Devon. For so long, the twins had ruled my universe when it came to the male species.

I said yes when Shawn asked me to be his girlfriend. We were officially the cutest couple to those who knew us. What's better? He was perfect. Sweet. Doting. Respectful. I even let him kiss me a couple weeks in. At the end of summer, he spoke of visiting me in Bonney Lake . . . so I broke up with him. As fun as our relationship was, my feelings never went beyond that of a crush—and crushes fade.

When I returned from Florida that summer, everyone was surprised I had let my hair grow so long rather than keeping my predictable shoulder-length style. My taste in clothes had changed too, thanks to my new love for fashion magazines and my trendy Florida friends. I still hated makeup, but I knew how to apply it now without looking like a clown. I'd filled out a little too, but not in a bad way. My mom told me curves were a good thing.

Apparently I also picked up a bad habit of being late over the summer, because I stumbled into my first class a few minutes past the bell.

After my lesson learned from the previous summer, I'd completely avoided the twins before school started. But that wasn't just due to the scalding memory of Devon's butt cheeks greeting me upon my arrival; it was important for me to free myself of my dependency on them. I wasn't twelve years old anymore and if my short-lived relationship with Shawn taught me anything, it was that I wanted to date.

Unfortunately, my newfound desire for independence was quickly challenged as the twins stared back at me from their desks with mouths agape.

I was torn between running away and laughing at the irony, so I settled for a simple smile of acknowledgment. I took the last seat left—front row center—and focused on my syllabus.

The bell sounded and the twins cornered me outside the classroom with biting looks in their eyes.

"Hey guys," I said easily, looking around them for an opportunity to escape.

"Looking good, Chloe!" shouted Blaine as he walked by. Thankfully he'd outgrown Stacy's crew soon after the twins befriended me, and my ventures past the playground were far easier without him as lookout.

I shot him back a flirtatious smile, thankful for the distraction.

"You didn't return any of my calls," Gavin said.

"Are you ignoring us?" Devon asked.

I clearly hurt them both. Realizing that, my strength quickly dissolved. "No, of course not." I stood up straight and glanced between them. "I just have a lot riding on this year. You guys know I'm not into the extracurricular thing, so I need my grades to be ridiculous if I want a scholarship. I'm just . . . focused."

Gavin looked doubtful but didn't argue. "Where's your schedule?"

I slid my bag from my shoulder and handed him the sheet of paper. His gaze lingered on me, moving from my hair to my clothes to my shoes. "You look different." His tone was accusatory.

"She looks fucking hot, dude." Devon's eyes seemed to be wandering over my body a little more aggressively than Gavin's.

I watched Gavin's expression harden, but he ignored his

brother and reviewed my schedule. A smile brightened his face, warming me. In that moment my reasons for wanting to keep my distance from them completely evaporated.

"We have three classes together."

I met Gavin's smile, unable to help it. Then Devon swiped the schedule from him and smirked. "We have three, too. Gym." He winked at me, and I knew immediately he was picturing my new body in short shorts, bouncing around the track.

"That's *one*, genius," Gavin said, shooting daggers at his twin.

Devon glared back. "English," he pointed to the class we just left, "gym, and chemistry. With you, loser."

I quickly evaluated what he'd just said. That meant I had two classes with both of them. *It's going to be an interesting year.*

"Let's go," Gavin growled, pulling me along. "We'll walk together. See you, bro."

Without a pause, I followed him to calculus. We sat beside each other, and it was almost as if nothing had changed. But when his eyes strayed from mine and landed on my lips, I knew that *everything* had changed. I was no longer the girl next door who needed bully protection.

It wasn't just me that had changed, though. Gavin was taller, his body thicker and more sculpted. He dressed more like Devon now, in dark jeans and a solid-colored t-shirt. And I'd never noticed how thick his lips were until that moment he was examining me. I guess I was examining him back.

Oh my God. I have the hots for Gavin.

I had felt an attraction to Gavin before that moment. I'd have been crazy not to, but he had always just been my best friend. Someone he took pity on and protected. I wasn't like any of the girls he dated, and he sure didn't look at me in that glazed over way that screamed lust and need. I'd seen that look before when Devon saw something or someone he wanted. I craved for someone to look at me like that.

When Gavin perused every detail of me in class that day I thought it was the beginning of something. A festering spark between us that finally hissed to life. The air around us sweltered so headily I could practically taste it.

"Tell me the truth, Chlo. You avoiding us?" His tone was serious, but the playful tug of his lips let me know he already forgave me.

"Maybe I don't want to be 'that girl who hangs out with the twins' this year."

"Oh, yeah? Who do you want to be?"

I shrugged. "That's the part I'm still figuring out."

"I'll help you."

Those words meant more to me than anything. Gavin understood, and he never judged me.

"How about Chloe Rivers, writer by day, superhero by night?" Gavin smiled as he dramatically waved his hands in the air.

I giggled and pointed out that Superman was already a thing. Unfazed, he immediately returned with more ideas, which we exchanged in notes and whispers until the end of class.

Things were just as they should have been, and maybe a little bit better. But still, something had shifted and I didn't know what to do about it.

Guys were noticing me, and not just Gavin and Devon. Some even asked me out. I surprised myself by going on a few dates in the fall, but like Shawn, none of them held my attention. The twins made sure to sabotage any chance of a second date anyway. They thought I was oblivious to their locker room threats, but I was well aware. If I was being honest with myself, though, guys didn't hold my attention because I couldn't get my mind off Gavin's lips. And everything else about him.

We had our opportunity to explore something more than friendship later that fall when Gavin and I went to Seattle for Comic Mania. He dressed me up in one of his crazy costumes, refusing to dress up himself, and we spent a day attending seminars, meeting random celebrities, and browsing the exhibits. We could have easily driven home after the event, but we were invited to a party in the hotel. We decided to make the most of it and purchased a room for the night.

The costume party wasn't anything spectacular, just a bunch of teens sneaking liquor and nerding it up as they talked comics. Gavin had a possessive hold on me all night, and I was certain things were changing between us.

We returned to our hotel room and collapsed onto the bed. I felt his arm hook around my body and pull me close so we were in our familiar friendship spooning position. For hours we lay awake, his hand gently stroking my exposed skin but never entirely crossing the steadily blurring border between friendship and something more. We didn't say a word. I couldn't sleep. Not with the electricity in the air and the buzzing in my brain. It screamed at me and I was disturbingly sensitive to all things Gavin. Every shift of his body, every change of pace of his strokes. And the way his breath released directly onto my neck, instantly raising the bumps on my skin . . . My own unsteady breaths were embarrassingly loud, but it was like I had lost all control over my body.

Eventually frustration won out, and I flipped myself around to face him. He froze and stared back at me with wide, fearful eyes. "Gav," I whispered, desperately wanting him to know it would be okay if he kissed me. When he didn't respond, I took his hand and placed it on my racing heart. His breath hitched and for a second, he began to lean in, our lips just an inch from confessing our feelings.

I should have closed the gap.

Instead, I slammed my eyes shut and waited. I waited while air danced between our readying lips, and while his hand slid from my heart to my neck. He could definitely feel my racing pulse now. There was no question in my mind that this was how things were meant to be between us.

Gavin didn't agree. He chose that moment to pull away and jump from the bed as if he'd been bitten. My eyes were still closed, but I could hear his quick moving retreat and the slamming of the bathroom door behind him.

And then something inside me cracked.

My heart.

I pretended to be asleep when he came back to bed. The truth is neither of us slept that night. I could tell by his restless movements beside me, but I refused to let him know I was awake too.

The next day, we drove home in silence. When he pulled into my driveway, he opened his mouth to speak, but I slammed the door and ran inside before he had an opportunity. He didn't fight for another one.

As much as I wanted to talk to Gavin about what happened that night, life got weird. I'd starting tutoring after school, and Devon was in desperate need of it. His explosions of anger on the field got him benched one too many times, and his grades were suffering too. Athletic suspension was inevitable.

So I agreed to tutor him, which was no easy task.

"School isn't my thing, Chloe. I just need that football scholarship so I can play. I don't need English class to help me succeed. I've got skills on the field."

"I'm sure you'll get your scholarship, and I won't argue with your skills on the field, but don't be ridiculous. You speak English. There's no excuse for failing your first language."

Devon glared at me. He glared at me a lot during those tutoring sessions. I learned more about him during that time than I had in all our previous years of friendship. For the first time, he confessed to me the painful details of his mother's suicide, and I could imagine the pain behind his eyes. It had to be there, festering somewhere deep, dark, and dangerous. I finally understood what provoked his angry nature.

But it wasn't just his mother's death that haunted Devon. Gavin had always been the academic in the family, and he was artistic too. To top it all off, he played the same sports Devon did, although he didn't dominate in quite the same way. It became clear to me that Devon was jealous of his brother. Although he never came out and said it exactly, I figured it out as I watched him closer. He felt as if he had nothing without his athleticism, and the suspension brought those weaknesses to the surface.

I was proud of Devon for pulling through his next few English tests with high enough scores to take him off suspension.

One chilly afternoon I was alone in the treehouse when Devon burst in, exam paper in hand and a larger-than-life grin on his face. "We did it!" he exclaimed.

He spun me around so many times that I landed dizzy on the couch. I laughed and looked at the 'B' he had earned for himself. "Good job, Dev! This is the best score you've gotten yet."

Devon took his energy out on the punching bag in the corner of the room while I beamed proudly down at his paper. As I shuffled from page to page, my finger slipped. I cried out in pain from the paper cut, then gasped at the line of blood thickening above my skin.

Devon was by my side immediately, inspecting the wound and smirking. "There's only one cure for this," he teased.

"What?" I looked up, confused. And then I understood.

Before I could stop him, he pulled my finger into his mouth. My heart stopped beating, the world stopped spinning, and I was staring into the eyes of my friend—a friend who had always annoyed me to the core, who had been inside more girls than I could track, and whom I never looked at as anything more than a friend. If anything, it was Gavin I'd felt that connection with. But on this day, Gavin was nowhere on my mind.

Devon continued sucking on my finger, pulling it deeper into his mouth with glazed eyes. My entire body grew hot under his spell. I finally understood how he did it, how he could woo an entire cheerleading squad into his bed.

I let him kiss me.

It wasn't my first kiss, but it was by far the best. I'd had no clue that touching someone else's lips with my own could cause sensations throughout my entire body.

I pulled away from him as his hands slid up my stomach,

between my skin and shirt. "Fuck, Chloe. You have no clue how badly I want you."

His words confused me, and for the next few weeks I avoided him at all costs. I thought time would help get my raging hormones in check, and I prayed it was just a one-time occurrence. Devon would forget about our kiss and run off to the next girl willing to fulfill his needs. Besides, I couldn't possibly have feelings for *Devon*, of all people.

It was Christmas morning when he finally knocked on my door. It was the first time I'd ever seen Devon vulnerable. He stood there, bundled up from head-to-toe to combat the winter chill, a hopeful expression on his face. My heart melted when I saw the holiday wrappings between his fingertips.

"You didn't have to get me anything."

"Just open the damn present." He pushed it toward me with a soft smile.

It was hard not to smile back. This was so un-Devon-like. I took the gift and peeled the paper at the slit to find a pendant necklace bearing the quote *Those who wander aren't necessarily lost.*

I cocked my head, unsure what the quote was supposed to mean. If I hadn't known Devon better, I'd have thought his cheeks went flush. "This whole time, I thought you were the weak one. It wasn't until recently I realized how wrong I was," he said. "You may be quiet, but you're far from weak. You've got your shit together, Chloe. I could learn a lot from you."

"Thanks, Devon." I smiled and slid the necklace over my head, loving his words, mostly because they surprised the heck out of me.

"I'm sorry for kissing you like that," he continued, forcing my eyes to meet his, listening intently. "I'm impulsive, which you know about me. But with you, I should have been more careful." He paused, as if debating how he wanted to word what he was going to say next. "If there's anyone for me out there, it's you. I'd like to try this. If it's okay with you."

And so it began.

Devon asked me on one date, and then another, and another, until it became obvious that he wasn't going to stop. Something was developing between us, which wasn't easy since we were keeping our attraction a secret from Gavin. I enjoyed this new side of Devon and was thankful he was willing to keep our relationship from his brother. I wasn't ready for Gavin to know about us because I was still uncertain what *us* was.

Devon treated me unlike I'd ever seen him treat any girl: with respect. It took him more than two weeks to kiss me again; *that's* how I knew he really liked me. It's not like we had much alone time anyway, and I definitely played hard to get. But on that particular day in late January, Devon earned his kiss.

He had the idea to walk the trails at Allan Yorke Park, surprising me with a picnic complete with blankets, soft drinks, and a basket of food. As we lay together under the stars, he turned and kissed me. That was the kiss that sealed the deal of our relationship. It was also the start of Devon wanting more than I could ever give him.

ONE MONTH LATER

Devon walked me to the parking lot after school. He was revved up about something that happened in Spanish class and couldn't stop yammering about it. I honestly wasn't paying attention to his words; instead, I was paying attention to Gavin, who was closing in on us from the other side of the parking lot. He was only ten or so yards away when Devon grabbed my hand.

Time stopped.

Gavin's eyes followed the movement.

And then my heart stopped.

I knew this was the moment everything would change. Or maybe it already had.

With a petrified glance up at Devon, unease crept through me. I'm not sure what I expected, but it certainly wasn't the slow-spreading smile that lifted his cheeks. His eyes were at a slant, zeroing in on his brother's reaction, enjoying every bit of it. The exchange made my insides knot with horror. Devon had been insistent on bringing our relationship out in the open, but I wasn't ready.

As I tried to tug my hand away, he tightened his grip. Gavin stopped in his tracks, his demeanor morphing different flavors of confusion, hurt, and then anger, until there was nothing else to express.

"Hey, bro!" Devon called out with a jerk of his chin, as if seeing our hands interlocked shouldn't shock his twin senseless. "Need a ride?"

I'm positive if the situation were different, Gavin would have accepted since his truck was in the shop. Instead, he shook his head, then searched the parking lot until his eyes settled on something. Or someone. "No thanks. I'm going to catch a ride with Stacy. See you later."

Without another glance in our direction, Gavin took off at a jog, catching Stacy right before she opened her car door. There was a thud in my chest as Stacy lit up at the sight of him. The ache worsened when he fell into the passenger seat as if he'd done it a million times before.

"Gavin!" Devon called out, releasing my hand and starting to jog in his direction. But before he could get his brother's attention, Stacy's car was backing out of the stall.

As Devon fumed about Gavin's non-reaction, my insides were shriveling to nothing. I considered ending things with Devon right then. As much fun as we had together, and as much as I liked him, I knew he wasn't the one I wanted to be with forever . . . and that's the exact moment I realized *why* my feelings for Devon would never go beyond holding hands and innocent make-out sessions.

I was in a situation I didn't know how I got into or how to get out of. *He tricked me.* Devon's sweet as honey game was over and the real Devon started to slip through the façade, little by little, until it was all I could see.

I wasn't his exception.

I wasn't special.

I was just . . . lost.

As Gavin grew distant, my walls went up with Devon. Meanwhile, Devon's persistence increased at a rapid pace. Apologies followed every argument about sex and the lack thereof. Flowers followed every screaming match that consisted of him spewing evil, hateful words at me.

Yet despite all these painful situations, I couldn't bring myself to just break it off with him. If I did, our friendship would be over —and since Devon was my only link left to Gavin, I selfishly wasn't prepared to let that go. Instead, I became numb to the relationship. To Devon's aggression.

Even after finding the growing condom wrapper stash in his car, evidence of his weak commitment to me, I let our paper-thin relationship continue. I knew it would take either me leaving for college or one final blowout to end things between us.

I was right.

CHAPTER 5

DESTROYED

GAVIN

I'd much rather be comforting Chloe right now than journeying into the dark woods to calm Devon down. Is that so wrong? My brother is and always has been a hothead. People ask me how twins, born and raised together, can turn out to be so different. I just shrug. Our shrink seems to think it has something to do with Mom, but it's been eight years since she ended her life. And Devon is still a dick.

Mom was a unique character. Laidback, loving, and always smiling . . . at least, that's what I remember from the first eight years of our lives. When Dad's schedule started to pick up at the hospital, I think Mom got lonely. He was gone almost every night the last year of her life, and she grew progressively angrier and more distant. Empty wine bottles began piling up in the recycling container. She slept through the morning and drank from the afternoon on, unleashing her darkness in fits of rage and abuse.

But she never laid a hand on me. Devon wouldn't allow it. It was Devon who protected me, so it was Devon who was victim to her flailing fists. It was also Devon who found mom passed out in bed for the last time, an empty bottle of prescription meds an inch from her fingertips.

When Devon has moments of darkness, I get it. I forgive it.

Usually, his anger doesn't hurt anyone but himself, and he always gets through it. But there's something different about tonight. This time, his malevolent behavior is hurting someone else— someone I love.

Now, as I'm stalking through the woods in search of my brother, I'm unable to come up with a good reason why I'm going after him. Our house is on the other side of the woods, but I know that's not where he is. Even at eighteen, our safe haven is still the treehouse, and I'm certain that Devon is there now, either punching his workout bag or having sex.

At this point, I'm only going after him to tell him to leave Chloe alone. It's time they both moved on. I might even tell him that he ruined my life by dating the only girl I'll ever love.

I know that usually when a guy falls in love at twelve years old, he's really just falling in love with the way his junk feels in his pants. Not me. I've been falling deeper in love with Chloe every day for six years for reasons way beyond my junk. I can't say the same for Devon.

He always does this. He has everything, yet he always finds a way to fuck it up. His football scholarship, Chloe . . . Okay, so I guess that's two things, but that's a hell of a lot more than I've been handed over the years. I have to work my ass off just to stay on any sports team, and everyone knows it costs more to study being an artist than it'll ever pay. Then there's Chloe. Sweet Chloe who defies logic with her beauty. Who I always considered to be more my friend than Devon's. I still can't comprehend how she ended up with my brother.

As I walk on, I grow angrier. Why does Devon always play the victim card? What gives him that right? I've granted him reprieve for years, but this time he crossed a line. The entire graduating class knows that Devon has been more faithful to the cheerleading team than he has been to Chloe, yet he's the one raging mad and accusing her of cheating. I let out a sarcastic laugh. Cheating with *me*, of all people. What a joke.

It's not a long walk to the treehouse but I take my time, giving both of us a chance to calm down before we finally talk. This time, he's going to hear me out.

I arrive at the base of the treehouse and look up. A faint glow illuminates the windows of our home away from home. Everything in me locks up: my steps, my blood, my breathing. It's not that I'm afraid of Devon; Devon doesn't scare me. No, I'm reconsidering confessing how I feel about Chloe.

Does Devon really need to know? Come to think of it, I bet he already does. It's probably what motivated him to go after her in the first place. He always did like a good competition. Only, I care more about Chloe's happiness than I do about fighting for something that isn't mine. Chloe chose Devon. That was the moment my feelings for her stopped mattering. Even now, there's no way Chloe and I can be together after she's been with him. That would be wrong on so many levels.

I put a great amount of thought into my feelings for Chloe every time Devon's come home after one of their fights and cussed her out. He thinks I'm being a good brother by listening to him, but in reality I want nothing more than to knock him out cold, go to Chloe, and say to hell with brotherly loyalty.

So then why, as I stand staring up at the treehouse, are my nerves hammering my heart into my throat like a confession is about to spew from me the moment I see my brother?

With a deep, calming breath, I start to climb the ladder. I hear the first crash before I make it to the landing.

"What the hell are you doing?" My scream of outrage rips through me as I enter the treehouse and see Devon holding my entire stack of CDs and hurling them one by one at the nearest wall.

He turns to me, reminding me of the Hulk: furrowed brows taking over his face, shoulders reared back and waiting to attack. It's the look he uses on the football field against his opponents. "I told you not to follow me."

"Why? So you could destroy our stuff?"

Devon lets out a grunt as his fist meets the wall. "Shit!" he cries.

"Just sit for a minute." My voice is calmer, hopeful. "Talk to me."

He begins to pace the length of the space, shaking his head, trembling with adrenaline. I've never seen him like this before. He looks partially on the verge of tears, partially infuriated. He kicked the steroids in the fall because of the suspension, but I had a suspicion he turned to them again once he lost his football scholarship. Now, everything about Devon screams rage, something induced by the drugs.

"I bet you're happy, aren't you? All this time, pining after my girl," Devon spits his words. "You didn't even wait five minutes before swooping in to—what did you say—comfort her?"

It takes everything in me to mask my frustration. He's right. It didn't take me long at all because I know how Devon is. Chloe deserves better. She deserves to be worshipped, to be awash in the glow of candlelight just because a guy wants to woo her. She deserves to be loved in every possible way a beautiful, unusual, sweet girl should be loved. She deserves someone loyal to stand beside her in even her worst moments. I've often imagined what being in a relationship with Chloe would feel like, and I know it's nothing like what she and Devon had.

"Do you love her?" I already know the answer, and it kills me.

"What?" Devon glares. "What the hell does that have to do with anything? She's my girlfriend, not my wife. I don't have to love her to want to fuck her."

I cringe. Physically cringe. If Devon weren't my brother I'd have tossed him out of the treehouse by now.

"*Was* your girlfriend," I correct him. I can't help myself. "You don't deserve or own a single piece of her."

Devon steps forward in my direction, puffing out his chest. "I'm right, aren't I? You want her. You always have. Have you two been fucking around on me this entire time?"

"No! Cut the shit, Devon. We both know you haven't exactly

been a loyal, doting, boyfriend. You two had your shot. It's over. Now you can move on."

Devon's face contorts into something I've never seen before. Sadness, maybe. Shame. "I wanted it to work. I wanted her to be the one."

My heart breaks a little. Devon may not know what it means to love someone like Chloe, but he wants to. I see that now. "Just give her some space. You two can't work things out when you're heated like this," I say. "The drinking doesn't help. Sleeping around on her definitely doesn't help. You think she doesn't know what you're doing behind her back? The whole school talks about it, Dev. If you really care about her—I don't know—maybe it's best to just let her go."

My words seem to have the opposite effect than I intended. Devon drops the last of the CDs in his hands and stalks toward me until the air from his nose sprays onto my face. "Is that what you were doing with Chloe earlier? Convincing her to give me space?"

"What? No!"

"You like the way seconds taste, bro? Go on. Have her. I've had my fill."

The first time I ever punched Devon was a complete accident. It was almost two years ago and we were taking turns at the bag, holding it in place for each other and letting off steam after losing a football game one night. Devon got distracted by his phone and stepped away from the bag, pulling it to the side, and I nailed him. Hard.

This time is no accident.

My left hand shoves him away as my right arm cocks back before ramming into his left cheek. It's a mechanical reaction to his words, but even if I stopped to think about what he said, I'd still punch him. I'm not sure if it's Devon's disrespect for Chloe or the truth he's revealing with such hateful words that affects me more. But whatever it is fills me with venom.

A surprised Devon falls onto the couch, then springs up just as fast. He lunges for me, but I haven't been drinking like him. His offense is weak and easy to shield. I step to my right and let him fall into the desk. I don't want to fight my brother. I just wanted to make him bleed for what he said about Chloe. Mission accomplished. Devon swipes his nose, smearing crimson across his face.

He growls, some feral, awful noise, before searching the room for something else to destroy. My sketchbooks sit in a stack atop my desk like always. They're the one thing in the treehouse that everyone knows is off limits. I'm practically shaking as he reaches for a book at the top of the pile. I already know which one it is, and it's as good as gone.

Devon holds it up, taunting me with it before attempting to rip it in two.

"What the hell are you doing?" I roar.

He pauses, and there's a flicker of something in his eyes. Maybe he's completely out of it. Surely he'll wake up tomorrow without a clue about the destruction he caused tonight. To the hearts he broke—including mine. I want to believe he'll feel guilty for his actions, but as much as I love my brother, I know there's something dark deep down within him.

When he realizes the sketchbook is too thick to tear whole, I sigh with relief, but it's short-lived. Next thing I know, he's opening the book and ripping each page out, one by one, until there's a flurry of paper falling around us. At least he's not shredding them. I rush to the desk, grabbing a stack of sketchbooks and toss them over the outside rail, keeping six years of work safe from Devon's obsessive rage.

As hard as I'm shaking with anger, I know it's time to walk away from this. "I'm outta here, bro. Don't even think about going after Chloe tonight." I turn to exit.

The treehouse might be in shambles tomorrow, but I can worry about it in the morning when everyone is sober. I'll stay with Chloe tonight to make sure Devon doesn't start another fight. Tomorrow will be a new day and I'll be of clearer mind to deal with him—with all of this. This ends tonight.

"Hey, *bro*," Devon says, letting the last syllable linger, causing the hair on the back of my neck to bristle.

I swing around, expecting a fist in my face. Instead, I watch as Devon slams his fifth of whiskey into the lantern above our heads, instantly cracking both the bottle in his hands and the glass protection of the lantern. An ear-piercing crash resounds through the air. My arms fly above my head, shielding myself from the shower of glass that sprays in all directions.

When I look up, Devon's face is disturbingly unfazed as he holds the broken whiskey bottle above his head, an angry sneer on his bloodied face.

We're locked in a stare-down, waiting to see who will make the next move, so focused that neither of us sees the lantern swing loose from the hook above our heads. It tumbles heavily against the floorboards with a crash and a clatter before fire and gas begin to chase the booze-drenched pages of my sketchbook. A trace of kerosene infiltrates my nostrils, the odor suddenly dominating my senses. The rest plays out in slow motion.

Devon's wicked smile as he lunges forward, the fragment of glass tearing into my shoulder.

Pages upon pages of my hard work going up in flames.

The rapidly growing fire.

Devon's scream as he barrels into me.

The fall . . .

Death.

CHAPTER 6

DARKNESS (PART ONE)

CHLOE

My body is physically shaking as I'm pulled from my sleep, a slumber that took me a surprisingly short time to fall into. The nearby sirens and flashing lights only add to the surge of adrenaline and confusion that Gavin left me with. My mind is restlessly spinning as the events of the past several hours come rushing back full force.

With a groan, I turn and sink back into my mattress, attempting to crawl back through the thick haze and into my sleepy dreams. The shaking continues, and this time it's accompanied by a voice. "Chloe. Wake up. We need to go."

"Jazz?" My mind is foggy, but I would know my best friend's voice anywhere.

"Come on, Chloe. Get up. Now!" Her voice is like a cold bucket of water being thrown on me.

I sit up and focus on her cute, pug nose and bright blue eyes, which look swollen even in the darkness. "What's wrong?"

My parents are in Florida, too consumed with a new property management venture there to attend my graduation. Knowing that, my friends tend to come and go as they please. Jazz, however, is always welcome whether my parents are here or not. She's been my best friend since our first day of high school.

She throws me a t-shirt and pair of jeans. "Get dressed. We'll talk in the car."

Once in the car I turn to her. She's crying. "What is going on? You're scaring me."

Jazz glances in my direction, not meeting my eyes, and then returns her focus to the road. Her fingers choke the steering wheel, and I watch as she struggles to take an even breath. My thoughts immediately move through the possibilities of what could have happened, but she speaks before my imagination has a chance to run wild.

"Devon was drunk and left the party mad," she says, her voice ragged. "Gavin must have gone after him, and Stacy found them both unconscious at the base of the treehouse."

I shake my head and relief floods my body. "They'll be fine—"

"The treehouse was on fire when she got there, Chlo," Jazz cuts in.

My heart stutters as I try to keep the panic at bay so I can hear the rest of her story. "Tell me they're okay."

Her fingers lift and then wrap around the steering wheel before she lets out a sob. "I don't know. Stacy was freaking out. She said there was a lot of blood . . . screamed for us to call 911." She shakes her head in disbelief. "They were taken away by ambulance. The paramedics were trying to get a heartbeat—"

A hand flies to my mouth. "No," I whisper.

Another sob escapes her as tears burst from her eyes.

CHAPTER 7

UP IN THE TREEHOUSE

CHLOE

W e spent the majority of our time up in the treehouse in our own respective spaces: Gavin at his desk drawing, Devon at the punching bag working out, and me on the couch writing. It was a constant battle between art and fitness as Devon and Gavin fought over the music playlist. Devon wanted heavy metal to work out to, and Gavin wanted acoustic to sketch to. I was forced to be the tiebreaker, which never ended well.

"Chloe, you have to choose. What do you want to listen to?" Gavin put me on the spot one day, but I was ready. After finding the playlist I created, I lay back on the couch and watched their reactions. Gavin grinned like the Cheshire Cat when his favorite Breaking Benjamin song came on. His reaction over something so minor filled me with happiness.

When the next song came on, though, Gavin's face changed and Devon cheerfully knocked his punching back straight into the wall. "That's what I'm talking about!"

The custom playlist was the best solution for us all, but I'll never forget the pang in my chest when I witnessed Gavin's disappointment. He'd thought I'd chosen him—that he was the winner. For some reason that moment played on my mind for years. I was only trying to make everyone happy, but if I'd had to make a choice, even that early on in our friendship, I would have chosen Gavin.

Other than some harmless squabbles, our friendship was simple. We did practically everything together and had fun doing it. The twins were polar opposites, but I was able to connect with each of them on different levels.

Devon brought out an adventurous side in me, teaching me to climb a tree, fish, and water-ski. If it weren't for him, Gavin and I would have spent days upon days holed up in the treehouse.

Gavin, although he enjoyed being spontaneous, had a greater passion for art and nature. His sketches were vivid in color, bringing the world around us to life through his unique perspective. His art lifted from the page and existed among us—among our reality. He paid earnest attention to the intricacies of each scenery object, exaggerating them, calling attention to beauty that so often goes unnoticed . . . like spongy green moss on a tree, revealing its age like worn felt . . . or the strength of the tree bark, etched with aged lines and crevices. Gavin once told me that while the roots of the tree support its structure, each branch carries a story of its own.

Every one of our adventures became a sketch, which in turn inspired my writing. I wrote—short stories mostly—based on our adventures together. But I wasn't the only storyteller. We soon found out that Gavin was capable of far more than one-off sketches.

We were fourteen when Gavin was hard at work on a comic book. He never offered to show us what he was creating while he was lost in his own world, and it felt too private to even ask. But at the end of that summer, Gavin surprised us by pulling us to the center of the treehouse with his sketchbook in hand. "It's not done yet, but I want to show you something."

With our stomachs pressed against the floorboards, we eagerly awaited the book's contents to be revealed.

The first sketch resembled the very tree structure we spent our long days in. It featured two boys, one dressed in ripped jeans and a tank top that revealed his bulging arms, and another with glasses, khaki pants, and a white zip-up sweater. A girl stood between them wearing a sundress, fists clenched tight and a fierce expression on her face. The title: *Up in the Treehouse*.

As the book went on, a bully cornered the girl, and the two boys came to her rescue. With help from the boys, the girl learned how to become her own superhero. They taught her to stick up for herself and face the bullying head-on by standing taller, speaking out, and walking away. In the end, the trio became superheroes for others undergoing bully attacks. Their hiding place where they would regroup and restore their energy was the treehouse.

It wasn't your typical comic, but it was powerful—so powerful I had tears in my eyes by the time the book was closed. Even Devon's eyes gleamed with pride for his brother's talent. When they hugged, I thought my heart would explode.

I was certain in that moment above any other that Gavin and Devon were as different as two brothers could get . . . and that their love for each other was perfect.

CHAPTER 8

DARKNESS (PART TWO)

CHLOE

W e arrive at the hospital to find the waiting room jam-packed with our friends, all of them heaving sobs of loss and devastation. My own screams drown out everything around me as I fall to my knees and let go. I'm assuming the worst from their reactions.

Guilt, heartbreak, anger, sadness, disbelief, rage, fear, and desolation . . . it all racks my body from within as I try to grab onto something—anything—to keep me from falling. But I can't find anything. I'm only aware that my hands are numb, my vision dark, my voice raw, and my tears scalding my face.

I don't know who peels me off the stark white linoleum floor of the hospital or how I eventually end up in the family waiting room with the twins' father and stepmom. But here I am. They're the ones who break the news to me.

Devon was pronounced dead on the ambulance ride to the hospital. It was a root at the base of the tree that broke his fall, the ultimate cause of his death.

Death.

I can't breathe.

I can't move.

I can't . . .

"Gavin?" I manage to ask, my voice cracking with heartbreak. I am terrified yet desperate to know if he is okay. By the Rhodes' silence, I know the news hasn't been delivered yet. When a doctor finally arrives an eternity later, we cling to each other for support.

"He's unconscious but stable," the doctor informs us. "His condition is not unusual after such severe trauma. Now, we monitor him and wait."

For day after endless day, we await Gavin's fate. When I'm not at the hospital I hole myself up in my bedroom, curtains drawn, practically motionless as I remain in a deep depression. Guilt gnaws at me. Everything hurts. Every move feels wrong. *Breathing* feels wrong.

Knowing that Devon was drunk out of his mind that night makes no difference to me. It's my fault he died. I'm the one who hurt him to the point of self-destruction. I'm the reason he was drinking excessively, the reason he lit the treehouse on fire and then fell to his death while trying to save himself. Everything leading up to Devon's death falls on my shoulders. And if Gavin doesn't pull through . . . I shudder to even think about it.

I stay with him every moment I can, crying by his bed, praying for him, squeezing his hand so hard he'll have no choice but to wake up and tell me it hurts. I wait for his dad to kick me out of the hospital, for my friends to yell at me for being the cause of all of this, but it never happens. No one but me knows why the boys were in the treehouse that night.

At least that's what I thought.

It's four days later when Stacy approaches me in the hospital cafeteria. I'm used to Stacy's glare, but this one doesn't just burn a hole through my head; it burns one through my heart, too. She had maintained a friendship with the boys all throughout school, so she has every right to be upset. Gavin was always too nice to shut her out completely, and I feared Devon always had the hots for her, even when we dated. I try not to think about the Stacy who smashed my head into the locker as she plops herself in the seat across from me.

"I know it was you." She speaks quietly, but it's clearly a threat.

My face must be beet red. It feels iron hot, and my palms immediately start to sweat. "What do you mean?" I manage to choke out.

I see the fire burning behind her eyes. "Devon told me what happened before he . . ." She swallows her words and shakes her head. "This is your fault. What do you think you're doing here? Do you think you're *helping* Gavin? If anything, you're guaranteeing he never wakes up."

Without even thinking, I reel my arm back and bring my palm across her cheek as hard as I can. A clear *smack* illuminates the air, and for a brief second it brings me justice for all the pain she's caused me. She clutches her cheek in shock and then looks back at me, meeting my furious gaze.

"What?" My voice, no more than a whisper, drips with ire. "It's not my fault." I force the words out because I don't want to believe them. I've been pushing my negative thoughts away to focus on Gavin's recovery, but what if she's right?

"Devon is dead," she hisses, tears brimming at the corner of her eyes. I feel tightening at the back of my throat. "Gavin is in a coma. You realize you're the reason he's unconscious right now, don't you?" The volume of her voice is escalating by the second.

I shift in my seat and my focus darts around the room as I plan my escape route. Stacy may have left me alone these past few years, but I know she's always hated me. I should tell her to go to hell, to leave me alone. I should stand up for myself the way the boys taught me to and tell her that nothing she says will bother me. Except, this time, she might be right.

"If you think I'm going to let you prolong Gavin's recovery, you are *dead* wrong," she spits. "You have no right to be here."

Tears fill my eyes, but I refuse to cry in front of Stacy. Like Devon, I know she sees tears as a sign of weakness.

And that's the exact moment she knows she's won.

"If you choose to stay, I'll tell everyone what you did."

"I can't leave. I need to know he's going to be okay."

"You'll leave now. If they knew what I know, you'd have been thrown out of here days ago."

Stacy's words are the final blow to my beaten and broken heart. I feel helpless, useless, and responsible for all that's transpired. It's time to let go. As much as my heart hurts for Gavin and Devon, there's nothing I want more than for Gavin to recover, and Stacy is probably right about his chances being better if I was gone. The guilt already burning a hole in my gut expands and consumes me in this moment. There's no use fighting anymore.

I nod as the tears begin to fall. "I'll leave." I stand and turn to go.

But apparently this isn't enough for Stacy. She stands, inches from my face, and narrows her eyes. "Gavin will wake up," she promises. "When he does, I'll be there for him. I'll make it my personal goal for him to forget you ever existed."

My parents' response to the tragedy is to fly home from Florida to pack my things and take me back with them for the rest of the summer. In August, they come with me to Oregon and help me get settled, convinced the change of scenery will finally pull me from my depression.

Everything is a blur. I meet my roommate, attend my first class, and even apply for jobs, but I'm just going through the motions. I'm living life like my destiny has been preselected and I'm fated to play it out on autopilot.

The first time I feel a jolt of reality, a reminder that life is continuing while I'm still stuck in the black hole I now know as my life, comes exactly five months after that horrific night. I receive a call from Jazz. It isn't the first time she's called, but it is the first time I've felt ready to answer. She's been a loyal best friend even through my radio silence. She's kept trying, and she finally succeeds tonight.

"I miss you Chlo," she says when I answer. Her voice carries strength, not sadness like everyone else who speaks to me. It fills me with something inexplicable, and it's the first moment since that awful night that I feel like more than a walking zombie.

"Did you get my messages?"

I did. I know that Gavin got released from the hospital shortly after my departure. I know he left with a broken leg and brownish-yellow remnants of his fall along the length of his side, his cracked ribs supported by a white gauze bandage. It took some time for his memory to return completely, which guts me more than anything. I should have been there.

"How are you doing?" she prompts when I don't respond.

A pang in my chest answers her question, although I know she doesn't hear it. "It still hurts."

"I know, Chlo. Do you want me to come visit? Or will you be home for Thanksgiving?"

I shake my head vigorously. My parents have already asked me to spend the holiday at home with them. Not that they would pay me much attention if I did go home. It would be much of the same. Me, coming and going as I please. Them, too into their own lives to care much where I am or who I'm with. But it doesn't matter because I've already made up my mind. "I can't." I don't need to explain why. It's just too soon.

"What will you do?"

"Stay here. There's a homeless shelter I'm going to volunteer at. And I have a lot of homework to catch up on."

I don't want to explain that my grades are suffering. I plan to spend the entire Thanksgiving break studying and doing extra credit work to catch up. After a couple months of neglecting my grades, I've found that burying my mind in schoolwork is actually a perfect distraction from the dark places my mind tends to wander.

Jazz is silent for a moment before speaking again, as if considering her words. "He was asking about you."

My heart ceases in my chest, panic rising, and I think I might be sick. I drop the phone and it lands on my bed, cushioned between my skin and my comforter. As I do every time Gavin Rhodes enters my mind, I begin to shake. A muffled sound comes from the phone beside me, but I know I can't continue the conversation. So I hang up.

If I've learned anything over the last few months, it's that guilt is a killer. I may never let go of the guilt I feel about Devon, but I am learning how to cope with it and maintain some semblance of a life. I understand this kind of guilt as the kind I can't control—at least, I don't know *how* to control it. Not yet. The other kind, the guilt I feel over hanging up on Jazz when she's just trying to be my friend, eventually snaps me back to life. I've missed my best friend.

When I call Jazz back a week later to apologize, I am terrified I've already lost her. She could easily dismiss me, her psychotic head case of a best friend whose life is in shambles with no hope of recovery. But of course, she forgives me. She forgives me and then flies to Oregon to help me in the soup kitchen over Thanksgiving break.

We make a pact during her visit that she will never mention Gavin to me again, and she won't tell him anything about me. I know she doesn't understand and is reluctant to agree, but if I'm going to attempt to move past the tragedy, the best chance I have is to leave the twins in my past.

That visit from my friend is probably what saves my life. The darkness I've been battling is too dark to fight alone. She breathes life back into me, and I'll be forever grateful. And even after she flies home, the light begins to seep back into my world, and I embrace it with open arms.

Still, I refuse to visit Bonney Lake. That's a reality I don't think I'll ever be ready for.

Branch Two

FOUR YEARS LATER

"Life is the art of drawing without an eraser." ~ John W. Gardner

Chapter 9

Bonney Lake, WA

Chloe

There are times I still awaken with wild eyes and my body drenched in sweat. I search the darkness for Jazz, my heart beating down the walls of my chest, waiting for the news to be delivered. News that would alter my future and haunt me every single damn day of my life. When I finally make sense of my surroundings I realize where I am and force the lingering images of that fateful night away.

Today marks almost four years since Devon's death, and I'm about to take the final exit off the freeway and into my hometown of Bonney Lake. I've made great attempts to suppress every memory of this place, but the familiarity of my surroundings proves my efforts have been futile. My car veers to the shoulder in reaction to the erratic pounding of my heart.

You can do this, Chloe.

When it came time for me to make arrangements to head back to Florida after college graduation, my parents broke the news that they would be traveling around Europe for the entire summer. They asked me to go to our house in Bonney Lake and watch over things while they tried to sell it. After this summer, Florida will be their permanent residence.

My first goal upon learning the news: find a new place to live as soon as possible. Knowing I would need some sort of income, I interviewed for jobs and was offered a position as a creative writer at BelleCurve Creative in Bellevue. It was a better opportunity than I expected. I certainly wasn't looking for a long-term commitment since I didn't know what I would do once summer came to an end. Still don't.

So here I am at the corner of Hancock and Robles, releasing my lunch onto the hot asphalt in the middle of June. I'm trembling from toe to mouth, anxiety weighing heavily on my mind, trying desperately to block the memories that come with being back here. Four years of avoiding this town was not long enough.

Once I've emptied the contents of my stomach, I crawl back into my car and maneuver it deep into the neighborhood until I arrive at the cul-de-sac of my childhood home. Not much has changed. My house still stands on the lake beside the thick of the woods. Beyond it lies what I imagine are still the burnt remnants of the treehouse the twins and I shared—and broken memories. Broken because every wonderful childhood memory I once had has been tarnished.

Everything is quiet except for a few kids playing hopscotch down the street. Two boys and a girl. I smile as the girl screeches when one of the boys nudges her. I long for the days of being carefree and innocent, clueless to the tragedy that surrounds us. At the same time my heart aches for that girl's future. Will she still be a friend to those boys in six years when hormones are raging and competition is fierce? Will she be forced to make a decision that could alter their lives forever?

My phone buzzes from my back pocket and I quickly answer it, hoping it's the distraction I've been waiting for. Looking at the caller ID, I see it is. "Jazz," I sigh with relief.

"Are you home?"

"Just pulled into my driveway. Please tell me you're coming over now."

"On my way," she assures me. "Just had to pick up a few things at the store, but I'll be there in five."

When I hang up, I debate whether I want to step into the house alone. But if I'm being honest with myself, it's not really my home that I'm afraid of. I muster the strength to gather my bags and let myself in.

I knew my parents were in renovation heaven recently, but I didn't realize the house I was walking into would be completely foreign to me. It's . . . refreshing and actually does wonders for my anxiety.

The family room looks bigger, and I realize it's because they knocked down the wall between it and the main entrance. The carpets have been replaced with large, deep brown tiles, and not one piece of furniture is how I remember it. The entertainment center takes up almost the entire wall now.

As I familiarize myself with my new surroundings, I find that I'm more at peace than when I drove here. Maybe this won't be so bad. And then I step into my old room.

It's just as I remember it.

A twin bed is nestled under the window, a tall dresser beside it. I turn back toward the door, and my eyes stop on the white desk. It's mostly empty, but the bulletin board above it glares back at me through Devon's eyes. So many eyes. His face is everywhere. Gavin's are there too. Both sets of eyes have haunted me for the past four years.

My head is spinning, and I can feel the sweat begin to form on my palms. I practically run out of my room, slamming the door behind me and catching my breath as I curl over my knees.

Another door slams, snapping me from my panic. "Jazz!" I scream.

"I'm here!" she shouts back, and the next thing I know her arms are around me, pulling me upwards.

My fists grip her shirt as I steady my breathing. "I was expecting it to look different. The whole house looks different," I choke out. "I just figured my room . . ."

Jazz pulls me back out into the living room and sits me on the couch. It's the first time I'm really taking in her appearance. She told me she was letting her hair grow out, but I wasn't expecting such a drastic change. Her pixie cut is now shoulder-length with wispy layers. But the changes don't stop at her hair. She's ditched her many earrings for just two on each ear, and her clothes are, dare I say, classy.

Apart from her style, though, I know my friend hasn't changed much. We talk every week on the phone, and she's still the same caring yet blunt person she's always been.

"Your room? What is it that hurts the most?" she asks gently, but the question might be more than I'm capable of responding to. I've asked myself the same thing for years, and I've never been able to give myself one straight answer.

I give her the best response I can conjure up, one that my therapist helped me realize. "I'm terrified of the darkness and anything that reminds me of it." This is true. Devon's death gutted me, and the patchwork that made life livable again was poorly manufactured.

"Well, my goal for the next week is to make you totally comfortable here before I leave."

I groan. That's right. Jazz and her hot, olive-skinned fiancé, Marco, won't be around for the summer. She sure struck gold with that one. We were all friends in high school, but it wasn't until Marco and Jazz ran into each other on a camping trip the summer after graduation that they started dating. He recently accepted an apprenticeship at some hotshot company on Wall Street. She's following him out to New York, where they'll live for at least three months. Maybe forever if Marco is offered a job.

"Is it just your room that bothers you? I say we pack it up and redecorate for the summer," Jazz says with much more enthusiasm than I feel. "Let's work on it this week! You can have my bed, too. I'm sure my parents will drop it off this weekend." She's practically jumping up and down with excitement. She loves a good project.

As much as I love my best friend, she's much too giddy for me this afternoon. "You are not spending your last week here redecorating my room. I'll take the guest bedroom," I say with a smile. "Anyway, I need to go to the grocery store to get some things."

Jazz grins. "Already done. Wait here."

I stare open-mouthed as Jazz walks to the entrance and hoists up two recyclable bags filled to the brim with food. We race to the kitchen to unload. If I know my best friend well enough, she's already stocked up on my favorites.

One look at the contents of the first bag makes me frown. "Vegetable stir fry? Jazz, you've lost your touch." I feign disappointment.

Jazz snatches the bag from me and sets in on the other side of her. "That's the boring stuff. You know, the stuff you have to eat to maintain that ridiculously perfect figure of yours. This"—she gestures to the other bag—"is where it's at."

One by one she begins pulling out the contents. Easy Cheese, Lemonheads, Twigs, bagels, strawberry cream cheese, Pop Rocks, coffee flavored ice cream, Cinnamon Toast Crunch . . . By the time we get to the bottom of the bag, I'm rolling with laughter. Jazz is grinning from ear-to-ear, obviously pleased as she tears open a box of kettle corn and throws it in the microwave. Then she opens the fridge, grabs two of my dad's Pyramid ales, and hands one to me.

We take our kettle corn and beers and sit on the back patio that overlooks the lake. Now this is a memory I forgot without meaning to. Mount Rainier sits high above us, towering gloriously over the rows of evergreens and the homes on the other side of the lake. A reflection of the snow-capped mountain appears to be painted on the water. Boaters and jet skiers are gliding by, taking advantage of the warm day.

I take a deep breath, and for the first time in four years I actually feel my lungs expand and take in the air around me. I've tried hard to forget so much over the past four years that my memory took the good stuff with it. This beautiful sight is a perfect reminder of everything good that still exists . . . that might still exist within me, too.

CHAPTER 10

REUNION

CHLOE

gainst my wishes and better judgment, Jazz and I are walking from our taxi into Babalouie's, a sports bar in the heart of our small town. The local dive is warm and oddly charming with its mismatched décor comprised of neon signs and beer advertisements that clutter the walls. The jukebox is playing some rock tune I recognize but can't name. The pool tables are full, and every table is already taken. Overwhelmed by the boisterous voices and thickening crowd, I get immediately anxious.

I haven't seen or spoken to any of our friends from high school since I left town. And after numerous emails telling me so-and-so wanted to connect with me on some new social media platform, I changed my email address. I had already deleted all of my old social media accounts before leaving town, set on cutting ties with the heart of my guilt.

Jazz's gaze wanders the room until she finds what she's looking for and smiles. She pulls me behind her, weaving us through the energetic crowd until we're standing in front of two high-top tables that have been pushed together. Marco's arms snake around her, pulling her to his lap. He's definitely one of those hard-to-look-at types with his dark, powerful eyes. Their pairing would have seemed odd in high school, with her radical ways and his focused professionalism, but she's lightened him up a bit and he's toned her down some. Not in a way that changes who she is, but I've already noticed she's more comfortable with her natural appearance than she was in high school.

"Chloe!" Blaine is the first to stand and wrap his arms around me. The rest of my friends follow as we exchange hellos.

At one point during the greetings I search for Jazz and glare at her. She just throws her head back and laughs. She told me it would be just a few of our closest friends. I don't even remember half these people. And the ones I do know I haven't spoken to in years, yet here they are acting as if I didn't abandon them all for my own dark world of self-absorbed, psychotic depression.

"There's a chair back here, Chlo!" Phoebe shouts.

I smile at the sight of her tucked in the back corner, exactly where I want to be. I begin weaving my way around the crowd to reach her and give her a hug before I sit down. Her hair is still as blonde and beautiful as it was in high school. I bounce one of her ringlets with my palm like I used to do, and we laugh.

Time goes by and I don't have to speak much. My chatterbox friends are recounting the last four years of college and bragging about upcoming jobs and internships. I remain silent and sip my vodka soda, listening and smiling at all the right parts, just as I taught myself to do at the social events I attended during my tenure at Oregon State. It's safer to blend in and avoid opening myself up to questioning. I'm not sure if I'm ready to give any answers.

"What about you, Chloe? Are you back for good?" Blaine's voice cuts through my thoughts, and all eyes turn to me. My face heats and I'm suddenly racking my brain for something to say. I know I've been recluse for the past four years, but surely Jazz hasn't kept everyone completely in the dark about my life.

"Yup. She's here for good." Jazz beams proudly at me. "Chloe graduated from OSU with a degree in journalism."

I take the assist and run with it. "I just accepted a writing job in Bellevue. My parents are selling the house, so if the timing works out, I'll be moving into my own place soon."

"Is this the first time you've been home since graduation?" Jen asks.

I nod, a forced smile plastered on my face. "It's nice to be back." I hope that's enough for them. As much as I want to restore lost friendships, I need to take things one step at a time. No one seems to find my response odd, and they don't make me elaborate. I look around the table, and I'm happy to see my friends turn and break off into animated conversations. Relieved to be off the hook, I catch Jazz laughing with Marco about something food-related, and I smile at their exchange as my gaze drifts around the room.

It's a head-on collision when our eyes meet from across the bar. He's walking toward our table but stops dead in his tracks when he sees me. I freeze too, captured by the fierceness in his green eyes. Even from a distance and after all this time, Gavin's eyes send a bolt of light directly to my core. The intensity dies when he turns his attention on who I'm sitting with, and then he frowns.

Just as Gavin turns to leave, Marco yells out, "Hey, Gavin! Yo, buddy. We're over here."

My eyes never leave Gavin, so I watch as he jerks to a stop and hesitates to turn back around. A second or two goes by before he faces us again, expressionless, and makes his way toward us. If I could get away with ducking my head and fleeing toward the exit, I would. But he's already seen me and my brain is too foggy to come up with a decent excuse to run, so I continue watching him, transfixed by his every move, his every feature.

Gavin has always been well built, but he never had a body-builder's stature like Devon. He clearly spends more time at the gym now. His neck is thicker, his shoulders are broader, and everything else matches perfectly. The light green shirt he's wearing fits his body just right. He's let his hair grow some too, creating a perfectly disheveled mess up top. Girls must love running their fingers through that shaggy nest. But it's the stubble on his face that throws me completely off my equilibrium. Gavin has always been good looking, but sexy is the word I would use to describe him today. Gavin Rhodes is sexy as hell—and still not returning my gaze.

I watch as he greets the group nearest him, giving them hugs and smiling as he says hello. A girl I don't know hugs him a little longer than the rest and my stomach tightens. Jazz is nearest to him when she darts a look at me and says something to Gavin. It's something about me, I can tell, because he looks up and his eyes land briefly on me. He gives me a nod but I don't have time to respond before he turns toward the bar.

My heart sinks into my toes. This is as good as it's going to get with Gavin, because Gavin Rhodes hates me.

I'm not a drinker. Never have been. I'm not sure if it's the college scene that turned me off the stuff, or if it's just that I don't enjoy losing control. Tonight, however, is an exception. Tonight, I drink.

Jazz carries the tray like a pro, effortlessly balancing eight shot glasses and setting them down near the pool table. When Jazz suggested pool, I jumped at the opportunity to get away from Gavin. Him ignoring me is worse than if he were to yell and scream at me. It means I'm nothing to him, and I can't handle that thought right now.

Blaine quickly offers to partner with me against Jazz and Marco, and I find myself loosening up during the game. Oddly, I can shoot a decent game of pool in my inebriated state. With laser focus, I line up my cue and tap the white ball without a second thought. When the white hits the solid blue ball in the wrong spot, I pout and shuffle over to the tray of drinks. Blaine hugs me from the side and tells me it's okay. I give him the brightest smile I can muster.

Throwing my head back, I toss down the sticky, sweet substance and pound the shot glass on the table. My friends cheer. Without thinking, my eyes dart across the room toward Gavin. I know exactly where he's sitting because I haven't been able to look away from him long enough to lose track. This time, his face radiates resentment as he glares back at me.

Oh, shit.

The liquid seeping through my system instantly turns to fire, and it burns like the flames of guilt that have consumed me for so long. His brother drank too much and died as a result, all because of me, and here I am slamming back shots right in front of him.

I think I'm going to be sick.

I run for the nearest exit, knowing Jazz is too wrapped up with her fiancé to notice. Throwing myself against the exterior brick wall of the bar, I gulp in a deep breath of air, forcing my stomach to get a handle on itself. I've already lost my lunch once this week. I'm not trying to make it a habit.

A buzzing takes over my body so strongly that I don't recognize the sound of the door opening beside me.

"Let's go," a voice barks.

When I look up, I find Gavin towering over me, fuming. "Wh-what? No, I can't leave Jazz. I'll be fine."

The intensity on Gavin's face is layered with red, and I swear I see smoke puffing from his ears. If I weren't so sick to my stomach, I'd giggle.

"You're coming with me. Now." He takes me by the arm against my alcohol-induced protests. I stop physically fighting him by the time we get to the passenger side of an unfamiliar truck, but I'm ready to spew some words in his direction when he opens the door, picks me up, and drops me into the leather seat. Literally drops me, like I'm a twenty-five-pound bag of sand. "Put on your seatbelt." He slams the door. A different door than the one I remember. Looks like Gavin's old truck got upgraded. There's a pang of loss in my heart.

"What about my purse?" I shriek when he climbs into the driver's seat. He tosses my bag at me before shifting his truck into drive, not saying a word.

"Jazz and I caught a taxi here, you know? We weren't planning on driving home if that's what you're so worried about."

Gavin is already crawling to the stop sign, but he taps on his brakes, pitching me forward. I catch myself on the dash with my palms and turn to him, returning his glare from earlier. "What the hell is wrong with you?"

"Put your seatbelt on," he says without looking at me.

I throw myself back and place my seatbelt over my shoulder. "Fine. But you know this is false imprisonment, right? You can't just force me into confined spaces with you because you disapprove of my behavior."

He doesn't respond, just waits for the click of the seatbelt before he begins driving again. I turn my head to face the passenger window for the entire ride home. Neither of us speaks, so the truck is filled with complete silence save for the roar of the engine. Gavin doesn't even turn on the radio to fill the emptiness.

By the time we get to my house I've calmed down some, but I still don't understand his anger. If he hates me so much, why give me a ride home? I would have been fine with Jazz, or anyone else for that matter. Gavin did not have to rescue me.

"Are you going to tell me what that was all about?" I watch his reaction to my question and gulp as I see his jaw remain rock-hard, the heat of his glare shooting lasers through the front windshield.

"Nope."

"Why not, Gavin?"

For some reason, the sound of his name gets his attention and his eyes turn to me. They're still heated, and if I were smart I would look away. But when it comes to Gavin Rhodes, I am obviously not smart. In the moment before he speaks next, I'm reminded of the last time we were alone, right before the accident. I remember the intensity of his warmth, certain he was going to kiss me . . . but then it sounded like he was saying goodbye. I didn't think I'd ever see Gavin again after that night. Even knowing I'd be back here for a summer, I figured he would be long gone.

"Chloe. I don't want to talk, okay? I got you out of that bar before you got any more shitfaced than you already are. You're home safe now. Go to bed."

"You don't want to talk to me now? Or ever?" I search his expression, the pain from the last four years flooding my vision. I know I brought this all upon myself, but facing Gavin is hard enough; having him tell me he never wants to talk to me again is unbearable. But I have to know the truth.

"Goodnight, Chloe." He turns forward, and I'm forced to do the only thing I've become good at: walk away.

CHAPTER 11

CHLOE RIVERS

GAVIN

As I back out of her driveway, I'm left battling a live wire that's come loose in my chest. Just the few moments I spent with her tonight have awakened something in me. Feelings I suppressed. Anger I've learned to let go of. Loss I've managed to cope with. And sadness I refused to let myself feel again.

Chloe Rivers.

I never thought I'd see her again, especially after the FOR SALE sign went up in her parent's lawn. When Marco broke the news that she was coming back to housesit for the summer, I might have lost it a little. Not in front of Marco, of course. And it's not like I punched a wall or started screaming or anything like that. That's what Devon would have done. Not me.

The riptides of emotions I've bottled up over the past four years are capable of sending me into beast mode if I so desire, but that isn't what happened. Instead, my heart began to race, sweat started beading at my scalp, and a flood of memories came sailing through, each one reminding me how badly Chloe Simone Rivers broke my heart.

I knew she'd be at the bar tonight. I also knew she would be surprised to see me. Marco has become a good friend—my best friend. He's loyal. Not even Jazz knows the things we talk about, and I'd prefer to keep it that way.

The truth is, before walking into the musty bar, I wanted to see her. After four years, I was curious. What does she look like now? How does she dress? Does she still do that cute hair flip thing when she's mad? Do her long lashes still scrape the top of her cheekbones when she closes her eyes?

But the moment I saw her again, something inside me, something that had been buried with my brother, rose to the surface. Everything about her screams familiarity, but she's somehow . . . different. Her hair is as long as I remember it. She was beautiful back then, and she was radiant in the bar—even with the pain in her expression, the slump of her shoulders, and the flush in her cheeks as her eyes locked on mine. It was too much, too soon.

So I turned away, considering that possibly another day, preferably in a private place, would be a better time for us to talk. Or maybe there didn't need to be another run-in. I got what I wanted. I saw her. She seems to be doing fine. But the pain in my chest won't fucking go away when I think of her. Four years ago, she left without a single word. When I was unconscious, no less.

What the hell was I doing? I was stupid to think that a surprise run-in with Chloe was the best thing for us. At that moment, as I walked away, my curiosity transformed into anger. Anger I thought I'd buried in a sacred place in my heart. Clearly it's been festering beneath the surface all along, and all it took was a little gust of wind, one stolen glance, to uncover it. Turns out it's alive and well, climbing rapidly like vines inside the walls of my chest, and it was threatening to take over my body as my eyes locked on hers.

"Hey, Gavin! Yo, buddy. We're over here."

Screw you, Marco. He'd seen me and knew I was trying to leave, and now I had no choice but to join the party. Then Jazz had to greet me with a hug, just to whisper in my ear, "She's nervous too."

At this, I cracked. For a second, I let my focus wander back to her, accidentally meeting her eyes, and I gave her a nod, acknowledging her. There was a glimmer of something in the glassy blues staring back at me, something behind the pain, and I wanted desperately to look deeper. But my own pain, the deep ache in my chest that *she* is the cause of, put a halt on any desire I had to get close to Chloe again.

For the rest of the night, I allowed my anger to dominate my actions. I ignored Chloe at all costs while her eyes burned a hole straight through me, sparking off the titanium shield surrounding my heart. It wasn't until she got up to play pool that I let my gaze wander back to her.

And then Blaine had to touch her. No, he groped her, pulling her close, taking advantage of her inebriated state. The attention he'd been paying her all night told me all I needed to know. There was no way in hell Chloe was going home with anyone but me as drunk as she was.

I found myself wondering if she's really okay. Emotionally, I mean. Devon's death didn't leave her unscathed; I know that. But is she dating again? If she is, what types of guys is she dating? Do they treat her well? These are the questions I never dare ask Marco for fear that he'll take them completely out of context.

I just want Chloe to be okay. I want her to be happy.

That's all.

She was turning green by the time I got to her. Too many shots, not enough water. While her drunken giggles might have been an adorable sound, her attractiveness would have plummeted if she got sick all over the asphalt. This wasn't the Chloe I knew. Then again, it had been four years. This may very well be the new Chloe. People change.

More anger as I lifted her into my truck, her small but tough limbs fighting me. That would have been cute if her breath hadn't smelled like the bottom of a sewer. But what else could I do? I knew Blaine would be all over her when she went back inside. Jazz was even more shitfaced than Chloe, and Marco would be busy taking care of Jazz. Just in case they got worried, I planned to go back and pick them up too. I convinced myself I was doing the right thing for the right reasons.

After a long, silent car ride, I got her home, evaded her questions, and watched her walk the entire way to the house.

Now, as I bury my head in my pillow, I groan. How in the hell am I going to stay away from Chloe Rivers all summer? Because there's no way I can be near her . . . not with the forbidden temptations bulldozing all logical thought from my mind.

CHAPTER 12

LOSING LIGHT

CHLOE

J azz and I are sprawled out on my living room floor. We've been this way for the past few hours, moaning and groaning but barely moving. I've been to the occasional college party, but I've never drank the way I drank last night.

"Holy crap, Chloe. It's never hit me like this before. I can't even remember getting home. I need Funyuns." Jazz rolls over and attempts to stand but curls into a ball instead.

"Gavin drove you and Marco home after he dropped me off. I don't know why he didn't bring us home together." I couldn't sleep when I got home last night, so I waited by the window, fuming over Gavin and worrying about Jazz. As soon as I saw his truck roll up again, I felt relief and confusion wash over me. Does he make it a habit of dropping drunks off at their homes? Or just the ones that live near him?

As she moans, I pull myself to my feet, feeling slightly better after my second nap of the day. I stumble into the kitchen and snatch the Funyun bag from the counter, then grab two waters from the fridge. I toss one bottle to Jazz and sit cross-legged beside her.

"Did you know Gavin would be there last night?"

Jazz tears into the yellow bag before responding with her

mouth full of rings. "No. He rarely comes out. I swear, Chloe. I didn't know."

She pours water down her throat and glances at me. "What happened between you two anyway? Gavin won't say much about it, but I can't believe you two haven't talked at all since Devon died."

"I couldn't."

"Why not?"

I cringe.

"Just tell me, Chlo. I'm your best friend. You can tell me anything, you know? I know what happened was hard on you both, but you two were good friends. I'm surprised neither of you reached out to the other after . . . you know."

One thing I love most about Jazz is that she's unafraid to be honest with me, but she still respects my boundaries. For four years, Jazz has done a fine job of avoiding this topic, knowing it upsets me. We made a pact. But suddenly she's full of questions.

"There's not much I can explain, Jazz. It's been four years, and I'm certain he hates me. You should have seen him toss me into his truck last night. Like a freaking gorilla. I think he growled at me too."

I made a face and Jazz throws her head back and laughs. "That's hot, Chloe." She fans herself. "Gavin growling is definitely yum."

I roll my eyes and steal the bag of Funyuns from her grip. "It was kind of scary, but I don't blame him. If I were him, I'd hate me too."

Jazz sits up and glares. "Seriously, Chloe, why do you say shit like that? Devon's death was not your fault. I thought you moved past all the guilt."

There's no use having this conversation with Jazz. If I were to tell her my true thoughts and fears, the ones that resonate deep within me, the ones that have caused me many sleepless nights, she would involuntarily admit me to some psychotherapy shit.

She will never understand my guilt because it's not something I will ever fully share with anyone.

No.

What Devon read in my journal that night will forever stay between the ghost of Devon Rhodes and me.

Jazz leaves a few hours later, just as the sun begins setting over the water. I'm tempted to watch it, but instead I shower and change into shorts and a t-shirt, then head out the back door.

There's something I have to do.

I slip into the woods, following the same path the twins and I created so many years ago. I'm not surprised to find that the trail is overgrown. Does Gavin still come out here? *Why would he?* What awful memories that would bring. I, for one, couldn't venture back into the woods after Devon's death. I had no desire to see the fire damage, to see where Devon fell . . . I've always assumed the entire tree had burned to the ground, destroying any evidence of that fateful night.

A noise in the woods slows my already lethargic pace. It's not the same noise that guided my original treehouse discovery. No. That was a happy sound of great memories being created. What I hear echoing through the trees now is filled with pure anger—a growl and then the violent hacking of wood.

When I reach the spot in the woods where our sanctuary once sat, I suddenly get dizzy. I have to grab onto something, so I reach out, placing my palm on the nearest tree trunk. There it is. The large wood panels that created the sides of the house are blackened at the bottom, but the house is surprisingly still intact. The structure never burned to the ground like I imagined, but by the looks of the outside, I'm sure most of its contents were destroyed.

A piece of wood flies in my direction, causing me to gasp. I look back up at the structure and see Gavin near the back rail, prying wood from its nails, hacking it apart, and heaving it outward. He doesn't see me, an eerie reminder of the first time I spotted him with Devon in this very spot. I continue to watch him work. He's mechanically ripping apart our very best memories, one wood panel and two-by-four at a time. If I had to guess, I'd say he's been here all day.

Whatever Gavin is doing seems to be therapeutic, and he's nowhere close to stopping. I hold my breath as he slides his shirt over his head and lets it fall to the ground below. He takes a swig of his water, giving me the opportunity to fully admire him.

Unwavering stance. Defined abs on top of a solid build. Strong jaw—all slick with sweat from head to toe. He's not a boy anymore. Gavin Rhodes is a god.

The ridged scar on his left shoulder almost brings me to my knees. There was a bandage on that same spot in the hospital after the treehouse fire. I'd always assumed it was a wound from sprayed glass. But the scar looks more purposeful, as if someone put it there. I shudder, knowing that someone could have only been Devon.

Memories of our time here haunt me. Just being in these woods brings me closer to my past . . . our past . . . and after four years, here Gavin is tearing it down. What I don't understand is . . . why now?

CHLOE, 17 YEARS OLD

"Can you turn your head that way?"

"Why? I've turned my head in every angle possible," I muttered. I'd been standing there in the middle of the woods, posing for Gavin in a ridiculous, custom-assembled superhero costume for over an hour, and he still hadn't finished his sketch.

Gavin laughed. "We're almost done. We're losing light, so let me capture a few things, and then we can go."

I smirked. "Why don't you just take a picture and then sketch from that?" Gavin froze. My hands moved to my hips. "Don't tell me you didn't already think of that."

"I didn't, smarty pants," he quipped. "I guess I could do that if you really want me to. It's just not the same. I like capturing things as they live and breathe in front of me. If I were to take a picture, it's like I'm just sketching a flat image rather than the angles." His face blanched and his eyes darted to mine. "Not that you have a lot of angles . . ."

I peered down at my outfit: a mini skirt and a short white tank top with a gray vest buttoned over it. My breasts were practically toppling out of my C-cups, and the white tank top covering them was see-through in the bright light. I placed my arms around my waist to cover my navel and pouted, suddenly self-conscious.

Gavin sighed and walked toward me. Placing his hands on my shoulders, he chased my eyes with his until I was looking back at him, fully focused. "Hey, it's just me. You're beautiful, Chloe. I wouldn't have asked you to do this if I didn't think you'd be amazing at it. But if you're uncomfortable, I totally understand. I can call Stacy or something." The corner of his mouth twitched with his last comment. He knew what he was doing.

A wave of heat washed over my cheeks the moment he said her name. With a glare, I shoved him and unwrapped my arms from my waist. "We're almost done. Just finish and then we can go."

As much as I acted like standing in the same spot for so long was torture, spending that time with Gavin studying my body was not. In fact, I secretly enjoyed every second of it.

Chapter 13

Too Much, Too Soon, Too Late

Chloe

P repping for a new job is a tricky process, especially when I have no idea where to start. New hire packets and employee manuals with processes and procedures are scattered all over the floor of my living room. Everything is here, from parking pass information to rules about which bathrooms in the building are off-limits.

I'm not complaining, though. BelleCurve Creative is taking a risk on me, and everything I've heard tells me it's a huge opportunity for my career. They hired me based on my writing samples and stellar recommendations from my college English professor. He was a University of Washington alum, same class as the founder of the company.

I may have received a journalism degree because of my passion for writing, but I have no clue if I'll actually use it to be a journalist. I'm finding a greater interest in creative writing, hence my interest in an agency that specializes in everything from video production to traditional advertising. Their PR division seems to be a perfect fit for me: news with a creative spin.

Sometimes I wonder what it would be like to have known what I've wanted to do since I was in diapers the way Gavin has. Gavin's an artist. He sketches and works a colored pencil like it's nobody's business. Writing has always been my passion, but I'm still trying to find my voice. I'm hopeful this job will bring me closer to it.

As I shut my laptop, my thoughts shift back to Gavin's half-naked body as he took his anger out on our old sanctuary. *He's tearing it down.* I can only imagine that seeing me again stoked his flames, and now he's destroying anything that reminds him of me.

Am I really the reason he's turning our old hiding grounds into a scrap pile? Our exchange the night before wasn't pleasant. I shouldn't have drank that much; I know that. And it's clear he hates me. But then why force me into the truck? If he just wanted to make sure I got home safe, there were other options . . .

My brain hurts from obsessing too much. Fresh air is just what I need, so I head outside. As I move down the drive toward the mailbox, I glance over at the woods separating Gavin's house from mine. I frown. At least . . . I think he still lives there.

Jazz pulls into the driveway just as I reach in to pull out the mail. She's beaming at me as she steps out of the car. "Lazy much?"

I know she's referring to my white shorts, baseball tee, and unkempt hair. "Ha ha," I say. "What's the point of graduating from college if you can't bum around the house before life in the real world begins?" I grin at her and trudge up the drive until we're at the front door. "I guess I have been lazy today."

"Today? You've been like this all week. Who studies for a job they already have, anyway?"

She's right. I frown. "Let's go somewhere. I need to get out of the house."

Jazz shrugs. "Sure. I'm up for anything. Well, almost anything." Her face contorts, and I already know what she's thinking. "No bars. I had my fill for the week."

"The week? Try a year. I didn't even know my body could consume that much alcohol."

"It can't," we say simultaneously, causing a fit of giggles between us.

I shower and dress quickly, more than ready to escape the confines of this house. I offer to drive since it was my idea to go somewhere, but we still haven't a clue where we're headed.

"What does everyone do on a Friday night around here?"

"There's a volleyball tournament at the park tonight. We could hang with everyone else if you want." I don't miss the sneaky look she gives me, as if she's afraid I'll be mad she asked.

"We could do that. Who's there?" As long as Gavin won't be there, I'll be fine.

"Everyone. But . . . it's kind of Gavin's thing." *There goes that.* "He throws events to raise money for the organizations he supports. Everyone has to give something, but it can be as little as a dollar. It's mostly about getting sponsors to pitch in and support community events like this to help raise awareness. They're a lot of fun, but I understand if you don't want to go."

I grip the wheel tightly. The fact that Jazz didn't want to share this with me before I asked brings on a wave of anger. "I want to go."

"Okay, then let's go. It's at Allan Yorke Park."

That's Devon's park. At least, it's the park he always dragged us to. "Why wouldn't I want to go?" I play the nonchalant card, wanting desperately to fit in. It's not something I ever strived for in the past, but for some reason, being back has me wanting all sorts of things I didn't know I wanted before.

From the corner of my eye I see Jazz shift uncomfortably. "Because this thing between you and Gavin is awkward enough. We all talk, you know? You two were best friends and then his brother dies and you never speak to him again. I'm sorry, Chloe, I never bring this up because I know it's hard for you, but I'm going to say something: no one understands why you left when you did. We get that you were torn up about Devon's death, but to stay away for four years . . . I know I enabled it, because I love you and I made a promise to you, but you're back now. Pact over."

"I left because—believe it or not—at the time I didn't think I had another choice." I don't want to go into the details about

Stacy. I've never told a soul about our confrontation at the hospital because then I would have to explain the fight with Devon and what he found in my journal. Then they would question if I was to blame for Devon's death, and I just can't go back to the darkness.

Now that Jazz has opened up the door to this conversation, she's not backing down. I feel her turn her entire body so that it's facing me. "So then what is it? Why avoid him now? If you know you made a mistake, you should be trying to fix it."

"I'm not avoiding him. He gave me a freakin' ride home the other night." I can't keep the annoyance out of my voice.

"You know what I mean."

How do I respond to this when I don't even know what happened? It's not that I didn't think of Gavin after the accident. I thought of him every moment of every day until I left for college, and then I still thought of him more than I care to admit. But every time I imagined what I would say to him, the response he gave me in my mind was not one I wanted to face in reality. Part of me knew that I would only be a reminder of the reason Devon died, and I didn't want to cause him any more pain than he'd already suffered. Instead, I locked myself away in my own misery, believing everyone was safer and happier without me around.

"He doesn't want to talk to me, Jazz. You should have seen the way he was glaring at me the other night. And when he took me home, he *told* me he didn't want to talk."

"The fact that he even got in the car with you should speak volumes. I think you need to try harder. Despite what the others think, I know you care about him, but you've done a real shitty job showing it. You should talk to him. You've both changed— and he's been through a lot, just like you."

"Is he happy?"

Jazz shakes her head. "Oh no. You're not doing that. Maybe when you were back at OSU, but now that you're here, you'll have to figure all that out for yourself. Talk to him."

Dejected, I pull into a parking spot and let Jazz go on ahead of me. "I just need a minute."

She hesitates for a second but eventually leaves me in the car. It isn't until she's out of my line of sight that I scream to let out the emotion that's been building in my chest.

Is Jazz right? Obviously I've been a shitty friend to Gavin, but wasn't that better for all of us?

CHLOE, 18 YEARS OLD

The day Stacy confronted me at the hospital wasn't the last time I saw Gavin. I couldn't leave him without saying goodbye, even if he couldn't hear me. I went back to see him a day later, slipped past the waiting room unseen, and waited until his room was clear.

I squeezed his hand, just as I'd done so many times before. But this time, I leaned over his body, my mouth directly next to his ear. I pulled in a shaky breath before beginning, tears already threatening to escape.

"Come back to us," I whispered. "Please come back."

There was no way to battle the heavy emotion of my words. My voice cracked and tear rolled down my eye. Just looking at his bruised body and the tubes entering and exiting different parts of him, mangled my heart. I couldn't imagine a world without Gavin Rhodes in it.

"This world isn't ready to lose you, Gav," I continued with shaky breath. "You'll change lives for the better; I just know it. And there are people here who need you. Who love you. Your dad, Linda . . . me."

I swallowed back the lump in my throat, desperately needing to get through this without letting go completely. "I know it'll be hard without Devon. I know, but you can do this. You have to."

My voice cracked again as I leaned my forehead against his. I couldn't get close enough. "When you wake up, you won't remember that I was here, but I believe you can hear me now." I take a deep pull of air. "No matter what anyone says to you, no matter how much you might blame me for everything, try to remember one thing. The most important thing. That I love you. You know I do, and only you know how much. And I *am* here."

My throat tightened again and I lost the battle when a sob escaped and more tears rolled down my cheeks. They were unstoppable now. "I wish I could stay. It's all I want. But we both know when you wake up everything will be different. I'll be the last person you'll want to see."

I pressed my lips softly against his warm cheek, then hesitated before moving my lips above his. Air scraped the path between our mouths. My body shook as I moved closer and placed my lips on his, skimming them gently with my final words. "You were my greatest friend. Goodbye, Gavin."

He woke up the next day. Jazz called to tell me and urged me to visit, but I'd already made up my mind. Gavin and I would never see each other again. Stacy was a bully, but she was right. Gavin needed to recover; he didn't need me reminding him of everything he'd lost. I couldn't deal with the hate I would see in his eyes, the torture I caused as a result of his brother's death.

Devon was everything to Gavin, and he was gone forever. I was certain that there was no going back to the friendship we once had.

A long string of lights sections off the parking lot from the beachfront of the lake where two volleyball games are in full swing. Onlookers gather around the boundaries of the games, some in beach chairs, some standing. A brightly lit tent stands at the entrance to the sand. Tables beneath it hold merchandise and donation jars. I slip a twenty into one of the jars and hang back from the crowd, leaning against the pole of the tent and forgetting why I decided to come in the first place.

You're showing everyone you're not the heartless asshole they think you are.

Ugh. If I could slap my subconscious self, I totally would.

I look around for a distraction from my thoughts. There's a flyer at the edge of the table, and I grab it, recognizing the art immediately. This is, without a shred of doubt, Gavin's creation.

Drink Water. Drive Safe. That's the name of his series of summer events for an anti-drunk driving campaign. The list of events and dates are on the backside; there must be dozens of them. Gavin has always been charitable—he was an active member of Key Club in high school, always participating in something to "make a difference"—but I can't help but wonder if this event has something to do with Devon.

The sound of shuffling plastic catches my attention. I turn just as Gavin pokes his head through the back entrance of the tent. He freezes when he sees me, but only for a moment. He looks away, staring straight ahead as if I'm not even there. I study him as he sets a box on the table and opens it to start sorting the contents.

"Can I help?" I should have thought about how my voice would sound when I opened my mouth. It's weak and airy, lacking an ounce of confidence. I take a deep breath, hoping to get a grip before I have to speak again.

Gavin shakes his head. "I'm good."

Against my better judgment, my feet carry me forward until he can't avoid me. I'm facing him, our bodies separated by the table between us. "I'd like to help." This time my voice is even, controlled.

I'm not expecting him to look at me, but he does and it's piercing. I'm injected with his reality. Devon went ballistic on graduation night, drinking excessively because of me. And here I am, standing before him, probably causing more damage than good. My only confirmation of that comes in the form of silence. Suddenly I want to clean out the last three hundred dollars from my bank account and give it to him. But I know that whether I could give him three hundred dollars or a million, nothing would give him back what he lost.

"Why are you here, Chloe?"

"Jazz invited me. She said . . ."

He shakes his head. "Not *here*. I mean in town. It's been four years. Why now? I was beginning to think you died right along with him."

I gasp, tears springing to my eyes. His words crack my already iced-over heart, and I turn on my heel and walk away so he can't see the pain he just inflicted. He doesn't need to tell me twice. Jazz is wrong. I don't need to try harder with Gavin. I need to get away from Gavin.

"Fuck." I hear his voice behind me before his footsteps follow mine into the parking lot. "Chloe, stop."

I don't stop. I was right to want to avoid this. Seeing Gavin is hard enough. Hearing him all but confirm my deepest fear—that he blames me for Devon's death—is a punch in the face, a blow propelling me back four years and into the darkness that protected me, that numbed me. All I want is for that numbness to take hold of my body so that I can sink back into it. Let it carry me through these next few months.

His hands are on my arm, swinging me around before I can grab onto the door handle. "I didn't mean that the way it came out."

"Yes, you did," I fire back. "You want to know why I haven't been back here for four years? You think I wanted to face *you* after what happened? After everything you lost because of me? Don't worry, Gavin. You're not the only one who wishes I died that night."

His face contorts as he reels back. "Don't say that. I don't wish that at all. Devon's death was hard enough."

I shouldn't have said that. Too much. Too soon. Too late. "I shouldn't have come."

He doesn't stop me from opening the car door and getting in. By the time I sit down and look back up through the windshield, he's walking away.

CHAPTER 14

WALKING AWAY

CHLOE

J azz won't stop staring at me. "What's your problem?" I ask
her as we approach the entrance to my neighborhood.

"You." She glares at me. "Were you hiding in the car the
entire night?"

"Not the entire night. I ran into Gavin and offered to help.
You know, work on my selflessness, a way of life my best friend so
delicately pointed out I've failed to embrace as of yet."

She narrows her eyes and nods slowly. "Uh huh. But I didn't
see you handing out any of those damn water t-shirts."

I'm trying hard to not laugh at Jazz's brazen ability to dig into
me. "Gavin declined my offer to help." I bite my tongue before I
tell her about our awful exchange. An exchange that confirmed
every fear I had about coming back to this place.

"So you hid in the car. You could have hidden in the crowd.
Show Gavin you're not a horribly depressed human being and
that you're trying to live your life. We all lost Devon, you know?"

I sigh. "I know. Hey Jazz, can we drop it? I promise, this isn't
forever, but being back here is hard enough. I need to deal with
this at my own pace."

She frowns but nods. "Okay. I'm sorry if I'm pushing you too
hard. I just want to see you both happy."

I put the car into park and hop out before she can continue. "Are you spending the night tonight or going home?"

She pouts, knowing the conversation is over. "I better get home. I still need to pack."

I'm the worst best friend in the world. Tonight is the last night before Jazz leaves for New York. Sadness and guilt wash over me. There I go again, putting my problems first.

"Can I take you two to the airport?"

"My parents are driving us, and then they're heading to the mountains for vacation."

I hug her tightly, not wanting to let go. "Thank you for helping me through this first week."

"That's what besties are for," she croons in my ear before pulling back and winking. "You better believe I'll be calling for updates on how things are going with your old-new best friend. Don't give up on him, Chloe. Gavin's a good guy, and I know you two still care about each other." She nods toward the woods before turning to leave.

The rest of the weekend is lonely without Jazz around. I put all my focus into researching BelleCurve's client list while warming up on the treadmill at the local gym. It's just a hole in the wall down the street, nothing like my gym at college, but it has what I need to keep active. After warming up, I sit at the free weights station, focusing on shoulder and back exercises. The burn is the perfect remedy for my frustration.

A creak of the door startles me. All has been silent for the past hour, and I've been grateful for the time to myself. The distraction becomes unsettling, bringing my anxiety back in full effect. I take to the corner station to cool down and stretch my muscles. About halfway into my arm stretches I relax on the mat and practice deep breathing, a technique the campus trainer taught me to alleviate stress. It's had a one-hundred-percent success rate so far.

On my last breath I recognize how quiet the gym has become and wonder if whoever entered already left. I pry an eye open to check it out, expecting the room to be empty again. No such luck. A flutter takes off in my chest, sabotaging the last fifteen minutes of meditation. A familiar figure in the corner of the room is staring back at me, his sleeveless white shirt showing off every muscular curve of his arm. I'd know that arm anywhere. Gavin.

He must want his gym back. That's why he's not leaving. I stand, wishing I had chosen more than a sports bra and leggings for my workout. I'm not ashamed of my body and I know that if anyone can appreciate it, it's Gavin, but the way he's burning a hole through me makes me feel . . . naked. And not just physically. Gavin's always had a certain way of making me feel like he sees more than a nice body and a pretty face.

After throwing on my short sleeve zip-up, I nod my head in his direction and make for the exit. "It's all yours," I call before the door shuts behind me.

Flattened against the brick exterior of the gym, I take several deep breaths to steady the palpitations beneath my ribs. He didn't say a word to me. But Jazz's words fill my mind. *Don't give up on him, Chloe. Gavin's a good guy, and I know you two still care about each other.* Maybe it's me who needs to speak, not Gavin.

With a push off the wall and confident march, I'm now facing the door that separates my heart from my ego. I throw the door open with a dramatic flourish, hoping to announce my assurance with an unforgettable entrance.

"Ahh! Fuck!" Gavin grips his forehead with his palm and backs away from the door.

"I'm sorry! Oh my God. I didn't mean—" I reach for him.

"It's fine." He swipes his forehead, revealing the reddening of his skin. He catches my horrified look and holds up his hands. "I'm fine. Did you want something?"

That's right. I'm on a mission. A mission that just feels ridiculous now. "I just . . . last night . . . I'm sorry I walked away like that without finishing our conversation."

Gavin chuckles sardonically. "You're sorry you walked away from me *last night*? Trust me, Chloe, I'm unaffected by your vanishing acts. Do what you want."

His words and stiff body language tell me one thing, but his eyes tell a completely different story. I know Gavin well enough to know his eyes speak the truth, and right now they're telling me he doesn't mean what's coming out of his mouth.

"You think this isn't hard for me? Coming back here took four years. Cut me some slack. I'm trying, Gavin. I'm trying to talk to you. I'm just not sure if you want me to talk to you."

"I don't."

I step backward, trying not to let the hurt reach my eyes, but the ball is already forming in my throat. "Okay, I can respect that. I'm not here to cause you any more pain. I'm just here for the summer to look over some things for my parents, and then I'm gone. You never have to see me again. I'm sorry, Gav. I really am."

I want to say more—so much more. I want to ask him why he took me home the other night. What he was doing by the door when I flung it into him just now. And then I want a turn to speak. To apologize. I want to tell him *why* I'm sorry. But I'm not sure I'm capable of speaking another word without bursting into tears. Instead, I walk away—again—but not before hearing the reverberations of his fist slamming against the closed door behind me.

GAVIN

"Damn it, that hurt."

My hand stings so much I'm afraid the blow may have fractured something, but I don't care. I needed to feel that. To wake up. I'm only making this thing between Chloe and me worse. She came back to talk, but for some reason I let my hurt and anger control my mind. They took over, refusing her and refusing myself. We can't go an entire summer without speaking. A summer is all the time we have left. Her parent's house will sell soon, a place that was like a second home to me. Because of her. When Chloe's house sells I'll lose yet another piece of her. The Chloe I remember, anyway.

Chloe was as sweet as a kitten, but fierce as a tiger when she needed to be. It's one of the many things I've always adored about her. It's something I hope I played a part in uncovering after Stacy smashed her head against that locker in seventh grade.

Today, her energetic rant should have put me off her. I shouldn't be finding her sexy as hell stretching on that blue mat with her flat stomach and soft curves staring back at me. I shouldn't want to devour her body whole at the same time I'm cursing myself for caring about her at all. Because she clearly doesn't care about me.

People who care about you don't walk away from you, and that's exactly what Chloe does. She walks away instead of facing her problems head-on. Fear has always been a driving force in her life, one I tried desperately to help her work through when we were younger, but she never grasped it completely. Instead, she hid under the security blanket that was Devon and me. Selfishly, I enabled it. I liked that she needed me—us.

That's one of the things that hurt the most after waking up in that hospital bed. It was at the bottom of the list—less prominent than, say, Devon dying and Chloe leaving for college without a word to me—but it was there. Chloe would continue living her life, and she would do it without Devon and me sheltering her from the bullies of the world. She'd outgrow us. Our friendship would become nothing but a sacred memory that ended far too soon.

Before Chloe attacked my face with the gym door, I was going

K.K. ALLEN

after her to finally have *the talk*. And maybe I'm just as conflicted as her, because as badly as I want this confrontation to happen, I'm afraid of it. It will be closure, and I'm not sure I'm ready for that.

100

CHAPTER 15

THE CONFRONTATION

CHLOE

M ore pounding. More prying. More heaving and crashing. The treehouse walls are no more. All that's left is a two-story platform bridging the tree's two largest branches and a single rail wrapping the circumference of the foundation. Gavin bounces on the plywood to check its sturdiness. Maybe he's considering tearing that down too. I mean, why would he keep it? I can't even imagine what Gavin must have gone through the night of Devon's death, or what was on his mind when he awoke to the tragic nightmare of his new reality.

I watch from my spot behind the tree, my new safe place, where I can be close to Gavin without disturbing him. As much as it's pained me to watch all week, the demolition of the treehouse seems to be therapeutic for him. It also reminds me of a time before Gavin, Devon, and I became friends. When I watched them in the woods, wanting so badly to be brave and engage with them but not having the guts to reveal myself.

Watching the destruction of my most cherished childhood getaway fills my heart with emotions I won't even attempt to sort through. Not right now. If Gavin wants to rip every last memory of ours apart, then that's his choice. But it's not the same choice I would make. For me, the treehouse is filled with more great memories than bad ones. For him, the bad most likely outweigh the good. In that case, I can't blame him for what he's doing.

We all do what we can to cope with the shit hands life deals us. The escape can be dangerous. Reality is our home, and the longer we're separated from it, the easier it is to forget who we are. Sometimes the way we choose to cope destroys who we are in the process—the twins' mom being a prime example. She clung to the escape until it swallowed her whole. She could have clung to the light. Her sons. Her husband. Her future. Even if the light is a sliver shining through the darkest cave, it's enough to guide the way home.

When Gavin moves to scale down the ladder, I make my turn to leave. As I do, my foot catches the edge of an unseen scrap of plywood, and I struggle to maintain my silence and my balance. There's no saving me.

The next thing I know, I'm plowing face-first into the ground, my shins slamming into the piece of wood. I let out a strangled cry as a searing pain rips through me and I barely keep from face-planting into the dirt.

There's no way I'm leaving this spot undetected.

The sound of dirt, dry leaves, and sticks crunching beneath Gavin's feet tells me he's approaching as I lie on the ground. With eyes pressed closed, I pray that Gavin won't be as furious as I imagine he'll be when he sees what a creeper I've become.

"I'm not even going to ask."

Suede boots caked with dirt and scraps of wood greet my eyes when I finally pry them open. Gavin reaches beneath my left arm and pulls me to a standing position. I'm certain my face is beet red with embarrassment, and I scramble to make an excuse. "I was just passing through—"

"Save it. I know you've been watching me."

I meet Gavin's eyes. No use hiding anymore.

"Fine. Then I won't beat around the *bush*. What are you doing to our treehouse?"

He doesn't pause to smirk at my joke as he once would have.

Instead, his eyes flicker as if they're about to pull away, but for whatever reason, they remain locked on mine. "What does it look like? I should have done this a long time ago."

"Why now?"

"I think you know why."

I knew it.

He surprises me by extending his hand, offering me the rusty sledge axe. "Go ahead," he prompts. "Take a swing. It feels good."

"It feels good to destroy our memories? What the hell is wrong with you?" I cross my arms and shake my head in disbelief.

Gavin shrugs. "Fine. I'll do it." He walks back to the tree and begins a one-armed climb up the ladder.

Adrenaline plows through me and I rush to him, yanking him down the first step by his belt loops. He turns and hands me the axe again, raising his eyebrows and challenging me. "Either you do it or I will."

With a glare, I elbow him aside, grab the axe, and make my way up the stairs, using only one hand to pull me up. Gavin is right behind me, and he kicks the edge of the rail. "Start here."

I stare back at him, silently asking him if this is truly what he wants. *Do you really want to destroy everything? Our memories? Our past?* He nods.

That's all I need. Zeroing in on the edge of the rail, I bring my arms to my right, reel back, and then throw everything I have into the hit. A crack sounds at the connection just as a shock of energy releases through my body, starting from my arms and surging outward. The pillar of wood unlatches from its foundation, only hanging on by the tip of a nail.

I can feel it. The intense collision of pain and letting go. I hit it again, sending the blackened plank of wood falling to the ground below. *I can smell it.* The burnt memories mixed with worn-down plywood. I strike another section of the rail. *I can hear it.* The explosion. A warning that their time is up. The axe splits another piece of wood. *I can see it.* The threatening flames of a fire that sends the twins tumbling from the platform.

Another whack. *I can taste it*. Blood and dirt as it coats the inside of their mouths.

Tears are rolling down my face by the time I'm halfway around the platform. I pause and look around at what I've done, then drop the sledge axe in shock and turn to Gavin. "Why?" I shout. "He may have died here, Gavin, but we all *lived* here. Why?"

"Look at it!" he yells back, pointing at the pile of burnt foundation at the base of the tree. "It's black. It's charred by the fire that killed him. You think I want to remember that? Don't you see? The good memories are all gone. *He's* gone!"

And then he reaches for the sledge axe and unleashes hell on the rest of the rail.

"I guess that's how long it takes to destroy everything you once loved," I spit. I'm physically shaking. "Is it that easy for you, Gavin? You think Devon will stop haunting us now?"

He turns his rage on me. I've never seen Gavin like this, with the rage of Devon in his eyes. "*Us*? No, Chloe. You don't get an *us* anymore. You walked out on *us*. You have no idea what it's like to be haunted with his memories. To be left all alone with nothing tangible to hold onto."

I shake my head, unsure of what to make of his words, unprepared for the feelings taking over my body. Maybe we're both stuck in a nightmare. Maybe that's why I just want to scream at the top of my lungs until Jazz wakes me up to tell me everything is okay. I just want everything to be okay.

"You think Devon doesn't haunt me every damn second of my life?"

"Save it. It's four years too late for me to hear what you have to say." Gavin wields the axe and smashes it through the plywood beneath us.

"No!" I scream. Without thinking, I jump on his back and yank his arm, forcing him to drop the weapon. He turns, forcing me back to my feet and goes to pick up the axe again.

"Stop!" I scream.

We spent so many days with our stomachs pressed against the wooden floor he wants so desperately to destroy. I can't let him annihilate the foundation of the treehouse.

"You once told me this treehouse was mine too. If that's the truth, then you'll honor this one thing. Please don't destroy our foundation. It's all we have left of him."

He scoffs. "This?" He stomps his foot, the impact reverberating through the woods. "It all has to go."

I push his chest as hard as I can with both hands. If he won't listen to me, then all I have is my physical strength. It's no match for Gavin's; I know that, but if he can feel me fighting, maybe he'll stop. Maybe he'll take a step back and realize what he's doing.

When he doesn't budge, I cock my hands back to slam my fists into his chest again. He catches them and pulls me forward until I'm falling into him.

"Go ahead," he booms, spreading his arms out wide. "Hit me, Chloe. Whatever makes you feel better. Let me be your punching bag." His muscles expand as if he's flexing them. "I promise you, I won't feel a thing."

When I make no move to hit him, he pulls me to him again, causing a cry to release from my throat. "Isn't this what you want?" he roars. "You want to be mad at me? You want to be the victim? Is that how you're going to play this?"

I feel him shaking above me, and it's my undoing. I try my hardest to block the tears, but the stream comes with my words. "No," I say. "Gavin, I don't know what I'm doing." I shake my head in frustration. "I'm here, but I don't know why. Every opportunity I have to talk to you, I fail to say what I really want to say. I've spent four years convincing myself that you hate me—that you never wanted to see me again. I didn't want it to be true, but it's the reality I burdened myself with in order to cope with it all. Now that I'm here . . . seeing you so angry just looking at me . . . it confirms my reality."

"Your reality? Do you want to know what *my* reality is?"

I don't respond. I'm not sure I do want to know, but I let him tell me anyway.

"The last night I saw you was the last night I saw my brother. Remember when I said it was like you died right along with him? I wasn't lying. I wasn't trying to hurt you. It's what happened. You vanished from my life when I needed you most."

As much as my body wants to relax into him, I can't. The guilt is too heavy. When I gain the strength to look up, his expression is different. Gavin has only looked at me with anger and rage since I've been back in town. Now he just looks tired and sad, his energy depleted.

Suddenly, I understand Jazz completely. For the last four years, I've kept to myself, protecting myself from pain by shutting everyone else out. I've been telling myself that my distance was for the best, because if it weren't for me, their pain wouldn't exist. But when I look at Gavin now, Gavin with his sad eyes, I realize that everything I've done to keep others out has only worsened their suffering. If Gavin needed me after Devon died, I never knew it because I selfishly convinced myself that I was the reason for it all.

"I only remember bits and pieces of the first few days after it happened," I say. "It hurts to remember anything. Physically hurts."

"I know," he says gently.

"When I found out Devon . . . died"—I choke on my words— "all I could think of was how there were so many things I should have done differently that night. Devon would have never gotten so angry. He wouldn't have left for the treehouse. You two wouldn't have—"

Gavin tightens his grip on my arms, cutting me off from delivering my confession. "In the past four years, I haven't once questioned who was responsible for Devon's death."

It's as if he's slicing through my heart slowly so that I can feel every inch of the blade.

"Devon started the fight with you," he continues. "Devon

chose to drink too much. Devon destroyed the treehouse. Devon caused the fire. It was Devon who lunged at me, tossing us both from the top. I love and miss my brother more than anything. I would have given my own life to save him. But everything that happened that night was Devon's doing. It was an unfortunate accident caused by reckless, alcohol-drenched decisions."

Hearing these words aloud is both heartbreaking and uplifting. Gavin doesn't blame me for what happened that night. But he should. "If he wasn't angry with me, none of that would have ever happened," I insist.

He pulls my chin up, his brilliant green eyes meeting mine and filling me with an odd mixture of hope and fear—hope that he truly doesn't blame me for Devon's death, and fear that he's wrong.

Without breaking his hold, he speaks again. "You want to know what I remember about your relationship with Devon?"

I shake my head. I don't, but I think he's going to tell me anyway.

"You two didn't go a day without fighting. He constantly accused you of sleeping around behind his back when he was no better himself. He called you awful names. Devon couldn't attend a social function without wrapping his mouth around a bottle of booze, and you always took care of him, no questions asked. You think you were responsible for him drinking that night? No, Chloe. He couldn't wait to party that night. You may have helped him justify what he was doing, but Devon was the one making all the bad choices."

I stare up, open-mouthed at Gavin. "How did you do that?"

He looks confused. "Do what?"

"In twenty seconds, you just rebutted an argument I've been having with myself for four years. I've been so afraid to face you, knowing my part in all of this."

Gavin drops his hands, freeing me. I don't want to be free from Gavin. I want his arms around me, where I feel safe. It's the first time I've felt safe in years. "I may not have been liable for his death, but I still feel guilty for other things. I could have been a better brother to Devon, especially in the last few months of his life. I could have supported your relationship. I'm sure you have some guilt too, but the guilt of Devon's accident doesn't fall on either of us."

"I thought you hated me," I say.

Gavin's jaw tightens, and he tears his eyes from mine. "I never hated you, Chlo. I tried. Hating you would have probably been easier than what I was actually feeling. The pain of losing Devon was agony, but layered with the pain of losing you, it was . . . insufferable."

"I'm so sorry." I don't know why the words hurt to say, but there's a tug at my heart when I speak them. Gavin doesn't meet my gaze, so I reach for his hand instead. He glances down at our adjoined palms, making no move to remove his from mine. Hope blooms in my chest. "I didn't realize it at the time, but I was selfish for running away. The last thing I wanted was to hurt you. In a sick way, I thought that by distancing myself, I was helping you while punishing myself."

A deep crease forms in Gavin's forehead before he looks up again and squeezes my hand. "I don't want you to punish yourself. Devon's death was bad enough. That's not blame you should own. No one thinks it's your fault."

I frown. "No one knows why Devon was so upset."

Gavin's face contorts. "They have an idea. I guess Devon was pretty vocal when he went back to the party to refill his booze. But his rage wasn't anything they hadn't seen before."

"What did he tell them?"

"I don't know. He was a loose cannon and I wasn't there. Rumors can get twisted so I try not to pay them any attention."

"What were the rumors?"

He holds my eyes for a moment. "He ran around telling everyone you cheated on him with me. I told them it wasn't true and they believed me. What I still don't understand is why he would have ever thought that to begin with."

The question in Gavin's eyes causes panic to flood my veins. My pulse reacts to my churning mind. I turn my head down and shake it, praying he'll drop it. "I can't remember."

Gavin doesn't push it, but by the look on his face, I know he doesn't believe me.

I'm gripping the back of his drenched shirt because I'm not sure if I'm strong enough to look any higher. "If I could go back, I'd do everything different," I say, my voice barely a whisper. "I would have stayed. I would have let you know that I was here for you if you needed me, but only if you needed me. I shouldn't have made that decision on my own." I bite my lip. "I'm so sorry, Gavin. I'm sorry for everything you lost, for being an awful friend, for being selfish. And I'm so sorry it took me four years to apologize."

It's quiet as neither of us moves. I take this as a positive sign. He hasn't thrown me off him or stalked off into the woods. He's still here, and this time, I'm not going to walk away.

SECOND CHANCES

"DEATH IS NOT THE GREATEST LOSS IN LIFE. THE GREATEST LOSS IS WHAT DIES INSIDE US WHILE WE LIVE." ~ NORMAN COUSINS

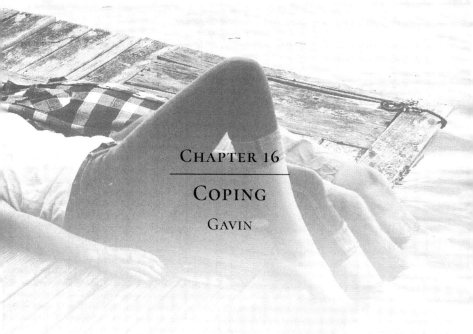

CHAPTER 16

COPING

GAVIN

The next few days make the past four years seem like a blur. Chloe's presence is once again the epicenter of my universe, and it consumes my every thought. I replay the treehouse confrontation a thousand times. Trying to make sense of her reasons for leaving, desperately wanting to accept her apology. But when someone does something so seemingly wrong that no morals can justify the actions, it's hard to gain closure.

What will it take to overcome the pain? Now is my chance to find out. I've spent a good portion of the past four years angry with Chloe Rivers for having a heart that would let her walk away. For making me question whether I knew her at all. I'll have to figure out how to let that anger go. But to do that, I'll have to let *her* go.

So much has changed in four years. My life has become one of a workaholic with little time for much else besides my closest friends and family. I like to keep my mind preoccupied with the things I can control.

There was a time, closer to the night of the accident, when I willingly accepted the pain just to see Chloe's face in my memories. I asked myself what she was doing, how she was getting along at school, if she would ever come home . . .

When my questions turned up void of a response, the pain would morph into anger. That anger led to a lifestyle in which I sought out ways to distract myself from the pain. Drinking. Sex. Working out. I was starting to remind myself of Devon.

Marco must have thought the same thing, because after one year of my toxic behavior, he was the one to sit me down and give it to me straight. "Buddy, you've been through a lot," he said, "and you handle this shit better than anyone else ever could, but you're starting to worry me. You've got family and friends that need you. Stop drowning your conscience with alcohol and randoms. Wake up and deal with what's important."

So I did.

I spent the next year focusing on getting my shit together, filling my life with good distractions: school, work, family, and friends. Like the mark on my shoulder, I knew that the scarred tissue of my past would always be there, still tender to the touch, but it no longer bled or caused me insufferable pain.

It was on the second anniversary of Devon's death that I first returned to the treehouse. I let myself relive life with Devon, from my first memories with him up to that night we tumbled from our safe haven. That was also the day I decided to let Chloe go. When I did, it was as if the walls closing around my heart finally completed its construction, and I was ready to move on.

Or so I thought.

Around that same time, I had recently received an associate of applied science degree in comic and sequential art, landed my first big contract job, and purchased my dad's Bonney Lake house. My responsibilities allowed little time for any distractions to get me through at night. Drinking and sex were still dominant outlets on occasion, but it was all about learning to balance the things I wanted with what I needed. I kept it simple. That's what my life became.

Now, relationships are short-lived with no strings attached. Drinking is reserved for celebrations and the occasional social event. In a way, it seems I'm coping with the shit hand of cards I'd been dealt fairly well.

But the moment I heard that Chloe was coming back into town, old seeds broke through soil, bringing me right back to the root of it all. The treehouse. Turns out those walls I'd built up around my heart were flimsy bastards. It took just one swing of her axe to bust it open, leaving my heart bare and vulnerable, just as the treehouse stands now. Apparently, no structure can withstand the force of Chloe Rivers.

Unfortunately for me, when she left she took a piece of me with her—and it wasn't until she returned that I realized just how big that piece was.

I want it back.

This is something I need to deal with, once and for all. Forgiving Chloe is my first step toward healing and moving on. Now that she's in town and we've had the inevitable first talk, there's opportunity for closure. Right? We can't change the past, but maybe there's still hope—for the both of us.

"Hey, Gav, baby. What'll you have?"

"A beer. The usual. I won't be here long. Just needed to get away from the office." It's almost midnight, and by *the office*, I mean my home office where I'm sketching a piece for an upcoming event.

I wink at Amanda, the brunette bartender with a body that's always reminded me of Chloe's, but that's where the similarities end. Amanda is pretty, I think, but it's almost hard to see behind the many layers of makeup. Chloe never hides behind makeup. It's easy to appreciate her heart-shaped face, accentuated by the natural pout of her lips; the corners of her mouth are always downturned unless she smiles.

I always loved making Chloe smile.

Amanda slides me a beer. I catch it with one hand and then bring it to my mouth, trying to shake the thought of Chloe's lips from my mind.

"You work too much," Amanda says as she folds her arms and rests her chin on them.

I shrug. "Work isn't the problem."

"So, there is a problem." She takes the bait.

With narrowed eyes, I set the beer down and lean in. "A *big* problem," I tease.

Amanda catches on and turns her flirtation up a notch. "My offer still stands, baby. I'm good for a release if you ever need one."

I knew she would offer; it's why I'm here. Not to take her up on the sex. No. I wanted to feel the pull to a woman other than Chloe. Amanda is stunning, but as she bats her fake eyelashes at me, I can't help but think of Chloe, who never had to flaunt or enhance a thing to be beautiful. Her beauty radiated from her core and touched every morsel of her exterior . . . and it only seems to have gotten better with age.

So, against my better judgment, I watch Amanda work the bar at Babalouie's, taunting the approaching males with her breasts in hope of scoring extra tips. She pays me special attention, giving me playful smiles at every opportunity. I allow the flirtation, begging something within me to stir.

At some point, Amanda stops asking me if I want another drink and continues to place one after the other in front of me until I've well surpassed my limit.

By closing, Chloe is still ingrained in my mind and I can only think of one way to push the image away. I search for my unfinished bottle, wanting nothing more than to drown out every thought of Chloe that's surfaced over the past few hours. I'm going to need it.

To my surprise, Amanda's already tossing my bottle into the trash and helping me from my stool.

"Come on, sweetness. I'll give you a ride."

People still say I remind them of Devon. Maybe that's what pain does to people. No one but me understands why Devon was the way he was, why he internalized pain until he couldn't hide it anymore and it burst from him in the form of rage. Our peers judged him, loved him, and hated him, but they never knew him like I did. They'll never know that Devon was my hero.

He's the reason I wasn't as fucked up in the head as he was. The abuse he suffered from our mother was something no one should ever have to deal with, especially at such a young age. But Devon took the brunt of it to save me from the same pain.

Our mother was an abusive drunk, psychotically depressed, and in the end, her death hurt Devon more than her fists. He couldn't fix her. He couldn't make her whole. And after finding her dead with an empty bottle of pills in her hand, he would never look at another woman with respect again. Not even Chloe.

When Devon died, I understood some of his pain. It was the most helpless, hopeless feeling in the entire world, and the thought of ever loving someone unconditionally again seemed impossible. Why would I want to put my heart in someone's hands when at any moment they could just disappear? Chloe is a perfect example of what I can't have in my life. I loved that girl too much. So much that it changed me when she wasn't there anymore.

Again, I ask myself how I'll ever be able to forgive her. What-ever Chloe's reasons were for leaving, it will never be okay, no matter how sorry she is.

So then why am I fighting so hard with myself to stay angry, when all I want is to head straight to her house and continue our conversation? Is it closure I'm searching for, or something else?

I wake up with a pounding head and unfamiliar surroundings. I sit up slowly, then see Amanda's tiny skirt lying at the edge of the bed and groan into my hands. I wasn't too drunk last night to know what I was doing, which is a good thing because after fooling around for a while, we both passed out without going too far. I just wanted to forget. I wanted the romantic tranquilizer that's been keeping me safe to seep back into my veins and work its magic. Because as good as I've gotten at keeping my heart out of relationships, I'm not so sure I have that same restraint with Chloe Rivers.

Chapter 17

Lucky Clover

Chloe

My stomach rumbles, a sign that my next adventure involves the grocery store. The realtor just called, and I'm being forced to leave the house for another showing. This is going to get old fast. After a quick tidy-up, I throw on an old flowery sundress and a pair of slippers from my bedroom closet and give myself a once-over in the hanging mirror behind the door. It's getting easier to walk into this room as the days go by, but I still won't sleep in my old bed.

I jump in surprise when I open my front door. Gavin is walking up the stairs of my front porch, a cardboard box in his hands. His intense stare greets me.

"Geez, Gavin, you scared the crap out of me." I place my hand over my heart, hoping to steady it.

He gives me a half-smile with a side of nerves. "Sorry. I boxed up some of your stuff from the treehouse and thought you might want it."

Three excruciating days have gone by since our showdown, our first real conversation since I left town four years ago. I didn't expect to find him at my door with a box of the past in his arms, and I'm not sure what to make of it. Is he really just stopping to deliver my things, or is this an excuse to see me?

"You didn't have to make a special trip. I could have grabbed it from you." I take the box and set it by my front door. "Thank you."

"Heading out?"

"I am." There's an awkward moment between us and then Gavin turns to leave without another word. Desperate and frustrated, I call out, "Did you just come over to deliver this box?"

He stops and swivels his head around. "I don't know why I'm here."

"It's okay if you're still mad at me, you know? It's also okay to admit you missed me."

He glares and I realize how arrogant I must have sounded. "Excuse me?"

My face flames with embarrassment. "I'm sorry. I just—"

"You just what? It's been four years. What chance did you possibly give me to make me *miss* you? I was too busy feeling other things."

Ouch. "Well, I missed you." I swallow the ball in my throat, not allowing myself to cry this time. "I'm not trying to take back what I did. I know I can never make this right, but you have to know how sorry I am. I'll do anything to prove that to you."

Gavin's eyes soften. "I was fucking pissed at you for leaving, Chlo. I'm having a hard time understanding how you could pick up and leave without a word—when I was unconscious, no less. I know you, and that's not *you*. What the hell happened?"

I open my mouth to respond, but he shakes his head. "Don't answer that." He takes a pause to clench his jaw and take a deep breath. "I'm trying. Not that you deserve it. I'm just trying to figure out a way to forgive you, because *I* need to. Not for you. For me. I need to move past this anger that surges through me every single time I think about you."

My heart sinks but I nod, knowing I owe him at least that much. "I can explain, but I don't think that's what you want from me."

"You've already explained it. As fucked up as it is, I get it. But it still doesn't erase the last four years. Honestly, Chloe, being around you scares the shit out of me."

"I don't know what you want from me. It was never my intention to hurt you. I guess we all deal with tragedy differently, and I apparently suck at it."

"Yes, you do."

We both let out a hesitant laugh. This admission is a weight off my shoulders.

Gavin seems to be contemplating something. I let him work things out in his mind before jumping in again, even though the silence is driving me crazy.

"You mentioned you'd be gone after summer, right?" he asks.

I nod.

"Maybe this means we have a chance to end things much better than we ended them four years ago. We can't change the past, but I also can't change the fact that I still care about you. This will be good for us. One summer. And then we can move on with our lives."

One summer. And then we can move on with our lives. I actually hate that idea. This time of year ten years ago was the start of it all. And by late summer, it will be the end.

I swallow, willing to do anything to bring Gavin peace. I've been selfish for too long. "Okay," I concede. As he shifts from foot to foot, my heart beats a bit faster. "I could actually use some company," I say tentatively. "I'm heading to the grocery store if you want to join me. They're showing the house, and Jazz did the shopping for me before she left." I make a face. "Let's just say I'm sick of Pop-Tarts."

He gasps, feigning shock. "You? Sick of Pop-Tarts? Let me guess: frosted blueberry with sprinkles."

I laugh, enjoying the chance to banter with Gavin again.

"I need to get a few things too. I can drive." He hops off the steps and walks toward his truck without waiting to see if I'll follow. I do. Of course I do.

"Have a good weekend?" I ask once we've pulled onto the road, because what else is there to ask in a moment like this?

I watch his broad shoulders lift, then drop. I'm practically salivating at the simple movement. "It was okay," he answers casually.

It's nice to see that the tension has dissolved since the last time I sat in this passenger seat. When he dragged me from the bar that night I was too drunk and angry to look at him closely. Now I can admire the scruff that covers his baby face, highlighting the glow of his green eyes. It's safe to say I've been attracted to Gavin from the moment I met him, but attraction changes through the years. We become attracted to different qualities, less obvious ones. I'm definitely attracted to those too, but right now I'm not afraid to admit that my thoughts about Gavin are majorly sexual.

"Just did family stuff," he continues. "Remember the Port Angeles house?"

"Oh, that's right. Your dad still owns that place?"

Gavin nods. "I went to visit them. They live there now. Since last summer, actually." He must sense my confusion because he continues. "I bought this house from them. Figured it was a good investment, and the art thing is going well, so . . ."

"You own a home? At twenty-two? Gavin, that's incredible."

A hint of a smile forms on his lips, and I can see that he's proud of his investment. "I was forced to grow up quickly. I'm lucky that my contracts pay well and I don't have to work full time. It's a good setup. Besides, I got a helluva deal."

Sounds like it. If only I could find something so accommodating. "Maybe my agency will hire you one day." I beam. "I start my job tomorrow, and they have loads of clients."

He raises an eyebrow in my direction. "Really? You writing?"

I nod. "Marketing and PR. They're sort of mid-sized, and they have a need for both, so they said my style of writing will need to adapt from project to project. It's not exactly the job I've always dreamt of, but I'm really excited."

He squeezes my shoulder, sending shivers through my body. "You'll be great at whatever they throw at you, Chloe."

An hour later we're checking out at the grocery store, and I notice the bagger placing our stuff together. "No, that goes in the plastic bag. The cottage cheese goes in the reusable one." My directions are useless. The bagger gives me a look that tells me she has no concern for my organization methods and she's going to continue bagging the way she knows and loves.

Gavin twists his face, playfully nudging me. "Get that cottage cheese out of my bag, Clover. What do you eat that with anyway?" The expressionless bagger holds up the can of pineapple chunks in answer to his question, and Gavin laughs. "I'm a fan of pineapple. Go ahead and toss that one in my bag."

When he winks at the bagger, I'm still flushing over hearing his nickname for me. No one has called me Clover in years. It's a name only Gavin knows . . . because he's the one who came up with it.

CHLOE, 17 YEARS OLD

Before I left for Florida the summer after junior year, Gavin finally received the letter he'd been waiting on for months. He'd submitted a full-color sketch in response to a competition that would land him two all access passes to Comic Mania in Seattle, an annual conference that usually costs thousands to attend.

"I'm not opening it." He shoved it into my hands.

We sat cross-legged on the highest tower at the community playground. Despite the chilly breeze, I swear there was sweat dripping from Gavin's forehead. I wanted to put him out of his misery, but I was starting to get nervous too. I didn't want to be the one to disappoint him. He was talented beyond measure, but he didn't see it. He just loved art. Maybe that was better for him than knowing how talented he was. People who know they're great at something tend to overcompensate, and that wasn't like

123

Gavin at all. Gavin was humble and skeptical about his own talent, and there was something endearing about that.

"Before I open this, you have to remember that they only choose one person out of thousands of entrants. Don't beat yourself up if you didn't win."

He pounded his head into the plastic wall behind him. "Just open it, Chloe."

I tugged at the large envelope and pulled out a formal letter on official-looking letterhead. Gavin sat across from me with his eyes squeezed tight and his hands clasped together. If I didn't know him better, I would have thought he was praying.

I wanted to burst with excitement when I read the first line. "Holy shit."

Gavin's eyelids flew open, and he tugged the letter from my grasp as my hand covered my mouth. *No way.*

Gavin had never been one to express extreme emotion. But at that moment, he pulled me to my feet and swung me around in celebration, screaming at the top of his lungs. When he finally set me down, we were laughing and breathless. I picked up the envelope to scan the rest of the contents and pulled out his two tickets to Comic Mania. Behind it was the full-color sketch with a four-leaf clover attached by a paperclip.

I glanced up at Gavin, who was admiring his passes. "What's this?" I asked, and he looked up at me.

His face grew even brighter, if that was possible. "Do you remember this?" He pulled the clover from the paperclip.

I squinted in disbelief. "Is that the clover we found in the woods?"

He grinned. It was a grin I would never forget because it did something to the hormones raging inside me. It was the first moment I thought I might have a crush on my best friend.

"Yup, that's the one. You made me attach it. You said it was a sign since we found it on the same day I was submitting my art. You were right."

I'm pretty sure I was returning his grin with a stupid one of my own. "It's your good luck charm."

Gavin shook his head. I watched open-mouthed as he crumpled up the clover and tossed it over the side of the rail. "I don't need a plant for good luck, Chloe. I just need you. You're my clover."

S omewhere between driving back to my house, sorting our groceries, and continuing our playful banter, Gavin and I start making dinner. Surprisingly, we manage to roll out the pizza dough before arguing.

"Tomato sauce or white sauce?" Gavin asks as I grab two bottles of water from the fridge. I wouldn't mind something a little stronger right now, but I still don't know how Gavin feels about drinking in general after that night at the bar.

I make a face. "Tomato. Who eats pizza with white sauce?"

He feigns shock. "What? You haven't lived." He proceeds to douse the dough with the entire bottle of Alfredo.

"What are you doing?" I laugh. "I said tomato sauce. Why even ask me if you are going to do the opposite?"

"That's exactly why I asked you."

I return his smug response with a glare, then reach around him, accidentally brushing his arm before grabbing the tomato sauce, opening it, and letting the contents pour like lava on top of his fancy white sauce. Now it's my turn to smile smugly, but the effect of our skin-to-skin contact is distracting.

Challenge is written clearly on his face as he reaches for the cheese. "Mozzarella or goat cheese?"

I'm appalled at the question. "Please tell me you're joking. No one eats pepperoni pizza with goat cheese."

He grabs the goat cheese and makes like he's about to let loose on the pizza . . . but then he laughs. "Gotcha! I hate goat cheese. Mozzarella it is."

I let out a relieved sigh, and all is calm until we start fighting over pepperoni or sausage. At least this time we agree on half and half.

We finally get the pizza in the oven and poke around the entertainment system for a movie to watch. "I give up," I say, splaying out on the floor. "Let's watch something on Netflix."

"Oh no, you pour the wine. I'll find something to watch." He pulls me up by my arms until we're standing face-to-face. My pulse begins to quicken the moment I stop to think about how familiar this all is. Then I force those thoughts to the back of my mind and turn toward the kitchen before I do or say something stupid.

I grab two glasses and pour our wine. Thank God he suggested it. I don't know how I'd be able to handle this night without some liquid courage. We've done a great job ignoring the tension so far, but that's the problem: we're ignoring what we should be facing. Then again, maybe we both need a night off from all the drama.

"What do we have here?" Gavin pulls his hand out the cabinet holding a familiar DVD just as I reenter the room.

I set our glasses down and shriek. "*Teen Witch*! Play it. Now."

Gavin chuckles as he starts the DVD and switches off the light. He joins me on the couch, purposefully leaving a few feet between us. There was a time when movie night consisted of "friendship spooning," as we'd call it. My favorite part was when we'd fall asleep only to awake in the most awkward positions, happily suffering pains in our backs and necks.

But things have changed.

As the movie plays, the room is still too quiet, and our proximity is growing uncomfortable.

I smile with relief once he begins to mock the awesome absurdity of the movie. He knows every word by heart. We both do, but Gavin especially likes to speak every line of every scene in fluent exaggeration. It's brilliant. The main character is currently twirling in circles, with her book of magic in hand, calling the wind.

"Shh," I tell him, placing a finger over my mouth as I search for his eyes in the darkness.

There they are. Good Lord, his eyes are beautiful . . . and they're staring back at me.

Just then, the beep of the stove timer startles me. I jump up, walk-skip into the kitchen, and grab the pizza from the oven. I pull myself up onto the counter and wait for it to cool instead of joining Gavin in the other room. I need a minute before facing him again.

We've been friends since we were twelve, with a four-year hiatus. I should know how to watch a movie with him without paying attention to every breath he takes. Am I even allowed to feel these things after all this time? The fact that Gavin still owns the flock of flutters in my stomach says something, but more-than-friendship is totally out of the question. Not with our history. Not with Devon's ghost still riding the wave of guilt in my mind. Besides, I should be glad Gavin is even talking to me, let alone attempting a second round of friendship.

"Chlo? Where'd you go?" He pokes his head around the corner and I smile shyly back at him.

"Just waiting for the pizza to cool off."

His expression tells me he knows me better, but he doesn't ask questions. He grabs two plates from the cabinet and grabs us each two pieces before pulling me off the counter. As he does, my body scrapes his, and I'm fully conscious of the sudden change in my breathing.

He tips my chin up with his fingers so I'm looking back at him. He's staring down at me tenderly. It's almost as if nothing's changed, but I know that *everything* has changed between us.

Before, the touching meant friendship. Now, I can't stop thinking of the night of Comic Mania when we had a chance to explore something more. We're having one of those moments right now. Aren't we?

In the short time I've been home, the feelings I once had for Gavin have only quadrupled. It doesn't help that he's brushing his thumb against my cheek with a heart-melting intensity in his gaze.

"You're going to miss the part where Louise turns her brother into a dog," he says playfully.

This does the trick. I let out a laugh and wrap my arms around his waist, my cheek resting against his solid frame. "Damn. What did you do to your body?" I tease, pulling back and rubbing the cloth over his abs. "And your stomach! Carve hills on this bad boy?"

He grins, obviously pleased with the attention. "You like?" He pulls his shirt up to reveal his bare torso. I almost hit the floor. I saw his stomach before at the treehouse, but up close and personal it's an entirely different story.

"It's nice," I say, knowing the flush of my cheeks is giving me away.

"Your turn." He lifts his brow teasingly. "Show me yours."

I laugh and shove him away. "Nothing's changed here."

He subtly roams the length of my body with his eyes. "I would argue with that."

My breath is caught somewhere between my throat and my mouth, and I'm certain there's a damn horse galloping in my chest. "Gavin Rhodes!" I scold, happy to have found my teasing voice despite my intense desire for him in this moment. All the while, I'm trying to remember if this was how we used to banter. I can't remember Gavin ever being blatantly flirtatious.

He winks and pulls me to him, then rubs my back with the palm of his hand in slow, steady circles. "Chloe." His voice is raspy, cutting me straight to the core. My entire body stills. "I don't want you to think I'm blowing past our issues. Four years is a long time. I want this to work. Losing our friendship was the second most devastating loss of my life, and if we can have that back for one last summer, I want to embrace it."

The way he glances from my face to my dress and back up makes me wonder if our friendship is all he wants to embrace. It's totally inappropriate, but I'm hopeful.

I grip him tighter. "I want that too." I look up, loving that at least we've come this far. What I feel for Gavin goes beyond friendship, and the blaze in his eyes tells me there's more for him too. So I say the only thing I can think of at a moment like this. "Pizza should be good now."

That breaks the spell. Without another word, Gavin turns his focus on the pizza and carries our plates into the other room. Our eyes stay glued to the movie as we scarf down our dinner. I take our plates to the kitchen only to come back to find Gavin curled up at one end of the couch. He watches me weigh my seating options before I settle for the center cushion. It's a safe distance from Gavin but not too far away to raise suspicion.

We're both laughing as we rap the entire Top That scene to perfection. My entire body lights up when he reaches around my waist and pulls me toward him. "I love this scene," he whispers, making me jump halfway out of my skin. The feeling of his breath lingers on my neck, causing goose bumps to emerge.

At first, I don't know where to put my hands. I think back to the hundreds of movies we watched together when we were younger. We sat in this same position: my back against Gavin's chest, his arm wrapped loosely around my stomach. It was all so innocent, nothing like how it feels today. I drape my arm between his legs like I used to, but this time I feel his body tense beneath me. It pleases me to know that I affect him, but I act as if I notice nothing unusual.

When a romantic scene comes on, I feel my own body tense, warmth spreading through me. I imagine Gavin and I reenacting the same scene, except instead of being in an abandoned house, we're in our treehouse. A tickle on my stomach distracts my thoughts, and I realize that his fingers are drawing slow circles around my navel. My breath gets caught in my throat at the touch. This is definitely not something Gavin would have done during one of our movie nights back in high school. My panic quickly subsides as I give into the fact that I'm aching for his fingers to crawl between the buttons on my dress, just to feel them on my bare skin. As if he reads my mind, he inches closer to the slits of my dress, clutching the cloth but hesitating to move further.

His breath tickles my neck, causing my ragged breathing to reveal how much I want this. Suddenly I'm aware of every sensation in my body, and I swear I hear him sniff my hair right before he presses his wandering fingers into my stomach so I'm flush against his body. With all this attention to my stomach and neck, I almost miss his other hand dragging along the length of my leg, pulling up the bottom of my dress as it feathers my skin. When his lips press against that sensitive spot between my neck and my shoulder, my eyes roll back into my head and I shudder.

"Shit!" Gavin retracts his hands, moves me aside, and pulls himself to his feet. He does a funny dance, jumping a little as he tugs on his jeans and then backs up.

Watching his sudden movements, I let out a deep breath as a wave of embarrassment washes over me. "What's wrong?"

"This is a mistake."

"Which part, exactly?" I ask, not trying to hide my hurt.

"All of it," he growls, and then he walks to the kitchen. I hear shuffling, and alarm fills me as I realize he's gathering his grocery bags to leave. I remain seated, afraid of what I'll say or do if I go to him. Instead, I just watch as he leaves the kitchen with his hands wrapped up in plastic bags, tosses my front door open, and slams it shut behind him.

CHAPTER 19

TEAMWORK

CHLOE

I tug nervously at my light blue, sleeveless dress as I walk into BelleCurve. It's my first day on the job as a creative writer. My anxieties are consuming but they are nothing compared to the disappointment I woke up to when I realized last night wasn't a horrible dream.

Luckily, I've learned how to tuck away my raw emotions until they harden, thickening the wall I've built over the years. All I have to do is keep my mind off of Gavin Rhodes. If anyone is capable of turning my walls to wax and melting them down, it's him. But with my new job in front of me and my sights set on moving out of Bonney Lake soon, I know I can get through this.

The creative agency is located in a three-story office complex in downtown Bellevue. BelleCurve is located on the second floor, sandwiched between a Top 40 radio station and a cellular phone company. With high ceilings and a wall-to-wall trophy case in the lobby, I know this is the real deal.

Monica, the perky receptionist with a most welcoming smile, shows me to my cubicle, which appears to be in the highest traffic area of the entire floor. A group of my new coworkers huddle at the hall's intersection, sipping their coffee and exchanging stories about their weekends.

Monica gives me the rest of the tour as if it's the most important job she'll have all day. Maybe it is the most important job she'll have all day. Either way, she's great at it. She's friendly, almost too friendly with a widely exaggerated smile and a bobble head that agrees with everything I say. I want to like her, and I don't *dislike* her; it's just hard to assess if someone with that much energy is actually being genuine.

She continues to show me around my computer: email, instant messenger, and my calendar, which is already populated with meetings from nine until five, including a lunch appointment with her. I'm already overwhelmed.

"Don't worry," she says with a smile, "these are just meet and greets today with the staff. Oh, and one vendor meeting for our upcoming event. You don't start meeting with clients until Wednesday."

I'm not sure why that should settle my nerves, but I smile in appreciation. When am I going to find time to actually write?

I glance at the time and see that it's already nine o'clock. Monica walks me over to a large conference room on the other side of the building. Immediately, I recognize the three executives I met during my interview on videoconference. They stand and smile brightly. I give them a firm handshake just the way Gavin taught me when we were young.

"Nice to see you again, Ms. Rivers. You remember Charles and Barker?"

I want to giggle when I hear their names again. How could I forget? "Of course. Nice to meet you all in person finally." I grin. "Thank you again for the opportunity. Your facility is beautiful. Is it new?"

We take our seats; mine is facing the three of them. Sandra sits between the men, and I can't help but wonder how the two males are able to conduct business beside a beautiful blonde bombshell. She's gorgeous. Stick skinny with bright blue eyes and a short bob that shows off her slender face.

"About four years new." She grins. "It was our ten-year plan for ourselves when we started the company, and we made it here in six."

I don't have to feign how impressed I am. That's an incredible accomplishment. "Sounds like I made the right choice."

Barker leans in. "You did, Chloe. We're very happy to have you. Professor Edwards was a colleague of mine some time ago." He winks across the table. "I won't tell you exactly how long, but let's just say, we go way back. And he had great things to say about you."

My heart grows warm. "I'll have to thank him."

We're interrupted by Charles, who I remember being the serious one in my interview. He's serious again today. Straight to the point, minimal small talk, and not missing a beat before kick-starting the meeting.

We move through the basics, mostly going over things I already read on the company website. When Sandra finally gets into the fun part, my ears are ready.

"Our next big fundraiser is a three-part series, one a month from August to October," she explains. "As you may already know, October is National Bullying Prevention Month. We're working with some of the top celebrities in the nation to support our cause and splitting the events up allows us to invite more attendees and sponsors to make the biggest contribution we can in October. We want to give back in every way possible, not just by collecting donations during each event. We want to recognize the victims, heroes, and families of childhood bullying and share their stories. We hope to give them the confidence to continue standing up and speaking out against bullying, and to just have a downright great time."

She really has her spiel down.

"We've nailed down the venue and the name: Heroes and Legends. Not fancy, we know, but it says it all. These kids attending are local heroes, and they should feel empowered to share their stories and help spread the love. They're proven advocates of the cause who have really sparked some light within the education system on how we view bullying, empowering kids to stand up for themselves and their peers. It's important to teach kids at a young age that they can make a difference."

I'm elated; I couldn't think of a better cause for me to be a part of. But it's a struggle to stay focused because the first thing I want to do is call Gavin to tell him about this. How is that possible? Especially after last night.

Sandra leans forward with a smile on her face. "That's where you come in. You, alongside our creative director, will bring the theme to life in any way you see fit. Sharlene will be your project manager, so all costs will be approved through her, but we don't want cost to limit your creativity. At the end of the day, you can't put a price on what we're doing, and there isn't much that isn't donated or already paid for by our sponsors. So . . . sky's the limit."

By the end of the meeting my head is spinning. My next meet and greet is with Sharlene, the event's project manager. She gives me more details about the event and the exact role I'll be taking on, which is beyond what I imagined for myself when I accepted the job. I'll be creating a show script for the entire event, from the invitations and artwork copy to the MC's announcements and videos we'll show. I can't wait.

The rest of the morning is a blur, and I'm relieved when it's finally time for lunch with Monica. As we eat, I conclude that she's a really sweet girl—genuinely sweet. By the end of lunch hour, I'm enjoying her company. Her positive banter and wild stories about people in the building make me laugh. Obviously I'm horrible at deciphering first impressions today. That, I blame on Gavin Rhodes. He left my mind a scrambled mess when he walked out the front door last night.

Giggling from our endorphin-induced walk around the building, Monica shows me to my next meeting, this time in a smaller conference room near my desk. As I take a seat, I scan my day's inventory for details about the meeting.

"Hey Monica," I call before she walks out of the conference room, "what's the name of the vendor coming in to see me now?"

A figure appears behind her. Tall, with broad shoulders and a five o'clock shadow I've recently come to find extremely sexy. Our eyes connect. My heart does that annoying racing thing as I rack my brain, trying to come up with a less obvious reason Gavin is entering my conference room.

"Here he is," she says with a grin. "Hey, Gav!" She throws her arms around him in a hug, much too unprofessional for my taste. I want to launch myself across the table and pull her away, but I think I might already like my job too much. "Gavin, this is Chloe, our new writer. She's going to be working with you on Heroes and Legends. Chloe, meet Gavin Rhodes, our uber-talented artist. You'll love him."

When she winks at me, I know she's indicating that I'll love him for more than his talent. If only she knew how right she was.

Gavin continues to stand awkwardly at the door and Monica looks between us with a fading smile. "Okay, you two. Get to work. I'll let Sharlene know you're both here."

When Monica leaves, Gavin steps across the threshold, meeting my astonished stare and taking a seat across from me. "Well, this is a surprise," he mutters.

He focuses on laying out his pad of paper and container of pencils before sitting back in his chair and crossing his arms. He looks everywhere before finally resting his eyes on mine. Are things so bad between us that he can't even be in the same room with me?

Well, if Gavin wants to be childish and ignore me, then so be it. We're not in this room to be friends. He's the artist. My vendor. *Ugh.* Why, of all the creative agencies in the world, did Gavin have to walk into mine?

Okay, technically he was hired on first, but that's not the point.

Sharlene breaks the silence by bursting through the door and taking a seat next to me. She reaches across the table to shake Gavin's hand. "Nice to see you again, Gavin. You've met Chloe?"

Gavin plasters a smile on his face and nods. "It's like we've known each other for years."

Sharlene is too busy shuffling through her three-ring binder to pay attention to his sarcasm. "Okay, let's start with the agenda, shall we?" She tosses us each a sheet of paper. "It's just a rough, so don't take it literally. This will help us create a story for the event. We want everything from the moment guests are greeted at the door to their send-off to be like they've been immersed in a story. We'll come up with all the marketing content later. First, I want us to have a solid idea of what the experience is."

An hour later, Sharlene leaves us for another appointment but asks us to begin addressing the theme. How will it look and feel? What will it say? The moment the door closes, Gavin sets down his pencil and rises. "I need to use the restroom. Be back."

Heat rises to my cheeks in response to his brisk departure—again. I stand with determination. I'm pushing through this. Gavin may have a problem with me, but right now it doesn't matter. We have a job to do, and it's for an amazing cause. Gavin will see that too; maybe I just need to remind him of it.

I search the room until I find what I'm looking for. When Gavin returns, I'm taping the final poster to the wall. I turn to find him staring back at the faces of children and teens who have been victims of bullying, a defeated look on his face.

"This is why we're both here," I say.

That gets his attention. His jaw loosens and he nods. "Yes. It is."

He takes a seat and flips open his sketchpad. I can tell he's thinking by the way he taps his pencil and nibbles the corner of his bottom lip. I always joked that I didn't want to be his lips when he was thinking. That wasn't entirely true.

After a few minutes he squints and tilts his head. "Can we use these photos of the kids in the art?"

I shrug. "I can ask Sharlene. I'm sure we already have their permission since we have these. Are you thinking about using them in the set design?"

He looks at me. "I could. Don't you think it would be cool to incorporate them into the art in some way, immerse them into the adventure? We could do a collage of them all . . . "

My mind is working, not completely loving his last thought, but it greases the idea wheel. "Maybe not a collage. That's too impersonal. We want to showcase these kids as the superheroes of this event. We should fill the walls with inspiring quotes—or create one long story that wraps around the entire event—with our superheroes guiding the story."

Gavin's right there with me. "A comic strip that wraps the event, or we could create stations of mini stories—grab quotes from each of them—and each quote or story could be part of a skit or video that gets played on stage. Or we could have immersive adventures throughout the party."

"Gav," I gush, "I love it! It'll be like a superhero carnival."

Gavin smiles. It's a beautiful smile that reaches his eyes, giving me a glimpse at his heart. He has a beautiful heart, too.

For the next few hours our minds are in fantasyland, deep into the brainstorm. Some of our ideas are wild-crazy ones that get cut before making it to the whiteboard, but I love that Gavin's already sketching some of our better ideas.

When Sharlene comes in to check on us, I think she's a little overwhelmed. Luckily, her job is to organize our madness and help us make sense of it. That's exactly what she does as she helps us tone down some of the wackier ideas and elaborate on the better ones.

By the time five o'clock comes, we've made incredible progress. At least I can leave today knowing that not only did I get through my first day, I got through it with Gavin.

I grab my bag from my desk and shut down my computer with a smile on my face. I'm hopeful Gavin will still be around when I'm heading out. After today, I don't think resolving things with him will be totally impossible. But my hope dims when I turn the corner and spot Gavin sitting on Monica's desk. He's peering down at something on her computer, hand perched on her back, grinning and then laughing.

If I could find a back entrance and dart out it I would, but the only way out I know of is past Monica's desk. I trudge forward, forcing a smile on my face when all I want to do is punch a wall.

"Goodnight, Chloe!" Monica beams up at me. "Glad to have you here."

Gavin is still staring intently at Monica's screen. After a second I give up hope that he'll acknowledge me and turn back to Monica. "Goodnight. Thanks for everything today."

As soon as I'm outside, the tears come.

CHAPTER 20

FRO-YO

CHLOE

The next morning before work, my closet is in shambles. I try on everything I own before finally settling on a pink sleeveless blouse, white capris, and strappy white heels. My hair falls in loose curls bouncing lightly against my back. I even apply extra mascara to compete with Monica's thick eyelashes.

The first half of the day is quiet around the office, so I take my time reviewing what Gavin and I put together yesterday and coming up with more ideas. I want to be on point for our one o'clock.

At one thirty, I'm still sitting in the conference room alone when the door finally bursts open. Monica walks through first, breathless. "Sorry, Chloe. Gavin and I lost track of time. He's here. So sorry we're late."

She lets him brush by her, but there's no mistaking the look of longing she gives him before exiting the room. All my strength and confidence crumbles. I honestly don't think I can hold in my calm another minute.

"We have a lot of work to do," I say over the thundering of my heart. I try for a professional tone, but I'm certain it was more of a whine.

I need to quit. I can't work here with Gavin. Not if every day is going to be a flirt show between wide-eyed-Monica and hates-me-Gavin.

But can I really quit knowing what I'd be leaving behind? I'm already invested in this event. Gavin may be a huge part of this project team, but so am I, and this is something I want to be part of too.

"Sorry," he replies. "Like she said, we lost track of time." Gavin faces down, beginning to quietly sketch in his pad. My heart wants to burst at the sight of him. "Monica has releases for all of the kids," he says without looking up.

For a second I have no idea what he's talking about.

"For the scenery."

I nod. "Oh. Okay. Great." I focus on my notepad, hoping to find intelligent words that will mask my jealousy. "So," I start, "I was thinking about the speakers. A few of them are kids. One victim. One hero. One is an ex-bully. We have their speeches already. Would it be possible to project a mini comic reel of them as a backdrop while they talk?"

Gavin just stares at me, wordlessly at first, and I wonder if he's going to tell me I'm a complete nut job who needs to seek a new career, one far away from him. "Yes, that's possible. I love that idea, actually. If you can get me their stories I can sketch something. When do we pitch our ideas to the executives?"

"Weekly," I say. "Every Friday we show them our progress."

"Okay, we can wrap this up next week, easy. I'll come up with a draft storyboard by Monday and we'll flesh out the rest together. We'll be able to walk them through the event outline from start to finish."

I nod and go back to my notepad, pretending to think more about the event. In reality, thinking about anything other than Gavin's possible relationship with Monica is difficult. I want to ask him. In high school, I would have had no problem asking him about his relationship status, but now . . . it means something different. And really, what business is it of mine? I waltz back into town and suddenly feel as if I own Gavin's heart? I know better than that. Gavin is a gorgeous, talented, smart guy. Any girl would be crazy not to flirt with him given the chance. I can't be mad at Monica for trying.

"Something wrong with your hand?"

"Huh?" I look up to find Gavin smirking at me. He nods at my right hand. I look down and find myself choking my pen with a death grip, the ball tip pressed so hard into the paper it's forming a hole three pages deep. "Oh, God." I drop the pen and stand. "I need to take a walk. Um, writer's block or something. Be back."

Once outside, I take a big gulp of air and take a seat at the entrance steps. This cannot be my life. Am I really pining over my ex-best friend? I need to get a grip. There are millions of men in this world, including some very good-looking ones who happen to work in the same building as me, but I can't seem to look at them long enough to find anything I like.

"I thought you were walking."

I stiffen at the sound of Gavin's voice. "I just needed some air, that's all."

"Come on. There's a fro-yo shop around the corner. My treat."

"Please tell me you did not just say fro-yo." I tried so hard not to smile, but Gavin's cuteness factor is off the charts, even when I'm mad at him.

"Sure did. Get up."

I stare at his outstretched hand for a second before taking it. Fro-yo does sound good. We walk slowly, arms dangerously close to touching as they swing by our sides. It's silent but I can tell Gavin has something on his mind. He does this deep, heavy sigh thing when he's about to say something he's been thinking about for a while.

"The other night—" he starts.

I know him so well.

"Don't worry about it, Gav. I get it."

"Really? You can read minds?"

I blush and shake my head. "No, I mean, it's okay. You don't need to explain why you ran away the other night. It was dark, we were lying down, there was a romantic scene on . . ." I should just stop talking now.

"We've always been friends. I don't know what came over me that night. Don't get me wrong. You're so damn beautiful. I've always thought so. But you're . . ."

Embarrassed even more than before, I turn from the sidewalk to the massive fountain in the courtyard. "I told you not to explain." I'm sure my face is a fierce shade of red.

"Wait a second." Gavin turns me to face him, his brow furrowed, creating a crease down the center. "Are you upset?"

"What? No. I've never been your type. I know that. I just . . ." This conversation is taking a strange turn.

He laughs. Gavin *laughs*. Jerk.

"If I didn't know better, I'd think you *want* to be my type." There's a smirk on his face, and I'd love to slap it off him. How can he think this is funny?

"Chloe." He grabs my hand and forces me to stop in my tracks. Raising his hands to either side of my face, he takes his thumb and brushes it across my cheek, then holds it in place while he searches my eyes with his.

What are we even talking about? Turning toward the fountain again, I shake my head. "No, I'm just saying I understand."

"Obviously you don't." This time Gavin comes to stand in front of me. "And stop turning away from me. It's rude. I'm talking to you." My gaze shifts everywhere but on him. "Chloe!"

I look up into his spider web and I'm trapped.

"Thank you. Geez. You should know something. Maybe it will make you feel better—or maybe it will make things worse. I don't know." He groans. "This is hard, actually." He shakes his head. "I wanted to kiss you the other night. I wanted to do more than kiss you." He takes a deep breath; meanwhile, I'm holding onto mine. "If I didn't leave . . . Chloe, you have no idea what was going through my mind that night."

Holy shit. Tremors rip through my body, and he's barely touching me. I can't imagine what would happen if he ever did make a move. I'd combust. "You said it was a mistake and you just walked out, like you were mad at me. What did I do?"

"Nothing," he sighs. "When I came over that day I had no intention of things getting to that point. You've always been off-limits to me. It was like there was this invisible line between friendship and everything else. Any time I thought of crossing that line, I talked myself out of it. I didn't want to lose our friend-ship; I didn't think you'd feel the same; it wasn't the right time . . . and then you were dating Devon."

"What does that have to do with the other night?"

"You're still Devon's."

All goes silent as I process the words that come from some-where deep in Gavin that I may never understand. I'm off-limits. He obviously wants to respect his brother; it doesn't matter that Devon was never *the one* for me. At least it's clear now why Gavin tore himself away from something that was so obviously there. But there will never be anything more between Gavin and me than friendship. I'd better get used to it.

I give him a tight smile, telling him I understand. "Well, now that we got that out of the way . . ." Now is a great time for a distraction, or a change in conversation. "Can we get that ice cream you promised me?"

"It's fro-yo." He smirks.

Gavin and I decide to work the rest of the day in the frozen yogurt shop. We find the perfect booth in the back next to enormous windows that overlook a park. The natural lighting is good for Gavin's sketching and for my thinking.

We neither move nor speak until Gavin's phone buzzes around five. "It's Monica. She wants to know if we've been kidnapped."

My mouth tightens in an attempt at a smile. *How sweet.*

When I look up, Gavin is viewing me strangely. Maybe the eye roll was a tell.

"I'll let her know we're having an off-site meeting so she doesn't worry."

So she doesn't worry about what? There's a sinking in my stomach as my mind begins to roam once again. Ugh.

His fingers blaze across the phone's touchscreen before setting it down, crossing his arms, placing his chin atop them, and looking at me. "What was college like?"

My eyes flicker between his eyes and his mouth as I try to adjust from work to his personal question. I can't help but appreciate him, especially when he looks at me like that—sweet, curious, and considerate.

"Fast. Busy. Different." I grin. "Or do you need details?"

He returns my grin. "Details. All of them."

"My classes were actually fun once I got past my electives. I almost switched majors to psychology when my roommate went psycho on me and threatened to throw me out a window if I wouldn't get up and do something with her. She was an interesting character. But I guess her threats worked. I started going out my junior year and met a lot of people. Dated some, kicked ass in my writing classes, and graduated magna cum laude."

Gavin cocks his head to the side. "How are the boyfriends in Oregon?"

I tilt my head, amused. Of course that's what he picks out of my entire response. "Tall, dark, handsome." I shrug. "Huge muscles. And even bigger—"

He practically jumps from his seat. "Whoa, no! I don't need those details."

I roar with laughter. "Hands! There's nothing wrong with big hands, Gavin."

With that, Gavin pulls out one of his hands and examines it. He flips it around and nods in approval. "Can't complain about these babies. What do you think?" He shoves it in my face and grins. "As big as Oregon?"

I wink. "I'll never tell."

Dejected, he pulls his hand back and continues. "Magna cum laude, huh? No wonder you got the job at BelleCurve. They only hire the best, top of the class."

"How did you start working at Belle?"

"Remember that anti-bullying comic I did of us in the treehouse?"

"*Up in the Treehouse*? You still have that?"

"Throughout my studies I kept going back to that one. I don't know why. Wanted to get it perfect, I guess. I'd learn new things and want to try them out. My last quarter of college was completely project-based, and we got to showcase our work at an end-of-year event that tons of recruiters and huge companies came to. Treehouse was my showpiece. I ended up connecting with an awesome recruiter who continues to land me the best jobs. He hooked me up with BelleCurve straight out of school, and most of my contracts have been with them."

"How did you not lose everything in the fire?"

He pauses and I wonder if he'll even respond. "I was actually able to salvage most of my work; I only lost one sketchbook that night. Unfortunately, it was turning out to be my favorite."

"Did you ever try to recreate it?"

He's taken aback. I can tell by the way his expression dims, as if a dark thought suddenly crossed his mind. "I did, but it wasn't the same. Either I'd get caught up in the reasons why I was re-sketching it, or I'd completely lose motivation."

"You should try again. Surely enough time has passed for you to get back to it."

He sits up straight. "It's getting late. We should head back before they lock up."

I'm not ready to go. I pout, but he doesn't see it because he's already sliding out of the booth. He holds out his hand again and helps me out after him. He gives my hand a squeeze, then releases it and leads the way out of the yogurt shop.

CHAPTER 21

STAR-STRUCK

CHLOE

Working at BelleCurve comes with some very desirable perks that weren't mentioned in the job description. I walk into the executive conference room on Wednesday morning, laptop in hand, and stumble over my own two feet the moment I catch sight of our celebrity guest.

Zachary Ryan, local celebrity, football star, and most eligible bachelor in all of Seattle (according to the local news stations) is standing across from me, holding one of Gavin's sketches. He smiles, and it's as if someone shines a spotlight on just him and me. Heads turn in the direction of his glance. A blush lights up my cheeks.

"There she is!" Sandra beams and ushers me to their side of the table. She places a hand on both my and Zachary's backs the moment I step within reach. "Zachary, this is our writer, Chloe Rivers. Chloe, I'm sure you're already familiar with Zachary Ryan, NFL quarterback and Super Bowl champion. He's an advocate for the cause, and he'll be a speaker and host at the August event."

"It's wonderful to meet you, Mr. Ryan." I manage my best smile as I reach my hand out to grasp his in a firm handshake.

"Please call me Zachary," he says before releasing my hand. "I look forward to working with you closely, Miss Rivers."

Sandra nods at Sharlene. "I'll be stepping out so you can get to work. Zachary, you have my number. If there's anything you'd like to discuss, please call. Anytime, dear." She hugs him as if they're old friends and then walks briskly from the room.

Zachary takes the seat next to me, and Sharlene begins the meeting. I almost don't notice Gavin on the other side of the table, trying not to make eye contact with me, but I see the curious glances he throws between me and the hottie to my left. Satisfaction washes over me as I realize Gavin might just be getting a taste of retribution right about now. He's the one who wants to brand me as Devon's off-limits girlfriend for the rest of our lives and put me in his friendship corner. He'll have to be okay with what that means.

For the next hour, I dazzle Zachary with many smiles while we discuss ideas for his part of the event. At the tail end of our interview, we're huddled in the corner of the room.

"Have you always been an anti-bullying advocate?" I ask him.

"Since I was a victim myself at a young age, I've been using my career as a platform to help raise awareness."

"You were bullied? I can't believe it."

"I was the kid getting thrown into the dumpster in elementary, the one getting chased down the street as rocks were pelted at my head. I'll tell you what: it could have gone many different ways for me. I chose to bulk up, play sports, and become so fierce, mentally and physically, that no one would even think of messing with me again."

"I'd say you succeeded."

"I'd say you're right."

I pretend to scribble something in my notebook as an excuse to tear my eyes from Zachary's.

"What's your story?"

I look up and blush. "What's that?"

"I want to know more about you. What's your story?" he repeats.

Giving him my best smile, I respond, "Another time, another place. Today is all about you, Mr. Ryan."

"Well then name the time and place, Miss Rivers."

Without responding, I stand politely, extending a hand. "I think our time together is up. Thank you so much for the brainstorm."

He shakes my hand, a wicked grin replacing his curious one. "The pleasure was all mine."

As I head for the door, Gavin's stare from across the room is unavoidable. The heat radiating from his body is scathing, and I'm tempted to stop and ask him what his problem is. Instead, I slip out the door and collide with a drooling Monica. It appears she's been snooping through the glass. She grabs my arm and pulls me around the corner.

"Were you two flirting?" she hisses.

I look around, hoping no one is listening to us. When I confirm the coast is clear, I turn back to her and laugh. "No," I hiss back. "We were talking about the event and I was interviewing him."

"He looked like he wanted to eat you."

With that, I throw my head back and laugh. "That man has no problem finding a meal. I highly doubt he's starving."

She scrunches her nose to show me she doesn't agree. "Well, maybe he just spotted something new on the menu. You know men and their food; they have to try a bit of everything before they're completely satisfied."

"Wait, what are we talking about?"

We both burst into laughter just as Gavin emerges with his sketchbook in hand. His brows furrow when he sees us huddled together. "Can you two act more juvenile? The man is here to work."

Monica shrugs. "I think he's into Chloe."

I nudge her, hoping to stop her from elaborating. Gavin stiffens before shaking his head and walking down the hall.

The rest of the week is filled with Gavin shooting me petulant glares across the table every time Zachary is around. Monica keeps a close watch on my time with the football hunk, whispering to me later how hot he is for me. I just jab her in the ribs and move on.

I'm still unsure what's going on between her and Gavin. I've started privately referring to her as googly-eyed Monica because anytime she shares a room with Gavin, her eyes look as if they are going to slinky from their sockets. She's so obviously into him, but somehow Gavin doesn't seem to pick up on it. He's nice to her, but Gavin is nice to everyone.

"C'mon, just one drink, Chloe." Monica is pressing her perfect boobs over the counter, waiting to attract attention from the male bartender. He doesn't notice her right away, but she has captured the attention of pretty much every other guy in the bar.

I shouldn't have agreed to come for happy hour. "Fine, but I can only have one. I need to drive home."

Monica finally gets the attention she's been working for and orders us drinks. She hands me a beer and yanks me over to a table of our coworkers. "You should move to the city," she says. "My place is just around the corner. I was living down south until a few weeks ago. Helluva commute. I walk to work now, and the grocery store is around the corner."

"Not a bad idea. I can probably start looking for my own place in August. Until then, I'm stuck with the sober commute."

We slip through the packed crowd and over to a table of our coworkers. She introduces me to the finance department and the entire video production team. "So you're on the Heroes and Legends project," says a guy named Mitch, obviously impressed.

"That's going to be one hell of an event. Such a rush to see what we do for those kids."

As I'm responding with equal excitement, my eyes flicker to a movement at the entrance of the bar. *How does he do that?* The bar is packed and I'm standing on the opposite side of the room from the door, yet I see him the moment he enters.

And he sees me too.

Gavin assesses the smile on my face, the beer in my hand—and Mitch, who has conveniently inched closer to me since we started talking. In typical self-conscious fashion, I lower my arm to hide the beer from his view. Something about this moment reminds me of the night at Babalouie's when he practically dragged me from the bar. Will this night end the same way? I can't say that would be a bad thing. As Gavin weaves his thick build through the crowd, I try to focus on Mitch, who has all kinds of things to tell me. He's been at BelleCurve for seven years and just received a promotion to senior producer. I think he tells a joke next, so I laugh to be kind, but I'm not processing much besides Gavin making his way across the bar.

Gavin approaches us, centering his body behind mine. The lack of distance is surely due to the crowded bar, but a tingling sensation creeps up my spine. Did he have to stand right behind me? It's an absurd thought, but it feels almost as if he's claiming me.

"Hey, man," calls out Buddy, one of the video guys at the booth. "Here." Buddy offers Gavin a beer from his ice bucket. Without hesitation, Gavin takes a long pull from the bottle.

"Thanks, Buddy," he finally answers. He turns his focus to me, and then he winks.

I swivel my head back to Mitch, embarrassed to be caught staring. Mitch is still talking as if I haven't been completely ignoring him. "Did you go to school around here?"

"OSU. Journalism."

Mitch widens his eyes to show his interest. "That's a great school."

He's actually a good-looking guy with his sandy blonde hair and short, stocky build. A little on the nerdy side, but I like that. In another place and time, I might have actually returned his interest.

I feel Gavin shuffle behind me and realize I'm far too aware of his every move.

"Hey guys, over here!" Robert from the graphics department has just claimed a high-top near us, and he's waving us over.

Relieved to exit the conversation, I grin at Mitch and grab a chair. Gavin is right on my tail, casually taking a seat beside me while he yammers on with another guy whose name I can't remember.

Mitch takes the seat across from me. "Do you live in Bellevue?"

I shake my head. "No, but I'll be moving at the end of summer, probably out this way."

That gets Gavin's attention, and he pulls himself into the conversation by leaning over so his shoulder presses into mine, eyeing me intently. "Really? Bellevue?"

I shrug. "I haven't started looking yet, but it makes sense. It's close to work. I wouldn't have to drive much." My mind wanders back to Monica's sales pitch of city living.

"It's expensive and packed with buildings. Wouldn't you miss —what did you used to call it—serenity at your backdoor?"

I shrug again. I think I might have a twitch. It's becoming my go-to action when Gavin asks me a question. Am I trying to be elusive? "Not really," I lie.

He seems surprised and leans back into his stool, turning away. My heart beats a little faster at his disapproval.

Just then, Monica rushes over to our table with two shots. "Bottoms up, girl. You have some catching up to do." She pushes one of the shots to me and it slides across the table without spilling. Impressive. Only bubbly girls like Monica can make drunk look sexy.

I shake my head and hold up my beer. "Just one, remember?"

Monica pouts and holds her shot glass to her lips. "Suit yourself. Gavin, it's all yours." She twists her upper body back and forth in a shimmy, smiling flirtatiously.

I slide the thick, caramel colored shot to him and smile. "Bottoms up, Gavin."

He slides it back to me and leans into my ear, so close that his facial scruff tickles my cheek. I shiver, and I'm certain he feels it. "Take it. I'll drive you home."

Tempting. With a glance at him, I smile. I wouldn't mind being in a car alone with him. Then again, maybe I should mind. "I don't need another, but thank you."

Are you crazy? Take the damn shot!

He leans in again, but this time his lips press against my ear. His proximity is definitely not an accident. If this is what being friends will be like, I'm not sure my sanity will hold out. "Have fun. I'll take care of you. Promise."

"Okay," I say as the breath rushes from me, hoping he's offering more than a ride home.

He smiles, sending another shiver racing through me.

Monica's expression has dimmed some since her peer pressure commenced, but she's all smiles again when I hold up my shot glass to hers. "To heroes who stand up to bullies because it's the right thing to do," I say.

"To heroes!" Monica chimes in and clinks her glass to mine.

We throw back our shots and Monica cheers loudly, raising her arms above her head. We all see her gorgeous stomach, and I can't help but glance in Gavin's direction. He's appreciating Monica's body along with everyone else. My stomach belly-flops instantly just as his eyes flicker to mine. He must see my disappointment because he slides his beer to me. "All yours."

"Trying to get me drunk?"

He laughs. "Hardly. Just distracting you from your own thoughts." He moves closer, going for my ear again. My arm hairs jump to life and my face is on fire. He really needs to stop doing that. "You've had a great first week. Celebrate a little, but don't throw up. If you do, I'm sending you home in a taxi."

I turn to him, wide-eyed, trying to hold back my smile. "Maybe I'll choose to take a taxi anyway."

He glares. "Not a chance."

Monica's on her fifth shot, giggling and falling into Gavin's lap when I stand, ready to call it quits. "I better start heading home," I say loud enough for Gavin to hear.

He gently leans Monica into a sitting position and stands with me. "Not you too," Monica pouts. She really sticks that bottom lip out. "I thought you wanted to see my new place."

Her words are a blow straight to my ego. I try to hide my hurt by turning and shuffling away from the table, my mind reeling. The good news: Gavin hasn't seen Monica's place yet. The bad news: Gavin wants to see her place.

Even with a free pass to drink tonight, I've paced myself, not wanting to be too drunk for the ride home. If Gavin wanted to go home with Monica, then he wouldn't have let me get drunk. That's all that matters.

While Gavin pries Monica off him, I take an extra-long bathroom break. Maybe I should give him an out, take a taxi home, allow him to have some fun of his own.

But he doesn't give me a chance to think about it further. When I come out of the bathroom, he's standing there, arms folded across his chest and a knowing look on his face. "Don't even think about taking a taxi. Let's go."

I let out an exasperated sigh and stumble toward him. Now that I'm walking around, I realize I've got a good buzz going. "I'm okay if you want to leave with Monica. Don't let me stop you."

Gavin narrows his eyes and grabs my arm. "C'mon, Chlo. Let's go before you say something you might regret."

"I don't want to be a cockblock."

Gavin lets out a nice, throaty laugh and tightens his hold on me. "Maybe I want you to be a cockblock."

Ahh. So he's onto Monica's advances and maybe isn't so keen. My curiosity is at its peak. Once we're outside, he removes his grip on my elbow and grabs my hand. We reach his truck in a few minutes and are on the freeway before I finally speak up. "So what's the deal with you and Monica?"

Gavin shifts, shoots a look in my direction, and then grips the steering wheel a little bit tighter. "We're friends."

"Like you and I are friends?"

Gavin shifts again. "No. You and I have something different. You know that."

My cheeks lift slightly, happy to hear him say it. "Then what kind of friends are you? I get the feeling she doesn't view your friendship the same way you do."

"We had a thing." He throws a look at me, as if expecting me to freak out. And I am totally freaking out—on the inside. On the outside, I'm frozen.

"Last summer," he continues. "We weren't official or anything, but there was something. I don't know; for me, it just fizzled."

"Not for her."

Gavin shakes his head. "No, not for her. That's partially my fault."

I'm shooting darts at his head with my eyes. "How so?" My voice is much harsher than I planned. He sighs.

"Chloe, I don't want to talk about Monica."

"I do."

He throws me a glare and turns back to the road. "Why? What does it matter?"

With a huff, I turn my entire body to the front. "It doesn't. Never mind."

"No, not never mind. Answer me. Why do you care about Monica and I?"

"Monica and me," I correct him, just as I've always done, but in the past it's always been a joke. I'm not laughing right now. "Don't turn this around on me. If you want me to answer your question, then answer mine first."

He groans. "Really? Is this a game? So if I answer your question, you'll answer mine?"

"Yes. Pinky swear."

"Give me your hand."

"What?" I look at him, baffled.

"You want to pinky swear; give me your pinky."

My hand crosses the distance between us and we link pinkies. "I pinky swear I will answer your question if you answer mine. Why is it partially your fault that Monica has the hots for you?"

Gavin doesn't let go of my pinky. He simply lets our hands rest between us, pinkies still intertwined. "Every now and then we still . . ."

"Okay, I get it." I tug my hand to escape his grasp, but he just grabs on tighter.

"You can't be mad. You wanted to know, and I'm not going to lie to you."

Why do I feel as if Gavin cheated on me when we've never even dated? This whole *just friends* thing didn't bother me when we were younger. Now, it's slowly killing me.

"Your turn to answer my question."

"I can't remember what it was," I lie.

He doesn't miss a beat. "Why do you care about Monica and me?"

My throat squeezes, but I swallow it down, not wanting to cry right now. I had such a fun night, and I don't want to ruin it. "Please don't make me answer that. I think you already know."

Gavin squeezes my hand. It's a long squeeze that somehow reaches my heart. "Okay."

A change of subject is needed, quick. "So what are your plans for the treehouse?"

"What do you mean? I wasn't planning anything."

"You tore down our treehouse," I say as if he should know exactly what I'm getting at. "You did that to erase the bad memories, right?"

He seems shocked at my question and answers tentatively. "Yes."

"And now that you don't have the treehouse anymore, you're still avoiding the memories like they never happened."

He furrows his brow, and I know I'm onto something. "I can't avoid them."

"But you're trying to avoid them. You thought tearing down the treehouse would help you move on. Like tossing out old photos or old clothes." I shake my head. "I hate to break this to you, Gavin, but that place will always be there whether you want to see it or not."

"What are you trying to say, Chloe?"

I sigh. I'm not exactly sure, but I know I'm on the verge of making a point. "Maybe instead of destroying old memories, you should find a way to make new ones. Happy ones. Hell, Gavin. Maybe you should build a new treehouse."

BRANCH FOUR

REBUILDING

"HEALING COMES WHEN WE CHOOSE TO WALK AWAY FROM DARKNESS AND MOVE TOWARDS A BRIGHTER LIGHT." ~ DIETER F. UCHTDORF

CHAPTER 22

TINKERING AROUND

CHLOE

I 'm exhausted and sweating as I roll from my bed and realize something is wrong. It doesn't take a genius to recognize that the AC isn't working. *Great.* The realtor is showing the house all day. I'm supposed to be out by ten.

After giving the realtor a quick warning, I slip on one of my old bikinis and skip out to the lake. My parents' spacious yard is a bright and healthy green, landscaped with white azaleas, garden rocks, Lodi apple trees, and beautiful shrubs. It's hard to imagine someone else living here. When this house sells, there will be no more sunbathing on the dock, skipping through the woods, punching out the screen of the upstairs loft and reading on the roof—not that I've done any of those things for years, but that's not the point. The point is those options will no longer be available and I'll be left with is a dullness in my chest.

Once I reach the end of the wooden platform, I pull my raft from the boathouse, secure it to the dock cleat, and hop onto the floatation to bake and relax for just a few minutes . . .

"Shit!" I jump from my raft. I must have fallen asleep. Under the blazing sun, no less. How long have I been out here? I pull myself onto the dock and run for my house. As I rush up the back steps, the patio door swings open. I duck behind the top few stairs and hold my breath. How am I going to escape this?

"Isn't this view beautiful? It's one of our best properties. With that view of Mount Rainier you can't go wrong. Especially on a day like today."

I slip back down the stairs and turn the corner. Now what am I going to do? Planted against the side of my house, I weigh my options: run through the woods to Gavin's and ask if I can hide out for a while. Or run inside my house for a change of clothes and my car keys, ultimately sabotaging the showing and revealing my poorly planned attire. I can always plead for forgiveness later.

My feet are moving before I know I've made a decision. I've run through these woods barefoot many times, but I was younger then. I don't remember it hurting this much. I curse a few times, land on several unkind rocks, and earn myself some splinters before I'm deposited in the center of the woods where our tree-house once stood. Today it's nothing but a big, beautiful tree that once meant the world to three children who knew how to dream lavishly.

I don't linger long. My feet hurt, my skin burns, and I'd really like to cover up. Gavin's house isn't far from here, and when I arrive at his back steps I start banging feverishly. The lights appear to be on inside, and as I press my face up against the sliding door glass, a warm buzz grows within me at the familiarity of the interior. I can almost picture Gavin, Devon, and me sitting at the dining room table, playing board games, and drinking copious amounts of soda.

Curious eyes appear on the other side of the sliding glass, causing me to jump back. Gavin opens the door, revealing an amused expression as he unhurriedly scans me from my head to my toes.

Instinctively, I fold my arms and tap my foot in annoyance. "What are you gawking at?"

He's laughing now. Doubled over, in fact. "I can't wait to hear this story." I push past him and walk toward the stairs that lead to the second floor. I cringe as I hear Gavin call out behind me, "And here I thought I woke up. Still dreaming, I guess."

"Stop." I yell back. "I need a change of clothes and a place to hang out for a while. I fell asleep on the lake and the realtor is showing the house all day. To top it off my AC crapped out on me."

Once upstairs, I pause in the hallway beside Gavin's old room. I realize he probably no longer sleeps here. I look to my left and frown. Devon's room? I reach for the door handle, but Gavin doesn't give me the chance to turn it as he breezes by me and toward his dad's old bedroom. I follow him through a wide set of French doors.

"Is it okay if I hang here until the realtor leaves?"

Gavin stops and turns, looking as if he's pondering my request. If he's about to make a joke, it dies on his lips as he nods. "Sure. I'll grab you something to wear until we can get your clothes."

As he's preoccupied in his closet, I look around the master bedroom he's taken over. The room is all man; that's for sure. White walls, brown comforter, gray rug, and absolutely nothing on the walls. A dresser and end tables with small white lamps are all that decorate the room. His bed is unmade, but other than that, his room is clean. Nothing to hide, it seems.

Gavin emerges moments later, tossing me a shirt and shorts. I'll have to tie the drawstring tight to keep those bad boys from falling off, but they'll do. "You can use my shower if you want to wash up," he says. "I'll be downstairs when you're done."

I take him up on his invitation and make myself comfortable in the shower, relieved to find that none of the toiletries hint at any presence of the female species. Geez, am I really this jealous of anyone who even looks at Gavin? Maybe it's a good thing we're not together. In fact, maybe this is why he doesn't have a steady girlfriend—because any woman lucky enough to call Gavin hers would need to have a little crazy in her to put up with all the competition.

After washing off the early afternoon's escapades, I exit the shower and slip on Gavin's clothes. My heart beats a little faster when I realize he chose his old football shirt for me to wear. In high school, if a guy loaned you his team *anything* it meant he was totally into you. We're clearly not in high school anymore, so it's crazy for me to read anything into this, but as I stare back at myself in the floor-length mirror, I can't help but smile.

When I head toward the stairs, I glance at Devon's room again. My drumming chest is warning me away, but I ignore it and turn the handle. It's been locked. I'm not sure whether I'm relieved or saddened by the discovery that Devon's memories are trapped behind his old door. With a heavy heart I turn away.

Moments later, I'm planting my feet on the bottom floor. Gavin is waiting for me holding a pair of my old running shoes and guzzling a bottle of water.

Holy crap. In all the chaos, I hadn't noticed what Gavin was wearing. He looks like he just got done working out in his bright green, sleeveless shirt and charcoal gym shorts. I don't care how shallow my thoughts are as I appreciate the way his muscles bulge in all the right places, and how effortlessly disheveled his hair is. I've been staring too long. As I come back down from my ogling, I acknowledge the shoes in his hands. "Where'd you get those?"

He smiles. "I ran by your house. The realtor was between showings. You'll need these for where we're going."

"Where *we're* going?"

He extends the shoes, and I grab them suspiciously, slipping them on my feet.

"*We're* going shopping." He grabs a folder from the entrance table and opens the door. "Let's go."

"Shopping? For what?"

"You'll see." He's grinning. I see that now. Gavin is up to something, and apparently I'm going along for the ride.

So here I am on a Saturday afternoon, dressed in a men's extra-large t-shirt and shorts, standing in the local hardwood store as Gavin fills the cart to the brim. He still hasn't told me what's going on, but by now I can guess it has something to do with the treehouse. Why else would he be stocking the cart full of plywood and containers of nails, screws, and other supplies I can't even name?

"You couldn't have grabbed me some clothes while you were at my house?" I complain as I move to tighten the string on the shorts for the hundredth time.

He chuckles but is too focused in his task to respond, so I begin to browse the aisles. When I see a hammock, I don't resist the urge to grab it.

When we meet back up at the check stand, Gavin starts laughing at me. "That's where you were? Buying a hammock?" he asks as he pushes items around the cart to see what other treasures I found.

I nudge his hand away, unable to keep the smile from my face. "No peeking."

When I hand the cashier my credit card, Gavin hands over his instead. She takes his while I shoot him a glare. "Hey! I'm buying that."

Gavin shrugs. "Today is my idea, so it's my treat."

I can hardly be mad at him, but I would have never grabbed the hammock if I'd known he was going to pick up the tab. He nudges me and points to the box I'm carrying. "So, you know what we're doing today?"

I smile and shrug. "If it's not what I think, hammocks are still cool."

"True."

When we arrive back at Gavin's house, he backs his truck into the driveway. We get out and he hands me a cooler from his garage. "Why don't you fill this up with food and drinks? Whatever you can for the afternoon."

Thirty minutes later we've filled a wheelbarrow with tools and wood pieces, and we're towing it and the cooler deep into the woods. My pace is a little slower than Gavin's, but I'm realizing I packed a lot of crap into this cooler. I'm heaving deep breaths by the time we've made our way to the spot in the woods where our treehouse once stood.

I'm standing there, staring up at the massive task ahead of us as Gavin comes up behind me. He wraps his arms around my shoulders and rests his chin on my head. "Sometimes," he starts, "I actually listen to the things you say." I can feel him smile, so I do too. "You had a good point the other day. If I want to hold onto the good memories and let go of the bad, maybe I should rebuild the treehouse. So that's exactly what we're going to do."

"We?" I tease.

He grins. "Yes, we. You don't get to sit back and watch like last time." As he steps away and leans down to grab a folded piece of paper from his pile of stuff, I check out the sweat that's already seeping through his form-fitting shirt. Back muscles like those should be illegal.

"I suppose I don't have a choice."

He hands me a piece of wood and winks. "Nope. Get up there. We need to fix the platform first. Some crazy person took an axe to it."

A burst of laughter erupts from me. Realizing his instructions actually excite me, I take the treehouse ladder two rungs at a time. It's not as daunting as it was last weekend. Devon's memory will always be here. There's no getting rid of that, but the fact that Gavin is ready to deal with it in such a significant way is a huge step—for both of us.

Gavin is still on the ground with his paper, studying it closely. "Is that the original blueprint?" I call down.

His eyes are shining when he nods. "Yeah. I want to replicate it as much as possible, but with some enhancements."

A grin takes over my face. "Enhancements? Like a solar-powered skylight?"

He chuckles. "Not quite, but that's not a bad idea. We could finally install that refrigerator Devon wanted so badly. I want to add some height to the second story and width throughout. Upstairs could be more of a loft with windows. I think it would be cool to sleep out here on cooler nights. You know, I used to crash here a lot after working late. I've never been more inspired than when I sketched here."

Gavin didn't have to tell me that. I remember catching him snoozing in the treehouse a lot. I'd often joke about him moving in and making it his permanent residence.

Conversation stops as we get busy working on the treehouse. Scratch that. Gavin is working on the house. I am back on the ground assembling my hammock.

"When you're done tinkering with that thing, come help me with the railing," he says.

Tinkering. I narrow my eyes at him, but he's already refocused on the treehouse. I'll show him.

Within an hour I've finished *tinkering,* and Gavin comes to check out my work. "Not bad, Chlo."

My smile starts from within, pleased that I may have impressed Gavin with my handy lady skills. Maybe he'll think twice next time before reducing my efforts to just tinkering.

Puffed up with adrenaline and confidence, I practically leap up the ladder to help Gavin with the railing. I test out the platform by hopping up and down a few times, then smile to let him know I approve. He's too busy chugging from a bottle of water to notice me, but I notice him. Sweat is dripping from his face, but he still wears a smile. He takes a long pull of water and uses the bottom of his shirt to dry his face.

I hope my gasp isn't audible, but it's uncontrollable as I get another up close and personal view of Gavin's defined body. He doesn't seem to notice my gawking as he offers me the rest of the water.

By early evening, I stretch out in the hammock and admire all that we—mostly Gavin—accomplished in just a few hours. We've repaired the main floor, rebuilt the railing, and started on the new frame, all in a day's work. We're both sweaty and exhausted by the time we decide to call it quits. He tosses a tarp over his supplies and places the more expensive tools into the wheelbarrow.

"You need a shower?" he asks me as we pull into his driveway.

"Probably. What's the plan?" I realize that will make three showers today, but after sweating several pounds off, I don't care.

"We'll figure it out."

So I shower again, surprised to find a fresh set of clothes laid out for me on the bathroom counter when I'm done. I try not to linger on the fact that Gavin walked into the bathroom while I was showering and dress quickly. He's walking up the steps as I'm leaving his room. A smile appears on his face, melting my insides.

We stand awkwardly at the top of the stairs. "Feel better?" he asks.

I nod, unable to tell him that I had felt better before he smiled at me. Now, all I want is to throw him against a wall and devour his mouth.

"Make yourself at home. I'll be out in a few."

It's not my imagination. Our eyes hold each other's for a few more seconds before we turn in our respective directions. When he closes the double doors of his bedroom, I'm finally able to let out my suffocated breath. It leaves my body ragged, and I feel the blood pumping through my veins. Gavin is crazy to think this will ever only be friendship. All these feelings . . . it can't just be me.

CHAPTER 23

ANGELS FALL

CHLOE

As Gavin checks his emails, I walk into the living room and flip on his stereo. It's already connected to an MP3 player that sits off to the side. I let it play, knowing that I'll love whatever Gavin's got queued up.

Yup. Angel's Fall is the first song on the rotation. I lie back on the floor and close my eyes. It's one of my favorite songs, one I listened to on repeat the moment it was released. It doesn't take a genius to figure out why this song is on Gavin's playlist. He's always loved Breaking Benjamin, but this song screams Devon. But more than that, this song reminds me of loss in general—lost friendships, missed opportunities, unfulfilled dreams . . . Today, the lyrics bring me closer to all my suppressed memories, and for the first time in years, I allow the memories to wash over me.

Magnetic energy fills the air and I know Gavin's there. Watching me. I look up and see him gripping the doorframe between the living room and the kitchen. His jaw hard and pointed at me, but his mind—it's somewhere else. Sadness, confusion, and even anger bleed through his features.

He doesn't need to tell me that he's contemplating asking me to turn off the stereo. I don't give him time to make the request. "Lay with me." My voice is gentle but pleading.

With a tentative step, he moves toward me, lying on his back so the sides of our arms are pressed together on the carpet. His freshly showered scent is intoxicating. I drink it in until I'm forced to release a breath. We're motionless, lost in our thoughts as the steady beat of the drums and the cleansing rock melody drown out everything else.

I've always thought lyrics had the power to heal, and maybe that's what our souls are trying to do now. There's a reason we're drawn to each other, even if it's only because we're meant to lean on each other to break free of the darkness. And maybe that's okay.

Flutters take off in my chest when his hand finds mine and gives it a squeeze. Without having to think about it, I weave my fingers through his. It's a subtle gesture, but one that I hope speaks volumes. Neither of us moves again, allowing the playlist to transition from one song to the next. An acoustic cover of How Will I Know filters through the speakers and my shoulders sag with relief. I'm not sure if I can handle another moody song.

I sneak a look at Gavin. The first thing I notice is the measured rise and fall of his chest. It squeezes my heart. I can only assume he's fighting to gain control over his emotions, just as I am. Sometimes confusion bleeds into pain and it's all too damn much.

My gaze drifts up to his face and I have to suck in a breath. He closes his eyes, but it's too late. I saw it. A sheen of moisture resting on his reddened eyes. My heart is already breaking. When I look at his distraught features I see it all. Pain. Heartache. Loss. Suffering. When Devon died, so did a part of Gavin. Who's to say how big or small that part is? Only Gavin knows. Only Gavin suffers the way he does.

How could I have been so selfish? Sure, Stacy told me to leave, but as Gavin often said about Devon, she was being Stacy. Ultimately, I'm the one who made the awful decision to leave.

I prop myself up on my elbow, leaning over Gavin and

brushing my thumb beneath his eye. Even though no tears have fallen, I want him to know it's okay if he lets go.

"I'm so sorry." My voice cracks, tears threatening to follow. I'm not sure if I'm apologizing for leaving or for Devon dying. Maybe I'm apologizing for both. I search his face, digging deep for a sign that he might find it in his heart to forgive me and end this angst between us.

My energy depletes when silence continues to swallow the air. I have to close my eyes to take a breath. When I do, I drop my head to his chest while my hands gently stroke his unshaven cheek. It's like sandpaper caressing my fingers. Rough. Calming. Addictive. Touching him like this—so freely—it lights up my senses. Exposes my vulnerability and opens me up for rejection. Again.

In this position I can feel his pounding heart between our bodies, my own keeping pace with his. A melody more beautiful than the one coming from the speakers. I don't want to hold back anymore. I slide my fingers through his hair, tilting my head. My mouth is so close to his neck I could taste his skin if I wanted to. *I want to.*

He wraps an arm around my center and releases what can only be described as a whispering hiccup. I know, without a doubt, that noise came straight from Gavin's heart. There are no actual tears falling, but that noise and the tortured look on his face are enough to completely unravel me. My throat is closing in around itself as I hold back tears of my own.

Before I can even think about it, I'm lifting my head and touching my nose to Gavin's. We're face-to-face. Eyes closed. Lips so close that air has to fight its way between us.

"Gav," I whisper. My heart's hammering something fierce within me.

We're just breathing raggedly into each other's mouths, neither of us taking that next step. Then he tightens his hold around my waist and I swear I hear a rumble come from his chest.

Soft lips graze mine. It could very well be an accident so I'm trying not to get my hopes up but I'm humming with electricity. Physically shaking with it. I'm not sure how to control it, so instead of trying, I go for a distraction and brush my mouth against his. This time there's no question of who started it. I won't let him question my need for him anymore.

He responds by splaying a hand just above the dip in my back as the hand at my waist slowly creeps up my spine. It's enough to feed my confidence. I take his bottom lip between both of mine and kiss him. I don't wait for a response before I'm using the suction from my lips to tug his mouth open, asking permission to cross the threshold. He pulls a strangled cry from me when he allows my tongue's entrance. It's safe and warm. Just the long-awaited shelter I was seeking.

He's kissing me back now and it's—*damn*. I moan into his mouth and run my fingers through his hair before gripping a handful, refusing to let go, terrified that at any moment he'll change his mind and—*poof*—just like that, make like dust in the wind and vanish. To my relief, he makes no move to pull away. Instead, he slips a hand up my shirt, his palm grazing my back as his thumb slides up my rib cage. With his free hand, he reaches up and places a fallen strand of hair behind my ear.

I'm all shivers in his arms as my knees slide to a more comfortable position between his legs. He groans, telling me I've done something right, and if our lips weren't sealed together, I'd smile. At this point he's carrying my weight because I'm too weak to support myself anymore.

I swear this man can read my mind. Gavin palms my head and rolls me to my back so his body is hovering above mine, our mouths never separating.

In this position, my hands are free to roam. Just as I can feel the smooth skin of Gavin's back, he tears his mouth from mine and plants it on the soft spot between my neck and my shoulder. He nibbles and sucks until I'm quivering beneath him.

"You smell so damn good," he moans.

When his mouth moves back to mine, his arousal presses into me, and then he's sliding his body against me until he's maneuvered his way between my thighs. He pushes into me through his shorts so I can feel just how much he wants me. Panting may be an unladylike response, but I'm not sure I have the sensibility to care much at the moment.

The shrill sound of Gavin's phone ringing brings us to a halt. I silently curse the little piece of technology as I feel him snapping back to reality. He peels himself away from me and reaches for his phone.

"Hey, what's up?" he answers, his heavy breathing the only evidence of what just happened between us. "I don't know; one sec," he responds and then turns to me, searching my expression for something. "It's Justin. Do you want to see the Jackholes tonight?"

For a second I have to think about who the Jackholes are again and why we would be going to see them. Then I remember they're Justin's favorite rock band from Portland. Gavin has me so flustered that I can't give him an honest answer to his question. I'd much rather stay here for the rest of the weekend. "Do you?" I ask, deciding not lay all my cards out right now.

To my disappointment, Gavin pushes off the floor to a standing position and helps me up too. "We should probably get out of this house. We can run by your place and pick up some clothes first. They're playing in Tacoma at nine, so we have some time to get there."

While a night out would probably be good for us, I'm hesitant to agree. I only do because it's clear he's already decided we're going.

He smiles at me and turns his attention back to his phone. "We're in." There's a pause. "Chloe's with me. We'll be there in a bit."

After hanging up, he makes his way into the kitchen. I hear the jingle of car keys, and then he's walking toward the front door. He waits for me to follow. Anxiety slowly creeps through my veins, but I hope I'm just paranoid. He doesn't make a move to touch me or even look at me during the short walk to his truck. I'm afraid all that just happened will dissolve into thin air and never be discussed again. I have the sudden urge to kick something, but there's nothing around except Gavin and his truck. My heavy steps down his driveway might not have the impact I'm going for, but I guess they'll have to do.

We're silent the entire thirty second drive to my house, and I jump out of the passenger seat without a word. I'm expecting a heat wave when I walk into the house, but no such luck. The realtor must have fixed the AC. Damn her. I was looking forward to using it as an excuse to spend more quality time with Gavin.

I search my old closet for something casual and sexy and smile when I lay eyes on the perfect outfit: a white romper with sheer, floaty sleeves that shows off more than enough leg. I check myself out in the mirror and try to ignore the fact that my bust is quite a bit larger than it was in high school. Maybe this is a sexier look than I was initially going for, but I know it'll drive Gavin crazy. I throw on gold heels and then strut back out to the truck with a smile that only brightens when I see Gavin glaring back at me.

I hop in, surprised to find his eyes glued to the front windshield. "Nice outfit," he says.

"Thanks," I respond casually, meanwhile patting myself on the back for causing his frustration. I'm not about to let Gavin forget our kiss that easily.

GAVIN

What the hell is she doing to me? I have to adjust myself about four times within the first five minutes after seeing her leave her house in that damned outfit that rivals Emma Frost's White Queen costume. Chloe wins. Only Chloe can make an outfit like *that* look like sin—a sin worth committing multiple times. It doesn't help that we just made out after listening to a playlist I created in memory of Devon. What's worse: I didn't stop her. God, I wanted her. I still want her.

Fuck. What am I doing?

If steering wheels could talk, this one would tell me he was choked out, dying, and on his way to the grave by now. I'm gripping the damn thing so tight, trying to relieve some of the tension building up inside me. Unfortunately, there's only one type of release that will fix me, and that's not happening right now.

The moment my phone rang, I knew it was a sign. We needed to stop, so I took the opportunity to get us out of the house. If Justin had never called, I wouldn't have had the strength to stop. I was seconds away from stripping Chloe naked and doing things I've only dreamt of for years. Of course, today I'm more experienced when it comes to pleasing women. Sex with Chloe would be mind-blowing. There's no question about it after how crazy I became just feeling her lips on mine. I shiver. Those lips are my addiction.

She leans over, playing with the radio knobs. I'm drawn to the natural glow of her smooth, toned legs, then to her long layers of brown hair. I have to sigh to relieve more of the need building inside of me—but my sigh comes out more like a groan, and Chloe swivels her head to look at me. I clear my throat and turn back to the road.

She settles on a pre-programmed rock station and leans back into her seat. I sneak another look at her as she gathers her hair and pulls it into one of those messy bun things that girls do so well. I now have an awesome view of her plunging neckline that reveals the curves of her plump breasts. I get a good eyeful as her back arches . . .

Fuck!

"How's the AC?" I ask in an attempt to distract myself from the half-dressed Chloe sitting beside me.

I see her shrug out of my periphery. "Still hot as hell. I'll figure it out tomorrow."

Liar. I won't call her out on it, but I fixed the AC when I stopped by her house earlier to grab her shoes. The wall unit just needed to be reset; nothing she needed to spend a small fortune on to fix. But her lie confirms what I was afraid I already knew.

Chapter 24

Friendship Spooning

Chloe

I know Gavin's not oblivious to my charms, but I'm disappointed by the lack of attention he's been paying me since we left his house. My stomach rumbles, reminding me that there are other important things in life—like food.

"Gav, I'm starving. We haven't eaten much today."

"They serve food there. Or would you rather stop somewhere first?"

"No, it's okay. I can eat there. Who else is coming out?"

"Phoebe, Blaine, and a few other friends of Justin's. Jazz and Marco are missing out. Speaking of which, have you heard from those two?"

I frown and shake my head. "Texts here and there. We've been playing phone tag. I've either been at work or away from my phone when she's called, and she always tells me she has to call me back when I finally reach her. I'm sure they're keeping busy."

"Same with Marco. I'm wondering if they'll come back," he says, speaking the same question that has been on my mind since my best friend left.

"They have to for the wedding, but I know what you mean. I hope so. I know this is a great opportunity for Marco and all, but

177

I miss Jazz. Who else will stock my fridge with the necessities and then eat it all?"

Gavin smiles. "That's right. No wonder you're starving."

I'm laughing as we pull into the venue's parking lot.

Our group is already at the bar, claiming two round tables at the back of the room. The only two spots left are at different tables, so Gavin lets me pick my seat first. He sits down at the other table and chats with Justin while I catch up with Phoebe. She introduces me to a couple of her friends from college, Izzy and Rachel. Both of them are gorgeous. Izzy's a fashion editor, and Rachel models locally. I notice Rachel's eyes moving from our table to Justin's, and I already know who has captured her attention. I look over to see Gavin, with his head tossed back, laughing with the guys and handing his credit card to the waitress.

For a second I think he's ordered a drink for someone at his table, but then he stands up and walks to me, a clear drink in his hands. "Vodka soda, miss?" he teases, looking happier than ever. Maybe getting out of the house wasn't such a bad thing.

"Thank you, sir." I give him a smile that dazzles before he turns to walk away.

"Wait, Gav, come meet my friends," Phoebe calls after him.

Gavin retreats to stand beside me, smiling as Phoebe introduces everyone. I am far too aware of the looks Rachel is giving him, hoping to snag his eye. He holds up a friendly conversation while I order a plate of nachos, excited to get some food in my stomach.

Eventually, someone gets smart and pulls our two round tables together. Just in time, because when the Jackholes take the stage the energy immediately shifts into pandemonium. The audience is clearly familiar with the group they're straining their vocal chords for. I've never heard of them, but I can understand the excitement. These guys are really good.

I'm totally focused on the band when I notice Blaine snag the spot beside me. Gavin is currently sandwiched between Rachel and Justin. Something needs to be done about this seating arrangement.

"So what have you been up to?" Blaine asks me, breaking me out of my mental strategy session.

"I started my job last week, and I'm helping my parents sell their house. I'm keeping busy."

Interest lights up his face. "That's right. What's the company name?"

"BelleCurve Creative, in Bellevue."

His forehead creases come to life. "Isn't that where Gavin works?"

I nod. "We're on the same project. So you know it?"

"Only from Gavin."

Just then, the band finishes their first song and there's awkward moment at the table as Blaine throws Gavin a look. I know this look all too well. He thinks he's staring at his competition.

"What about you?" I ask, trying to drag Blaine's attention back to me.

He has to think for a second, as if still caught up in his previous thought. "I do construction now. I'm working for my dad. Decent hours, great pay, and benefits. I'm loving it."

"That's great." I smile politely and take a sip of my drink, my insides churning with unease. My eyes dart to the other table, and I almost choke. Gavin's stare is on Blaine, zeroing in with intensity.

Our attention is diverted by the lead singer who starts talking to the audience, evoking complete insanity from the crowd. My food comes too, and I immediately dive in. A few songs later, Blaine gets up to order another drink, and Gavin doesn't miss the opportunity to steal his seat and devour half of my meal.

"I was hungry. Sorry, Clover. Want me to order you something else?"

I smile at his nickname for me and shake my head. "I'm good."

Blaine returns with a smile plastered on his face as he takes Gavin's old seat. "How's it going, Gav?"

"Great, dude. How are those new homes coming along? I was going to swing by soon and check them out."

Blaine leans back in his stool. "Oh yeah? What about the nice setup you have now?"

"Oh, it's not for me. A friend of mine is looking for more space."

The moment I think it's safe to tune out their conversation, I hear Blaine's next question. "How's Giselle? Haven't seen her around lately."

Giselle? The only woman I know of named Giselle is a model. Of course Gavin would date a model.

There's an awkward silence in the air before Gavin responds. "She's fine. Away on summer vacation. Hey, do you think you'll get football tickets this year? We should go again. My agency gives me Sounders tickets sometimes. We can do a trade."

Thank goodness Gavin changed the subject. I don't think I could handle a discussion about one of his many conquests as we try to get through this night, especially after what happened back at his place.

"Great idea," Blaine says. "Yeah, I'll get tickets. Just let me know what game you want to go to and I'll put in for 'em. We're going to dominate this year with our new receiver."

Bored of all the sports talk, I head to the bar and order us another round of drinks. As I'm waiting, I notice an older guy wearing a sports jacket, skin drooping beneath his eyes. He's sitting on the stool beside me, taking his time as he scrolls the length of my body. I shift toward the bar, giving him a less revealing view, but he's already interested.

"You need some company tonight, sweetie?" he slurs.

I give him a pinched smile and tilt my head. "No thanks. I got it covered."

He leans in, not accepting the hint. "You sure? I'll make it worth your while."

I gag as he shifts on his stool and places a hand on his lap, rubbing the bulge in his pants. Disgusted, I quickly turn away and slam right into Gavin's wide frame, surely looking as mortified as I feel.

"Everything okay over here?" Gavin's voice is an octave lower than usual as he gives the man a knowing glare. The stranger shifts uncomfortably in his seat and faces forward as if nothing had happened.

I bite back a smile, loving Gavin's possessive tone. It's sick and wrong for me to like that kind of attention, I know, but it's Gavin. We've never really been able to talk about our feelings, but if actions speak louder than words, then his actions just told me a great deal. If only I could know for sure that he won't change his mind this time.

We move to another section of the bar and Gavin maneuvers me in front of him. He flags down the bartender and orders a round for the table. A rush of energy flows through me when I feel his arms snake around my waist, pulling me back so I'm flush against him. Placing my arms on his, I allow myself to relax against his strength, to sway to the music, and to lose track of everything but him and the damn horses galloping in my chest again.

We're back at Gavin's by two in the morning, far more sober than expected after hanging out at a bar all night. He doesn't even ask me if I want to go home; he just pulls into his driveway and silently lets me in the front door. He hands me a new toothbrush and change of clothes for bed before nudging me toward his bathroom.

When I emerge, Gavin slips past me and shuts the door without a word. I'm still standing in the same spot. He stumbles, almost toppling into me. I look at him, a bit lost, and gesture towards the bed. "Are we both sleeping there?"

Gavin smiles and starts peeling back the comforter and flat sheet. "I'm sleeping in here. You're welcome to join me, unless it makes you uncomfortable. I can sleep somewhere else if it does."

One glance at Gavin and I know I'm not sleeping anywhere but next to him. He waits for me to join him and then pulls me into spooning position. "I don't think we're allowed to call this friendship spooning anymore." The words are out of my mouth so fast, I slam my mouth and eyes closed with embarrassment.

To my relief, Gavin's chest reverberates with laughter. He plants a kiss on my shoulder. "Go to sleep, Clover. We have a treehouse to build in the morning."

Too disappointed by the fact that slumber is the only activity happening in this bed tonight, it's a while before I actually fall asleep. As I'm drifting off, I'm vaguely aware of a draft as Gavin moves away from me and slips out of bed.

CHAPTER 25

DETOX

CHLOE

T reehouse activities are much harder to accomplish the next day because I'm absolutely drained from lack of sleep. After drifting off for a while, I awakened a short time later to find that I was right; Gavin had left the bed at some point in the night. I waited up for hours, hoping he'd come back, tossing around explanations for why he left in the first place. The only rationalization that seemed to stick, the one that haunted me until I finally fell back asleep, was that Gavin just isn't that into me. Maybe he was at one point in time, but now that he's older and more experienced, I'm just not *the one*.

What type of girl is Gavin attracted to, anyway? Is it a forward girl like Monica? Or is it a model with a perfect stick figure like Rachel? Maybe it's neither, or both. The only thing I'm coming to terms with is the fact that his type is not a five-foot-four, curvy brunette with a passion for the written word and a heart as big as Florida.

Our talking is limited as we focus on the task of rebuilding our childhood safe haven. It's actually quite remarkable watching it all come together. I just wish I could enjoy it. Gavin is more focused than I've ever seen him, and by the end of the day, the treehouse is a wireframe of what it once was, with some enhancements, of course.

"That's it for today," Gavin announces proudly as he admires our work from the base of the tree. "Next week we put the walls up."

I force a smile and begin repacking the cooler.

"You staying over tonight?"

His question throws me off guard. Maybe it's my wild imagination, but something about his tone tells me he doesn't want me at his house another night. I'm learning how to take hints. "The realtor sent a message earlier and told me the AC is fine now," I lie. "Not sure what happened, but I'm going to head home."

He doesn't argue. "You want to grab some dinner before you go?"

I shake my head, resisting temptation. "Not tonight. I'll see you tomorrow at the office, okay?"

With a final smile and wave, I leave Gavin at the treehouse, dragging my tail behind me.

Cleaning and cooking are the only things that seem to distract me from the swirl of confusion running circles in my mind. Two dozen cookies, one chicken pot pie, and a guava turnover later, I put my apron away and settle in with my dinner, a movie, and a glass of wine.

After two pathetically romantic movies, my eyelids begin to feel heavy. I force myself to leave the couch and head to bed for some rest. Heaven knows I'll need it because my Gavin Rhodes detox starts tomorrow when I see him at work.

"Damn, Chloe, the cookies are a hit. I don't think you realize what you just did. You're officially the holiday cookie maker now. And anytime we have a potluck, you're screwed if you don't bring anything." Monica is perched up on my desk giving me one of her famous earfuls as crumbled cookie pieces fall everywhere but in her mouth. The girl doesn't eat much, but when she does, you do not want to be around her.

"Geez, Mon, get any of that in your mouth?"

She rolls her eyes and moans in mock ecstasy as she pushes the last of the cookie past her lips. I laugh, unable to control myself. The girl is ridiculous, but she's growing on me quickly. It's not hard to see why Gavin likes her. She's down-to-earth and fun to be around. It's also endearing that she doesn't acknowledge what others think. It's not that she doesn't care; it's that she just doesn't pay attention to it. I like that.

The week has been hard to get through because Gavin's current mood is that of someone who is devoted to his work and only his work. It's not just me; he barely talks to anyone, so I can't take that personally. He's focused, which is more than I can say for myself. I've been scatterbrained and struggling to focus on anything I need to write, even in draft form. So when Monica takes me to lunch later in the day and blatantly asks what's up with me this week, I tell her. Everything.

There's something about Monica that tells me I can trust her. She's receptive to everything I say, although I detect a hint of disappointment as she realizes she isn't the only one having issues with Gavin. But she recovers quickly and even offers some words of advice.

"When that Zachary stud comes in tomorrow, you better flirt him under the table. One of two things will happen. Either he'll be so turned on he'll ask you out, and you can't say no because, well, that would just be rude. Or Gavin will be so furious he'll start a fencing match to win your heart."

I burst into hysterical laughter. "You think Gavin will *fence* for me?"

She nods dramatically, as if she actually believes what she's telling me. "Yes. All the true romantics do it."

"I'll keep that in mind," I say sarcastically. "But you're forgetting the other options: I lose Gavin because I'm flirting with

Zachary Ryan, or I lose them both because I make a fool of myself."

Monica shrugs. "It's worth the risk, I'd say. They're both hot."

"I don't love Gavin because of his hot factor."

"Did you just say love?"

I should have known Monica would latch onto that one. I want to reach into her brain and erase my words. "No. I didn't mean it like that. Gav and I have been friends so long; of course I love him as a friend. I didn't mean *in* love. That's totally different."

"Shit, I'm in love with Gavin Rhodes. I'm in love with Zachary too. You just take your pick and I'll have my way with the other." Monica laughs at her own joke, and I join in.

By the time we're walking back into the office, I feel better. Not because things are resolved between my heart and my mind—they're still waging a silent war—but because it's the first time I've been able to talk about all of this. Even if Jazz were here, I'm not sure if I could divulge the depth of my feelings. She's been so judgmental about Gavin and me that I'd rather figure this out on my own while trading jokes with a new friend.

The most I talk to Gavin all week is when we're trapped in the conference room, just him, Zachary, and me. As Zachary and I bounce around ideas for his speech, Gavin stays mostly silent, sketching ideas. "Obviously you'll tell your story about being bullied too," I start, but Zachary is quick to interrupt me.

"Actually, Chloe, I wasn't going to tell that story. I want my speech to be more about the kids who are dealing with those issues today. I want to speak about their bravery, not mine."

"Don't you think the best way to do that is to share your story? You're a hero, Zachary. You dealt with what millions of kids go through every single day, and you came out of it with a hero mindset. And look at you now! You're playing for a team that's on the way to winning back-to-back Super Bowl championships. If anything is going to drive some fire in these kids, it's listening to your story."

He stares across the table at me, and for a second I think I may have pissed him off. But what he says catches me completely off guard. "Have dinner with me."

I can't help it. I look at Gavin, who has stopped drawing and is clenching his pencil as tightly as I was the day he took me to get fro-yo. When I look back at Zachary, I'm at a complete loss. "Wh-what?"

He looks embarrassed for a second as he glances between Gavin and me. "I'm sorry. I should have asked you in private. It's just—you just shocked the hell out of me, and people don't do that easily. You have a way with words, Chloe Rivers." He chuckles. "Which is a good thing since you're a writer."

Blushing is something that's become second nature to me lately. I do it again and curse my emotions for being so damn obvious. I have to admit, even with Gavin sitting here with me, I'm inclined to accept Zachary's offer. It's refreshing in comparison to the push and pull Gavin's been giving me. It would be nice to go on an actual date with someone rather than chasing after a guy who has told me many times over that he isn't interested in more than friendship.

Gavin must sense that he's the cause of the awkward silence, so he slams his sketchbook down and slides his seat noisily behind him. "I'll give you two time to talk. Just buzz Monica when it's safe to come back." He doesn't meet my eyes as he speaks to me, although I'm silently pleading for him to.

"Well, what do you say, Chloe?" Zachary asks as soon as the door is closed. "I'm free tomorrow if you are."

Tomorrow is Friday. I have absolutely nothing going on. "Thank you, Zachary. I like you, but I've recently gotten out of something and I'm not ready—"

He shakes his head, telling me it's okay. "I thought I'd ask. A beautiful girl like you won't stay single long. You know where to find me if you change your mind." He gathers his things and smiles, seemingly unaffected.

"You don't have to leave . . ."

"I have to get going. Practice in an hour. I'll be back next week with my speech. Great ideas today." I stand with him and walk him to the door, still reeling from the events of the past hour. He faces me before leaving, hand perched on the doorknob. "Whoever holds that heart of yours is a lucky man. Just make sure you get it back soon. You deserve to be fully in control of what happens next. See ya, Chloe."

Zachary's words stay with me long after he walks out the door. He's right. I've carried this thing I have for Gavin for too long now. I can't control what happens next, but I can control whom I give my heart to. When someone has already made their choice, you just have to be smart enough to know they made it and have the strength to walk away.

DEAR CHLOE

"ALL THE WINDOWS OF MY HEART I OPEN TO THE DAY." ~ JOHN GREENLEAF WHITTIER

CHAPTER 26

CHLOE'S JOURNAL

DECEMBER 25, 2006

W hy do people start off their journal entries with Dear
Diary? Really, I should be saying Dear Chloe, since
I'm writing this for my eyes only. Dear Chloe. This is
12-year-old me, speaking to the ~~you~~ me of the future.

So here's the deal, Chloe of the future. Your friend Gavin
Rhodes gave you this journal for Christmas. It's a massive journal,
but no need to be intimidated. He knows you love to write. Because
he's Gavin and Gavin knows everything about you. He's also a nerd,
which is probably why you refer to him as a kindred spirit. We're
alike in a lot of ways, but not in obvious ways. He's super smart and
creative. I just like to read books and write. But when we talk about
the things that we love, we're both passionate about them. We can
talk each other's ears off for hours. Now that I think about it, that's
probably why he got me this giant journal for Christmas . . .
hmmm. Maybe he's hinting that I should stop telling him everything that goes through my brain.

Anyway, Gavin's rules (because Gavin always has rules) are for
me to write honest thoughts in my journal. He calls it a safe space
where no one can judge me and I can say anything. I can just write
about my feelings and thoughts. I can even cuss if I want to because
no one will read this! SHIT!

Gavin also says that I must only write about the significant events of my life. He says I'll know when they're significant and no one can tell me what's significant or not, so really, I could write every single day and no one will know or care. Man, Chloe of the future is probably annoyed at Chloe of the past right now.

All you need to know is that Gavin Rhodes is your best friend. I hope he'll always be your best friend because there will never be anyone like him. Well, except maybe his twin brother, Devon. They kind of look alike. Other than that, they have nothing in common.

CHAPTER 27

NEVER STOPPED

CHLOE

The front door slams behind me, shaking the walls of my house. An entire workday went by again and Gavin completely ignored me. Not even a hello or a goodbye. That makes an entire week of silence, but today was the worst. We sat in the same conference room for hours and he couldn't even look at me. I thought we moved past the part where he was hurt and angry. How are we suddenly back to where we started?

Twenty minutes later, just when I've finally managed to turn my boiling anger into a simmer, my phone rings. I grab it more frantically than I'd like to admit, but my heart plummets when I see Phoebe's name on the caller ID. "Hey."

"Geez, you okay? You sound like someone squished your hamster."

I make a face, not liking that comparison at all. "I'm fine. What's up, Bee?" I used to call Phoebe "Bee" all the time. Everyone thought it was cute, but since we lost touch over the years, I'd all but forgotten about the nickname—until just now.

"We've got a date, you and me. Can you be ready in thirty minutes?"

I frown, not sure if I'm in the mood to hang out but not

entirely discounting it. Sulking will not help me. "Where are we going?"

"Somewhere you haven't been in years. C'mon. Just get ready. I'll be there at seven. Don't make me come inside and drag you out by your hair."

Ouch. I hang up the phone and throw it on my bed. Phoebe's threats always sound so painful.

Without knowing where we're going, I make a decision to dress up, at least casually, for the occasion. When I spot a blue dress hanging in my old closet I know I've found a winner. It's nothing short of amazing that my clothes from high school still fit. I think that's why I turn to my old closet every time I hang out with old friends. It's my chance to relive the good times before everything got so complicated.

Phoebe honks her horn at seven o'clock on the dot. I run out, flashing her my best smile before hopping into the passenger seat. She whistles as she backs up. "Dang, girl. Where do you think I'm taking you? Speed dating?"

I groan in frustration. "Where *are* we going?"

"To the drive-in!" she exclaims as if it's the most exciting adventure she's been on in years.

I turn to her, convinced my friend should be committed. "Why the hell didn't you warn me? Turn around. I want to change."

"Oh no, no way. Blaine is going to love you in that." She winks and my stomach flips—or maybe it flops.

"What do you mean, Blaine is going to love me in this?"

Phoebe throws her head back and laughs. "Oh, c'mon, Chloe. You're always clueless when it comes to the opposite sex. Blaine is so into you. He's been begging me to get you two together again since last weekend. At first he assumed you and Gav were together, but I told him he was way off. Everyone knows Gavin Rhodes has only ever loved one girl, and that's Giselle."

There's that name again.

She suddenly grows quiet, as if she can hear the questions forming in my mind. I do my best to move past the *love* bombshell Phoebe just dropped in my lap. "Who else did you invite on this surprise date of yours?" I glare at her, but I don't think a glare is fierce enough for how angry I am right now.

"Everybody!" she exclaims. "Justin, Blaine, Gavin, and my friends Rachel and Izzy. We all thought it would be fun. And Rachel is all about Gavin these days. I figured I'd hook them up tonight too while I was at it with you and Blaine."

"Phoebe!" I think I'm going to be sick. She's the worst matchmaker ever.

We pull into the drive-in line, pay, and pull over onto the shoulder where Blaine and Gavin's trucks are waiting. Damn it. To make things worse, I see Rachel jump out of Blaine's truck and strut over to Gavin's. She lets herself into the passenger seat with a kittenish smile, and then I can't watch anymore. I face front and reach for my phone to help me plan my escape.

By the time our caravan moves into the lot and we're searching for a row to park, I've already got my finger on the call button. I'm taxiing my butt out of here. Not wanting to make the call in front of Phoebe, I wait until we're parked to jump out of the car and walk toward the concessions for some privacy.

Blaine blocks my exit as he beams an impressive smile. "Hey, Chloe."

"Hey, Blaine." I smile back.

"I think Phoebe and Justin are going to watch from her car. You're welcome to hang in my truck if you want."

"Um, I totally would, but I don't want to be rude to Phoebe. She asked me to come and all . . ."

His hopeful expression falls. "Right, yeah. Of course."

Just then, I hear Rachel and Izzy giggling as they climb into the back of Gavin's truck behind him. Out of my periphery, I watch to see what he does. When he does nothing, a surge of adrenaline rushes through me.

"On second thought"—I turn back to Blaine with a sugary sweet smile—"Phoebe and Justin probably want their privacy."

Blaine's beam has extra wattage this time. I put my phone away as he leads me to the bed of his truck. I hop onto the tailgate, letting my feet dangle below me. To be honest, I never thought I'd be in the back of anyone's truck besides Gavin's. He was the only one I ever watched drive-in movies with. That thought alone will surely spoil the rest of the night for me.

"Chloe, catch."

A tin can whizzes toward me, smacking my left eye before I have a chance to react. My skin stings, goes numb for a moment, and then starts to throb where I was struck.

"What the hell, Justin?" Gavin moves like lightning from his truck to Blaine's. Rachel and Izzy are in hysterics behind him. I don't think they are mean girls. I just think they're drunk and borderline clueless about how to get a guy's attention. They're both so beautiful that they've probably never had to make any effort to snag a guy before.

Blaine's beside me by the time Gavin arrives, pulling my face toward him to check out my eye. I yank my face away and put the chilled beer can to the sting. I avoid Gavin's stare, feeling a rising ball of emotion creeping up my throat.

"Sorry, Chloe!" Justin calls from the cooler.

"It's okay," I respond quickly. I want everyone to stop paying so much attention to me.

"Let me see it, Clover," Gavin whispers, triggering the ball in my throat, effectively releasing a tear I didn't know I was holding back. I cover the moisture with the can and swallow forcefully, pushing the rest of the fuckers back down into my stomach.

Gavin pulls the beer away just as I look up at him. His eyes are carrying the weight of everything good I feel when I'm with him, all bundled into one beautiful package. *He does care.* So then why the weeklong silent treatment?

"I'm fine, Gav." The can makes a satisfying hiss when I crack it open, and I smile before taking a sip. "See? All better."

He gives me a look telling me he knows I'm full of shit and retreats back to his vehicle without a word.

I stay at the tailgate of Blaine's truck for the entire movie, afraid if I back up I'll accidentally glance over at the giggling girls and Gavin, all snuggled up together. My stomach aches the entire movie, and I'm horrified when I realize we're attending a double feature. As soon as the credits begin rolling, I lurch out of the truck and hightail it for the concession stand. If I'm going to sit through another two hours of this, then I'm going to need some sustenance.

My timing is horrible. The line is practically out the door. On the bright side, I have more time away from Blaine, who has been trying to hold my hand all night.

I jump when something prickly rubs against my cheek. "What the—" I turn around to find Gavin laughing, until he sees that I'm not.

"Did you follow me here?"

"Yes."

"Why?"

He tilts his head. "Because I was afraid you were getting ill in the back of Blaine's truck. Your facial expressions during the entire movie reminded me of that time you almost puked all over my shoes. And you ran out of there so fast . . . I wanted to make sure you were okay."

"Since when do you care if I'm okay?" I turn around, hating how reactive I become around him.

He surprises me by sweeping the hair off my shoulder and leaning in, pulling me toward his chest in one swift move. "I have never stopped caring, Chloe. You drive me insane, and it's taking all of my willpower to stay away from you." Chills blaze a trail along all the skin his breath touched. "So here's what we're going to do: we're going to get food and walk back to our friends, and then you're going to climb your beautiful ass into my truck because I'm not sitting through another damn movie unless you're with me."

His words effectively melt the ice wall I've been building all week. "What about the girls?"

"They'll figure it out."

CHAPTER 28

CHLOE'S JOURNAL

JANUARY 15, 2007

*A*wful, stupid, worst day ever. I'm so tired of Stacy and her evil glares. At least she's not trying to shove me into lockers anymore, but in other ways, she's worse. Stacy is one of those girls that if you give an inch, she'll take a mile. Since the twins never completely cut ties with her, she's been finding ways to torture me that don't cross some invisible boundary she's made up in her head.

The leftover scar on my scalp has become a distraction from my worked-up nerves. I realized today that I touch it every time I'm nervous. Today, Stacy saw me and announced to the entire class that I was scratching dandruff and that I'm contagious. I don't know if she's dumb or stupid. First, I do not have dandruff. Second, dandruff isn't something you catch. Nevertheless, everyone laughed, including Devon. He seemed to have gotten the biggest laugh out of everyone. That one really hurt. Sometimes I think Devon's just as bad as Stacy. If it weren't for Gavin, Devon would be just like her. That's a scary thought, and it makes me wonder what makes a person choose to have people fear them rather than like them.

It's frustrating that Gavin sees Devon as someone who just needs a constant nudge in the right direction. What will happen when *we're out of school and the twins aren't living under the same roof anymore? Gavin won't always be there to protect his brother. Devon will have to start making decisions on his own. One day Gavin is going to realize he's an enabler because Devon will no longer have a safety net when he goes too far.*

CHAPTER 29

ALMOST HOME

CHLOE

W e stock up on popcorn, drinks, nachos, hot dogs, and candy. As we head back to the truck I'm tense wondering how this is going to work. I don't want Blaine to think I'm being rude by leaving his truck for Gavin's, except that's exactly what I'm doing. I should have never gotten into his truck to begin with.

Blaine is leaning on the side of his vehicle, searching the darkness for something when he sees Gavin and me approach. His eyes bounce between us, figuring out what I didn't want to come out and say. I try to shoot him an apologetic look, but he's too engrossed in the ping pong match his eyes are playing.

"You seem to have some effect on the male species lately," Gavin says softly. "Want me to talk to him?"

"No. What do you mean *lately*?"

I can't see him but I can sense his smile. "You were clueless in high school."

I pivot to face him now. "Why is everyone using that word to describe me? It's like you all joined the Chloe is Clueless Club in high school and forgot to invite the guest of honor."

Gavin chuckles and hops into the bed of the truck first. He reassembles the blankets and pillows before sitting back and patting the spot next to him. It's hard not to be around Gavin and get little hot flashes every now and then. I'm having an episode now as I climb onto the tailgate.

I'm happy to spot Rachel, Phoebe, and Izzy giggling around the cooler, sipping one of Justin's mysterious, boozy concoctions. Either they picked up the hints Gavin dropped or they're just too interested in socializing, but they seemed to have given up on claiming Gavin's attention. I smile as I take a seat next to him, leaving a few inches between us—for safety purposes.

"Nice dress," he comments.

I blush, wondering if he remembers the last time he saw me in it.

"Senior homecoming pep rally." He answers the question I didn't speak aloud. My heart hammers in my chest and I stare in awe as he explains. "You walked into the gymnasium and all eyes were on you. The things some of the guys were saying—let's just say I had to threaten a couple lives. Even the girls wanted to ask you out," he teases.

I smile. "I can't believe you remember what I wore that day."

"There's not much about you I don't remember, Chloe."

I nudge him with my shoulder, trying to hide my grin. "Did you know I would be here tonight?"

He nods. "Justin mentioned Phoebe was setting you up with Blaine. I thought I'd check out her matchmaking skills."

"Oh, yeah? What did you think?"

He frowns. "Boring. I was hoping he'd try to cop a feel so I could rescue you."

My shoulders shake with laughter. "He's not like that and you know it. You just have a hero complex. It's all those comics you sketch."

He smirks playfully. "What did you say?"

The glimmer in his eyes causes me to scoot away with laughter, afraid for what's coming next. I see a tickle war in my future, and my dress will not be forgiving. "I'm kidding, but you should really be nice to Blaine," I say. "He's not the one who pummeled my face with a can."

I expect Gavin to laugh, but instead he takes my face between two fingers, gently turning it sideways to examine the damage. It's a sweet gesture and I don't pull away like I did with Blaine. "Your face is perfect. Does it hurt?"

"Nah. It was more of a shock thing."

He places a light peck on my left eye before releasing me, the searing heat of his fingertips leaving flames in their wake. "Good. Now hand me the popcorn, woman."

GAVIN

During the final scene of the movie, I look down to find Chloe asleep in my arms. *My Clover.* With blankets draped over her and my arms wrapped around the blankets, she's secure and adorable. I don't want to wake her, but I've learned from experience that once the credits are done rolling, the vehicles must leave.

I shake her softly. After a few moans, her eyes finally flutter open, melting my heart. Then she pouts, forcing me to bite back a smile.

"What is it, Chlo?" Her pout threatens to bring out the vulnerable side of me, just like every other thing she's done lately. Chloe has always had a serious effect on my heart, but lately . . . lately, she's stolen pieces of it, bit by bit. Or maybe she's had them all along.

"I slept through the movie?"

"Yes, and I wasn't about to wake you. It brought me back to when I'd catch you sleeping in the treehouse." I chuckle at the memory. "You have the most restful sleeps. Except for those cute little moans." I lean in and delicately run my thumb over her nose so as not to disturb the slight pink she's recently earned from the sun.

Her eyes lock on mine, stealing my breath. "Kiss me."

Her words catch me off guard. After our kiss last week—the frenzy that overcame us—I've been doing everything in my power to hold back. I promised myself I wouldn't lead her on any more than I already have. As much as I want to react to what my body and heart want, it's just not right.

But her damn pout . . . and her words that reach deep down inside me . . . words that say to hell with what's right or wrong, just kiss the girl.

They win.

My nose grazes hers, and I smile before kissing her soft exposed cheek. There's slight hesitation on my part before I move to her lips, but I'm too far gone to stop myself now. My lips press into hers gently, caressing them with all the words I want to say but can't.

I'm not sure who deepens the lip-lock, but it's me that's unraveling the blanket, aching to get my hands under that little blue dress. To touch her silky skin. To feel her tempting warmth.

Mission accomplished. I pull her into my arms and toss the blanket over us with nothing but bad intentions. My hold on her tightens around her waist, knowing there's no way to hide my arousal in this position. If it wasn't clear before, she knows I want her now.

My thoughts become jumbled as my hands react with a mind of their own. They're all over her, sliding underneath the thin fabric, up her legs, past the hills of her backside, then up her waist until my fingertips touch the wires of her bra. My tongue wants to be in all of those places too.

Chloe lets out a moan directly into my mouth and I lose it. I want her. Here.

I don't think either of us cares that we're having one of the most erotic moments of our lives in public, in the wide-open bed of my truck. I sure as hell don't.

Once I've memorized every inch of her waist, I bring my hand back down, grazing the straps of her thong, considering its strength and whether or not I can shred it with my teeth. I skip that for now and squeeze one of her thighs, which is pressed firmly against the other. I tease her skin with feather light strokes, hoping she'll grant me access to her forbidden parts. As if she can read my mind, she loosens the tension at her thighs and trembles beneath my palms. I brush my fingertips toward her center.

As much as I want to keep going, I need to be sure. I remove my mouth from hers and lean into her ear. "Tell me to stop and I will," I whisper.

She releases a shaky breath as I wait in a form of torture named anticipation. When she grabs my hand and presses it deeper into her own thigh, I know this is happening.

"What are you going to do?" she breathes.

I kiss her temple and then speak into it, my heart pounding eagerly in my chest. "I'm going to slip my fingers into your panties and slide them down. You don't need them anymore."

There's a hitch in her breath as her hands press mine deeper into her thigh.

"I'm going to touch you and push my fingers deep inside you."

Her body begins to shudder in response to my words, begging me to make good on my plans. The anticipation is killing me, but I'm not done. "As I'm pumping you with my fingers I want to feel every inch of you until I make you moan. Do you want that, Clover?"

She nods and releases a strangled sigh. *Shit. I haven't even touched her yet.* A shaky hand releases the grip she has on my hand, giving me permission to make good on my words.

Without a second of hesitation, I'm lifting the side of her thong and sliding it down below her knees until she's free of it completely. I shove her panties into the blankets and groan into her mouth, wanting her to know what she's doing to me. My hand moves back to her thighs. I glide up toward the go-zone as she's spreading for me as her breaths release in quick pants. *She is so ready.* Just another inch up her leg and I'm home.

"Take it to the bedroom!" Phoebe shouts as a car revs up beside us.

I pull away from Chloe, gasping for air. My head falls to her chest as I try my best to regain my sanity. She's gripping my waist now as if afraid to let go. This is so wrong, but fuck if it doesn't feel right.

Once I've got my breath back, I lift myself from the blankets and glare at Phoebe, but she's not there. The screen is completely dark and there's already a line of cars heading toward the exit. Our friends are gone.

When I look down at Chloe, her eyes are closed and she's taking long, deep breaths. "We should get going," I say, knowing we're seconds away from getting kicked out.

Without a word she opens her eyes but I look away, already knowing I'll see disappointment flooding them. It's the same disappointment I feel. And as I slip my hands from her and pull down her dress, I'm also relieved we didn't have a chance to take things further.

I help her up and realize she's looking at me, waiting for me to respond with anything to validate her feelings. But I can't return her gaze. I know Phoebe's interruption was for the best. Once again, I almost fucked everything up.

Even when she's mad at me, even when I'm mad at her, every day I am around Chloe makes the battle between my mind and my heart that much harder. I want her in every way possible. Physically. Emotionally. But as much as her hold dominates every rational part of me, there's something bigger festering within me. The reason I can't go any further with her than a heated kiss is one that's haunted me for years. And beyond that, the life I live now is one she's yet to know about, one I'm not sure I can keep hidden for long. One I'm afraid she will never understand.

CHLOE

He doesn't see the moisture blurring my vision. He doesn't see the pain behind my eyes. Because he doesn't even look at me. Not as we join the line of cars to leave the drive-in, and not as we drive home in silence.

It's not until I climb out of his truck that he finally turns his eyes toward me. I can feel him watching as I quickly close the gap between his truck and my house. Although I rush to close and lock the door behind me, letting the weight of my embarrassment come crashing down . . . I notice the bright glow of his headlights lingering in my driveway. If my pounding heart could speak it would convince me that Gavin would return my feelings if he could. That's what I believe. What I also know is that there's a force, bigger than us, that plays defense to our desires, and it's a battle only Gavin can fight. If he chooses to.

CHAPTER 30

CHLOE'S JOURNAL

OCTOBER 17, 2011

S enior year is shaping up to be the best year yet. Walking into English class on the first day of school to the dropped jaws of the Rhodes brothers gave my confidence a boost in the right direction. I guess I was going for the shock factor when I held off seeing them until school started, but I didn't expect to feel the things I did for Gavin. Sure, I've had a crush on him since I was 12, although I didn't realize it. At 12 I had a crush on everyone. Besides, it's hard to not have feelings for the guy who single-hand-edly altered the course of my social life for the next six years. I'm convinced that if Gavin hadn't stuck up for me the way he did with Stacy, I would have figured out a way to end it, but I may have never been as close with the twins as I am now. So thank you, Stacy Berringer, for smashing my face into my locker with your backpack.

This is the year. I can feel it. Something big is going to happen, and I can tell you what I hope that thing is. I'll never forget the way Gavin looked at me on the first day of school because he hasn't stopped looking at me that way since. It's not just me. He knows there's more than friendship there, but he's just as afraid as I am. He's got to be. It's the only explanation for why he's holding back.

Next month is Comic Mania, and Gavin invited me to go with him. Devon is pissed he wasn't invited, but he'll get over it. All he *would be interested in is checking out the costumes anyway—and not because he's into fashion. I can't wait to see Gavin's face light up when he meets his favorite artists and discovers new work. It'll be great for him to talk to others about his own work too, about how he sketches the way he wants to see the world. That's what Gavin does. He sees the positive in people and places that no one else recognizes, and he brings them to life through his vivid drawings. I try to do the same with my writing.*

I wonder how Gavin would draw our relationship. I know how I would write it.

CHAPTER 31

THAT NIGHT

CHLOE

My eyes feel as if rocks are weighing them down. Even when I'm able to peel them open, I just want to shut them again. The evil light of morning is mocking me. What a shitty night. Not all of it. Just the tail end. What a shitty end to a great night. We connect on so many levels and then in the end . . . it's just never enough.

I put myself out there for him. Again and again. At first, we seem to be on the same page. And then he pulls away and acts as if nothing happened, as if I made up all this chemistry in my head. I've always hated science.

The back and forth is wearing me out. Why is he holding back? Why is he keeping us in this awful limbo? Why do I even care anymore?

After hours of contemplating the same questions, I decide I need a release, so I put on my tennis shoes and run until my legs lose their strength. By the time I stumble up my driveway I'm in a better headspace, but it's crushed completely when I spot Gavin sitting hunched over on my front steps.

"Where have you been?" he asks, concern written all over his face. "I've been waiting for you at the treehouse all day. Is your phone off?"

I can't look at him. He's already cracked my foundation. It's just a matter of time before the whole damn thing crumbles into a million vulnerable pieces. That's the remarkable effect Gavin Rhodes has on me. He seems to be the puppeteer of my emotions. But this is it for me. I'm not letting him take hold of my strings again. Whatever is causing his wavering confidence in us is something he needs to deal with. Not me.

My steps are swift and my strides are long as I walk by him without a word. I aim for the front door, which I plan to close and lock behind me, distancing myself from Gavin's fickle heart. It's not a long-term fix, but it will have to do in this moment.

"Chloe, stop."

I'm almost to the door when I hear footsteps behind me and feel an arm wrap around my waist. His face is in my hair, and his energy is bleeding desperation. "Stop."

For a split second, I want to cave. Sink into Gavin's embrace and melt. But the fantasy dissolves quickly because I already know how it will end. Swiveling around, I push him from me. "Why?" I demand. "So you can pull away from me again? What kind of game is this to you?"

"It's not a game. Not at all."

"Then what are we doing?" I demand. "One second you want me, and the next you're pulling away like you're trying to get back at me for something. You don't want to date me but no one else is good enough for me. Do you like me or do you hate me, Gavin? Because it kind of seems like the latter. I'll accept whatever you want, but I won't play this game anymore."

His face twists as if he's in pain, then he steadies himself by pressing his hands on the door, caging me in. "I was trying to be your friend."

A laugh escapes me. "We're not in high school anymore, Gavin. Stop trying to be my friend." I shake my head, wanting to scream. Maybe I *will* scream. My hands move to his heart as I peer up at him. "Why can't you just admit that there's something between us?"

Gavin squeezes his eyes shut, and it looks as if he's trying to stop a dam from bursting. "We got carried away."

"No!" I scream, then push against him. Like a stubborn mule, he doesn't move. "Don't do that. It's not us getting carried away if it keeps happening. Why are you fighting this?"

A look of fury crosses his face, sending my adrenaline racing. He pounds the door with his fist and opens his eyes again. They're wild and filled with intensity. "Things are complicated between us. You know that. And you're right; we're not in high school anymore. Being friends used to be so easy, and now, I can't be around you without . . ." He shakes his head. "We just can't go there."

"Why?" My voice cracks and I curse it silently. I can't break down now. Gavin needs to see that I'm strong.

He groans. "Life happened. It's fucked up, but it happened. My brother is dead, yet I'm still mad at him for stealing the one person that held the key to my dreams. And now it's too late."

My heart ricochets in my chest, and it takes all my energy not to spring into his arms at his words. "It's not too late, Gav. We can make this work."

"Don't you get it, Chloe? It hurts to be around you."

I blink. That's not an answer anyone can ever be ready for. Let the shattering of my heart commence. Unfortunately, these are words I also understand. They aren't the ones I want to hear, but they are honest.

"Okay," I respond, but this time I turn away, unable to meet his gaze. I'm about to give up and push my way through the front door when I hear something chilling come out of his mouth. It's a whisper, but I hear it.

"You're Devon's."

It's not the first time he's said this, but it's the first time I'm beginning to understand the meaning behind it. I stare up into Gavin's green eyes and shake my head. "But I'm not. I haven't belonged to Devon for a long time. You were there that night. You comforted me. Our relationship was over, and the breakup was long overdue." I squeeze my eyes together, silently cursing myself. "I'm not disrespecting Devon. I'll always remember him as a childhood friend, as someone who taught me how to take risks and enjoy life, but anything we ever had beyond friendship was a mistake."

Gavin shakes his head. "That's the thing. In my mind, you *are* his. You'll always be his. And whether or not it was a mistake, that doesn't change the fact that it happened. How disrespectful would that be for me to make a move on my late brother's girlfriend?"

"We're well past the point of no return when it comes to making a move, don't you think?" My thoughts inappropriately drift to memories of last night and the feel of his hands exploring my skin. Of him dragging his mouth across my neck until my entire body tensed with pleasure.

The pain in his expression snaps me back to the present just as his hands rush to my hips. I gasp. His head bows down so his forehead is touching mine. "Damn it, Chloe. I'm not talking about kissing. I'm talking about Devon and you . . . being intimate. As much as I want you, there's no moving past that for me."

As his words sink in, Gavin pushes himself off the door and begins his retreat into the woods.

"Gavin, no. Devon and I . . ." The words die on my lips as I realize it's pointless. He's not going to believe anything I say because he's already convinced of another reality. I watch him disappear into the wooded area between our homes before taking a seat on the porch and contemplating what to do next.

All of this build-up hasn't been my wild imagination. We both feel it, but Gavin can't act on it out of loyalty to his brother.

If I had known years ago what I know now, I would have never let Gavin assume there was any intimacy in my relationship with Devon. And I would have explained *why* I could never go there with Devon—because my heart belonged to someone else. I would have done everything differently.

That night after graduation, when Gavin confronted me in

my room, I didn't think my silence would haunt my future in this way. All I knew at that time was that I was trying to protect Devon from getting pounded by his brother while finding strength within myself to move on from a horrible relationship. I had already moved past hoping Gavin wanted me in that way. After the night in the hotel, I was convinced he wanted nothing more than friendship. So what would it have mattered if he thought I slept with his brother?

What Devon found in my journal was more truthful than I've ever been with either of them, but that truth was for no one's eyes but my own. It was my one secret that should have never been exposed, and that secret died with Devon that night. Or so I thought. Four years later, I'm realizing that revealing my secret might be the one thing that could bring Gavin peace.

If Gavin were to read those same words from long ago, he wouldn't question things. He would know that no one could *take* someone unless they want to be taken. That night of graduation, when Gavin mentioned I *chose* Devon, I wanted to scream. There was no choice. Gavin made sure of that. And now the repercussions of our actions have given us no choice but to face them. It's time to end this, once and for all.

I jump up, unlock my front door, and walk straight for my old bedroom. It doesn't take me long to locate the brown leather journal. It's right where it's been for the past four years after Devon got his hands on it and read my most personal thoughts. I put it right back in my underwear drawer and never touched it again. Figured there was no sense in hiding it anymore.

In the amount of time Devon had my journal, he didn't have time to read everything, but the pages that he did read were the only ones that could crush him the way that they did.

When I hand my journal to Gavin, he can read it all if he wants. There's no reason to hide anything. Not when there's so much at risk.

I can't believe I'm about to do this.

Gavin is standing on the top platform of the treehouse when I see him, his head cast down, arms folded. He must hear my footsteps approaching because his attention shifts to me and then to the brown leather book in my hands.

"What is that?"

Clutching the journal to my chest, I climb the ladder until we're face-to-face. I hope he can't see me shaking. I pause to take a deep breath. "That night—"

"Chloe, this isn't going to—"

"Let me talk, Gavin. Please. You said your piece. I understand where you're coming from, but now I need you to do something for me."

"What?" Gavin is focused on the journal. He recognizes it and understands it's significant. I can see that in his eyes, but he's trying to put the pieces together before I can tell him.

"I need you to listen to everything I have to say."

He lifts his head until our eyes lock, and then he nods in agreement.

"The night Devon died, he was in my room before you got there."

"I know, and you two had a fight."

"Yes. We had a fight at the party. I hadn't even taken my graduation gown off before he started in on me. People had been talking, I guess. Slinging jokes at Devon about our relationship and how I must not be that into him if I wasn't on his arm. He confronted me the moment I got there. Told me how badly I embarrassed him. Called me names." I sigh, hating the memories. "So I broke up with him. Or, I *tried* to break up with him. I told him it was over. That it had been over for a long time. He wanted to take me somewhere private. *To talk.*" I shudder. "I walked away from him and found a deep corner at the party where I hid out for a while, hoping he'd calm down. Eventually I came out of hiding and found him in my room reading this." I hold up the journal with shaky hands, and then pull it back down, not ready to let it go.

"The things he read . . . they weren't for his eyes. He called me out on some things. Things that hurt him . . . and other things he misinterpreted. And there was a passage about him that I don't think he liked very much. He disagreed with my recollection of a certain event. That's why we were fighting in my room before you showed up."

I hold out the journal to Gavin, but he doesn't reach for it. Instead, he looks directly at me. "This will tell you everything you need to know about the relationship Devon and I had . . . and why he was so furious at you that night."

Gavin shakes his head. "That's your journal."

I nod, taking a step forward to press it to his chest but he takes a step back. "I don't want to read your journal, Chloe. Just tell me what you want me to know."

"I can't. Just take it, please."

He tries to press the book back into my hands, but the warning in my expression stops him. "Why?"

"Because I can't say these things out loud. You need to know, and this is the only way I know how to tell you. Trust me. Please."

When he still doesn't grip the journal, I set it on the rail and slip quietly back down the ladder and off into the woods.

Chapter 32

Chloe's Journal

November 17, 2011

Regina Wild?! I'm a freaking mess. My heart is sick and I just want to hibernate until this week is over. Does he really like her? She's hot. A cheerleader. Typical. If I didn't know better, I would assume bad intel and that it was Devon who asked Regina to the fall festival.

Just one month ago, before Comic Mania, Gavin was spooning me while we watched a movie together. Nothing outside of normal, but this time I swear he sniffed my hair. How can someone go around sniffing one girl's hair and then asking another out? I should have never gone to that convention with him. That night ruined everything.

Gavin has been avoiding me. Disappearing during lunch hour. Doesn't even show up at the treehouse. To top it off, I've started tutoring Devon, which is no fun at all. The guy has the attention span of a toddler.

At least the tutoring distractions have been helpful, but I just want things to go back to how they used to be. Then again, maybe things have been changing for far longer than I've wanted to accept.

Chapter 33

Surviving

Gavin

W hat the hell am I going to do with Chloe's journal? She left hours ago, and I immediately threw it at the base of the tree, burdened by its weight. And then I picked it up again. But I can't read it. I don't *want* to read it. The odds of finding something I don't like are too great.

As my feet dangle from the unfinished treehouse, I'm enveloped by darkness, which only seems to illuminate my thoughts. I replay graduation night for the first time in a long while. Two years to be exact. The fact that the memories are still so vivid terrifies me, and I'm not sure I'm ready to go back there.

My phone buzzes in my pocket. I reach for it and stare at the caller ID. Marco.

"Funny timing, dude," I say into the phone.

"Hey!" Marco exclaims, his Italian accent seeping through the speaker. It's so good to hear his voice. "Did I catch you in the middle of sexy time?"

I chuckle and shake my head. "No, dude. Not quite. What have you been up to?"

He divulges all the details of life on Wall Street, the tiny apartment he shares with Jazz, and all the sightseeing they've been doing. He tells me Jazz wants Chloe to visit and I should come too. I ignore that suggestion and listen to his stories of the celebrities they've bumped into and the movie sets they've stumbled upon.

Once Marco's satisfied that I know every detail about his life since he left town, he asks me what I'm up to.

"I don't think you'd believe me if I told you," I say.

"Try me."

"Okay, but this one stays between us."

"Of course," Marco agrees.

So I tell him about my time with Chloe. The anger, the fighting, our kiss. I leave out the steamy make-out session and the details of our drive-in movie experience. Knowing how loud Phoebe can be, I suspect he already knows.

When I finish talking he pauses for a moment, then says, "She just gave you her journal? What are you going to do? Are you going to read it?"

I slide my thumb across the pages, fanning them like a moving picture book. "She asked me to, but I don't know if I can. She said I could trust her, but—"

"Then you need to trust her. If she handed it to you, you're not betraying her privacy. When a girl gives you her heart and tells you to trust it, you don't question it. You don't waste a second. You just do it.

"Think about it like this," he continues. "The things you didn't understand about the night of graduation gnawed at you for two years. You never understood why Devon was so angry with you."

"Yeah."

"Maybe this journal holds those answers."

"But I dealt with all of that, dude. I moved on. There are things we'll never know sometimes, and that's okay."

"Have you dealt with it? Or have you just been surviving all this time? Ask yourself that, because I guarantee those questions have always been there. You don't bury questions like that without them resurfacing later in life. Thank your lucky stars that you have this opportunity."

We hang up a short while later, leaving me with more weight on my shoulders than before. I do have questions from that night. Questions Chloe refused to answer. One in particular. Why was he so convinced that Chloe was cheating on him with me when we'd never so much as kissed?

I look down at the journal again and try to imagine the events playing out how Chloe described them. Devon read Chloe's journal and got so angry it sent him into a spiral of rage. While that might be partially true, I know better.

Devon was a good brother until he wasn't anymore. Until he resented being a good brother and realized that I wasn't suffering the way he was. The anger Devon felt toward me that night was the result of years of pent-up pain, which seemed to be escalating. He was going to blow eventually, and he blew that night.

It's well past midnight by the time I decide to open the journal. I've finally convinced myself that it's the only way. It's what Chloe wants, and I'm curious to find out what's hidden between the tattered pages.

I could just skip to the end. But if I do that I'm completely disregarding why Chloe gave me her personal thoughts, so I use my cell phone flashlight and start on page one.

CHAPTER 34

MY FAVORITE DAY

CHLOE

Three days of silence. *Three.* Sunday was complete torture after I handed over the journal and left him at the tree-house. Monday, Gavin called in sick to work. Tuesday he said he was working from home so as not to spread his virus. A virus? Is that what my journal is to him? Or maybe he really is sick. I'd feel horrible if that were the case. If things weren't so strained between us, I'd bring him his favorites: chicken noodle soup and fruit punch-flavored Gatorade.

At one o'clock on Tuesday, Sharlene dials him into the conference line. "How you feeling, Gav? We need you healthy and working tomorrow, so hopefully you're taking care of yourself."

"Oh, I'm feeling much better. Thanks, Sharlene. Just a little tired and dehydrated. I'll be there tomorrow."

No one questions why Gavin and I don't address each other during the call. We speak directly to Sharlene because it feels safer. I'm clearly the only one who thinks it's a special event every time Gavin and I speak. Proof of that is in my journal.

There was no getting out of the location visit Sharlene set up for us today. I tried. She said it was important to get to know the space before our presentation to the executives on Friday. She's probably right, but I'm dreading it. By now, I can only assume Gavin has read a good chunk of my journal—six years of my life crammed into one big book. As promised, I only wrote when there was a significant event. But let's face it: I was a teenager, so there were a lot of significant events.

"Gavin's meeting us there. Let's head out." Sharlene is fast approaching the exit as I enter the office. "I have appointments so I can only stay until noon. I'll show you the space and we can work through some things before I have to take off."

My head is already spinning as I follow her to the elevator leading to the parking garage. "I can take my car."

"Don't be silly. Ride with me. We have some things to go over on the way. Gavin will give you a ride back to the office."

Managing my poker face well, I reach for my keys. "That's okay, he might still be sick. Better I not ride in the car with him. I'll just—"

"He's fine. He said he's kicked whatever he had, but he's been deep in the art cave and just wants to meet us there. No biggie."

"Does he know he's bringing me back here?"

Sharlene stops and turns to me just before we reach her car. She gives me a sideways glance and starts to turn away, then thinks better of it. "Is there something going on between you and Gavin? Something I should know about? I can't have my artist and my writer butting heads. Tell me now so we can nip this in the bud, whatever it is."

I shake my head, frantically. "No, of course not. Everything is fine. I just didn't want to assume Gavin was bringing me back. He may have other plans."

Sharlene waves a hand in the air and turns back to her car. "Don't be silly. It's Gavin. Let's go."

I'm sure my interpretation of "it's Gavin" is much different than Sharlene's, but I shut my mouth. Without another argument

I climb into her SUV and pray that Gavin doesn't think I had anything to do with this arrangement. When he's ready to talk to me, he'll make it happen.

My hands make horrible stress relievers. They ache from pulling and twisting so hard by the time we approach the venue, Melrose Market Studios, an industrial space tucked away on the west edge of Capitol Hill. It's a beautiful, truly historic 1920s building just blocks from downtown Seattle. I think I'm in love. Everything about it, from its exposed red brick walls and polished concrete floor to its Douglas fir beams and towering ceilings, screams history and class. It's a small building, but the natural lighting makes up for the lack of space.

"How many guests will be in attendance?" I know my voice comes out in a breathy rush, but I'm soaring in this moment as my mind works its magic. Writing a story for the event to this gorgeous backdrop is going to be one of the highlights of my early career. I can already tell.

"No more than two hundred." Sharlene goes on to explain that we're going with banquet seating and that a small stage will take up the back of the room. Before now, I had imagined a grand ballroom with endless space with room for thousands of guests. I was way off. Gavin and I will need to rethink a few things and tailor our ideas for a more intimate audience.

The sun streams through the rustic windows above us. I'm admiring the height of the room, feeling giddy with inspiration, when a familiar voice speaks. I'm instantly pulled back to the here and now. "This is incredible."

I don't look at him right away. I *can't* look at him. I'm still recovering from my brain's whiplash at hearing his voice. And now I'm panicking. *Has he read it?*

My intentions were good. For me, handing him my journal meant closure. He would finally understand why Devon and I didn't get along. It might even show him a side to his brother that he never wanted to see before. Sometimes people would rather accept a lie than know the truth. Life is a whole lot easier to swallow that way.

Leave it to me to make the wrong move, to spill my guts in a passive way and ruin whatever is going on between Gavin and me. Something I know in my heart has always been there. Now here we are. I still can't look at him. Instead, I pretend to examine the intricacies of the brick closest to me, touching a flawed section and running my finger along its length.

I'm so focused on zoning into the block that I lose track of the rest of my senses. I don't hear Sharlene step out of the room while Gavin closes in on me until his breath hits my neck. My entire body tenses.

"Hey, Clover." His voice is raspy, filled with something I should not be thinking about right now.

I circle to face him, not prepared to be inches from his chest. At least it's something to look at other than his eyes. Still, I need to make eye contact. I do, but it's a flicker of a connection because the moment our eyes meet, my body threatens to fail. Luckily there's a solid brick wall behind me that's proved its worth for close to a century. I fall back against it and take a stuttered breath.

Gavin's expression is the opposite of what I was expecting. There's a gleam in his gaze and a playful smile on his lips. He seems to be anything but pissed off. Has he just been torturing me with his silence on purpose? Is he enjoying it?

My insecurities of the past three days are all-consuming. Gavin may very well know years' worth of very intimate details of my thoughts about him. And I have no clue how he feels about me.

"Feeling better?" It's all I can think to ask to divert my embarrassment and get him to wipe the smirk off his face.

"Much."

"Good." I nod and try for a smile, but it feels more like a cringe.

The way he's eyeing me now makes me think he has something to say, but he's holding back. I want to scream for him to just come out with it. I've waited long enough. Then again, it's Gavin who's waited over four years to understand the depth of my feelings for him and the truth about my relationship with Devon.

"Let's check out the specs, shall we?" Sharlene walks back into the room with a stack of paper. Gavin quickly backs away from me and turns his attention to Sharlene.

I take this moment to regain my composure before peeling myself away from the wall and joining them on the floor. Have I ever seen Gavin's confidence fail? Never. Not even when he's upset. He seems to gain strength from life's turbulence. Why does everything about him have to be so perfect?

In front of us is a lineup of Gavin's sketches, my story outlines, and drawings of the buildings' rooms and their layouts. Gavin picks up the last sheet of paper and waves it in the air as if he's just discovered buried treasure. "What are these? Room drawings? Would have been nice to have these sooner, Shar."

I don't know why he calls her that, but she giggles. *Holy shit.* Sharlene just giggled. The woman is always so serious. I can't help but shoot Gavin a look of amusement. He winks, causing my already flushed skin to deepen a shade or two.

I take a moment to review the space around us again, glancing from wall to wall and envisioning what could be. I speak my vision and Gavin immediately builds off it through his sketches. We get lost in our world of brainstorming as if there's nothing else going on between us.

"We should cover up a section of brick and let guests spray paint their feelings. 'What do you think of when you think of bullying?'" I suggest.

Sharlene's eyes grow wide. "I'll get estimates. Great idea, Chloe."

"You know, that spray paint wall just got me thinking," Gavin says. "In the videos, we could have the comics come to life from the brick."

"Like that Paula Abdul video?" I'm laughing, but I still love the idea.

Gavin's eyes go wide. "You love Paula Abdul. Don't you dare act like you didn't dance to Cold Hearted in the tenth grade talent show with Jazz and Phoebe."

"I love it! You two make the perfect team," Sharlene says as she scribbles in her notes. I look up at Gavin.

We do make a damn good team.

I'm the first to break the silence as I spout off more ideas for the scenery. By the time Sharlene has to leave, Gavin is going to town on his sketches so he has everything he needs for our presentation on Friday. I find a corner in the room to write in my notebook.

Two hours pass before either of us moves. I'm sensitive to all things Gavin, so when his jeans scrape the floor my pen freezes. *Damn, I was on a roll.* Out of my periphery, I catch him in mid-stretch and have to force my focus to remain mostly on my notepad in front of me.

"I'm going to grab a bite to eat."

I look up because he doesn't ask if I want to come with him, so I just nod.

"You hungry?"

Yes. But what would we talk about for the next hour? I'm not ready for his rejection. "No, that's okay. I bought some snack bars."

He hesitates but doesn't press me further. "Okay, I'll be back."

I've just gotten back into my writing groove when he returns twenty minutes later with a pile of deli food. He tosses the bag on the floor and sits beside me, leaving me little room to breathe.

Gavin hands me a paper-wrapped rectangle. I already know what it is. With a small smile, I peel the tape from the top and peek beyond the layers of wrapping. "Chicken salad sandwich, toasted," we say at the same time.

We laugh. It's not an awkward sound. No. Awkward is everything else about this moment. But this shared laugh is familiar and comforting. It's a subtle reminder, not that I need one, that Gavin knows me better than anyone.

He knows me even better now that I've handed over my journal, that's for sure. I want to ask what he's read so far. What he thinks. It's possible he's read the entire thing, but I'm certain he wouldn't be reacting this way if he had reached the end.

"Thank you," I say between mouthfuls.

"You didn't write about the first time we went skiing at Crystal Mountain."

So, he's read through some of sophomore year. The memory Gavin is alluding to is one of my favorites, one I didn't have to write down to remember every single moment.

Gavin and Devon had turned sixteen that October. Their dad had an old blue Wrangler Jeep and an old truck he'd been saving for them. As soon as school let out for the winter holiday, we were in that Jeep on our way to the mountain. None of us had skied before so we spent hours stumbling around, falling all over each other. Not surprisingly, Devon was the first one who picked it up. He found some snow bunny to teach him. Watching them from afar, I was certain Devon was charming her with fake vulnerability. He was a born athlete. There's nothing he couldn't pick up, and he would never admit it if he couldn't. He and the girl disappeared for a while, leaving Gavin and me alone.

We finally decided to brave it and take the lift up the mountain. Gavin was at least able to hop off the lift first to help me down, but when I jumped, I lost my footing and toppled onto him. We were laughing so hard we could hardly hear the ski lift operator yelling for us to move.

After rolling to the side in a heap of laughter, we regained our composure and stood up. At least we'd chosen the easiest trail, so the falls weren't so bad as we half-skied, half-tumbled our way down. At the bottom of the hill we traded in our skis for sleds and joined the kids on the shorter slopes.

It was late afternoon and we were chilled to the bone. Snow had made its way between the opening of our sleeves and our wrists, and even through the thickness of our ski suits, the cold had managed to seep under our skin. We decided to head inside to the main lodge and warm up with hot chocolate and food. Without even looking at what he was buying, Gavin grabbed two random sandwiches so that we could stuff our faces as soon as possible. They turned out to be two chicken salad sandwiches, toasted. He thought it was disgusting; one bite and he nearly threw up. I devoured mine and then ate his, too.

We warmed our bodies by the fire after that, talking about art, school, and what we wanted to do for the rest of our lives. It was our fourth year of friendship, and it was probably my favorite because of moments like those, when we constructed our future in simple conversations.

"That was my favorite day."

"It was significant." His play on the word significant brings back the chill of that day on the mountain. It means everything to me. It means he remembers.

"It was significant, but do you remember what happened when we got home?"

"Pops fell from the ladder." Gavin visibly shudders. "We were in the hospital with him for a week. You were with us." He sighs. "Devon couldn't handle it."

The sadness in Gavin's voice overpowers me. I reach for his hand and squeeze. "Devon was never good at stuff like that. You know he cared, though. He was just worried. He told me so.

"You know, our trip to the mountains was one of my best memories with you, but after that week in the hospital, I felt guilty," I admit. "We had so much fun, but I couldn't bring myself to write about it. I was so afraid you two would lose your father, too."

Gavin turns to me. "I was an idiot, Chloe. There was never anyone else that compared to you or my feelings for you, but I never had the guts to give into what I wanted for the fear of losing something greater. Our friendship was like glass, fragile and irreplaceable. One moment of weakness . . . one mistake . . . and it might have shattered completely. Our friendship was worth too much to me to risk even the slightest crack."

Holy crap.

He must see my face because he immediately backtracks. It's obvious he doesn't want to get my hopes up. "But Chloe, you have to understand something. I'll keep reading your journal if that's what you want. But our history, our connection . . . none of that changes the fact that you chose Devon," he says. "And I don't want you to feel bad about it. I just want us both to move on from this because I can't give you more than friendship."

"You've said that before," I snap.

My emotions whirl through me at lightning speed, and I try to make sense of how Gavin could be so stubborn about my relationship with Devon. *He still must not know the truth.* That thought somehow calms me.

"Just keep reading, Gavin." I say it quietly.

"You realize I'm going to get to the significant part of your life where you fell for my brother, right? I'm not sure I want to read about your first kiss and everything that goes along with that. Especially since you two lied about your relationship for so long."

I shake my head. "You need to trust me. Unless you'd rather accept your own misguided perception of what Devon and I were. Forgive me for reaching into your brain and thinking for you, but you're never going to get the closure you're seeking by avoiding the truth."

He doesn't disagree. I search his eyes, mosaic tiles in gradients of jade, filled with confusion and heartache. I'd do anything to rid him of his pain. That's what I'm hoping my journal will do for him. God, I hope I'm right.

Chapter 35

Significance

Gavin

When Chloe tells me to trust her, I do just that and I keep reading, ignoring my fear of what I will find behind every page. Turns out, Chloe wrote about me a lot. My ego is actually healthier than it's been in years as I read my name connected to most of her significant memories.

Significant. I smiled at her reaction today when I used that word. I'd completely forgotten about giving her that journal until I saw her tight hold on it. After that, it was like the memories were as fresh as the day she unwrapped it.

That smile. She was so happy to receive a thoughtful present. Even at twelve years old, Chloe understood the difference between sincerity and pretension. Even then, giving each other gifts wasn't about how much we spent or how big they were. It was about making each other feel special.

That same year she got me my first set of professional colored pencils. They were only twelve dollars at the office supply store—I know because I had been eyeballing them for months. She must have noticed. The point is, before she gave me those, I'd only sketched with number two pencils. Chloe has always noticed things that were of no benefit to her, and that's what made her significant to me.

She occasionally wrote about nothing in particular and then admitted that I'd be mad if I found out. That would make me chuckle. The thing is, I am still intrigued to read them because Chloe always could make *nothing* sound like the best story in the world.

There are entries that make my chest hurt when—through a great memory—Devon is here with me. Other entries, the ones that reveal Chloe's anguish while encountering Devon's hostility, piss me off; but I'm more pissed at myself for making decisions that hurt Chloe, all because I was trying to protect us both.

I'm disappointed our weekend at Crystal Mountain isn't documented. Even after all this time, I remember the flutters in my heart when Chloe fell out of the ski lift and onto me, her eyes crinkled with laughter. And then again back at the main lodge when we relaxed by the fire and I watched her talk about her dreams of her future. I remember hoping I was a part of them . . .

Chloe and I cut out of the venue today earlier than we'd planned. We were both drained. I took her back to the office and then returned to her journal, ready to give it another shot. I read about Chloe's first low grade, about which I was the first she told, and then about her summers in Florida. This I was savoring.

During these months, it was both enjoyable and torturous to not have Chloe in town. When she was around it was hard for me to even look at another girl. I didn't give anyone a chance because no one stood out the way Chloe did. But when Chloe was away, I felt free. Free to consider other options, free to let my heart decide what it really wanted.

I dated a lot over the summers, but the moment Chloe returned, my heart always found her again. Even as I dated throughout the school year, no one compared to her, and it bothered me, especially as I got older and realized that I wanted a real relationship. I wanted to fall in love. It took seeing her with Devon to realize what I wanted all along was to have what I already had with Chloe . . . because I was already in love.

Instead of asking myself why Chloe's presence halted any feelings I had for any other girl, I looked for other options. I never realized how much my dating hurt Chloe until I read her journal. She never wrote specifically that it hurt her, but it was in the way she described her encounters with me and other girls that spoke volumes.

At one point during junior year, Chloe admitted to going on a date to hang out with a guy other than me. Maybe Chloe had feelings for me even then. I know I had them for her. But how does one admit to their best friend that they want to try for more? And what if more doesn't work out? I knew that would have ruined my friendship with Chloe, and I wasn't about to set myself up for that type of heartbreak.

After a passage where Chloe describes how Devon and Stacy picked on her, I want to bring Devon back to life just so I can throw a fist in his face. My mind must have been in a damn bubble to not see that Devon and Stacy were bullying her. From what I learned after my brother's death, those two had teamed up for more reasons than to pick on innocent people.

Thankfully, Stacy has changed a lot since our school days. She's shared with me that she has regrets about how she treated Chloe. I always hoped one day she'd have a chance to apologize. After reading these journal entries, though, I have a feeling winning Chloe over will be tough . . . especially once Chloe learns what transpired after the night of Devon's death.

I shudder.

No, I can't go there right now.

I get through an entire year of Chloe's diary before debating once again if I should skip to the end—but then, I never have been the kid who peeks at his presents before Christmas. That was Devon. Besides, reading about the past is kind of fun. So many of Chloe's memories are triggering my own, and it feels good. Like the time we decided to streak from our house to the treehouse and back. Chloe was the last one to the finish line, covering her naked bits and huffing for air. At thirteen she had a decent enough body to earn me my first chub over a real live naked girl. Thank God I was able to hide it before she saw anything. That would have traumatized both of us forever.

Reading about Chloe's first date and kiss with some Florida dude bothers me. There were many times I'd wondered if she had a boyfriend over the summers, if she'd been kissed before Devon. I never had to worry about it during the school year because Chloe didn't date much. And when she did, Devon and I had words with whoever asked her out. They knew not to touch her or they'd have us to deal with. Kind of messed up, I know. But I knew that if she met someone that really fell for her the way she deserved, whoever it was wouldn't let two possessive friends stand in their way. As hard as it would be, I'd stand aside to see Chloe happy. That's all I've ever wanted.

Still annoyed by Florida Boy, I toss her journal to the edge of my bed, head to the kitchen, and stuff my face with leftover chicken Marsala. After a long shower, I debate picking up her journal again. I shouldn't. Tomorrow is an important day for all of us: our pitch to the executives. I catch sight of the time. *Holy shit.* It's five in the morning.

I sprawl out on my bed, sighing. For a second my eyes lock on the thick, brown leather binding that lies open at the edge of my bed. I groan at it because it's taunting me, tempting me to keep going. There's not much left. Just springtime, which I know will be the hardest to read. I decide to allow myself one more passage and then I'll drift off . . .

CHLOE'S JOURNAL, APRIL 25, 2012

I can't do it anymore. I'm shaking so hard, I can barely write this, but I have to tell someone. You're the only one I can tell this to, Future Chloe. You're the only one that will listen.

We were at Justin's lake party. Everyone was there since it was one of the last parties for us seniors. We hung out long enough for Devon to slam some drinks back, and then he told me he wanted to show me the greenhouse. Things have been rocky between us for so long, I wanted to give him the benefit of the doubt. I thought it was a sweet gesture. It reminded me of our first couple of dates when he took me places and tried to impress me. At first we just walked around in a circle, looking at the colorful plants and flowers. I thought it was all so beautiful and could imagine having a green-house of my own one day.

Then he kissed me. It caught me off guard. It was one of those aggressive kisses I've always hated. This time, he wouldn't let me pull away. He tightened his hold on my neck and shoved his tongue in my mouth. Panic awakened every nerve ending in my body. I pushed away from him and his teeth bit into my lip like an animal. He even roared like one. Then he slammed me into a table. I screamed so loud, certain someone would hear us, and then I was sobbing uncontrollably. Devon's strength was frightening. He wanted to shut me up. When his hand muffled my aching voice, I could taste my blood against his dirty palm. That's when my fear turned to anger.

Things have never gotten to this point before. Usually, we kiss a little and he tries to touch me. Most of the time it's a struggle to push him away, but he always ends up stalking off frustrated. No harm done. This time he was determined to finish the job he started. He told me he'd waited for this long enough, then called me a stupid bitch for crying and flipped me around. He hates my tears, but I also think he gains power from them. Weakness fuels his need for control and the moment he sees me vulnerable, he manages to find a way to make me feel worse.

He bound both of my hands with one of his and pressed them into the wooden table. He used his other hand to dig into my hip as he shoved his body onto mine. I felt sick. Betrayed. Angry. The louder my sobs got, the tighter he latched onto me. Crying wasn't earning me my escape. If anything, it was filling Devon's gun with ammo. I had to get away from him.

When one of his hands slid between my legs, I did the only thing I could think of. I grabbed the nearest pot and smashed it full force over his head. He grunted and flew backward, hitting the *table behind him and falling over. His eyes rolled back until his lids closed over them, and I ran. I ran three miles until I was home and locked all the doors.*

I'm shaking because it's been four hours and I haven't heard from him. He could be dead for all I know. I'm also scared because I wouldn't put it past him to try it again. He's stronger than me. Graduation can't come fast enough. That's the night this all ends. I'll finally tell the twins I'll be leaving for college. Away from them. Devon won't be able to touch me. Until then, I'll have to figure out a way to survive.

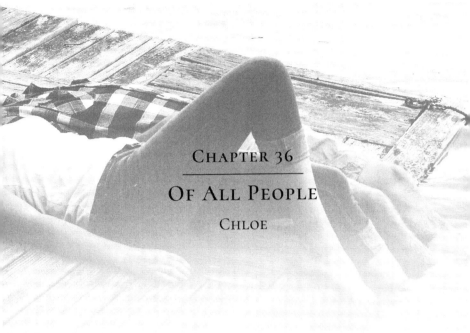

CHAPTER 36

OF ALL PEOPLE

CHLOE

Gavin walks in two hours late, less than an hour before we're supposed to present. My insides are about to explode with panic. "Where the hell were you?" I'm seething.

Something about the way he's looking at me forces my anxiety to magnetize and pool in my chest. His eyes are bright and wide, but the outer rims look dark, as if he hasn't slept in days. I swallow a big gulp of air, trying hard to focus.

Sharlene blows into the room. "Where have you been?" she demands.

Gavin's gaze doesn't leave mine when he answers. "I was up late . . . reading. Lost track of time."

"You're two hours late because you were reading? I can't believe you just admitted that to me. Gavin Rhodes, so help me. If this presentation isn't on point today . . ."

Gavin shakes his head. "I'm sorry. It'll be perfect. Chloe's got this. You just need my sketches, and I'll back you both up." He finally turns to Sharlene and gives her his panty-melting smile. "Everything will be fine. I'll hang the posters with Chloe."

"No, I need Chloe to run drafts of the script off at the printer. Ten copies, please," she snaps.

"Don't take it out on Chloe because I was late, Sharlene." Gavin's calm but terse tone brings me back to seventh grade all over again.

Always standing up for me.

"It's fine," I jump in, unsure of what might come next. "I'll get the copies and be right back." With one final glance in Gavin's direction, I leave the room, my heart racing, wondering again how far into my journal he's read.

The room is a bit calmer when I return, and I see that Gavin's posted his sketches on pop art backgrounds across the entire back wall. "Nice touch," I compliment him.

"Thanks. Want to do a dry run?"

Sharlene is still fuming in the back of the room. "There's no time," she snaps.

I raise my eyebrows at her, only because she can't see me, and watch her as she distributes the stack of papers onto the conference table. I take this moment to scan the sketches from left to right, a bright smile on my face. Gavin is even more talented than I remember. The intricacy of his lines. His usage of color. I can visualize the entire piece hanging on the Melrose Market walls so vividly.

Completely consumed by his work, I don't hear Gavin approach until he's leaning into my ear like he loves to do. "We need to talk." That's all he says before he walks out of the room, blazing a trail behind him.

Chills sweep over my body like a brush fire. There's no stopping the erratic wind that is Gavin Rhodes. Fear bubbles inside me. I have an idea what this is about, so I hesitate to follow, not knowing how I'll respond to whatever questions he's about to sling at me. But I do follow. I'm the one who asked him to read my diary, and I can't shy away from the consequences.

Gavin finds a dark office and pulls me inside, shutting the door behind him and flipping on the lights. We're in one of the editing suites. The walls are soundproof, which is probably a good thing by his expression.

He can't even look at me, and the room is heating up quickly.

"What's wrong?" I ask cautiously.

When he turns, I can see that he's shaking and his eyes have a watery glaze over them. "Why didn't you tell anyone what happened in the greenhouse?"

His fists are white, and his nails dig into the skin of his palms. *Shit.*

"I couldn't. I didn't know who to talk to. You and Jazz were the only ones I could think of, but I couldn't talk to either of you. You both would have killed him."

Gavin grinds his teeth and furrows his brows in anger. "You're damn right I would have kicked the living shit out of him. Why didn't you break up with him, at least? My God, Chloe!"

A lump hardens in my throat. "I didn't want to set him off." I know the excuse is shit, but it's honest.

"How many times did he touch you like that?"

"It doesn't matter. It's over." I'm shaking my head, afraid of what Gavin will do next.

"I want to know," his tone seethes.

"Just once." Now I'm on the verge of tears. "That was the worst of it," I assure him. "After that I only hung out with him in groups. I was so close to moving away for college—"

"So you let him get away with it?"

I shook my head. "I was scared. What was I supposed to do?"

"Report it. Tell me. Tell someone!" Gavin moves forward and takes my face in his palms. For as angry as he is, he's gentle when he touches me. The tears are streaming down my face when he looks at me again. "So he never—?"

I shake my head. "No. Never. I'm stronger than everyone thinks, you know?"

Gavin's jaw hardens. "Yes. I know that."

He seems to have calmed down some when he pulls me into his arms. "I wish you had come to me. I know he was my brother, but that didn't make him perfect. I knew he was an animal, but I never thought he would hurt you. Of all people. You were the one we always protected."

"No, Gavin. I was the one *you* always protected."

He strokes my hair and kisses my head, as if silently asking for forgiveness. My sigh that follows is a deep whoosh of air as the balloon I've carried for years finally deflates in my chest.

The presentation is, just as Gavin assured, perfect. More than perfect. The executives love the creative approach, fawn over Gavin's art, and thoroughly devour my script. Their notes are minor, and we're approved to continue working in our desired direction.

Sharlene takes the entire department out for dinner to celebrate after work. Gavin made an excuse to leave as soon as the presentation was over. No surprise to me. He looked exhausted. Can't say I'm not disappointed, though. I would have loved to overdrink on accident again.

"Are you going to Gavin's party tomorrow?" Monica is bouncing on the stool beside me after dinner. We decided to have an after-party since we were buzzing from the wine at dinner.

That's right, Gavin's Stay and Play party. The reminder causes an ache in my chest. "I don't think so. It's been a long week, you know?"

Monica ceases her bouncing and plasters herself in the seat beside me, all up in my bubble. "Don't you live right across the street from him?"

"On the other side of the woods. That doesn't mean I'm obligated to go to his parties."

I try to avoid the look Monica gives me in return. I almost forgot how perceptive she could be. Her face, half-smirk, half-accusing, tells me she sees me. Really sees me. "You realize you have to go, right? You can keep your eyes on your man. By now you should know me, and I'm upfront. If you're not there, there's no stopping me from laying it on him."

I cringe. Does she really need to go there? "Seriously?"

She laughs and winks, turning my fume into a smile. "I'm kidding, obviously. I have a thing for someone else." I follow her gaze across the bar. They land on Javier from the legal department.

"Really? Javier?"

Monica's expression turns sultry. "Oh yes. Javier." The way she rolls her tongue on the "r" has me in hysterics.

As we're about to take a shot, limes poised in our mouths, Monica's phone buzzes. We both look at it and see Gavin's name pop up on her display.

Gavin: Call me.

Monica's face turns pale.

Call me. That's all it says, but that's all I need to take the shot and order another round for us both.

"She'll be fine here. I'll make sure she stays put until tomorrow . . ." Monica's voice filters through the darkness and trails off at the end of her sentence. She's just taken my phone and walked it into another room.

My surroundings are unfamiliar, and rough fabric scrapes my face as I turn my head. A couch. I must be in Monica's apartment.

At least I'm not driving right now.

I pout. Gavin texted Monica. Why didn't he text me?

"Yes, I'll try, okay?" Monica's in another room, but I can hear her clearly. "That's all I can do." Another pause and then a huff. "Fine. Okay. Yes. Goodnight, Gavin."

I must doze off for half a second.

"Chloe?" Monica appears in front of me. She's all kinds of blurry. "Do you need water or anything?"

I moan again. Words are not my friend.

"I'll get you some." She moves to stand but I grab her wrist, pulling her down.

"Did you ask Gavin to come get me?"

Monica leans down and brushes a hand across my forehead. That was sweet. "That's probably not the best idea tonight, Chloe. Just sleep, okay? We'll talk in the morning."

My phone. She has my phone. I'll call him. He'll come. My hand searches clumsily over her body. "Phone," I moan.

"I have it, and I'm holding it hostage until the morning to save you from drunk dialing Gavin again."

"Again?"

"*Again*. Don't worry; I got to it before you could say anything stupid. You just called, he picked up, and I snatched the phone away. He insisted on coming here, but he's been drinking too. Just sleep on it. Y'all can figure your issues out in the morning."

"So he wasn't trying to sleep with you?"

Monica laughs, and somehow the sound calms me enough for my eyes to flutter closed.

STAY AND PLAY

"ALL THE WINDOWS OF MY HEART I OPEN
TO THE DAY." ~ LAO TZU

CHAPTER 37

SCRUNCH BUNS & BAND-AIDS

GAVIN

For three years now, Stay and Play has been an annual summer event. I invite my closest friends and then some to hang at my place all day and crash all night. No one is allowed to leave once they hand over their keys. We blast music, hang by the pool, take boat rides on the lake, barbecue, play poker, sit by the campfire at night, and basically drink until we pass out.

But the best part? All proceeds go to the charity of my choice. This year, it's the anti-bullying project.

Guests begin arriving at noon. There's no official start time, and I like it that way. For the most part, my friends do all the heavy lifting, organizing it entirely on a social media group they started. They bring the booze. They bring the watercrafts. They assign duties. They buy the food, the beer, and the buttery nipple shots, whatever the hell those are. My role: provide the party space, collect the keys, manage the charity jar, lie back, and enjoy.

As much fun as this party has become, it's also a time when I reflect heavily on Devon. This is a party Devon would have loved. My brother could be fun; at least I can admit that much. He brought a unique energy to events like this and never let anyone sulk in the corner. Although my thoughts of him are even more

245

muddled than before after learning what he did to Chloe, the event still serves a purpose, both in remembrance of my brother and as a way to give to a great cause.

My view from the dock is an image from a movie. The sun is shining, clouds are nowhere in sight, and my lakefront property is beginning to fill up with hotties in little bikinis. This year, though, Chloe is all I want, and I'm hoping she'll be here today. If she doesn't show, I'll break my own party rules and go find her. There's so much left I need to say.

Yesterday was rough. Being so angry at Devon puts me in a difficult situation. I can't turn back the clock. I can't have words with my brother. I can't do anything except deal with this and figure out a way to move on from it. One thing is for sure: I failed as a friend to Chloe if she didn't know that she could come to me about anything, even something as painful as Devon forcing himself on her.

After Chloe's journal, I realize that so much of what I accepted as truth was wrong. The biggest shock? My brother and Chloe never had sex. My one hang-up since they started dating was a false reality created by my overactive imagination and Devon's crazy insinuations. Devon wanted me to know that he'd claimed Chloe as his. "Claiming her" and "owning her" were phrases he threw around pointedly. The conversations are so vividly present in my mind. He'd stumble home after a party and make a point of boasting about his sex life. "That girl will be lucky if she can walk tomorrow." He'd throw himself on his bed, heaving laughter before finally passing out, and then I'd remove his shoes and throw a blanket on him.

I imagined punching him while he slept so many times that I could almost trick myself into believing it really happened. I should have punched him. I should have called him out on his bullshit before it was too late. There are so many things I should have done.

Last night, before I texted Monica, I was waiting on Chloe's doorstep. I knew she was going out to dinner with the department, but I figured she'd be home by ten. When she wasn't, I texted Monica, knowing they would be together.

Gavin: Call me.

Monica: Why are you texting me?

Gavin: Are you with Chloe?

Monica: LOL. Good. Yes.

Gavin: Are you two drinking?

Monica: Do monkeys sling their poo?

I cringed before responding to that one.

Gavin: Gross. She shouldn't drive home. Where are you?

Monica: She can stay with me tonight. Go do boy things.

I was frustrated, but I know I can't control everything. As much as I wanted to talk to Chloe right then, it would have to wait. Still revved up on all that I'd uncovered, I drove home and dove into the whiskey. I needed something to help me through the night.

By two in the morning, I had a good buzz going and headed upstairs to bed. When Chloe's name registered on my screen, I panicked a little. "Chlo, are you okay?"

"Hey—" Chloe's voice drifts further away and is replaced by Monica's.

"Sorry, Gav, I'm hiding her phone. You can talk to her tomorrow. She's drunk."

So am I.

"Are you sure? I should come get her."

"She'll be fine here. I'll make sure she stays put until tomorrow."

"Okay, thanks. Can you do me a favor?" I recognize that my words are coming out a little slurred, but I continue. "You're coming to my party tomorrow, right? Can you make sure Chloe comes with you?"

"Yes, I'll try, okay? That's all I can do."

"Try hard. It's important."

"Fine."

"Please," I pleaded one last time for emphasis. Because after reading the final entry in Chloe's journal, I was more eager to see her than ever.

"Okay. Yes. Goodnight, Gavin."

The phone went dead before I could respond. And then I read her final entry again before drifting off to sleep.

Chloe's Journal, May 10, 2012

This is it, Chloe of the Future. My last entry before I hide you away and move on to a new adventure. Thank you for six years of support.

Since I opened this diary with a passage about Gavin, it's only fair to end it that way. He's been my brightest light during my darkest days. Things may have gotten complicated this year, but he's still my constant. Even when he's not speaking to me, or not returning my feelings, he's still the same person. But as sure as I am about our connection, and as much as I trust him, there is a secret I keep. And it's my deepest, darkest one. In my mind, it's bigger than that unspeakable night in the greenhouse. I lived through that night and I'm stronger for it, but I'm not sure I can live without him.

I wanted to tell him all my secrets, but he became one of them instead.

My secret is one I hold closest to my heart, no matter how distant we are.

My secret is the love I can never confess. My secret is Gavin.

I am in love with my Gavin Rhodes.

That passage was the one I was most afraid to read because it was her last, but it ended up being my favorite. To learn how Chloe had felt about me in high school, and the fact that I felt the exact same way, is frustrating and satisfying all at once. Knowing that it's something I can act on now is where the anticipation comes in. I suddenly feel like I'm in junior high all over again, unsure of how to approach a cute girl.

Steve, a friend who has seen me struggle to approach many a cute girl, snaps me out of my thoughts. "Dude, you in for a game?" he calls from below. He's tossing a volleyball between his hands on the steps leading into the pool.

"Sounds good. Be right there," I shout down to him. I pull out my phone to text Chloe.

Gavin: Are you coming to my party?

Her answer isn't immediate enough, so I text Monica next.

Gavin: Make her come.

The three dots appear telling me Monica is already responding.

Monica: I'm trying. But isn't making her come your job? And drop the caveman speak or I'll tell her your balls are inflatable.

My face heats and it's not because of the blazing sun.

Gavin: I owe you one.

Her wink face in response satisfies me enough for now.

CHLOE

Monica sits cross-legged in the middle of my room with a wicked grin on her face. She's texting someone, and I don't even want to imagine what she's saying. I've been privy to Monica's text battles, and her wit always wins. I turn back to my bathing suit drawer and touch the strap of a fuchsia two-piece with ruffled edges. Facing Monica, I hold it up, asking for her approval.

Her eyes go wide and then she nods. "Yes."

I smile before stripping down and stepping into the tiny pieces of fabric.

"Is that a scrunch bun?"

I blush, reaching around to feel my backside. The material gathers in the middle, accentuating certain features. "Is it too much?"

"Definitely not." Her tone of admiration convinces me, so I

reach for my black cover-up. "If you're trying to kill Gavin," she adds with a chuckle.

I sigh and slip on the black dress. "Gavin's seen me in a bikini before."

"And I'm sure he didn't want to have sex with you then, either."

I throw my beach bag at her and laugh. "You are not helping at all. You're the one dragging me to his stupid party."

I'm full of it. Playing it off like I don't want to go to the party is much easier than admitting that I do. After our conversation yesterday, I'm curious if things have changed for him. Now that Gavin knows the truth, it could change everything for us—for better or for worse.

"Technically," I continue, "I'm not allowed to go because I don't plan on staying."

"You have to stay."

Shaking my head, I slip on my sandals. "Nope. I don't. I'll go because it's for a great cause and I get to hang out with my friends." *And because I desperately want to be near Gavin again.* "But then I'm coming home."

Monica shrugs. "Whatever you say, sexy. Let's go get our day drink on."

We trek through the woods, and on the way I show her the infamous treehouse, which on the exterior looks to be complete. I'm not so sure about the interior, but now isn't the time for an inspection. I'm glad Gavin decided to keep working on it without me. Besides installing the hammock and staring at Gavin as sweat rolled down his hot skin, I wasn't much help anyway.

By the time we reach the edge of the woods, we can already hear the party in full swing. Music is thumping, water is splashing, partygoers are cheering, and motors are revving on the lake. The weather gods couldn't have chosen a better day to bless our city.

We walk straight into the barbecue area where we're stopped by a group of guys tossing a piece of meat on the grill and trading jokes. "Hey, ladies," booms a voice that sounds somewhat familiar. I squint and recognize him immediately.

"Hey, Rod," I say with a smile.

"Chloe, is that you? Holy shit." He sets his beer down and picks me up, swinging me in a full circle before setting me down. "Where have you been, woman?"

Rodney was one of the twins' closest friends in high school. I remember Jazz mentioning that he'd moved to Vermont and gotten hitched.

"I graduated from OSU and I'm back. Working in Bellevue now. What about you? I heard you moved to Vermont."

He nods. "Still there. Just home for a couple weeks' vacation with the wife. She's over there. I'll have to introduce you to her later. You'll love her."

I'm happy for him. He looks tamer than he was in high school; that's for sure. Maybe the wife had something to do with that.

Our conversation is interrupted by Blaine as he approaches to welcome me with a hug. It's clear by his friendly demeanor that his expectations of *us* have changed after the night at the drive-in. There's a slight pang of guilt in my chest, but it helps that he's making an effort to still be friends.

Monica and I take our time before moving on, and when we do, I find myself searching for Gavin. There are distractions at every turn. Old friends stopping to say hello, polite winks from unfamiliar males . . . and then we bump into Phoebe and her friends near the back patio.

I'm still in my sundress, which makes me the oddball of the group. Monica stripped down to a little more than nothing the moment we arrived. I don't know why she was making a big deal about my scrunch bun when her strapless top resembles a Band-Aid. I have to hold back laughter when I catch Izzy giving Monica the death stare. I'm not sure if she disapproves of her attire or is jealous of it. It's funny either way.

I tug Monica's hand to move on when we're intercepted by a

dripping wet and shirtless Gavin. Kill me now. He's just inches from me, smiling as if I'm the highlight of his day.

"Hey," I say.

"Hey."

Of course his damn eyes sparkle in the sun.

"Here we are!" Monica exclaims, plastering her hip against mine. "Where's the beer? I'm ready to play catch-up. You all look like you've been at this for a while."

Gavin's hands move, gesturing to somewhere behind us. "By the kitchen door. You'll want to take it easy, Mon," he calls after her. "We'll be here all night."

"Looking forward to it!" She winks as she leaves us.

Gavin's eyes are locked on mine, and they hold an unspoken message. He's happy I'm here, and for the first time, he's not going to hide it.

CHAPTER 38

STAY

GAVIN

Distracting myself with volleyball seems like a great idea until I see Chloe and Monica approaching.

"Shit, dude. Is that Chloe? She's hot as fuck." Steve is holding the ball in his palm before his serve, gawking at the girls as they approach the barbecue.

My world stops at the sight of her and I allow myself to soak in everything I'm feeling. No more trying to suppress it. It's as if I've been looking at Chloe through a two-way mirror this entire time—aware of her and always feeling her presence, but never allowing myself to break through the barrier.

"You okay?" Steve grins.

Whatever bubble I'm floating in pops at the sound of his voice. "Yeah, I have to go check on things. Replace me."

Steve chides me as I climb out of the pool, but I can't hear what he says. My focus is on Chloe as the girls make their way up the porch steps. I arrive just as Monica heads off to grab a drink, so I'm left staring at Chloe with so much to say and no clue how to start. I've already promised myself that today is about having a good time. No serious shit.

Between the time Monica leaves and returns with three beers, Chloe and I haven't said a word to each other. We don't have to.

Monica presses a cold beer into my palm and grins. "I'm stealing your girl. You can have her later." She winks and tugs on Chloe to follow her.

Chloe doesn't move right away even though I've stepped to the side to allow her to pass. When she finally does, it's as if she's stealing my air as she goes. She's so damn beautiful.

Steve talks me into another game of volleyball and I happily oblige, seeing that Chloe and Monica have claimed two pool chairs and near the net. Wherever Chloe is, that's where I want to be.

The game gets fairly heated, seeing as we're all former athletes, and there's a crowd surrounding us. Nothing amps us up more than an attentive audience. When Steve spikes the ball one final time, we throw our hands up in victory and the crowd cheers. From my periphery, I spot Chloe laughing and clapping her hands. Just then, someone takes a flying leap into the pool, tucking their body just in time to cannonball. Water goes everywhere.

Chloe's cover-up gets soaked and my heart constricts as she reaches for the hem to lift it over her head. "Fuck me." The words are out of my mouth before I can process Chloe's tan skin and rocking curves. She tosses the drenched dress to the side and turns her back to me, giving me a view of the rest of her suit. *Kill me now.*

I take a casual swim to her side of the pool and cross my arms at the ledge to get a closer look—and to block any encroaching sleazeballs that try to hit on her. So far, it appears I'm the only one.

Monica sees me first and raises a brow knowingly. Chloe turns too and wastes no time sauntering over. Instead of jumping in like I'd hoped, she sits and dangles her feet in the water, peering down at me with her glimmering eyes. "Impressive game out there. Your team definitely had the bigger muscles."

I puff out my chest. "Damn straight."

She throws her head back to laugh, and my focus drops to her long necklace . . . and then to other things . . .

"Aren't you supposed to be hosting? Slacker."

"This event runs itself. Everyone's in charge of something."

"Oh yeah? What about me? You didn't give me a job." Even with the sun adding filter to her face, I can see her playful smile.

"Your job is to get your sexy ass in this pool with me." It feels good to flirt.

She reels back on her hands and grins. "You're a very demanding boss. I'm not sure I'm going to like this job."

Her defiance stirs something below my waist. I push up with my hands so we're nose-to-nose. "It pays well." I'm fully aware of how raspy my voice sounds. I'm also aware that Chloe's cheeks flush because of it. I wink, and then pull her off the ledge and into the water with me.

She goes in up to her nose, sputtering and gasping playfully when standing. "I think you just referred to yourself as my pimp." She purses her lips and shakes her head. "But I'm certain you're smarter than that, Rhodes."

I grip her waist and pull her toward me until her amused face is a close few inches to mine. For a moment I forget that we're having a conversation, too lost in her blue Bambi eyes. I'm a total goner. "I'm learning."

After our pool escapades, I make a point to not follow Chloe around like a puppy dog. Instead, I fulfill my share of hosting duties by ensuring everyone is taken care of.

Lucky for me, Chloe is always just a glance away. That doesn't stop me from finding ways to be near her. Like now, after realizing she's been nursing the same beer since she arrived. I exchange her warm can for a new one, but she declines it. "I kinda overdid it last night."

I nod, understanding completely. "Me too. Water instead?" She nods.

When I return with her water, I find her at the edge of the dock, waving to a departing Monica who's on a Sea-Doo. "Does she know what she's doing with that thing?" I ask on my approach.

"She'll be fine, but Blaine will stick with her."

I wish I had my camera. Chloe's face is glowing from the sun and pieces of her long brown hair fly around her head. From this angle her eyes are as deep as an ocean.

I'm so captivated by the sight of her, I almost miss what she says next. "My secret hiding place."

She's pointing, so I turn in the direction she's gesturing to and smile. *The boat shed.* She's recalling one of my favorite memories. "You were awful at that game."

"I was not!"

"That was your only hiding spot." I argue.

Chloe laughs. "But I fooled you guys every time."

"Yeah, because you were so small you could fit in the tightest spaces. You were like Houdini, but without the magic."

She scoffs playfully. "You're just jealous."

The corners of my mouth turn up in a smile as a surge of electricity travels through me. I grab her hand and pull her into the small wooden structure. It's blanketed in darkness except for the stream of light pouring in through the tiny window near the ceiling. The musty, moldy smell that used to irritate my senses only enhances the memories of our past now. So many good memories; some I had forgotten until reading Chloe's journal.

I have the door shut and her back pressed flush against it in two seconds. Her shocked expression makes me grin.

"What are you doing?" she asks nervously.

I lean in, dizzying at her scent, a fusion of citrus and cherry blossoms. She squirms beneath my nose, which is now buried in her neck. My hands smooth at her waist as my tongue dips and scrapes her skin, stealing a taste. So fucking edible.

I bring my mouth up to her ear to answer her question. "Something I've been wanting to do since the moment I saw you today."

She shudders, only causing me to smile again. My lips brush across hers and I watch them part in front of me, welcoming me as her lids fall closed. So I kiss her, deepening it enough to let her know I mean it. I've never meant anything more in my life.

She shakes in my hold. The movement is slight, but noticeable. I love that I can do that to her. Her moans are soft and pleasing to my ears.

Fingernails dig into my shoulders, then drag up to my scalp and through my hair. A leg wraps around mine, pulling me closer. She gasps at the feel of me. A groan rumbles low in my throat. It's exhausting all my strength to not take her against the door right now.

Maybe I should.

Her lips, skin . . . it's all so soft and tastes so damn good. But I've already made up my mind. This isn't the time or the place, no matter how good it might feel.

I tear myself from her warmth, my body aching for her. She must feel it too. She whimpers before letting her head fall back against the door.

With a chuckle, I tug on her hand and turn the handle. "C'mon, Clover. We've got a party to get back to."

I slip my fingers between hers and give them a squeeze, my smile promising more kisses to come.

CHLOE

Someone builds a campfire in front of me as the sun begins to set. That's my cue to ponder the decision that's been eating at me all day: to stay or not to stay. I track Gavin's movements as he darts off toward the dock. He starts to clean up the rafts and other flotation devices from the lake, most likely removing the temptation for drunk, late-night escapades. The party is already much more chill than it was earlier, and I'm surprised to find myself enjoying it more as the evening goes on.

The anticipation I felt earlier faded after our kiss in the shed. Gavin surprised the hell out of me by not tackling me like he could have. I would have responded without a fight. But what he did was much more meaningful, and it makes me want him that much more. He was gentle and passionate without any of the uncertainty I've felt from him in the past. It was as if he had finally given up his internal battle and there was something bigger on the horizon for us.

By the time everyone huddles around the campfire, Gavin squeezes in beside me and hands me one of his zip-up hoodies. "Your dress got soaked. Thought you might want this."

I take it from him, the right side of my mouth lifting with amusement. I think Monica was right about my scrunch bun. I've just slipped my hands through the sleeves when he leans in and kisses my cheek. It's such a light touch, but I feel it throughout my entire body. I turn to him, hoping now is the time he'll ask me to stay with him tonight. In a way, it's implied, because where else would I sleep? I can't imagine Gavin allowing me to share a sleeping bag with someone on the living room floor while he's upstairs in his big bed.

Along with anticipation comes the fear of what happens after I make the decision to stay. Things have been complicated between us for so long. Could this be the night that changes everything?

Before I have time to say more than thank you, Gavin stands to make his rounds, checking on his guests and ensuring no one breaks the rules and tries to drive home. His hospitality is endearing, but even after he walks away the sensation in my chest lingers.

Monica approaches, licking chocolate from her fingertips.

"So, you're still here. Does that mean Gavin and I have to wrestle over who gets to sleep with you? I vote Jell-O fight."

"You're telling me you haven't found yourself a man by now? You're losing your touch."

She twists her mouth in agreement. "Don't remind me."

"You can always come home with me."

"You're not leaving!" she hisses.

"I'm debating it."

She glares. "There's nothing to debate. Gavin is crazy about you. Stop being such a chicken and put him out of his misery already."

I know she's right, so I search the dark for him. My breath catches in my throat when I spot him standing at his bedroom balcony, eyes intently focused on me. That's the look that tells me everything I need to know. Maybe I don't need him to tell me to stay. Maybe *I* need to tell *him* that I want to stay.

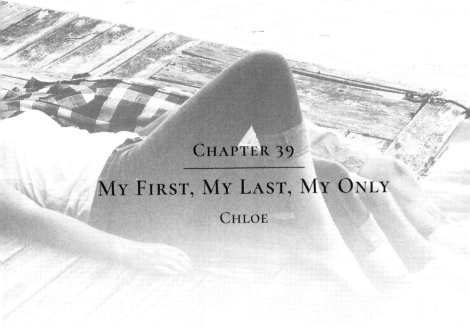

CHAPTER 39

MY FIRST, MY LAST, MY ONLY

CHLOE

Gavin stands on the balcony watching me, his chin perched on folded arms atop the rail. The intensity in his eyes awakens the butterflies in my stomach. Without another thought, I lift myself from the bench, walk up the porch steps, and enter the kitchen. It's a slow and heart-pounding walk the entire way upstairs.

And then I see him. The adrenaline racing through me instantly slows. He's opening the door before I can knock, a slow smile spreading across his face. "Hey."

I blush. What does he think I'm up here for? What *am* I up here for? And why am I so nervous? *Shit.* "I was looking for my things," I start, working up the courage to tell him that I want to stay.

Gavin's smile falters, and he steps away from the door to let me into his room. "Come in."

I follow him, getting a good view of his king bed and swallowing the nerves that have just hijacked my body. I've been in here before. I've slept in that bed. Only, this is so different.

He reaches into his closet, pulls out a plastic bag, and holds it out to me. I take a few steps closer; curious to see if he's really going to let me go so easily. I don't want him to let me go at all.

I'm the worst type of girl, always running away, always acting hard to get. Always playing it safe. Never going after what I want. In this case, all I've ever wanted was Gavin.

"Your dress is still wet." He waves a hand around. "Borrow whatever you need and I'll walk you home."

I grab the bag, disappointment filling me as I turn toward the bathroom. *Wait. This isn't what I want.*

"Or"—his voice halts me in my tracks—" you can grab a shirt in my closet and stay with me tonight."

"Do you want me to stay with you?"

He looks at me as if I'm insane. Maybe I am. I already know the answer but I want to hear it. And then he's approaching, his eyes never leaving mine. The intensity on his face makes my entire body quiver.

He's in front of me now, just an inch away. Still too far.

"Gav." My voice is breathless. I'm glued to his every move. "What are you doing?"

"Answering your question."

I'm abuzz with his raspy words as his hands take off at an agonizingly slow pace, unzipping and releasing me from his sweatshirt. It crumples to the floor and my eyes flutter closed. Not a second later, hands are gliding down the side of my neck, to my collarbone, then over my shoulders. The trail of his fingers leaves a chill in their wake. I feel like one of those anesthetic awareness victims—paralyzed, yet I can feel every damn thing.

Thumbs move to my cheeks, stroking, pleading for me to open my eyes. So I do. The lust-filled gaze I'm met with could be the end of me. My lips part in response.

All of this touching and he still doesn't kiss me. I need him to kiss me. The chills are beginning to burn.

He grips my wrists and pulls them over my head, pinning them to the wall behind me. Securing me with one hand, the other continues its tortuous movements down my side. I let out a moan. This seems to drive him crazy because he grasps my waist and pulls himself toward me, pushing me flush against the wall.

There's no question of his arousal as I feel him digging into my belly.

In one quick move he's got one of my legs wrapped around his waist and his teeth drag along the dip of my neck. He begins sucking and pulling the blood to the surface, but I don't have the mind to stop him. I'm letting him convince me to stay even though I never needed convincing.

With a release of my hands, he reaches around my backside and lifts me, supporting me with his palms. Now both of my legs are wrapped around his waist and with a roll of his hips he's grinding into me. My mouth goes wide at the friction. *Holy hell.*

My heart is beating down the walls of my chest when his mouth reaches the swell of my breast and kisses it. Working his way down, his hot, sticky breath silently hovers over the cloth of my bikini top. I want to push my breasts into him, but he seems to be distracted, contemplating something. To my utter disappointment, he growls and pulls away.

No. Why are you stopping?

My eyelids are pressed tightly together, so I don't see him, but I can feel our breaths colliding when he speaks. "Have you made your decision yet?"

His voice is full of pure sex, and it radiates through me.

I nod and swallow, unable to speak. After several moments I unwrap my legs from him and stand. His eyes are soft and hopeful. I melt. Completely melt all over the floor like a puddle of warmed ice cream. "I'll be back." And I escape into the bathroom behind me without ever answering his question.

Away from Gavin's intensity I'm able to clear my mind enough to give my mirror image a pep talk. The rapids of my every desire have captured me, and I'm headed straight for the damn waterfall. I can either grab onto the nearest tree and pull myself to safety, or I can follow the stream that is my heart. My mind sides with my heart this time, screaming for me to continue toward the edge and jump. I can't think of a reason not to. Before

I have time to come up with one, I'm untying the strings of my bikini and letting the pieces fall to the floor.

I turn on the faucet and splash water everywhere, washing away the chlorine and sunscreen from the day's activities. I step into Gavin's closet and slip on a shirt from junior high that barely reaches my upper thighs. For a second, I consider prancing out naked, but I quickly shake the thought away. My nerves are a freaking wreck as it is.

With a deep breath, I turn the knob from the closet to Gavin's bedroom. He's sitting at the end of his bed, facing me, but his head is bowed down, elbows resting on his knees. He looks up when I enter the room and scans my body from top to bottom. I hold my breath. The man staring back at me is as familiar as he's always been, but the expression on his face is new. It's one I've only imagined in my dreams. Unrestrained lust, desire, and want. He makes me feel sexy even though I'm dressed in only an old t-shirt.

"Come here." His voice is gravelly. Commanding.

Holy shit.

My feet move; I don't know how, but I'm in front of him in seconds. His hands reach the backs of my thighs and barely brush my skin as they travel up my leg. He stops when he reaches the bottom of the shirt. "I need to see you," he croaks. "Will you take it off for me, Chloe?"

I shiver at his question and reach for the fabric, pulling it over my head. His shirt falls and hair cascades around my shoulders.

Eyes take me in as hands move up my skin. "So fucking perfect."

Gavin's strong arms pull me closer until he's kissing my belly. Sweet kisses that drive me just as insane as his hungry kisses. The fact that I'm completely exposed for him releases a tremor throughout my entire body.

He must sense my nerves because he stands until he's towering above me, his gaze locked on mine. I don't dare look away. He pulls his own shirt over his head, revealing his masterpiece of a body, chiseled from the very best of God's makings. I trace the length of the scar on his shoulder with my fingers and then lean in, pressing my lips against it. His next breath is a shudder.

Abandoning the scar, I reach out and brush my fingertips across the length of his chest, memorizing every bit of skin. And then I move down to the V that dips below his waistline. I drag a finger across the edge, between the elastic and his skin, causing something to stir beneath the fabric.

"I've wanted this for so long," he says. "I don't want to take it slow, but I'm going to. For you." He presses his lips to mine. They taste like cinnamon and smoke from the campfire, a flavor I'm left craving after they leave my mouth and roam my neck. I take hold of the waistband of his shorts and slide them down until they fall to his feet.

A hiss seeps from his mouth as he pulls me to him, our naked bodies crashing together. "It's been a while for me, so this might go quickly," Gavin warns.

My cheeks flush. "Well, it's been forever for me, so I don't think I'll notice a difference."

Gavin freezes, his mouth on my neck. "How long is forever, exactly?'

"I meant it literally." I'm too afraid to see his reaction.

"You mean you haven't . . ."

I shake my head. "You read my journal."

Gavin pulls back, a look of shock registering across his face. "But that journal stops at the end of high school. What about the last four years of college?"

After everything, I assumed Gavin knew. I'm a virgin at twenty-two. I wasn't going to make a big deal of it, but that's what seems to be happening. *Is he put off?* Oh God. He's obviously experienced. And now I'm humiliated.

My eyes flee the scene first, but I can't seem to find my borrowed shirt fast enough.

"What are you doing?"

I snatch the cloth from the floor, wanting nothing more than to leave and bury myself in my own bed. "I should go."

"Chloe, stop." Gavin reaches for the shirt, but I tug it away. He fumes. "Stop running away from me." He finally gets a grip on the shirt and tosses it across the room, so I move to the closet, but Gavin gets there first and slams it shut. Before I make another move, he lifts me into his arms and wraps my legs around his waist. "Look at me," he pleads.

I do.

"I don't want you to leave." His eyes search mine. "I'm sorry I reacted like that." A hand caresses my cheek, and his breathing is almost as heavy as mine. "I'm glad you told me. I didn't think it was possible to want you more, but I do. And it gives me even more reason to go slow . . . if you'll let me be your first."

I sag with relief. "Oh, Gav." I swallow, mustering the strength for words. So far tonight, they've been hard to come by. "Not just my first. I want you to be my first, my last, my only."

And then the talking is over.

In one swift move, Gavin carries me to the bed and sets me down. He's slow, allowing his tongue to explore my mouth, giving and taking all at once. There's need behind every kiss, every touch. There's also a gentleness that transcends everything and speaks directly to my heart.

His roaming hands find a breast and knead it, triggering a ripple of sensations directly to my core. When his mouth leaves mine and lands on my nipple, I gasp. "So beautiful," he murmurs into my skin. He moves to my other breast like he wants to taste every bit of me. I grow dizzy, especially when he uses his free hand to explore the sensitive region between my thighs.

I'm shaking at his touch. Everything is warm and buzzing.

The heat of his body above mine. The needful breaths we take. The determination in his features. It's all too much. My hips react and he lifts his head, moving his mouth to my neck just as he slowly pushes one, then two fingers into me. I have to remind myself to breathe, especially when I feel the burn spread, tensing all my muscles.

"I can't wait to be inside of you," he whispers.

I'm deliriously aware of his words and it's too late to muffle my cries. The burn spirals through me and I'm not sure when it will stop. I'm praying it does soon because I'm a little afraid of just how good this feels. I'm shaking and gripping his shoulders so tightly that I'm certain my nails are doing some damage.

Before I can come back down to earth, Gavin positions himself so he's hovering over me, his palms pressed into the bed on either side of my head. He's concentrating on adjusting his knees and poising himself at my entrance. I'm caught off guard when he notices me staring and smiles softly. He dips his head to plant a soft kiss on my lips.

He's about to enter me when he freezes. "Shit." He jumps off the bed and hops to his nightstand where he retrieves a condom. I watch in amusement as he tears the plastic with his teeth and rolls the condom on before moving right back to where he was before. I wish I'd timed that. I'm certain he just broke a world record.

Gavin is breathing heavily above me when he focuses on my face. Then his mouth presses against mine, and he pushes into me slowly. The movement is unhurried, gentle, and seems to last forever until we're joined and can't possibly get any closer.

"Breathe, baby," he reminds me.

My first ragged inhale fights to take air into my constricted throat. He's patient as my breaths even out, allowing my body to eventually relax around him.

Once he starts moving, I take it all in. The impressive athleticism of his movements, the satisfied concentration on his face, and the natural rhythm our bodies create together. So perfect. Every now and then he'll lean down and kiss me. Or he'll gaze into my eyes. But with each look, each touch, each gesture, he reminds me how every moment between us matters.

Our pace is steady, but our appetites are increasing. He seems to be pushing further into me, but I don't know how that's possible. Our breathing quickens until we're standing at the edge of the cliff, holding hands, ready to jump together. I'm tensing against him as the build takes over my body, and I wonder how it will end. In pleasure or pain? Whatever the outcome, I think something within me is about to burst. And it does, in a wonderful explosion of warmth as the buzzing evaporates into my every fiber.

"Chloe," he moans. His lids press together as he shakes above me, then presses himself into me twice more before collapsing onto my stomach.

Somehow, with our eyes closed, in between gasping for air, his lips find mine. "That was . . . so worth the wait," he says with a sigh.

Gavin is gentle the entire night as we explore each other's bodies. He takes his time and pays close attention to my responses to ensure I'm enjoying myself. I think it's impossible to feel anything but joy when I'm being intimate with him.

I often imagined what sex would feel like—if it would hurt; if it would feel good; if it was overrated. All I know after tonight is that sex with Gavin Rhodes can only be as great as it is because of everything we've been through together. The wait was most definitely worth it.

When we finally drift off to sleep in each other's arms, I'm more certain than ever that I want Gavin Rhodes to be my first, my last, my only.

CHAPTER 40

RESERVATIONS

CHLOE

K isses trail from my belly to my neck, waking me from my deep sleep. I moan before opening my eyes, shifting in Gavin's comfortable bed just to feel my muscles respond the way I thought they might. Everything is beautifully sore.

"Good morning," he whispers in my ear. I sigh happily, somehow feeling both well rested and exhausted.

In a swift move, he pulls me on top of him so my belly rests on his. He pushes back my hair and peers up at me. "I was afraid to go to sleep last night. I've dreamt of being with you so many times, but those dreams are no comparison to last night."

It's impossible not to smile. "Are you saying I'm no longer your dream girl?"

He shakes his head. "You're every bit my reality, and that's so much better than dreaming."

I kiss him. I kiss him hard and don't stop kissing him until he's rolling me over and proving just how good our reality is together.

An hour later we've managed to fall asleep again, our bodies tangled together. I only know this because it's me that wakes up first and slips out of bed. Gavin's gorgeous body is sprawled out, and I take the opportunity to admire him before going to the bathroom.

I return to his still sleeping body, freshly showered and changed into a pair of his shorts and a t-shirt. I didn't notice it last night, but my journal sits on the nightstand by his bed. I pick it up and flip to a random page.

I start to read, smiling sadly at the mention of Gavin's art. I remember this entry. It was shortly after he found out about my secret relationship with Devon. I found him holed up in the tree-house, sketching more intensely than I'd ever seen him. I tried to sneak a peek, but he must have heard me because he flipped around and slammed his book shut. When he saw it was me behind him, he stood without a word and left. It is one of my worst memories. I let him leave, not knowing what to say or do to make anything right. To this day, I remember the look of pain in his expression and what that did to me. It told me there was no going back.

Gavin stirs and reaches out his hand, feeling the sheets for something. I set my journal down and slip back into bed, snuggling into his hold and kissing his chest. "Gav," I groan, kissing him again. "I'm hungry. And you still have guests here." I giggle quietly, embarrassed that up until this moment I'd completely forgotten about the party. He tightens his hold on me but doesn't open his eyes.

After a minute I slide from his grasp and walk downstairs to assess the damage. It's actually not bad. Gavin has a great set of friends. The clock in the living room reads eleven. A dozen or so people are still sleeping, but others are actually cleaning. I look around in amazement. There are guys taking bags of trash out the garage door, a couple people sweeping, and a girl mopping after them.

Monica breezes by and smiles at the sight of my dropped jaw. "Hey, sexy. It's late. Get much sleep last night?"

I try to bite back my grin, but with the way her amused face is perusing my body, I can't. "This is incredible. Everyone stayed to clean?" I change the subject.

She follows my eyes. "Last year Gavin threatened to shut the party down after his place got trashed. It's everyone's favorite party of the year, so that got their attention. This year all the plans were made online, and cleanup was part of the deal."

A set of arms wrap around me from behind and a nose lands in my hair. I laugh as Gavin sniffs my hair, then growls, "I wanted to shower with you." He kisses my head and nips at my ear. "Next time."

I'm certain I'm turning a deep shade of red as he walks off toward the kitchen. Monica laughs at me, and I roll my eyes. "How can I help?" I ask.

"It's pretty much done. I was just heading out."

"Your car is at my house. I'll walk you," I say as I try to remember where I put my sandals.

After saying our goodbyes, we head for the woods. Gavin said he'd call after everyone leaves, so that at least gives me time to get a few things done around the house and exchange his clothes for mine. Monica and I go for breakfast, and she leaves shortly after. I'm glad she doesn't pry for details about last night. What happened between Gavin and me was so much more than sex, and I don't think anyone but the two of us could understand that.

It's late in the afternoon when he finally calls. "Will you have dinner with me tonight?"

"Of course."

"Good, because I just made reservations. Meet me at the tree-house at seven thirty and we'll go together."

I'm not sure if I should question why he's not just picking me up in his truck. "Okay," I laugh.

"I can't wait to see you." The softness in his voice totally makes me melt.

I immediately search my closet for something to wear and start getting ready. I have a few hours, but I want to be prepared for whatever happens tonight. I choose a black strapless dress, and my stomach flips at the mystery ahead. Knowing Gavin, whatever we do, he'll make it special.

It's a little after seven thirty when I text him to tell him I'm on my way. The straps of my heels are secured between two fingers, while my flip-flops take me through the woods. The sky is darkening in color when I step into the small clearing where the treehouse sits.

My heart flutters rapidly in my chest when I see him standing there at the edge of the rail, a smile on his face. The entire treehouse is illuminated by strings of white lights that wrap the exterior.

"Gavin," I say in awe, "it's beautiful."

He bites his lip as he takes in my appearance. "You're beautiful."

I blush and take the last few steps to the ladder, where a single red rose sits on the bottom rung. Taking a deep breath to settle my rising emotions, I pick it up and climb the ladder to greet my handsome man.

He's waiting for me and immediately pulls me close. I slip my arms around his neck, then slide my lips across his, finally planting a soft kiss on his cheek. "Thank you for this."

Gavin can't stop smiling and neither can I. He pulls me inside where more lights cover every surface but his desk, which he's repurposed as a dinner table. It's covered in cloth and holding various pots of food. Whatever it is smells delicious. As he distributes the food, I just watch him, wondering how on earth it took so long for us to get here.

"Before I forget . . ." he says once we've finished dinner. He reaches under the cloth and into his desk. "I wanted to give this back to you."

My journal. I touch it but don't pick it up. "Thank you for trusting me," I say.

There's a flicker of something in his eyes. "I wasn't going to read it, but I'm glad I did. Reading those memories of yours reminded me of how perfect we are together. We were perfect back then too. If only we had just told each other what we felt . . ."

I place my hand on his. "Look at where we are. We're right where we should be, Gavin. No more secrets, no lies, no betrayals, no anger." I smile. "We get our second chance."

A look of panic crosses his face, but it's so fleeting I almost miss it. He pulls me onto his lap and places his head above my heart while he secures his arms around me as if he's afraid I might vanish. I think he's about to say something, but as time goes on and silence surrounds us, I realize with a heavy heart that whatever is on his mind is not something he's ready to divulge . . . and it seems to be slowly closing in on us.

Branch Seven

GISELLE

"Passion rebuilds the world for the youth. It makes all things alive and significant." ~ Ralph Waldo Emerson

CHAPTER 41

BAD WEATHER

CHLOE

Washington has a reputation for its constant cloud cover and endless number of drizzly days. Those of us who have lived here our entire lives are prepared for a little rain and snow when it comes our way. In fact, we make the most of it. We throw on our rain boots and jackets, stomp through puddles, and use the grime-covered snow piles as our sledding hills . . . anything to continue living life. And in life, every now and then, there are conditions that throw us off balance. We're hit by a hailstorm or snowed in on the freeway. Life isn't always predictable. But it's how we survive the bad weather that defines us.

It's Friday evening and Gavin is driving us to The Rock, our favorite pizza place in Tacoma. The memories of random hang-outs in this area hit me full force. It's a college and business district infused with history, art, and music. Back in high school, we'd come here often just to get away from our small town. We'd duck into the local coffee shop to listen to live jazz music or walk the bridge of the glass museum. We could spend hours hopping around a water fountain or walking through the college campus just to feel what it would be like to be a student there.

So far, our first week together has been close to perfect. We've worked out a great creative flow at the office while trying our best to keep things professional. I know I'm not the only one going crazy by the end of each day when we can finally be alone and smother each other with kisses.

Dinner together has become a regular occurrence. Some days we go out; some we stay in and cook. Our sleeping arrangements are the only disagreements we share. Gavin thinks we should be together every night, but I don't agree. Falling into a relationship with your best friend is tricky enough. Working with them—even more complicated. The moment we start sleeping over during the week, we're that much closer to moving in together. As much as I want that for our future, I'm not sure if I'm ready for it now.

As I stare across the table at Gavin, a half-eaten brick oven pepperoni pizza between us, I'm taken back to our high school years. One could drown in such memories by regretting how things should have played out back then. And yeah, maybe Gavin and I were slow to divulge our feelings to each other, but whatever this is between us now is meant to be just as it is.

"Did you ever consider attending Seattle U with us, or were you always planning to run away to Oregon?"

I smile. "I wasn't always planning on *running* away, but I'll admit that's what I was doing. With things so toxic between Devon and me, I didn't know what else to do."

"Were you ever going to tell us?"

"I was going to tell Devon the night of graduation before he went off the deep end. And you weren't talking to me, remember?" I smile since I'm trying to keep my response light. "I told you in the hospital . . . I know you couldn't hear me, but I spent hours telling you everything and anything to try to get you to wake up." I laugh, saddened by the memory.

"My dad mentioned you were there every day. And then one day . . . you just stopped coming. I tried to tell myself it was probably just too hard on you, but it still hurt like hell."

My throat tightens, but I force a nod. I've been conflicted about this story, whether I should tell him or not. He looks like he wants an explanation, so I take a deep breath and begin. "I've never told anyone this, but you deserve to know. I was there every day. My intention was to stay until you woke up. I had to know you were okay." I swallow my nerves. "But someone confronted me at the hospital. Told me they knew why Devon was angry that night. Said it was my fault and that they would make sure everyone knew I was to blame for his death."

Gavin's jaw drops and I can see anger and hurt on his face, but he lets me continue. "I don't know why I succumbed to the fear this person put in my mind, but I did. I turned back into that weak girl who got her head slammed into a locker back in seventh grade."

A tear slips from my eye but I wipe it away and continue. "I left the hospital, but I came back. No one knew, except maybe you." I smile. "I said goodbye to you. Told you I loved you and that you were my greatest friend. I desperately hoped that you heard me. You woke up the next day." My chest expands and collapses with relief. It feels so good to get the truth out. In the back of my mind, I've always wanted to believe that I had something to do with him waking up.

Throughout my story, Gavin's expression changed from angry to hurt to soft and loving. His Adam's apple bobs as if he's trying to suppress his emotions, and then he meets my eyes. "I heard you." I freeze. "At least I dreamt that I heard you. Maybe it was real."

"I'm sorry I wasn't there when you woke up, Gav."

He must hear my voice crack because suddenly he's out of his bench and sliding into mine. He cups my face, peering back at me with nothing but forgiveness. "Listen to me. Whatever happened, it's the past. I trust you with everything in me, Clover. You're my forever. My always. If it makes you feel better, I'm happy things turned out the way they did. As hard as it was to go through, I love my life now, especially now that you're in it."

Gavin's words are like CPR to my failing lungs. I press my lips to his, loving that I can do this without hesitation. He responds by pulling me in and deepening the kiss, using the tips of his thumbs to stroke my cheeks.

When the dizzying kiss is over, Gavin moves back to his side of the table with a grin.

"Anyway," I start with a laugh, ready to move back to our discussion. "OSU was a great school. I wasn't too into things at first, but I accomplished what every college student should."

"What's that?" he asks, smiling at my response before I say anything.

"I landed a great job." I tilt my head at him. "What are you smiling about?"

He shakes his head. "I've always loved your positive outlook. You may have been running from Devon, but you weren't running from life. That's the important thing. I'm proud of you."

I take another bite of pizza, rinse it down with a sip of Coke, and look at him. "What about you? You seem to have done well with college and finding work right away. You even bought your own house. You always were the level-headed one out of all of us, but your accomplishments are impressive."

He laughs. "Impressive, huh? That's what you call mortgage payments and getting hired contract by contract? BelleCurve may not have work for me after this event, and then what? I'll have to search for something else."

"You'll have no problem finding work."

"Is that right?"

"I have no doubt."

Gavin takes a sip of his water. "There's something I haven't told you."

An eyebrow raise is all I can give him as I try to assess his tone. I'm glad he can't see the way my stomach twists. "Well, since we're being honest. Let me have it."

"My comic, the one about the bullying and the treehouse . . ."

"Yes," I prod.

"I told you I reworked it during college. Well, after graduation I submitted it for publication and it got picked up by one of the big publishing houses. My signing bonus was significant. I was even able to pay off my house. That's partly why I do so much charity work, because I don't have to make a nine-to-five paycheck every week. After this contract with BelleCurve, I can take some time off if I want and I'll be fine."

"Gavin! That's amazing. Can I just go to the store and buy it?"

He nods. "Pretty much. Online, most of the big retailers. It's actually getting great recognition from schools too. I'm not always going to do the contract thing. Eventually, I want to focus solely on comic books—ones that raise awareness. Ones that make being a hero fun."

I tilt my head and smile. "'Make being a hero fun.' I love that! I'm going to use it in the event script. Thanks, Gav."

He winks and throws down a half-finished slice of pizza, wipes his hands, slides out of the booth, and stands. "Let's take a walk."

We cut through the university, hopping and dancing down the brick steps. Literally. Reggae music plays loudly from the campus speakers. Gavin twirls, dips, and then kisses me smack on the lips.

We laugh arm-in-arm along the 500-foot-long overpass that links to the Chihuly Bridge of Glass, a museum that helped revitalize the industrial wasteland that Tacoma once was. Bringing art and beauty into the city through unique glass displays was a mission most well accomplished. Now, the contemporary art museum is a local landmark. One Gavin and I frequented often back in high school.

The museum is closed at this hour, but the sights surrounding it are still beautiful. The blue Crystal Towers illuminate the bridge, hinting at the stunning glasswork inside. The standing wall leading to the museum, also known as the Venetian Pavilion, offers a unique floor-to-ceiling view of glass sculptures in window-lit cubes.

"This energy." I spread my arms out like wings by my side. "I remember this feeling. It's everywhere." Closing my eyes, I take a deep breath and spin, feeling lighter than air, enjoying the freedom of whatever has been keeping me prisoner for the past four years. I don't even care that clouds are rolling in and thunder is rumbling in the distance.

Laughing, Gavin catches me in mid-twirl. "C'mon, Chlo. There's a coffee with your name on it at the Spar. Let's go."

I shriek with glee and throw my arms around Gavin's neck. "We're going to the Spar?"

He laughs. "It's getting late, but yes. There's a band playing rock covers tonight."

The Spar is an old brick saloon that sits off Ruston Way and dates back to 1792. It's full of history, both for the city and for me. We cuddle up next to each other in the back of the room, listening to music and drinking coffee. An hour into it I'm laughing at the crowd as everyone sings along to the lyrics. Gavin, who stands beside me, gives me an amused look.

"What?"

He just shakes his head and leans in, pressing his lips to mine. He starts to pull away, but then in what seems to be a last-second decision, he deepens the kiss and places the tips of his fingers on my knees. The moment they start to slide up my thighs there's a crack of thunder outside and he freezes. When he pulls away, my heart is racing. "We should get out of here."

I nod vigorously, going from coffee buzz to Gavin buzz just like that because I know the thunder was not the reason for our escape.

We arrive at Gavin's house in less than thirty minutes. He leans back in his seat with his head facing me. "Is this okay?" he asks, referring to his house. "I missed having you in my bed. I get why you had to be home, but I'm hoping you'll stay with me tonight. And maybe tomorrow."

His hopeful expression brings a smile to my lips. "I want to be with you too, Gav. Let's go inside."

Without hesitation, Gavin is out the door and over to my side of the truck. He helps me out and holds my hand all the way to the front door. His mouth is on mine before the front door has even shut. I hear it slam and click behind us as Gavin lifts me into his arms and carries me to the nearest surface. I giggle as he sets me on the dining table and climbs on after me.

"This week has been torture," he moans, kissing my neck and fumbling around for the button of my shorts. I help him with his shirt so I can paint the canvas of his chest with my fingers while he removes my shorts and panties.

"I want to taste you," he says, his mouth so close.

I lift my hips, telling him it's okay, and he doesn't hold back. I'm immediately writhing in pleasure. He grips my thighs, pressing into them while his mouth pushes down on me. I use both hands to grab for his hair while shifting my hips to control the intensity.

It's too much. Gavin is on a mission to kill me. I squeeze my eyes shut as the build-up burns and then spreads like a rush of wildfire. I'm crying out at my climax and falling over the edge quickly. Luckily, Gavin's right there to catch me.

We don't waste another second before removing the rest of each other's clothes. He reaches for the back pocket of his jeans and rolls on a condom before pushing inside me, this time eagerly. I believe him when he says this week has been torture. I can feel how much he missed me with each rock of his body. The sweat dripping from his face is sexy as hell, too. I bite into his arm, causing him to grunt, and the intensity spirals through us, sending us soaring.

We're wrapped in each other's sweaty arms, unmoving and happily overexerted.

Lightning strikes near the woods with a deafening crack, causing us to jump and then laugh.

"Looks like a storm is headed our way," Gavin says, moving off the table and toward the sliding doors.

I practically have to pry my eyes from Gavin's naked body to follow his gaze. "Looks like it."

Chapter 42

Confessions

Chloe

Sandwiches and snacks are packed tightly in the small cooler, but I leave it on the ground as I climb the tree-house steps. Light music is playing in the background, but otherwise it's quiet. Gavin's back is to me, and I doubt he heard me approaching. For a moment I peek in at him from the entrance just like I used to, admiring his arm as it glides across his sketchpad with gentle strokes.

"Hey, hot stuff," I say as I approach him from behind.

He swivels in his chair. "Hey back." His eyes sweep over me and his smile grows. "Have I ever told you that I think you're my muse?"

I shake my head and take a seat on his lap. "If I was really your muse, wouldn't you know for sure and not just *think* I was your muse?" I wrap my arms around his neck and lean in to kiss his cheek.

"How else do you explain how fast I'm drawing? I've never created this quickly before." He nods to the desk and I turn to see the scattered artwork all over his space. There have to be dozens of drawings. I pick up one, and gasp.

"Gav." His name is just a whisper as I look at the sketch in my hands, then replace it with another, and another. I work my way through every new drawing until I'm holding the final one. "These are so good." I shake my head. "I don't think *I'm* your muse. But this girl—" I hand him the sketch in my hand featuring a young, redheaded girl with pigtails and a ninja suit on. I'm trying to ignore the pounding in my chest. I've never seen her before, but it's as if I know her somehow. She's in almost every one of the drawings. "She just might be your muse. Who is she?"

Gavin barely looks at the sketch I've handed him before he tosses it on the table and brushes the hair from my neck and kisses it. I sigh as pleasure spreads through me.

"One of the Heroes and Legends' guests," he grunts, still buried in my neck. "Let's eat."

I giggle and pull back. "You know, I brought an actual lunch. My neck is going to fall off if you keep doing that to me."

He chuckles and stands, taking me with him. "What did you make me?"

Grinning, I pull him toward the ladder. "Come find out."

"You know I'd follow you anywhere, right?"

The look I throw him over my shoulder is an attempt at flirtation, but when I see his face wearing complete and utter honesty, my cheeks grow warm and my smile softens.

We sit on the blanket beneath our tree and begin sorting through food. Gavin moans in exaggerated delight as I pull out sandwiches, cookies, and a platter of vegetables and fruit. I toss him a bottle of water and give him his sandwich options while he provides a drum roll. "Peanut butter and jelly, tuna melt, or . . ." I raise my brows for dramatic effect as he drums louder waiting for the final choice. "Roast beef on rye."

He snatches the roast beef container from my hand and gives me a knowing smirk. "I haven't had a roast beef on rye in years."

"I used to make these for you guys every weekend." I chuckle. "My mom would get pissed every time we ran out of roast beef."

"Snapple!" Gavin picks one up excitedly, exchanging it with his water. "You used to bring us six packs of Snapple all the time. Devon tried to get dad to install a fridge."

I laugh. "I remember that. Your dad thought you wanted to sneak beers in here. He started doing random treehouse checks. I don't think he liked that I was a regular visitor. As we got older, he started eyeing me a bit more suspiciously."

Gavin shakes his head. "My dad loved you. But he definitely thought something was bound to happen. When he found out you and Devon were together he tried to ban you from the treehouse."

"What?" I shriek. "You guys never told me that!"

Gavin shrugs, chewing a mouthful of his sandwich. He moans and mumbles how delicious it is. "Devon wasn't about to tell you because he knew you'd stay away. His thoughts were not totally pure when he'd bring girls back here, including you."

I shudder as I remember seeing what he was doing with Stacy when I walked in on them. "No sex in the treehouse," I say dryly.

Gavin narrows his eyes. "You know, now that we've rebuilt the thing and no one is monitoring our treehouse activities, we could probably amend that rule. I know you've thought about it."

My cheeks flood with blood. He's recalling a memory from my journal. "I may have had a thought or two." I clear my throat, trying to get my heart rate to slow. "But I kind of like the no sex in the treehouse rule."

Gavin is visibly disappointed. "Really?"

"Yeah. This place reminds me how innocent it all once was between the three of us. When all that mattered was how invincible we could make ourselves when we were together. And that rule meant a lot to me."

He smiles softly. "The first time I knew I had feelings for you was the night I finished *Up in the Treehouse*. The original. I swore I would never be done with that thing." He laughs. "We were fifteen and I was already crushing on you like crazy. But that night, I remember looking over and you had dozed off on the floor. You stayed with me all night. You had no reason to still be there, but you were."

"I wanted to be there when you finished your first masterpiece." Flutters take off in my stomach as I think back on that night. "I just liked being with you, Gav. We didn't have to be doing anything at all for me to enjoy our time together. It's the same today."

"I think I realized the same thing that day. Something about it was special. I thought about kissing you then, and from that point on, you can pretty much guess that kissing you was all I wanted to do."

"So much time has passed, yet so much remains the same. Our hobbies have turned into careers, but that's the only difference. We still work well together." I wink.

A calm washes over him, visible from the drop in his shoulders and serene look on his face. He leans against the tree and pulls me toward him until my back rests on his stomach.

"If you could go back in time and do anything over, what would it be?" I ask.

He's silent for a moment, thinking about my question. "I would have kissed you at Comic Mania, or on the hike. I wouldn't have been such a chicken shit with my feelings. Such a waste of time."

I scrunch my face as I think back. "Hike?"

"We went on a hike. Devon was being a complete jackass that day because we were too slow. Remember? He made it to the top of the mountain first and got sick of waiting for us, so he trekked back down by himself."

My heart speeds up. "You were only going slow for me, and I was determined to make it to the top."

He squeezes me a little tighter. "Yep. We made it and you were so happy. I remember hugging you and not wanting to let go. You were staring out at the horizon, telling me how it was the most beautiful thing you'd ever seen, and I was staring at you thinking the exact same thing. The urge to make you mine that day was beyond anything I'd ever felt."

"I can't believe I didn't write about that day. I was waiting for you to kiss me, but at the same time I was terrified. That's why I didn't look up right away. And when I did—"

"Devon's scream was so loud." We burst into laughter. "That bear shit he stepped in was no joke."

"We always warned him to stay on the path. He was so stubborn." I smile, remembering how much I learned to love Devon's stubborn side. He experienced so much more than the average person because he refused to conform in any way.

"Wasn't that the night you had me try on my first superhero outfit?"

Gavin groans, and it takes me a moment to realize it's because he's turned on. "Now that was my favorite thing ever. Sketching you while you posed for me in those costumes—you had no clue what you did to me."

"Now that I think about it," I say with amusement, "each outfit seemed to get smaller."

Gavin is silent, and I know it's a form of admission.

"I can't believe you!" I swivel to face him. It takes a great deal of effort to hold back the laughter. "I didn't want to disappoint you. You made me think it was the only way you could get inspired. You took advantage of me. I just wanted to help."

"Clover." He pulls me in and kisses my head. "You could have never disappointed me."

"I was so gullible. I wore every single one of those damn things, and there you were, using me for selfish means."

He chuckles and shakes his head. "You didn't wear all of them. Trust me, I remember."

"Oh my God. What outfit was that, with the silicone? It wouldn't even fit over my boobs!"

Gavin's gaze drops below my neck. He catches himself and looks up. "Please don't talk about Witchblade unless you're ready for me to drag you into that treehouse, caveman style."

I swallow. I'm changing the subject.

"Did you ever do anything with those sketches?"

"No way. My initial intention was to share them, but once

they were on paper . . . I didn't want anyone seeing those but me. It was great practice, though."

I laugh as I realize Gavin's zoned out thinking about the memory. I lean forward to put the lids on the food containers, letting him have his moment.

"Where are you going?" he asks, taking the blanket from my hand.

"Settle down there, Batman. I was going to head back and let you work."

Gavin peers up at the treehouse and then back at me. "Okay. I'll only be another hour or so."

I kiss him on the lips and smile. "I'll be waiting."

CHAPTER 43

COSTUMES

CHLOE

The moment I get back to the house, I start tearing through his closet, curious to see if he kept my old costumes. I find a garment bag in the corner and my heart rate spikes, knowing I've just hit the jackpot. Every single one of my costumes is here. I sort through them until I find *the one*.

I'm giddy as I shower, performing the longest primping routine I've ever endured. My legs are as smooth as silk. My hair is blow-dried and styled in messy waves. I apply moisturizer everywhere, wanting to glisten at every odd angle. I pluck, I pat, I pucker . . . all until I've groomed myself to my satisfaction. Gavin is going to lose his mind.

When I hear a door slam, I finish tugging the outfit around to cover all the important areas. Most of the costume is made of silicone, decorated with a veiny layer of black and metallic silver texture. It teases in just the right places and reveals every dip and bump of my curves. Witchblade seems to be Gavin's weakness. Probably because she's the most sexed up of all the comic book characters. The one-piece consists of two full-length sleeves, like a jacket but with little in the front. Two much-too-small cups hold up my breasts, and a thin cloth of a bikini bottom covers me below. I'm shocked I'm not falling out of the thing.

"Chloe?" Gavin says as he tries the closet door, but I've locked it. I don't want him to get a sneak peek.

"Be right out. Wait for me there." I smile at myself in the mirror and open the door to find Gavin taking a seat on his bed.

When he looks up, his jaw falls and his eyes scan my body quickly, then slowly, greedily and with resolve. "What are you trying to do to me?" His hand moves to his heart, but he doesn't stop examining every inch of my attire.

I glide toward him at a catlike pace, hoping to ingrain this moment in his memory. "You're right. You never got to see me in this one. Do you like it?"

He finally meets my stare. The desire in his expression darkens and I'm suddenly the leading lady of his favorite fantasy. He nods.

"Well"—I place my hands at my hips—"aren't you going to sketch me?" I twirl slowly, allowing him to take in the entire outfit. Before I'm even facing him again he's moving toward me, then grabbing me by the hips and pulling me against his hard body. My heart is trying to catch up to his eagerness as we fall onto the bed.

"I've done all the practice sketches I can handle." His hands are all over me, exploring the details of my exposed skin until breathing becomes the hardest thing ever. I'm frantically trying to remember how to inhale and exhale. He drags his lips down my neck and along the line of fabric until he's teetering near my breast.

There's not much foreplay after he latches onto my skin with his mouth. He's savoring me as he always does, but his hands are roaming other places, confusing all my sensations. Tying them in knots until it's all a beautiful, energetic mess.

"Chloe," he pants as he slides off my costume, "you're about to see a different side of me." The heat of his words shoots straight to my center, and then he's inside me, making good on his promise. I press my hands against the headboard to keep myself from flying as he loses himself in his fantasies. In me.

Gavin was right. This is definitely a side of him I've never seen before. It's primal in the sexiest way I could have imagined. Still, I can tell he wants to take care of me. I hear it in the warning he gives me right before he reaches his climax. I'm right there with him, calling out his name.

He doesn't roll over immediately after. Instead, he hovers over me, propped up with his elbows, relieving me from the full weight of him as he kisses my neck. "You've seriously ruined me for anyone else, you know that?"

I smile and kiss his nose sweetly. All I know is that I'm glad I didn't wear this costume when I was seventeen.

Playing house with Gavin is fun. It's Saturday night and I'm cooking pesto chicken and squash. My favorite. The entire house smells like heaven, and Gavin's MP3 player is shuffling through songs in the background. Gavin said he had to go out to the garage to work on something, but when he doesn't reappear by the time I'm ready to pop the bread in the oven, I go looking for him. He's not in the garage anymore, so I take the stairs two steps at a time and find the double doors of his room cracked open.

Just as I place my hand on it to push, I freeze. He's talking to someone, which shouldn't be a big deal, but he's whispering, and it *feels* like a big deal. I back up and then I pause, changing my mind. Pressing my ear against the door, I wait. I just want to hear him say something so the quickly forming knot can unravel in my chest.

"I can't talk right now, just—just tell Giselle I love her, okay?"

Just. Tell. Giselle. I. Love. Her.

What.

The.

Hell.

I start to reel back, the sucker punch to my gut too much for me to handle, but the optimist in me wants to hear more. Needs to hear more. Maybe there's something I don't understand.

Giselle. I knew that name meant something when I heard it spoken by others. I knew Gavin had loved her. At least that's what Phoebe said. She said she's the only girl Gavin has ever loved.

I thought he loved me.

We haven't come out and said those words, but isn't that what this is? We haven't gone through a decade of torture and heartache for things to end like this. Because of Giselle.

"Yeah. Tomorrow would be better. Call me when you're with her and we'll video chat. I miss those dimples."

That's all I hear before I flee downstairs to the kitchen. I'm shaking as I try to finish cooking dinner.

I should leave. I should confront him. I should . . .

No. I shouldn't have to do anything. It's Gavin who needs to be honest. What the hell is going on?

I'm so close to tears, but my anger is keeping them at bay. I shakily pour myself a glass of wine in hope of calming my nerves when I feel his arms snake around my waist. I stiffen. "Dinner smells great. How's my girl?"

My girl. How can he call me that when he misses someone else's dimples? *I don't have dimples.* I frown. This just doesn't add up. Gavin has done nothing but fight his feelings for me since I've been back. He wanted to spend the weekend with me . . .

"Whoa," Gavin says, grabbing the wine bottle from my hands just before I overpour. "You okay there, Clover?"

Don't call me that.

I bend over and sip from the top of the glass without saying a word and then slip from his grasp to check on the chicken. There's silence as Gavin senses something is wrong. I don't care. I can't pretend right now, but I can't bring myself to leave either.

I'm still hoping that whatever is going on isn't about to break my heart.

"Hey, Chloe," he says from where I left him. I turn, trying not to lock eyes with him, but of course I do. It's Gavin. "You okay?"

"Yeah, just feeling a little funny. Do you want to put the bread in while I finish the pasta?"

I don't believe you, say his eyes. He moves toward me, takes the wooden spoon from my hands, and kisses my forehead. "Let me take over. It's been a long day. Maybe you just need to rest."

No. I need you to be honest with me.

I take a few steps to leave the kitchen before I think better of it and turn to face him. His back is now to me when I speak. "Gav, we've spent the last six weeks playing cat and mouse because of secrets and misunderstandings." He throws me a surprised look over his shoulder but doesn't move as I continue. "I hope you know that giving you my journal wasn't just me getting some stuff off my chest. It was me showing you that I trusted you. One day I hope you can trust me just the same."

He starts to open his mouth and then shuts it immediately. His brow furrows as if he's trying to make sense of something. I walk toward him this time until I'm right under his chin. His arms wrap around me naturally.

Like I'm made for him.

I'm not losing hope that I am.

I stare into his eyes—eyes that are now swimming with contemplation and concern. "Something is going on in there." I run my hands through his hair, gently scratching his scalp. "It's okay if you can't talk about it right now, but don't leave me standing in the dark for too long."

His jaw moves as he breathes in through his nose, and I know he's grinding his teeth again. "There's something—but, Chloe . . ."

I shake my head. "Only when you're ready to tell me."

His forehead drops to mine, lids pressed closed and hands gripping my waist. "I don't want to lose you."

The tears that have been pooling slowly begin to fall. "I wish I could promise that you won't, but I have no clue what's going on. All I know is it's big enough for you to keep it from me, and that's significant."

Neither of us speaks at dinner. I barely touch the food on my plate. I manage to drink four glasses of wine, though. Gavin drinks none. He's showering as I climb into bed with one of his shirts on. That's all I've worn to bed since the first time I slept at his house. I love that there's a piece of him with me throughout the night, even when he's not there.

I'm snuggled into my pillow when he emerges. I hear him, but I don't look up. I can't. He looks and smells the best right after he showers. I usually want to devour him. Hell, I still do.

Gavin lifts the covers and slides into bed, immediately moving to my side to wrap his arms around me. He's naked. His hands are slipping under my shirt and his mouth is on my neck. I should push him away. I shouldn't want this right now. But I do.

He leans me up slightly to remove my shirt and tosses it far behind him, as if he's going for another world record.

He's kissing me now. I'm kissing him back. It's as if our mouths are saying goodbye. Everything is happening in slow motion, and my heart is beating so fiercely within the confines of my ribs that I think they might break. When he finally enters me, I'm quivering with anticipation, expecting our destruction to follow.

Gavin takes his time. Every movement is gentle and thoughtful, even sad, because now I'm wondering if this is it. Maybe this is goodbye. Maybe whatever he's hiding will define our entire relationship. Maybe it's too big for the both of us.

I put my focus back on Gavin and the attention he pays to sending us both over the edge. The emotions are coming on strong now, and while I can't hold back, Gavin is right there catching my tears with his kisses.

I don't know what time we finally fall asleep, but I know that I don't ever want to wake up if this really is the end of Gavin and Chloe.

Chapter 44

Celebration

Chloe

If I thought the week it took Gavin to read my journal was like hell, I obviously didn't know the pain of this week was coming. It's definitely worse to be just inches from the man you love and feel as if you can't touch or talk to him without breaking some undefined wall of silence.

We haven't talked about Saturday night at all. The morning after we made love for what felt like the last time, I went home to give Gavin space. He didn't object. The only problem is that Sunday's silence turned into a three-day period where Gavin did his disappearing act again.

He's in the office today for our meeting with the executives, and he's sitting right beside me because it was the only seat left when he walked in the door. Sharlene shot him her famous death stare, but he was too focused on the empty chair to notice. He's deliberately avoiding me.

Charles is at the front of the room explaining a licensing opportunity. Gavin's drawings attracted attention from our main sponsor, a major comic book publisher. They want to purchase the entire collection of comic sketches as well as the event script. Their big plan is to distribute the event as a template for others to use to help raise awareness for anti-bullying.

This is huge for the company, and for Gavin especially. Not only does the publisher want to purchase all of his work, there's even discussion about hiring him on to elaborate on what he's already created.

I turn to see if he's at all excited for the exposure. He's definitely listening, but there's something about his appearance that seems off. He's smiling with gratitude but doesn't seem as ecstatic over the news as he should be.

"We should hear back on Friday," Sharlene says. "Let's keep our fingers crossed and plan to celebrate then."

The executives walk out and there's a round of chatter focused on Gavin's work, which is now spread across the walls. Only a few of us have seen his latest designs, so there's a flurry of conversation and excitement.

Gavin and I are the only ones that remain seated. I turn to him again. "Congrats, Gav, this is huge."

He looks at me, and my heart explodes. It's there in his eyes. Love for me. There's a cloud hovering over him, but I'm not too dense to know Gavin is torn up inside from whatever this secret is. His hand barely touches my leg under the table, but I feel it as if he's touching my entire body.

When he leans in closer, I think he's going to thank me. But he doesn't. "Friday night," he says, "will you come over? I have something I need to tell you."

"Okay," I respond immediately. I'm relieved, happy, anxious —but more than anything, I'm scared.

The moment I get home from work, I do the math and figure it's ten o'clock in New York. Jazz will still be awake, and we haven't talked much beyond the occasional text message since she left. She was the first to text me after the night at the drive-in. Phoebe's mouth is too big for her small body. I wanted to be the one to tell

Jazz everything . . . once I knew *what* everything was. I've only given her bits and pieces of the happenings between Gavin and me over text message. I was saving the juicier stuff for when we could finally talk. Now is a better time than any.

"Hey, Chlo!" Jazz answers excitedly.

"You answered!"

She groans. "This time difference blows. Every time I call you you're at work. I'm glad you called now, though. I have so much to tell you."

"Me too. You first."

Jazz jumps right into her days in New York. She and Marco are definitely taking that city by storm, as they should. I'm envious of the constant activity and entertainment at every turn. It sounds like fun, but it's not something I could do daily.

"Don't tell me you guys are moving there," I groan. That's the last thing I need. I'd be happy for my friends if that's really what they want, but I miss Jazz.

Jazz lets out a breath. "No way. Marco and I had a huge fight about it the other day. He thinks they'll offer him a job here and it would be a great opportunity, but I can't deal with a tiny box of apartment and sirens for the rest of my life. Ugh, Chloe, it's a constant circus here. I'm going out of my mind."

I laugh because up until now I thought she was in love with the place. "Hopefully you can talk some sense into that man of yours. Are you even going to have clients when you come back?"

Jazz is a massage therapist, or as she calls it, the Rub-Down Expert. I have to say, I've received the rub-down, and she's earned the title.

"I'm sure I've lost some, but I don't want to talk about that. How have things been going with you and Gavin boy? Please tell me you've chosen less public places to explore your *interest* in each other."

I groan. "There have been . . . developments."

"Tell me," she demands.

"We're kind of together."

"What?" she screams. "Together as in how? Like, now, in the same room? Or like, a couple?"

I cringe. This is harder than I thought it would be. "A couple. But I said 'kind of' because some things have been going on."

"Holy shit. Chloe Rivers, have you had *sex*?"

She's practically screaming and I want to hide in a corner even though I'm alone in my own house. Instead, I curl up on the couch and nod instead of answering.

"You're nodding, aren't you?"

I laugh. "Yes."

"Oh my God. Chloe, I don't know what to say. I want to know all about it."

"I'm not telling you the details of that."

"Okay, then tell me what the drama is. What's going on?" Her excitement dissolves into something else. Concern, maybe. "Wait, so you've met her?"

There's a lurch in my chest. "Her?" I whisper.

"Giselle."

I'm silent for a moment as I try to make sense of how Jazz knows Giselle and whether I should just ask her what the hell is going on. "I haven't met her. Gavin hasn't told me about her. That's the problem. I heard him on the phone last weekend, talking about missing her . . ." I get choked up and pause to take a deep breath. "You knew about her, Jazz?"

"Well, yeah. Everyone knows about Giselle. Chloe, do you know who she is?"

"No. He's telling me on Friday. At least, I think he's telling me about her. Jazz, I don't know."

There's silence on the other end now, and I think Jazz is wondering if she should spill the beans. She's my best friend; of course she wants to tell me. She probably never said anything before because I made her swear to never talk about Gavin.

"Jazz, I know this could be the end of my relationship with him. As much as I just want you to tell me, I want to respect

Gavin. He wants to tell me on Friday, so I'll find out then. Please, just tell me it's not bad."

She's silent again.

"Okay, don't say anything at all."

My heart is already breaking.

"It's not bad, Chloe. It's just—it's just going to be a shock, and you two definitely have some big discussions ahead of you. I'm so sorry I'm not there right now. I should have waited for you to mention her. Gavin swore us to—shit—I'm sorry."

I swipe a tear from my cheek, wishing Jazz were here with a bag full of Pop-Tarts and Funyuns to accompany her swear-filled apology. I don't have the energy to be upset at her, and she has the magical ability to make me laugh even in my worst moments.

"Look, call me this weekend and we'll talk. And I'll talk to Marco again about when we're coming home. The wedding is in a few months, so it's not like we can just pick up and move here right now anyway."

When I get off the phone with Jazz, I notice I have a new text message. My entire body is on alert when I see Gavin's name.

Gavin: Go to your door.

After a few deep breaths, I take small steps to my door and pull it open. Gavin's not there, which immediately fills me with disappointment. Instead, on the landing of the porch stairs there's a single red rose and a piece of paper. I reach for it, looking around to see if there's any trace of him.

The paper burns a hole through my fingers as I step back inside and set the rose on the kitchen counter.

Chloe,

I'm so sorry for the past few days, but thank you for giving me this time. I realize none of this is fair to you, and I'm a hypocrite for keeping secrets. Just know that since Sunday morning, all I've done is think of you and how I can possibly tell you what I need to without hurting you. I meant what I said the other day. I don't want to lose you. This rose can't possibly make anything better, but it's important that you know how crazy I am about you. Not having you in my life is the worst fate I could possibly imagine.

It's Friday morning and I'm a complete wreck. I've changed my outfit at least ten times, and now I'm redoing my hair. I can't decide which style Gavin would like better: straight hair or a ponytail. When I realize how late I'll be, I leave it up and grab my purse. Work isn't what has my nerves zinging back and forth like a pinball machine; it's the fact that tonight is the big reveal.

"Chloe," Monica hisses as soon as I walk in, "everyone's already in the conference room."

Shit.

I try to sneak in, but everyone's focus snaps to me the moment they hear the door. It's like they were waiting for me. *Double shit.* Certain my face is a perfect apple red, I sink into the first chair I see and force a smile at a pissed off Sharlene. "Sorry," I say it to her, but loud enough for everyone to hear.

"No sweat, Chloe. We were just about to get started." Sandra is beaming at me from the front of the room. Immediately, I feel a little bit better.

Then my eyes find Gavin, and the relief I just felt is refilled with an ache. This is about to be the longest day of my life.

And it is.

We find out that the sponsor is not only contributing a significant amount of money to the event series and the charity itself, but they have purchased the entire collection of comic sketches and the event script.

The executives take the entire project team out to dinner and then to an early happy hour. Not an ounce of work was done at the office today because everyone was too busy celebrating the success of all our hard work. Monica gets to participate too since she's also contributed a substantial amount of time to the event.

She's doing her thing, trying to get me to take a shot, but I refuse. For the first time, Gavin is the one drinking a little too much, so I approach him and reach for the front pockets of his jeans. His eyes are burning into mine as he lets me feel my way around. I smile coyly and hold up his keys. "I'm driving tonight."

He smiles back.

I think I'm floating. *God, I've missed that smile.*

When he presses his lips to mine, I'm totally caught off guard, but I've missed these lips so much. I'm melting into his arms. Our coworkers are cheering loudly around us. Apparently, we're putting on a show. If they didn't know we were a couple before, they do now. Except Gavin seems to think we won't be a couple much longer.

Something happens to me in the few moments when Gavin's lips are on mine.

I change my mind. I don't want to hear Gavin's secret. Not tonight, anyway.

It's close to ten when I finally drag him out of the bar. It's not that he wanted to stay, but he was the man of the event. No one can say for sure how Gavin's career will take off from this, but we all know it's momentous.

Gavin finds a station on the radio and leans back in his seat. I can feel his gaze on me, and it doesn't seem like he has any intention of pulling away. "You're so beautiful, Clover."

My chest tightens.

"You should drive me around more often. I get to look at you and you can't do a damn thing about it."

I know he's drunk, but I smile anyway.

"I've missed you."

"I've missed you too, Gav." *So much.*

It's silent the rest of the way to Gavin's house. I much prefer staying with him. I don't know why. Probably because his house feels like *ours*, but I would never admit that to him. He manages to get to the door and unlock it without my help. The ride home probably helped him sober up a bit. Now we're standing awkwardly in the doorway.

"Chloe, as much time as I've had to think this week, I don't know where to start."

I shake my head and wrap my arms around his waist. "Let's not do this tonight. Tonight should be about celebrating. Give me one more night with you."

He brushes my cheek with the back of his hand and nods. "Okay."

We take separate showers and climb into bed, immediately wrapping our arms around each other. "Chlo," Gavin says in my ear.

"Hmm," is all I can muster in reply.

"I love you."

Those three words. The words alone make me want to rip his boxer briefs off and pounce on him. But the way he says them—as if there's no hope for us—crushes me.

"I love you too, Gav."

He holds me tighter, but he doesn't say another word. We drift off to sleep like that, clinging to each other like our lives depend on it.

CHAPTER 45

TIME

CHLOE

Time ticks on whether we like it or not. Time gives us the power to heal, but it also creates distance. That distance gives us the freedom to make new choices. Better choices. It gives us an opportunity to reflect on what we've lost along the way and whether it was worth it at all. I've come to realize that distance is not an obstacle when it comes to love; it's a bridge to something better. Something significant.

Time is what I give Gavin on Saturday morning while he sleeps off his hangover. At least I think he has a hangover. I've never seen him drink so much before, but he deserved his night of fun. This morning brings the much-anticipated conversation. Or maybe confession is a better word. I don't know what to expect.

Instead of lying in bed and waiting for Gavin to wake up, I go downstairs and make breakfast. We might as well eat a decent meal before my stomach decides to go on strike. I can't imagine wanting to eat ever again if this is really the end.

A light knock comes from the front door as I'm pouring a glass of milk. I take a quick chug before rushing to see who's there, opening the door with no expectations.

My mouth goes slack. My heart starts pounding. My first instinct is to slam the door, but I'm paralyzed with shock.

"Stacy?"

She looks the same, but different. Her red hair is brighter, and there's a certain glow about her. She's wearing a sleeveless top, and I can see that she's been somewhere getting sun. After I've done a full sweep of her body, my eyes land on hers. She looks surprised to see me, but not as shocked as I am to see her.

"Chloe. Hi. I wasn't expecting to see you again like this."

What? Why would you be expecting to see me at all?

"What are you doing here?" I can't help it. All of the rage from junior high and high school blows through me like a gust of wind. My defenses fly up and I want to completely unleash on her.

"We're here to see Gavin." She smiles as if this is the most normal thing in the world, and that's when I register she's not alone. A young girl about three years old stands beside her, wearing the same color hair and the same bright blue eyes. Her little eyes are trying to see past me into the house.

That face. I've seen that face before. She's the girl in Gavin's new sketches.

You're Giselle.

"Chloe?" Gavin's voice echoes down the stairs.

Then the footsteps stop. "Stacy." He sounds like he's been punched and that was the last ounce of air left in his body.

I look up to see Stacy's horrified expression. She realizes something is wrong. She knows about me, but I don't know about her, and Gavin wasn't expecting this.

I glance back at the little girl, who is now shoving her way past my legs to get to Gavin.

"Daddy!" she screams and jumps into his arms.

And then, for the first time in my twenty-two years, my knees give out and I faint.

He has a daughter. With Stacy Berringer. His daughter's name is Giselle. Giselle is the same girl from the new sketches he's been working on in the treehouse.

Gavin and Stacy.

Gavin and Giselle.

Gavin, Stacy, and Giselle.

Those are my first thoughts when I come to. My next thoughts have everything to do with the pounding in my head and aching in my body with every movement I try to make. Once I'm able to pry my eyelids open, I see a blinding white light from the ceiling. I squint with pain until Gavin moves to block the light. I glare at him.

"Chloe, you're awake." He looks relieved and calls out over his shoulder. "She's awake."

"It says to keep her down until she's breathing normally and then slowly help her up. But watch her in case she faints again." That's Stacy's voice.

Why is Stacy trying to help me?

"You fainted, Chloe. Don't stand up, okay? Just stay here until you feel better."

The concern in his tone should soften me. But I'm angry. I'm hurt. I'm everything but soft.

"Are you okay?" A little voice worms its way next to me. Now, the concern on Giselle's face might make me a *little* soft. But just a little. Nothing can erase what I just learned.

"Sweetie," Gavin says, gently guiding her away, "we need to give Chloe some space. She'll be okay." It hurts to watch the father-daughter exchange. It's beautiful too.

I struggle to prop myself up. Gavin's right back by my side, helping me sit up. He sits with me and holds my hand. "Babe, are you okay? You were out for less than a minute, but we were freaking out."

I look at him and then over at Stacy, who's watching us calmly. She looks different. Happy. Relaxed. Nothing about her presence screams "bully" like it used to. In fact, if I hadn't just fainted I would have sworn that she'd been smiling at me when I opened the front door.

"Giselle," Stacy says, "say bye to Daddy and Chloe. We'll be back tomorrow."

"No, I want to stay with Daddy." Giselle looks like she's about to burst into tears.

Gavin goes to her and picks her up. He takes her into the other room, and all I can think is that I'm the reason Giselle and Stacy are leaving so soon. It doesn't feel right.

"She can stay," I say to Stacy. "I should be going home anyway."

Stacy shakes her head. "Oh no, we only stopped by to say hi to Gavin. We've been away all summer, and she was dying to see him the minute we got off the plane. We're going to my sister's tonight, and then Gavin will have her for the week . . ." She trails off, and I think it's because she's still not sure how much I know about all of this. "I'm sorry we dropped by unannounced. I wasn't expecting . . . I knew you two were together. I just didn't think you'd be here."

Is Stacy Berringer blushing?

Giselle comes running out from the kitchen with a smile on her face. Stacy grabs her and picks her up. "It was nice seeing you again, Chloe. I hope we can catch up soon."

The way she's looking at me tells me she means it.

"You too," I manage. "I hope I didn't scare Giselle."

Stacy laughs and pokes her daughter in the ribs, causing her to giggle. "She'll be just fine. Bye, Gavin."

Gavin walks them outside and shuts the door. He's gone for a few minutes before he returns, but by then, I'm upstairs changing my clothes. He doesn't approach me. Instead, he sits on the end of the bed and waits. I don't know what he's waiting for. For me to say something, probably, but what am I going to say? *Hey, it was great meeting your daughter and seeing my high school bully who happens to be the mother of your child?* No. I'll pass and let him speak first.

"I didn't know they were coming by this morning. You know I was going to tell you. I'm so sorry you had to find out like that. Are you okay? Your head, I mean."

He stands, and I know he wants to inspect the damage, but I hold my hand up. He's incredible. "After all this time, after two months of everything we've been through . . . After me giving you six years of my private thoughts and trusting you with it, you didn't think I could handle this?"

"You're not mad?"

My jaw drops at how clueless Gavin is—or maybe he's just hopeful. I honestly have no idea which it is. "I'm *raging* mad," I say, "but not for the reasons you might think. You kept your daughter from me. Your flesh and blood because . . . why? Because you and Stacy were together? Because she was awful to me in school? Because you couldn't wrap it up to prevent a teen pregnancy? Yeah, all of those things are shocking and it will take some time getting used to. But what could possibly motivate you to jump into any relationship with someone who didn't know you had a daughter?"

In the ten years I've known Gavin Rhodes, I've never seen him cry. Emotional and close to tears, yes, but never tears. Today will be a first. He's trying to hold back, but his eyes are filled with liquid remorse and there's no way they won't start spilling. I want to go to him, to tell him it's okay. But it's not okay. Everything is wrong.

"Does Stacy know you've been keeping me in the dark about Giselle? She obviously already knows about us."

Gavin shakes his head and squeezes his fists tightly together. "I wasn't trying to hide her—"

"You weren't?" I explode. I wave my arms, gesturing around the room, but really I'm talking about the entire house. "You have a daughter. Why didn't anyone tell me about her? I guess I know why you didn't, but what about our friends? Did you ask everyone to lie to me? Where are her pictures? Where are her toys? Do you have a room for her? Let me guess: your old room, right?"

I walk into the hallway, wanting to prove myself right. Gavin comes after me, grabbing my arm as I reach his old room. He tries to turn me around, but I'm already opening his door. I throw it open, expecting to find all the evidence there. But it's a guest bedroom now. Nothing more.

"She sleeps in Devon's old room."

His voice is quiet, but I hear it. I also hear his footsteps as he walks to the opposite door. I turn to find him reaching for something at the top of the doorframe. He jams the key into the hole on the knob and gestures for me to open the door.

My heart is pounding so loudly in my chest; I have to take a deep breath. I look up at him. His head is down and his breathing is heavy. The tears falling onto his cheeks hurt to see. I push open Devon's door and stand stunned into silence. There it is. All the evidence that a little girl does exist is locked away in this one room. The walls are pink and purple with yellow sunflower accents. Her bed is small with a rail on the side. There's a cabinet stocked with toys. And there, lying on the floor, is a stack of picture frames.

"I never meant to keep her a secret. You walked back into my life and I was set on hating you. When we became friends again I was planning to tell you. Every time we were together I thought about telling you, but there never seemed to be the right time. When we finally admitted to each other that we wanted to be together . . . Chloe, at that point I wanted to wait as long as possible because I'm a chicken shit and I wanted to give us a chance before you knew everything. Because then maybe you wouldn't walk away again."

"Don't you dare blame this on me, Gavin. I promised you I wouldn't walk away from you again. I meant it. I'm still standing here now, aren't I?" I'm shaking and I don't know how to stop it. He reaches for me, and I step back. My anger begins to dissolve into hurt, and that's when my own tears start falling.

"You told me you loved me," I cry. "With love comes trust and honesty. You gave me neither of those by keeping this from me.

Just to be clear, Gavin, I'm not pissed that you have a daughter. I'm not even pissed that you had a kid with Stacy. I'm pissed at you for lying about it all while we were building something amazing."

I push past him now and aim for the stairs, but Gavin is too fast. He pulls me back and grips my face with his hands, his eyes pleading with mine. "I did it to protect you."

"Protect me?" He must be insane.

"Yes, to protect you."

"How on earth is lying to me about your baby protecting me?"

"Because Giselle isn't my biological child. I've been there for her since birth. I adopted her as soon as I could so she could have a father."

Oh my God.

"Devon is Giselle's father. Stacy was three months pregnant on the night of graduation, and she was going to the treehouse to talk to him about the baby. She decided to keep her and told Devon earlier that night. That's why he was raging mad. He was pissed at you, but he was more pissed at himself for what he'd gotten himself into. He went around that night picking fights with everyone."

He takes a deep breath and pours his heart into mine with each word. At least, he tries. "I hid this from you to give us time to be together before you found out. To show you how much I love you and what you mean to me. Every day that I kept this from you it got harder to tell you. You make me so happy, Chloe, and I honestly can't imagine the rest of my life without you in it. Please say you'll stay in it. I know this isn't an easy pill to swallow, but it's what has become of my life, and I love that little girl like she is my own. She *is*."

The weight of all the rocks that have been placed on me today is too much to handle. I desperately need air. I need to distance myself from Gavin. *I need time.*

"Can you take me home? I don't think I can walk back right now, but I need to go."

"Chloe . . ." he pleads, pulling my face toward his.

"Please take me home, Gavin," I cry, feeling shattered and lost. A lot like how I felt when I arrived in Bonney Lake a couple months ago. Only this might be worse.

HEROES & LEGENDS

"COURAGE IS FIRE, AND BULLYING IS SMOKE." ~ BENJAMIN DISRAELI

CHAPTER 46

REFLECTION

GAVIN

Before Stacy slammed her backpack into Chloe that day in seventh grade, I could see what was about to happen from a mile away. I tried to stop it, but Devon held me back. At the same moment Devon's arms stiffened against my body, I recognized a shift in our bond.

Being twelve, I paid little attention to the gripping in my chest and the fleeting thoughts running circles in my mind. Looking back on that moment now, I know what that feeling was. For a split second, I thought about following his lead. To be part of the gang. Because we were supposed to be a team. My brother had spent so many years protecting me from the horror that was our mother, it felt as if I was betraying him by straying from the crumbs he had laid in my path.

Maybe my mind was too strong to follow him into darkness. Maybe watching Devon take my beatings for so long gave me a certain perspective. I realized that he *was* a victim at one point, but somewhere along the way he became a bully. Sure, Stacy was doing all the dirty work, but that didn't make the bystanders innocent—including Devon. *It made them weak.* I saw weakness that day in the person I looked up to the most, and it scared the hell out of me.

I helped Chloe because she was hurt. It wasn't a hard decision to make. I was also angry, and it was easy to direct those emotions toward Chloe. I aimed my frustration at the fact that she did nothing while Stacy treated her that way. I wanted her to know this was something in her power to control. I also wanted to show my brother how good it felt to help someone. In reality, I was angry at Devon for disappointing me. Heroes don't stand there and watch. They don't make excuses. They step up.

Chloe was part of my plan to divert Devon's path from dark to light. In some ways it worked, but maybe I was just delaying the inevitable. Devon lived life like he didn't care if there was a tomorrow. He was reckless beyond reason. If you had asked me four years ago if people could change, I would have said with one-hundred-percent certainty, absolutely not.

I was wrong. People can change for the better, and we're allowed to hope that they will.

If you were to ask me that same question today, I would tell you with one-hundred-percent certainty, absolutely yes. People can change for the better, but no one can make the decision to change but them. Sometimes the tornadoes of life vacuum us up and chuck us onto unfamiliar ground. We can work toward building a sturdier foundation or let the dirt settle over us in defeat.

Stacy is the best possible example of someone who used the bad weather to rebuild her life. After thirty-two complicated and horrific hours of labor, Giselle was born with a full head of red hair. She screamed her little lungs off, proving more than any paternity test could that she was Devon's daughter. As Giselle was whisked away for a cleaning, Stacy was getting an emergency blood transfusion. For a moment I thought that might be the end of her life and she might never get a chance to rebuild it. Thankfully she recovered, and it was Giselle who changed her.

Stacy became a mother—someone who, without question, was about to devote the rest of her life to caring for another being more than she ever did herself.

"Gav, are you okay?" Stacy's look is soft. We're at the playground with Giselle to let her play before Stacy takes her home. It's good for our daughter to see us together, even if it is only for a couple hours out of the week. Stacy and I often joke that we've got it better than most divorced couples since we have no animosity toward each other.

Stacy hasn't said anything to me about that day she arrived at my door unannounced, but I can tell she's concerned. It's been a week since Chloe found out about Giselle. A week since I've seen her. I promised I'd give her time, and I've kept my promise. But my patience is waning.

I'm not okay.

I answer with a quick nod and then change the subject. "I've got some time off until I get busy with another job. I can watch Giselle more."

Stacy smiles at me with appreciation, her freckles bright in the sunlight. "I'd rather not spoil her by pulling her out of daycare another week. Plus, she loves that social time with her friends. We can work out a different schedule, though, if you'd like to see her more often."

I nod, because I would like to see Giselle more often. Seven days is too long without my little girl. The easiest decision I ever made was to be her father. That decision didn't come right away, though. Stacy's parents kicked her out of the house when she couldn't hide her pregnancy anymore at nearly eight months. My dad and my stepmom, Linda, took her in with no questions. I got used to seeing Giselle every day after she was born, caring for her when Stacy got too exhausted, taking her on short trips to the store, and escorting Stacy and Giselle to every doctor's visit. People quickly assumed that Stacy and I were together, but that was never the case.

After a year of living under my dad's roof and taking real estate classes, Stacy scored a job as a sales associate for a local builder. She moved out shortly after, and I missed Giselle like crazy. We met for lunch the same week she moved out, and that's when we discussed adoption. Stacy was hesitant. We discussed the possibility of her finding someone who she would want to love Giselle as his own. We discussed what Giselle would think of the situation when she grew up. We discussed a lot of things, and there just wasn't a single con that I couldn't dispute or turn into a positive. But I backed off, knowing ultimately it was Stacy's choice and not something that could be decided in a two-hour lunch.

It took something as small as Stacy having to work late one day and calling me to pick Giselle up from daycare that changed her mind. There wasn't anything I wouldn't do for that little girl, and Stacy knew it. That's what mattered most.

So the yearlong process began.

It was around the same time the adoption went through that I went back to the treehouse for the first time following Devon's death. With my art degree complete and plans for getting the tree-house comic published, everything seemed to be falling into place as best as they could be.

"Gav," Stacy says, bringing me back to earth, "there's something that's been on my mind for a while. Since the moment you told me Chloe was back in your life, I've wanted to tell you . . ."

I tense because I think I already know what she's about to say. "Is this about you confronting Chloe at the hospital?"

Stacy's face turns a disturbing shade of white, making my stomach roll. I never asked Chloe who it was that threatened her, because I had a suspicion that I wasn't ready to confirm. "She told you."

"She told me the story but never said it was you. I had a hunch. What the hell were you thinking?" I'm trying to hold back my anger, but it's a force that can't be stopped. There's too much history in this conversation. "You know what? It doesn't even matter. I wouldn't take it back because of Giselle, but I'm having a hell of a time understanding how you could purposely set out to destroy so many people."

I think Stacy's searching for the right words because she

doesn't speak right away. "I have no explanation other than that I was a horrible person—"

She sounds as if she's on the verge of tears. Now I feel like shit. Stacy has done a hell of a job turning herself around and should feel proud of her accomplishments. My head and chest feel so full they could burst.

I let out a sigh and shake my head. "You were, but you're not anymore. I don't need an explanation. I'm just so damn tired of dealing with the past. It's dark; it's ugly; thank God it's over."

There's an uncomfortable silence, but I know Stacy and I will be fine, even if we're not okay today.

"Giselle, sweetie, let's get going. Mommy needs to start dinner," Stacy calls.

Giselle is in mid-step up the stairs to the slide. She shakes her head so hard that hair sticks to every sweaty surface of her face.

I chuckle and go to her, picking her up from the sandbox and touching my nose to her cheek. "Remember what we talked about. Be a good girl and listen to mommy. I'll see you soon, okay?"

Giselle doesn't say anything. Her hold around my neck tells me everything. *I'll miss you too.* Her hold on me becomes a game, so I tickle her to release her grip. She throws her head back, giggling and twisting from me. "Daddy!"

I set her down, brush sand from her bum, and release her. Giselle happily runs into the waiting arms of her mother. They're both smiling now. We say our goodbyes and I take off in my truck, knowing I can't return home without a quick grocery trip.

The parking lot is packed. Sunday might as well be the only shopping day of the week because every car in town seems to be here. I sigh, in no mood to deal with a crowd, but step out of my truck anyway. Giselle and I managed to eat through my entire kitchen this week.

The moment I enter the store, a selection of Pop-Tarts greets me as a featured item of the day. For no reason at all, I toss Chloe's favorite flavor in my cart and move on. She's everywhere I go.

Every day. All the time. So when I see a petite woman wearing a baggy shirt with black leggings and sporting a messy bun, I have to blink a few times to ensure I'm seeing what I think I'm seeing. It's definitely her. My heart feels as if it's in my throat. Somehow her thrown-together look is the most beautiful sight I've seen . . . ever. Chloe is always beautiful, but this look is my favorite. Especially since the shirt she's wearing is mine from junior high.

Her eyes dart away from the orange she's holding and make a beeline for me, as if she can sense my presence. I'm sure she can; I'm staring at her like a damn stalker. Instead of turning away like I should since I promised her I'd give her space, I close the gap between us. She doesn't move, but her little fingers prove to be no match for the poor citrus fruit she's repurposing as a stress ball.

"I think you have to pay for that before you juice it," I tease.

She's confused for a moment before looking down at her palm and releasing the orange onto the floor. "Oh, crap." She picks it up and looks around her as if she doesn't know what to do with it. Pink stains her cheeks as she finally tosses the orange into her cart and looks up at me.

My heart is definitely not where it should be. Just one look at her and I'm ready to take back the promise of space. One week is one week too long to be apart. There are a million things I want to say, but how am I supposed to bring them up now? This is hardly the place to have a conversation. "I just wanted to say hi. I won't keep you." I'm hoping she knows without a doubt that "just saying hi" is the last thing I want.

After a few moments, she still says nothing, so I turn to leave. A hand grips my elbow and I freeze. "Gavin, wait."

I turn slowly, unable to hide the hopeful look on my face.

Her expression appears strange, though, like I abandoned her to deal with this on her own. *God, I hope giving her time was what she really wanted.* My hope dwindles. "Were you and Stacy ever . . ." I watch the crease of tension in her forehead as she's unable to finish her sentence.

"No." I answer immediately, wishing I had at least told her

this much. It didn't cross my mind at all that she might think Stacy and I were together at any point. She's probably been thinking about it all week. "Never. Nothing remotely close to it. It's all been about Giselle and Devon."

A deep sigh seeps from her. There's a tightening of my insides at the thought of causing Chloe pain. Suddenly I feel just like that poor, juiced orange lying in Chloe's cart.

"She's changed; you know?" I say. Chloe looks confused. "Stacy, I mean. She's a good person. Giselle was the best thing that happened to her."

The tension on Chloe's face seems to disappear, and I'm surprised to find that she's nodding. "I can tell. I'm happy for her. And you."

She's unable to meet my gaze. It takes everything in me to not reach for her and tilt her head so she can't help but look me in the eyes. Maybe then she'll see how much I love her. How much I *can*, but *don't want* to give her the space she's asking for.

"Have dinner with me," I say. Chloe shakes her head, but I won't accept it this time. I've given her a week. Doesn't she want to know the whole story by now? I step forward, giving into what I want, and brush my knuckles against her cheekbones. "Just dinner."

"Where's Giselle?"

"Stacy picked her up today." I plead with my body to calm down with a deep inhale and exhale. "I'd like to tell you everything, if you're ready."

Chloe genuinely looks torn between what she feels for me and the secret I kept from her. I can't help but think of what she kept from me for four years, but it doesn't seem fair to compare the two. What I read in her journal were her thoughts and hers alone. What I kept from her had an impact on her heart. A heart she trusted me with. The way I see it, the distance between us could do one of two things. It could end us, or it could make us stronger.

Chloe shakes her head. "I'm not. I'm sorry, Gavin." She takes a step back and my hands fall to my sides in defeat.

"I'm not asking you to forgive me this second. I'm not even asking for you to understand. Just dinner, Chloe. You've got to have questions, and there's so much I want to say. Please." I'm begging now.

"You're right. I have a million questions, but I don't think I'm ready to ask them today. Besides, I have to spend the weekend packing. The house sold, and they're closing at the end of the month. My parents asked me to get a jumpstart for them."

Timing couldn't be shittier.

"I can help you," I try.

She shakes her head, no.

"Where are you going to live?"

I feel like breaking when she hesitates. "I'm going apartment shopping this week. My parents come home next weekend, and then they'll pack up the rest of the house."

That means she'll be far away. Not that I know where she'll be living, but I do know she'll be too far from me to just hike across a half mile of woods to see her. Why does it feel as if everything is unraveling?

There's nothing left to say. She doesn't want to talk about this, and she's moving. There's nothing I can do except stand here like an idiot. I don't want to feel angry, but it burns. "I guess that's it, then."

She looks stricken at first, and I want to take back my words, but then she nods too quickly and backs away. "I should go."

And then she walks away, leaving me with nothing but a strangled orange and her abandoned cart.

CHAPTER 47

MOVING ON

CHLOE

My intention was never to walk away from Gavin. I didn't exactly have a plan when I asked him to drop me off that awful Saturday or when he caught me by surprise in the supermarket. Over the course of the week my anger fused into hurt, then sadness. Now I can't stop thinking of what would happen if I did sit down and have that conversation with him.

I have no doubt I can forgive him for keeping Giselle a secret. It hurt at first, but Gavin had good intentions. No, that's not what's holding me back from throwing myself into his arms and moving forward. The problem is, moving forward now consists of one more person—two if you count Stacy.

I'm twenty-two. I just graduated from college and landed my first real job. I'm about to move into my own place for the first time in my life—college dorm rooms don't count. And I've fallen in love. Madly, crazy, deeply in love with my childhood dream boy. And he's fallen in love with me. The one thing keeping us apart is a fear that I am not ready for a life with him and his daughter.

My household growing up wasn't filled with affection and warmth. My parents were physically there with me, but entirely absent when it came to things that mattered. We didn't do family time and they certainly didn't meddle in my social affairs. When I'd come home crying about Stacy, my mom brushed it off as me being too sensitive.

My parents have no siblings and I'm an only child, so I have no cousins, no nieces or nephews. I was never the type who babysat all the neighbor's kids. I've never even held a child. I've pretty much grown up without ever having to come into contact with the little critters. I figured I'd have kids one day and worry about the details then. But right now? I wouldn't even know how to interact with Giselle. What if she hates me? What if Gavin realizes I'd make a horrible future mother of his babies after seeing me fail with his daughter? The insecurities just keep coming.

It's early enough the next morning for me to wince when there's a knock at the door. I'm already downstairs chugging a glass of water when I hear it, but only because I wasn't able to sleep at all. I was hoping to go back to bed for a few hours once I got rid of this dry mouth.

Sharlene was surprisingly understanding when I told her that I had to pack my things and find a new place to live within a week's time. She's allowing me to take Monday off and then work the rest of the week from home. Since we're waiting on edits for the event script and there's not much for me to do anyway, she was extra accommodating.

When I swing open the door, my eyes go wide and let out a shriek. "Jazz!" I throw myself into her arms and then immediately start crying. "You're back. Why didn't you tell me?" I don't let her go. No way.

She's laughing and trying to pry my arms off her. "I wanted to help you pack and find a place. If I knew you'd welcome me like this, I would have reconsidered."

I pull away, wiping my tears. "I'm sorry, it's just been an emotional week. I missed you so much. Where's Marco?"

She makes a face. "Still in New York. He has a couple more weeks before his apprenticeship is over, and then he's going to make a decision."

"That doesn't sound good. That means you two are considering moving there permanently?"

Jazz shrugs. "I pleaded my case and he heard me. I don't think he necessarily wants to live there, but he does love his job, and it pays really well. He's not sure he can find something here right away if he comes back."

"Wow, that could be a huge step for both of you."

She laughs. "No, marriage will be the huge step. As much as I'd rather be here, I'll follow Marco anywhere if it means I get to spend my life with him."

And here come more tears. "That was sweet." And now I miss Gavin—not that I ever stopped. Damn it.

Jazz pulls me inside and straight to the kitchen. She opens the fridge and curses the moment she realizes I have nothing but a tub of butter.

"Sorry. I went to the grocery store last night but I ran into Gavin and—"

"You two talked?" she interrupts.

I shake my head. "Not really. He asked me to dinner, but I'm not ready."

The look she gives me is filled with all the things I feel: disappointment, sadness, surprise. She always has been a fan of Gavin, ever since high school. In fact, she was the first one to call me out on my attraction for him, but of course I denied it.

I'm happy when Jazz doesn't comment and instead takes me out to breakfast. We stop at the grocery store on the way home and then start packing. My parents asked me to box up whatever I wanted to take to my new place and put it aside before they arrived. They said they would either sell or give away the rest. They already have everything they need in Florida.

Jazz is helping me pack up my bedroom when I hear a hitch in her breath. "Oh my God," she says, holding up my leather journal. "Is this *the* journal?"

I frown and snatch it from her. "Hands off."

She glares at me, but there's more amusement there than anger. "So Gavin can read it but I can't?"

She's kidding, but sometimes Jazz words things in ways that frustrate me no matter the tone. I return her glare and throw the book on my bed. "I was proving a point to him."

"Which was?"

"That it was always him, even when it wasn't. Every entry, every dream . . ." I flush, realizing I'm saying more than enough. "You get it."

Jazz nods. "I do. I get that you two are more perfect for each other than anyone I've ever known—besides Marco and me—yet you're doing your distance thing again. It's unhealthy, Chloe. I'm your best friend; I'm allowed to give it to you straight. And you know what? I love you more than I need you to like me right now. You're ruining a perfect love. What you two have doesn't come around twice. Hell, for some it doesn't come around at all."

She's right; I don't like her very much right now. I'm allowed to be hurt after all that's transpired. I'm allowed to be confused. And now I'm angry too. "It's not so perfect if he thought he had to lie to me, now is it?" I kind of hate myself for asking this question. I know what Gavin and I have is rare, but that doesn't make this any easier.

She scoffs. "Right, because if he had told you about Giselle sooner you would have been fine with him having a daughter? With Stacy, of all people?" When I don't answer, she raises an eyebrow. "I didn't think so."

After our heated exchange on Monday night, Jazz and I ordered a pizza and watched movies until we fell asleep on the living room floor. I'd say it's just like old times, but everything about it feels different. She is careful to not bring Gavin up again, making for a smooth week, but it's obvious she's not happy about keeping silent. Jazz cares for Gavin. He's Marco's best friend, and she—unlike me—was there for him after Devon's death, so she was witness to his pain. She also knows me well, and my stubbornness has always driven her insane.

As mad at me as she probably is, she's also extremely helpful. Within a week's time, she's helped me pack my things, find a place, and move into my cute, new urban apartment in Renton overlooking Lake Washington. There are boxes everywhere and I can barely walk through the mess, but I'm here.

Monica stops over to check out my new place on Saturday night and gives me her approval. She was devastated when I told her I wasn't moving to Bellevue, but moving from the lake to the city just didn't sit well with me. This is a better compromise.

"We should check out the casino down the street," Monica says excitedly. She's got her phone in her hands and is lying on my couch, the only piece of furniture without boxes spread across it, looking up nearby restaurants for dinner.

Jazz hops over a box to glance at Monica's phone and nods. "That could be fun."

I wrinkle my nose. "A casino? It'll be filled with smoke."

Monica shakes her head. "No, it won't. It says 'smoke-free' on their website. Let's go. Looks like their food is dirt-cheap. I want to try it and then gamble a little."

I'm not in the mood at all, but I can't deny this to my two best friends, who have been nothing but amazing to me since I told Gavin I needed time. It still crushes me to think about how long it's been since we've talked. The worst part is that it's all in my hands. But every time I think to pick up the phone because I miss him, I wonder if I'll be intruding on his time with Giselle.

We stuff ourselves with cheap fried food and drink one too many cocktails, happy to know my apartment is only a short taxi ride away. Monica gushes over every detail of Zachary Ryan's visits to the office this past week, and then tries a game of poker. She does more flirting and giggling than actual playing. As much as the old guys love ogling her, they are far more serious about winning than checking out Monica's awesome rack. We take the hint and call a cab, fully ready to pass out wherever we find space.

As we're waiting outside for our ride, Monica leans on me and pulls out her phone. I can't help but notice Gavin's name appear on the screen. A sinking sensation creeps under my skin. I say nothing as she checks the message, but I look over to see what he's saying.

Gavin: She did? Tell me where.

Monica peers up at me, her long lashes fluttering with exhaustion. She hands me the phone. "Write him. He wants to know where you live now. Pretend you're me."

"What?"

She shrugs. "If you can't talk to him, then pretend you're me. You can ask him anything you want without him knowing it's actually you.

That thought doesn't sound entirely bad. I have missed him —a lot. I take her phone just as the taxi arrives, then climb in the front seat to guide the driver to my apartment.

Once we're all inside, I lead the girls to my bed. They're passed out the moment I drop the blanket on them. I laugh and sneak out to the couch with Monica's phone clutched in my hand. I raise it up and see another message from Gavin.

Gavin: Don't tell her I'm asking.

Gavin: Monica?

My heart races as my fingers move to the touch pad.

Monica: A cute apartment in Renton. What are you doing?

Gavin: Where in Renton? The ghetto? Why?

Monica: On the lake. It's really nice. And safe. You'd like it . .
.

It's a minute before he responds.

Gavin: That's good. What did you do tonight?

Monica: Casino for dinner.

Gavin: That area is not safe!

My heart is pounding.

Monica: We took a taxi.

Gavin: Shit, Monica. I'm going crazy. Did she say anything about me?

Monica: No, but only because she's stubborn and doesn't know what to say.

Gavin: Does she miss me?

More than you know.

Monica: What do you think?

Gavin: She hasn't contacted me. I don't know what to think.

I picture him gritting his perfect teeth.

Monica: She misses you.

I bite my lip, wondering if that last text blew my cover.

Gavin: Do you think I should call her?

My fingers freeze, unsure of how to respond to that one. If I say yes, then he'll call, and I'm still not sure how to handle that conversation. If I say no then he won't call, and that just might crush me even more. I'm in full-on panic mode.

Monica: I can give her a message if you'd like.

Gavin: No, I need to talk to her myself.

There's a definite ache in my heart when I think of Gavin. Of having someone to wake up to on weekend mornings, someone to cook with, to eat with, to laugh with. Of Gavin's kisses trailing my bare chest in the morning, waking me to play. I frown, suddenly going crazy with the thought of staying away from him anymore.

Monica: Call her tomorrow then.

I throw the phone like it's scalding me. It's already too late to take back the last text. By the time my racing heart rate slows and my eyes flutter closed, I've already decided that even if Gavin calls tomorrow, I'm still not ready to answer the phone.

The girls leave early Sunday morning to take care of their hangovers and leave me to finish unpacking. I'm surprised by how much I get done, but keeping my mind busy is the only option as

I wait for Gavin to call. I've tossed my choices back and forth—to answer or not to answer—and by the time late afternoon rolls around and he still hasn't called, I know there's no way I can ignore him when he does.

My heart does an erratic disco dance when I hear a knock on my door. It must be Gavin—who else would it be? I run to the bathroom and dab some concealer under my eyes, then move to my room to throw on a sports bra and tank top. I'm sure Gavin wouldn't mind me braless, but the conversation we're about to have will require our full attention.

I look through the peephole first because I'm not an idiot, and my disco moves become a clunky two-step when I see Stacy standing here. Her red hair is pulled up into a ponytail, and by the look of her shifting stance and constant deep breaths, I can see that she's nervous.

What is she doing here?

Heat sears through me at the sight of her, but then I remember how nice she was to me when I fainted and what Gavin said about how she's changed. I sure hope it's true, but I'm not a saint. I'm not sure if I'll ever forget the pain she's caused me. I finally open the door to greet her nervous smile. I don't smile back.

"Chloe, forgive me for barging in. I was hoping we could talk. If you're not too busy." She peers into my space over my shoulder and then looks back at me with a hopeful expression.

I sigh. "Come in. Excuse the mess."

She follows me inside and we sit on my couch. "Nice place."

I give her a smile now, but it's a tight one, far from reaching my eyes. "How did you find me?"

Stacy cringes. "Jazz, but please don't be mad at her. I was very convincing."

I'll have words with her later. She can't just be handing my address out like that. "Can you please keep it a secret? I'm not ready for Gavin to know where I am."

A pained look crosses her face. "Of course. I will keep it to myself. I actually wanted to come here to apologize to you. For so many things. I guess I'll just start at the beginning."

I nod, unsure of what else to say. The girl is already in my apartment, sitting on my couch. I haven't offered her tea yet, so I'm still winning.

"So much has happened in the last four years, and I'm so distant from the person I used to be." She sighs. "This is harder for me than you think. I try not to think of the awful person I was, but Chloe, I was awful." There are already tears in her eyes. "Once I had Giselle and after going through some intense therapy, my need to control my life and everyone else's didn't matter anymore. All that mattered was my little girl and what I would do to protect her.

"When I was little, I was so incredibly unhappy at home. I'm not here to tell you my sob story, but you should know that my story and Devon's are very similar. It's what connected us. Except my sister was in college and rarely came home. That's why I spent so much time at your house when we were little."

Oh my God.

"You were so mad at me when I came back from vacation."

Stacy sighs. "My father was evil, Chloe. I took the brunt of his abuse at home, and then I delivered a different type of abuse at school. When you left for vacation I had nowhere else to go but home. It was awful, and I shouldn't have, but I blamed you for the worst days of my life. I made a vow to myself that I wouldn't be a victim of his anymore. Instead, I became a bully. I ended up making friends with whoever would help me seek revenge, and when you came home, you became my prime target. I'm so sorry for it all. For the comments, the jokes, for touching you. Gavin was right to stick up for you, but at the time I was enraged.

"You know, I loved Devon. I crushed on him all through junior high, but we started seeing each other in high school. As you know." She blushes, probably remembering what I walked into in the treehouse. "Devon wasn't a one-woman guy though. You know that too. Hell, everyone knew that, but that only made me want him more. I had this false sense of security with him because of our pasts. I was delusional, but I thought we were truly in love. Things got pretty heated between us the summer before senior year and I thought that was it. I thought we'd finally be a couple. But then you came back from Florida and started tutoring him . . . and he lost all interest in me. Well, at least until he realized he wasn't going to get more from you than a peck on the lips."

Reliving this is not something I thought I'd be doing today. It does all sorts of funny things to my stomach, and I grip the couch intensely.

"He really did care about you," she rushes to say. "He kept telling me you deserved someone better, and I only ever agreed with him. Not because I thought Devon wasn't good enough for you, but because I wanted his heart to be free to love me. And I was convincing. I know Devon was always angry and not the best in school, and he was a horrible boyfriend to you, but he was the one for me. I was so desperate to keep him in my life I gave him the one thing you couldn't."

She takes a deep breath before continuing. "Devon knew about the pregnancy a week before graduation. We hadn't talked in over a month before that. I tried to get him to break up with you, but he refused, so I decided to finally walk away from it all. I was eleven weeks and had just found out. He asked me to get rid of it." She's wiping tears from her eyes now. "We were fighting about it constantly. The night of graduation I texted Devon to tell him we needed to talk about the baby because I was definitely keeping her. He called me a while later and told me to meet him at the treehouse . . . said he had evidence that you were cheating on him with Gavin. It seemed like he was more upset over that than he was about me keeping the baby. I went to him, but by the time I got there . . ." I'm glad she ends her sentence there. I know what happened.

How Devon went from fighting with Stacy to searching for my journal that night still makes no sense. "Do you think he was picking a fight with me that night because of the baby?"

Stacy nods without hesitation. "He mentioned something about how you were never faithful to him either and he was going to find evidence. He was rambling about it, like he was trying to convince himself that he wasn't a bad guy for having a baby with someone else."

So, Devon was looking for a way to justify his actions. Sounds very Devon of him.

I'm still connecting the dots. "Then why keep me away from Gavin when I saw you in the hospital?"

Her face reddens again. "Out of everything, that's what I'm most sorry about. I was devastated by Devon's death. I wanted to blame someone. I *needed* to blame someone. There I was, nearing my second trimester of pregnancy, and the father of my unborn child had just died. He was the only one that knew about the baby. I hadn't even told my sister. When I saw you at the hospital that day, something took over me. Him being at the treehouse was my fault, not yours, but I couldn't accept that."

"Stacy, he asked you to meet him there. It's not your fault he was too drunk to control his actions."

She nods through her tears. I walk to the bathroom and grab a roll of toilet paper. When I sit back down, she wipes her eyes and thanks me. "The night of the party I thought he was just deflecting, but that moment in the hospital, standing in front of you, I realized what Devon feared was true. You loved Gavin, and I feared that when he woke up you would probably have him. Then I would be left with nothing, except life as a single mother."

I've been understanding throughout her entire story, even on the road to forgiving her . . . and then she said that.

"Stacy, did you make me leave the hospital because you wanted Gavin to become the father?"

Her eyes go wide. "No! Oh my God. No. That never crossed my mind."

I take a deep breath, relieved.

"It's never been like that between Gavin and me. I love him now, but only because of what he is to Giselle. He's an amazing father. I know it was a shock for you to find out the way you did, and this isn't a conventional sort of deal that you've walked into, but it's important that you know how much Gavin has done for us. Because you deserve to know everything, and you deserve to be happy too. I also want Gavin to be happy, and it tears me apart that he's not right now."

It's amazing how honesty can turn a decade's worth of frustrations and anger into forgiveness, just like that. I was confused and hurt over Stacy for the longest time. Even more so lately knowing she and Gavin share Giselle. But I'm not angry anymore. It's like a cement block has been lifted from my chest and I'm finally breathing again.

"I'm sure hearing this from me means absolutely nothing, but I have to say it. I don't know a time since the twins moved to town that Gavin hasn't loved you. After you left"—she winces— "I saw him date plenty of women, and we even fought over his lifestyle at times. Gavin has never been interested in settling down, but he is now. Maybe I'm being selfish again, but my daughter deserves for her father to be in a happy relationship. And there would be peace in my heart knowing that you two chose each other. So, for what it's worth. I think you should talk to Gavin and know that, at least from my perspective, there's no better man in this world. Besides my fiancé, of course."

She's smiling as she wipes the last tear away. I smile back. I didn't realize Stacy was with someone, but I see the ring now. There's a glow in her eyes and a tiny bump on her belly. She's so tiny though, it could very well be a donut she ate for breakfast.

She must sense the questions behind my stare because she pats her stomach. "I'm only four months. Can you believe this?" Her tummy is definitely rounded out. "I was so tiny for most of my first pregnancy . . ." She smiles at me.

"You're engaged?"

Her eyes are wide as she nods. "He adores Giselle. We're getting married after the baby is born so I can fit into a decent dress."

Wow. Life sure has changed drastically in four years.

"Thank you for coming here and talking to me. I may not be ready to run back into Gavin's arms, but this conversation has been really enlightening."

She frowns. "I understand. If there's anything else you ever want to know, just ask." She slips me a piece of paper with her name and contact information on it. She must have planned this part. "Call me any time. Please. I hope we can be friends one day, Chloe. I truly mean that."

"Thank you."

I'm surprised to feel Stacy's hand wrap around the top of mine. "Everything will be okay." Her deep breathing is contagious, and my breath is rising and falling with hers. *I hope she's right.*

Chapter 48

Every Single Day

Gavin

BelleCurve is strangely quiet on Monday morning. Then again, I usually don't arrive to the office until early afternoon or later, so the quiet could be completely normal. Chloe will be in the office today, and truthfully that's my only reason for being here. My sketches are done and with the artist who's going to digitize my work. From there, Sharlene will arrange the printing, and the decorations team will place them around the room as planned.

"Gav, you're here early," Monica says with surprise. "Isn't your work done?" She's always the first one in the office. She also makes the coffee, and although I don't usually drink the stuff, I could use a shot or two of espresso right now.

"I figured I'd see if the team needed anything. I didn't want to just disappear."

Monica gives me a knowing smile. "Chloe isn't here yet."

I sigh and lean over the front counter of her desk. "I chickened out."

"I'm not following," she says. She tilts her head and I chuckle, realizing she was probably drunk when she was texting me the other night. Something seemed off with those texts, but I was so focused on getting answers about Chloe, I ignored the signs. Monica is never subdued; she's usually giving me shit and cracking awful jokes. It seems now she has no recollection of the conversation.

"Our texts. I was going to call Chloe yesterday, but I chickened out. How drunk were you on Saturday night?"

Monica's jaw falls open, and she scrambles for her phone. After she opens up the text exchange she looks up at me and shakes her head. "Gav, I'm not one to out my friends but you should know, I didn't write any of this."

"Then who did?" I stand up straight.

"I think it was Chloe." She says it like it's a question, distracted by her own thoughts.

I shake my head. "Are you sure you just weren't too drunk to remember?"

Monica sighs. "I was drunk, but I didn't text you this. I know I didn't. I'm pretty sure I handed Chloe my phone and told her to pretend she was me and write you back. I'm sorry, Gav. Chloe was sulking the entire day and Jazz told me I wasn't allowed to bring up your name."

I look at my own phone and reread the conversation. "She told me to call her." *Oh, shit.* "She wanted me to call her?"

Monica's eyes take up almost her entire forehead. "You didn't call her." She doesn't ask, she's just restating what I said as if it's just now clicking. "Shit, Gav," she whispers.

"I wanted to, but then I figured I'd give her more time. Besides, Stacy dropped Giselle off earlier than usual, so I knew I wouldn't have privacy." I groan and let my head fall into my hands. "Mon, I don't know what I'm supposed to do. She told me to give her time. She refused to talk to me last time I saw her; and now she's pretending to be you and telling me to call her. What the hell do I do?"

Monica is quiet. When I hear the door open behind me, I immediately guess why. I look up. Chloe has already spotted me. I know because she diverts her stare to Monica. "Morning," she says to neither of us, or both of us. I'm not really sure. I just watch her pass by, looking beautiful as ever in a light pink floral dress. Only Chloe can get away with wearing classy pattern like that and still look sexy.

Monica slides a box of Kleenex from one end of the counter until it's just under my chin. I look up at her. She has a glimmer in her eyes and a smirk on her face. "For the drool."

I groan and push off the counter, determined to talk to Chloe before the day is up.

Of course Sharlene walks in right behind Chloe and sends her downtown to meet with the editor for the morning. Of course I don't see Chloe when she comes back because I'm sent to the editing studio to review the almost-final event videos. And of course by the time I leave the studio, Chloe has already headed home for the day.

Monica is giving me sad eyes when I jog by her desk. I hope I might be able to cut Chloe off in the garage, but her car is nowhere to be found. Gripping my phone, my fingers fly over the touchpad in search of her number—but then I stop myself.

I jog back into the office and catch Monica as she's locking up behind Zachary, a blush on her cheeks as he leaves her with one last flirtatious glance.

"Where does Chloe live?"

Monica jerks up in surprise and shakes her head. "No, I can't. Gavin, you need to call her."

"She probably won't pick up. I want to see her and talk to her face-to-face."

She cringes. I can see she wants to tell me, but her loyalty to Chloe is strong.

"You know she wants to talk to me. You know she misses me. She told me herself the other night. You know how stubborn she can be. She'll drag this out for years. I gave her time like she asked. I respected her space. But I'm afraid if I don't go after her now, she'll never budge and call me first. I have to keep fighting for her."

Monica sighs, and I think I've won. "I won't give you her address," she says, "but I will help you contact her."

"What?" I'm exhausted.

"You need to remind her why she can't live without you. Whatever is going on in Chloe's head is driven by fear. She gets hung up on decisions until it's easiest for her to just walk away. I'm not saying that's what she's doing right now; in fact, I think she's trying like hell not to, but you need to convince her that walking away is the worst possible thing for everyone."

"How am I going to do that if I can't talk to her?"

"Remind her why she can't live without you," Monica repeats. "She always tries to walk away and you always let her. One of you needs to break the cycle." She pauses for a moment and then says, "What defines your love? Whatever it is, remind her of it. Every single day."

CHLOE

By the time I settle into bed, my tear ducts are dry from crying and my chest is heavy with ache. When I walked into BelleCurve this morning I was already sad Gavin never called. I'm tired of pushing him away, and I miss him desperately. I've always been able to talk to Gavin about anything—well, almost anything—I should, however, be able to talk to him about my fear. We can get through this together.

He didn't call, though. For whatever reason, he had a change of heart, and seeing him first thing in the morning with his head on Monica's desk as if they were in deep discussion didn't help my emotions. I was grateful when Sharlene sent me downtown. I don't know what I would have done if faced with Gavin.

It's just past ten o'clock when I hear a slow knock on my front door. Living alone can be scary. I tiptoe to the door and look through the peephole. My heart sinks when I realize it's not Gavin. I pull the door open, leaving the chain attached, my cell phone in my hand hidden behind the door—just in case. A man in regular clothes greets me with a nod and hands me a clipboard. The name at the top tells me he's from a courier service.

"Sign, please, to confirm your receipt."

I sign as he asks and then take the package from him. After shutting the door, I stare at the thin, plain manila envelope in my hands, completely puzzled. Then I tear it open. As I reach inside and pull out two slips of paper, Gavin's handwriting is revealed.

I begin to read.

Clover,

These past two weeks have been insanely lonely without you in them. I understand your need to have this time, and I've struggled giving that to you. In my mind, it's not time apart we need. We've had enough of that. Whatever you're going through, I want to go through it with you. Whatever I've done wrong, I want to apologize for it. Whatever fears you have, I want them to be ours. Clover, there's nothing I wouldn't do for you. We've both made mistakes. We're so far from perfect, but we're perfect together. Isn't that all that matters?

I'm not writing you this letter to beg you to take me back. I want to do that in person. I'm writing this letter to tell you that there won't be a day that goes by, from now until forever, that you're not reminded of my love for you.

Years ago you caught me sketching something. I hid it before you could look at it, but it was the sketchbook that meant the most to me. The one that burned along with the treehouse. That sketchbook was my version of a journal. It had everything to do with my heart—page after page–and the person who had captured it. She was beautiful, and smart, and sexy, and kind, and loyal. She thought she was invisible, but in fact, she was the brightest light.

She was you.

Although that sketchbook was lost in the fire, the drawings are as etched in my mind as they were the day I drew them. I redid this sketch today. It was one of my favorites because it was the first day I realized you were my muse. The only lucky charm I needed. My Clover. I still believe it's true.

Love,
  Gavin

My eyes are fresh with tears as I set aside the beautiful letter and reach for the drawing behind it. Everything goes warm. My chest, my neck, my cheeks. It's a sketch of me with my back turned toward Gavin while I look over my shoulder at him. I don't recall sporting shorts that gave me a wedgie, but the look on my face is one I remember wearing clearly. I was seventeen, wondering if Gavin saw me for more than a piece of his artwork. My expression is bright and hopeful. The wings strapped to my back were white at the time, but in the sketch they're made of four-leaf clovers.

The letters and the sketches don't stop there. For the rest of the week, Gavin makes good on his promise. That's one thing he's always been good at. Since he doesn't come into work, I look forward to the packages that arrive on my doorstep every night, sometimes before I get home. And every time I rip open an envelope, I'm in tears by the time I finish the letter. He sketches so much, and not just me in costume.

There's a sketch of my profile composited on top of Crystal

Mountain, my hair windblown and my cheeks flushed. There are a couple of me in the treehouse, one of me laughing, and another of me with my stomach pressed into the floorboards as I slept. Each one brings on a rush of emotions until I can't see anymore. By Friday, I'm determined to drive straight to Gavin's after work and fall into his arms as I apologize for taking so long. I've thought of texting or calling him to tell him how much the sketches mean to me, but I'd rather do this in person. I want to be there to see him smile. To feel his arms around me when he realizes I never actually left him.

Friday marks our last meeting before the first Heroes and Legends' event. Sharlene and I are looking over the final brochures and artwork in one last spot-check. I'm almost as nervous about the event as I am about seeing Gavin again. We're closing the last few shirt boxes when I hear someone enter the conference room.

"Hey, Gavin. This is a surprise. You ready for tomorrow?" Sharlene asks.

My head whips around at the sound of his name. The galloping in my chest commences. He's in jeans and a button-down shirt, looking far better than I feel.

"I am," he says with a smile. A gorgeous smile. Gavin's teeth are movie star white, and looking at him hurts sometimes. He's so damn gorgeous.

His eyes don't move to mine, filling me with disappointment, but he walks over to take the box in my hands, getting so close that his shoulder brushes mine. He sets the box on a stack of the others in the corner of the room. "Need help taking these down to storage?"

Sharlene shakes her head. "We've got a truck coming in a bit. We're going to store everything at the venue tonight. The event crew starts decorating at five in the morning." Sharlene scrunches her forehead like she forgot something. "Chloe, can you print out the schematics? A few of each should be fine. The crew has them, but having some printed may be helpful."

"You got it." I walk to the door, glancing at Gavin as I do. He's trying to look anywhere but at me . . . except he slips. For a moment our eyes lock, and I know nothing has changed between us—not the things that matter, anyway.

The rest of the day is almost worse than the days before it because Gavin is so close by but not speaking directly to me. He busies himself in his cubicle on the other side of the wall. At first I thought maybe he came in to see me, but clearly he's busy. I'm surprised when he follows me into the parking garage at the end of the day. He's silent, and I try to ignore the warmth creeping through me as I place my laptop bag in my backseat. When I'm done, I turn to face him. He's leaning against the driver's seat door, a look of deliberation washing over him.

"Hi," I say.

"Hi," he answers.

Okay, I guess this is on me.

"Thank you for the sketches. And the letters. They're beautiful."

His forehead creases and I wonder if I've said the wrong thing. "There's one more."

The galloping has turned into tiny flutters. "Gavin—"

"Wait, Chloe. I'm not sending you the last one."

"You're not?" *Oh my God. He's giving up.* Heat begins to rise in my chest. I open my mouth to speak again, to stop him from whatever he's planning to do, but he continues.

"My intention was to send them to you until you realized that this isn't something we get to mess around with. This is our future, and I'm not letting you sabotage it anymore. Yes, I have a daughter, but that doesn't mean anything between us has to change. I tried the silent treatment. I tried the daily dose of romance. After today, it's your move."

He reaches behind him, lifts the back of his shirt, and pulls out a manila envelope. As he hands it to me, I can't help but notice his entire body is radiating with energy. He releases the paper into my hands.

I open my mouth again to say something, but Gavin stops me with one look. Sometimes his intensity scares me, but not because I'm afraid of him. It's because one day I may not be on the receiving end of it.

"I thought I'd deliver this one to you myself," he says.

I bring the envelope to my side. I think he's about to leave, but instead he steps forward and slides a palm to the back of my head. "And this."

He lowers his mouth slowly, giving me a chance to back away. I don't. No freaking way. His lips are soft, warm . . . so perfectly familiar. I think I'm melting into a puddle on the floor. Everything is tingling. I might even let out a tiny moan. Usually this would make Gavin tighten his hold, press his body against mine, and bury his lips deeper. This time he pulls away, and before I know it, his footsteps retreat and a door slams. I watch him drive away, and then I tear the envelope open to see what's inside.

Chloe,

For the past week I've been sketching memories of you. Memories I thought were forever lost in a fire. Turns out the embers of that fire have somehow lived in a special part of my mind all along. I made a decision this week that as happy as those memories are, I'm tired of sketching the past. I'm ready to create our future. Together. So, here it is. My last sketch to you. This one is neither past nor future. This one belongs to our eternity.

There was a passage in your journal that stood out to me above any other. You wondered how I would draw our relationship. I've put a lot of thought into this because there is no single symbol, or emotion, or place that defines us. We're just us, and what we make of our past shouldn't define our future. We should use it as our foundation.

So, here's my sketch of our foundation. The treehouse is where we live—past, present, and future. It's our innocence, our friendship, and our initial bond. It houses our secrets, our growth, our passions, and all that inspires us. There is still room to build more memories, Clover.

Fire destroyed us. Love brought us back together. I hope it's enough to keep us together every single day for the rest of our lives.

Love,
 Gavin

CHAPTER 49

DANCE WITH ME

CHLOE

Monica hands her keys to the valet and walks to the bottom of the entrance stairs where the red carpet and roped-off area begin. Photographers are already in action snagging photos of everyone's arrivals. Our guests will be treated just as the title states—like Heroes and Legends.

The title of the event hovers above the entrance door in a huge, bold, colorful 3D display. As my focus lingers on the sign, Monica tugs on my arm eagerly. She pulls me into the venue just as someone dressed in a hero costume hands me a comic book. At least it looks like a comic book, but I know better. It's an event guide, designed by Gavin and written by me. I've already seen the final proof, but this is the copy I will keep to remember this event. I haven't even looked at the room yet, but I'm already immersed in the theme. I skim the cover with my fingers and smile, feeling tiny bubbles of pride float through me. Everything from the title to the page borders was sketched by Gavin. Beyond the bubbles, my heart is pounding dramatically against its walls.

And then I look up.

I gasp, clutching Monica's hand for support. Everything we created on paper is here, staring us in the face. "Wow," she says as her eyes float the room. Mine follow, taking in every intricacy of the designs. Not just Gavin's designs, but the scenery too. The decorators nailed it.

There are sketches on pop art backgrounds, some in black and white and some in color, scattered around the walls of the room. From left to right, they tell the story of the heroes, the kids in attendance at today's event, who become legends when they honorably defeat the Bulldog. The Bulldog is a bully who attacks because he is scared and weak. But when he puts on the face of the Bulldog he feels powerful, and he torments those around him. The Bulldog attacks the weak by barking at his victims, rendering them defenseless. Until the heroes come in, that is. The heroes teach the victims to help themselves. It's like a lifecycle of heroes, creating more heroes as they stand up against the Bulldog. In the end, those heroes become legends, and the Bulldog loses his mask and ability to torment.

Monica drags me to one of the comic photo booths where we take a slew of silly pictures. Then we visit the various stations with celebrities and hired comic heroes, which are scattered around the room for photo opportunities. We run into some coworkers and get distracted for a few minutes. The large screen at the front of the room starts playing a slideshow of the guests of honor at the event, each photo edited with comic elements featuring them as superheroes.

When Ferras and Katy Perry's song Legends Never Die plays, I know the event has officially started. As the chorus streams through the speakers and my coworkers are chatting excitedly, I'm trying to control my breaths. I know Gavin will be here soon if he hasn't already arrived. My focus moves from left to right, trying to maintain a casual look—but then I spot him. He's walking through the entrance hand-in-hand with Giselle. The butterflies take off like their first sign of light in my chest.

"He brought Giselle," Monica says quietly beside me.

I didn't know he was going to bring her, but seeing them together now is like a straight-up smack in the face. Gavin's handsome dominates the charts. I didn't think that was possible. The smile on his face as Giselle reacts to their surroundings; the way he picks her up so she has a better view of the art; the way she giggles when one of the heroes in costume approaches her . . . I've never seen anything so beautiful in my life.

"You okay?" Monica asks.

I nod, blinking back the tears, unable to look away from them.

Without another thought, I'm crossing the room and approaching the duo, a smile on my face. Gavin freezes, as if afraid of my reaction. Giselle just stares at me curiously. "Hi, Giselle."

She is already smiling, so I'm just happy that she doesn't stop when I speak to her. Gavin jostles her a bit and then touches his nose to her cheek. "This is my friend Chloe. Do you remember her? She's the one that fell on the floor."

Giselle giggles hysterically. Gavin smiles and meets my amused expression. "It's only funny because you're okay," he assures me.

He sets her down and holds her hand instead, then takes in what I'm wearing. I'm happy to see him slyly appreciating the ensemble. Monica and I decided to dress the part in the most professional way possible, but I think we look super hot in white button-down dress shirts tucked into our fitted, black pencil skirts. The buttons of our dress shirts are undone as if we've just ripped them open to reveal Superman shirts underneath. The suspenders were Monica's idea, purchased last minute from a thrift store to complete the look.

"You look amazing, Chlo."

I blush and thank him, suddenly remembering the last time he saw me in costume. I do my best to shake that thought from my mind. "You did a great job, Gavin. Everything looks so good." I want to ask him if he's heard anything more from the comic book sponsors and what's on the horizon for him. Or if he'll continue on another contract with BelleCurve. When I open my mouth, though, nothing comes out, thanks to my nerves.

"Well . . ." My eyes dart from Gavin to Giselle after a few moments of silence. I don't want to ruin their time together.

"Have fun tonight. Take lots of pics." I back away and almost crash into a cat suit-clad server holding a drink tray. Luckily, Gavin sees it coming and pulls me toward him, which means I crash into him instead. "Sorry," I say before trying to step away again.

Gavin's hold on me tightens. "Dance with me later."

"What about Giselle?" I ask.

He smiles. "I'll find her a dance partner too."

I blush and step away again, this time looking behind me first. "Okay."

I've never wanted to dance so much in my entire life.

When I find Monica again, she's taking a selfie with a costumed man covered entirely in green spandex. She hugs him a little longer than necessary and then runs over to me. "Oh my God. Did you check out his package?"

"This is a children's event!" I hiss, unable to stop my own laughter.

She shrugs. "I'm following him backstage. You never know what you'll find under those costumes. I may have just found my own Clark Kent."

She's ridiculous, and I love her. And now that I've approached Gavin, I feel better. I flip through the event program to see when the dance portion of the night is. There. The last hour. I frown. I have to wait three hours until then. What if Giselle gets tired and wants to go? What if Gavin changes his mind? What if he meets some hottie in costume and completely loses interest in me? Maybe I should have worn that Witchblade costume.

Just then, the emcee takes the stage and welcomes everyone to the event. One of our videos plays, and then Zachary Ryan steps out to the podium. The gushing commences as he begins his speech. Monica is particularly interested in every syllable of what's spoken. I know she has a crush on Zachary, but I'm starting to think this one goes beyond the norm for her. He might even return Monica's feelings. I've seen the way they flirt at work and how he always finds an excuse to talk to her the moment he spots her.

I turn my attention back to the stage. I've heard his speech before, and it's intense. In the end, Zachary agreed with me that he should tell his entire story so others can relate to him and see what possibilities life holds if you stand up and do the right thing. He brings the first tears of the night and an insane amount of applause. Just knowing I played a part in receiving that kind of reaction is all the reward I need. Without a doubt, the event is a huge success.

I hadn't really thought about how emotional tonight would be, but it is. The music picks up promptly at eight o'clock, directly following dinner, and my attention drifts around the room, hoping Gavin is trying to find me as well. We're always on the same page like that. But to my disappointment, Giselle is asleep in his arms and he's carrying her toward the exit.

My heart sinks to the bottom of my stomach and festers there, reminding me that Gavin's life is different now. He has a daughter who comes first—at least until she's eighteen, but then she'll still be all he worries about until she gets married . . .

I want to cry, and not because of the emotional speeches. I was looking forward to dancing with Gavin tonight and telling him that I want us to work, although I don't really know how. I just want him, and we can figure the rest out as we go along.

"Where's Gav?" Monica must sense my sudden sadness.

"He left with Giselle."

She wraps an arm around me. "I'm sorry, Chlo. Come on, let's go dance."

I shake my head, too afraid to speak and open the floodgate.

"Come on. You're not sulking the rest of the night. I'm sure she was exhausted. It's late for a three-year-old. You'll get your chance to talk to Gavin another day."

I don't know why that doesn't make me feel better. I guess I just had my heart set on talking to him tonight. After much coaxing, I allow Monica to manhandle me on the dance floor. She never does go after spandex man, and I love her for it.

Monica's the same height as me, so when she drops her head on my shoulder I burst into laughter. We slow dance until a hand on my waist brings me to a stop. "May I cut in?"

Can hearts stop and restart the same way computers need a good reboot now and then? I think that just happened. Gavin eases me away from Monica, who is already shuffling off with a grin on her face. He grips my waist with one hand and weaves his fingers through mine with the other. "Dance with me, Chloe."

I nod, trying to not make my swallow so obvious. I move easily into step with him as if we've been dancing together for years. In a way, we have. "Where's Giselle?"

"I asked Stacy to pick her up. I wanted to spend this hour with you. I hope that's okay."

Instead of answering, I release his hand and wrap my arms around his neck, pulling him closer so I can breathe him in. I've missed this scent. His arms tighten around my waist. I've missed these arms. When I lay my cheek on his chest, he kisses my head before resting his chin there. I've even missed his chin.

"The last drawing was beautiful. And the letter . . ." I pause and take a breath. "I'm really trying not to cry right now."

He lifts my chin so I'm looking into his eyes. "Don't cry, Clover. Just stop fighting this." He smiles hopefully. "There's no one else for me. Can you say the same?"

I nod without hesitation. "There's no one."

"Then what are you afraid of?"

"I don't know anything about kids, Gav. What if Giselle doesn't even like me? What if I suck at whatever my role will be? You're going to find out that my parenting skills are null. You should be with someone more . . ."

His laughter is silent, but he's definitely laughing at me. "I'm not asking you to be Giselle's mother. She's already got one of those. I just want you to be my girlfriend, and then my fiancée, and then my wife, and then one day hopefully the mother of our babies. Knowing you, you won't even have to try. It will come naturally. But don't worry about all of that today. Giselle will love you because I love you and because you'll love her. It's really as simple as that."

I'm still stuck on the words *my fiancée*. "You're serious? You want all that with me?" He's laughing again, so this time I smack his shoulder. "Stop laughing at me."

He lets out a frustrated groan and puts his mouth on mine, but he doesn't try to kiss me . . . yet. "I want you, and only you, for the rest of my life. You can call yourself whatever you want. We can go out and buy you a ring tomorrow. Chloe, I just want to love you, and I'm never going to want to stop."

Tingling snakes crawl up my spine and into my neck, releasing warmth throughout my entire body. His lips still don't move to kiss me, so clearly I attack him first. There's simply no other option. He returns my gesture and then pulls away, placing his lips against my ear. "If we keep going I'll get carried away, and I might scare off the kids."

I stifle a laugh and bury my head in the crook of his arm. When the music transitions into a fast song, Gavin leads me outside to the rail of the balcony that faces the brick wall of another building. It's not the most romantic view, but at least we're alone. He wraps his arms around me from behind and I mold myself to his front.

"I can see why you dedicate your art to supporting organizations and causes like this one," I say. "You must feel pretty damn good all the time. I don't think I've ever felt so . . . fulfilled."

"It all started with you. You realize that, right?"

I'm not sure I did. "You were drawing long before me."

"Yes, but my first comic book was about a girl who overcame bullying with the help of her two best friends. You inspired my first comic that dealt with real issues. And trust me, I realize comic books aren't meant to be serious, but what we're doing for these kids . . . I really think people will pick up on it. Instill good morals and values through unsuspecting mediums where violence usually betrays humankind. We have the opportunity to turn it into a positive."

His words plow into me, crushing my ability to breathe for a second. Gavin is sexy, and not just because he has a rock-hard body and an enchanting smile. His words are sexy too. I turn, wishing I could have watched his face when he said that. "That's all you, Gav. I may have inspired your first story like that, but this is what you're meant to do."

He nods, slowly, contemplating my words. "I think you're right, but I'm only happy doing it if you're beside me."

I smile. "Then you have nothing to worry about."

"You mean it? Are we doing this?"

I nod emphatically, unable to contain my excitement. "Yes."

He twists his face. "This was too easy. I don't believe you."

I laugh and pull his head down to mine. "Take me home and I'll make you believe me."

Gavin's eyes go wide, but I only see them for a second, because he's quickly tugging me through the event and out the front door. With one final glance around the room, I find Monica wrapped up in Zachary's arms, gazing up at him with a look that tells me she'll be full of stories for me in the morning.

CHAPTER 50

LOVING ME

CHLOE

Gavin won't stop kissing me, and normally I wouldn't argue with that, except it's been a while and I'm ready to pounce on him. "Gav," I say, trying to take a breath and plead with him at the same time.

He groans and pulls my blouse out of my skirt. That's better, but I'm still not naked. I help him out by tugging down the zipper of my skirt to pull it off, but it catches on my blouse and it's not going anywhere. "Shit," I moan.

Gavin tugs at the zipper, curses under his breath, and then looks at me. "How much do you like this skirt?"

"I hate it."

He gives me his sexy smirk and grabs the zipper, ripping the skirt in half in one swift motion. The fabric flies down my legs and then over his head, landing somewhere on the other side of the room. Gavin's mouth is already on me again. He rubs himself against my body and I feel every part of him. I've missed it all. His strength, his passion, and his endurance when it comes to our favorite kind of workout.

He's still not close enough. I reach for my blouse but it's too hard to unbutton while he's on top of me. Sensing my urgency, he leans back and allows me to slide it over my shoulders and down my arms. He tosses it to the side. I think he just likes throwing my clothes as far away as possible. I don't wait for him to attack me with his mouth again. I slip off my Superman shirt so that all I'm left with is my black lace bra and thong.

He groans when I reach for my heels. "Leave those on."

I pause, his demanding tone catching me off guard. It's kind of hot. "Okay." I scoot back on the bed, waiting to see what will happen next.

His shirt comes off first. Drool-worthy as always. I touch the corner of my mouth subtly, hoping I'm not actually drooling. And then his pants come off. I reach for my panties, but Gavin shakes his head. "That's my job."

Oh.

With the exception of my shoes, we're both in nothing but our underwear when Gavin crawls on all fours until he's hovering over me. I could get used to this view. My hands have a mind of their own, and they caress the lines of his chest and then his abs. My hand continues down to the V until my finger latches onto the waistband of his underwear. His breathing hitches, and I look up. He's just as ready as I am.

"I was going to take care of you first tonight," I say, giving him my best version of puppy dog face.

He closes his eyes and moans as my hand slips further down into his underwear. "Baby," he starts but isn't able to finish because of the visitor down below. "Ah." I can feel his muscles shake above me. I slide down the bed so my mouth is directly below him. With a tug of his underwear I take him in my mouth. "Fuck, Chloe. What are you—?"

I'm not exactly sure how to do this, but I did a little research and I'm taking cues from his moaning and cursing. When he tries to control the movements I use one hand to grip his thighs and the other to guide him into my mouth. "Ah." His shudders become more violent, telling me he's close. He pulls away, rolls onto his back and pulls me with him so I'm on top. "No more. I need to be inside you. Now."

I smile and gesture for him to help me take off my underwear. He shakes his head, his expression telling me he's changed his mind about him being the one to remove them. I think he's starting to warm up to me taking control. His hands move behind his head as he watches, eyes hooded and curious. A moment passes as I lower my panties to my ankles and I hear another curse. "You've never done that to me before. How did you know what to do?"

It's an afterthought. I can hear it in his voice that he's worried I'm not as innocent as he wants to believe. I shove my underwear aside, climb back onto him, and tell him the truth. "I asked, and I watched."

His lids shoot open so wide they practically fall out of his head. "You watched porn?"

My blush is burning the skin off my cheeks. "Maybe."

"Why?"

I shrug. "Because I wanted to know what to do when I—"

He pulls my head down so he can kiss me. I'm surprised when he pulls away soon after. "You're a great student."

Laughing, I wriggle above him. "Thank you. Can I show you something else I learned?"

"I'm all yours."

One swift maneuver later, the condom is secured, and with the help of my hands, I'm pushing down on him slowly. We both exhale loudly once I'm seated. I hold out my palms and he follows suit, holding his hands up to meet mine. I wait for our eyes to connect and then lift and sink down again until Gavin groans. Quickening my pace, we meet each other with every move until the space between my legs begins to burn, creeping into my stomach, and releasing in an intense explosion. I feel it everywhere, and it takes forever to fade. Not that I'm complaining.

Gavin's not far behind me. I try not to slow down but it's been so long, and my legs are weak and wobbly. He must sense this because he takes hold of the top of my thighs, controlling each movement until he lets go.

I fall on his chest, wondering why I waited so long to forgive him. My lips brush his and I sigh.

"What is it, Clover?"

Staring down at him, I'm overcome with love and happiness. "Thank you for loving me."

He pushes a strand of hair behind my ear before gazing back into my eyes. "You say that like I had a choice. My heart was made to love yours and vice versa. That's why, even when we were apart, there was always something missing. No matter how successful we were on our own."

"That's because there's no use enjoying *what* you love if you can't be with *the one* you love."

He smiles and presses his lips to mine. "That's exactly right."

EPILOGUE

GAVIN

She's my constant, the only light I need to keep my eyes on the road ahead. With her, I don't look back. If there's a fork, we choose the direction together, and if there's a bump, we hold hands and get through it as a team. Today, there is most definitely a bump, but the most beautiful kind imaginable.

After almost two and a half years together, I have fallen more in love with Chloe than ever before. It's intense, our love. It always was that one-in-a-million kind that doesn't come around for everyone, but we found it when we found each other.

I asked her to marry me in the spring on one of our afternoon hikes. While she was basking in sunshine and the euphoria of making it to the top, I knelt down and extended the ring box. She said yes, and we were married that fall. Today our love is even stronger. Now it's more like one-in-a-billion. Chloe Rivers is now Chloe Rhodes. It sounds good. Chloe joked that Rivers and Rhodes never did make much sense anyway. This way, we're sharing a pathway.

The beeping of machines, the sweaty hand in mine, and the voices talking excitedly in the room don't drown out the thumping of my heart. I'm certain my heart is beating louder than hers, and she's the one carrying our baby. *Our baby.* We're at the twenty-week appointment and we're supposed to find out the sex. Neither of us wants to be surprised. We're both anxious to begin preparing.

Chloe's certain it will be a boy, since my mom had two boys. I wouldn't mind if I had another girl for Giselle to be a big sister to. Stacy's baby boy is one now, and Giselle adores him. She's the best big sister.

"Mr. and Mrs. Rhodes?" We both look up, along with Chloe's mom, who has been more present since I proposed than all the years I've known her. It's been great for Chloe, especially now that she's pregnant. She has someone to talk to about it all— besides her friends and me, of course.

Chloe and Jazz have always had that sort of sisterly bond, and now Monica fits into the equation as if she was the missing component all along. Monica is putting herself through fashion design school at the Art Institute of Seattle while still working at BelleCurve with Chloe. And after Marco's apprenticeship on Wall Street, he accepted a job in Seattle as an accountant. He and Jazz are still waiting to have kids. With Marco's demanding work hours and Jazz's rub-down business picking up, they're perfectly happy.

"Hi, Dr. Langley," Chloe says in a sing-song voice. She does that when she's nervous. I bring her hand to my lips and kiss it.

"Let's get started, shall we?"

As the doctor rubs the device around on Chloe's rounded belly, which is sexy as hell, she's adjusting something on her computer. "So it looks like we're just after twenty weeks, and so far, all has been healthy. Is that right, Chloe?"

"That's right," she answers. "Why? Is something wrong?"

Dr. Langley laughs and shakes her head. "No, Chloe. Just asking the usual questions. How do you feel?"

Chloe shrugs. "I never really got morning sickness, I take my prenatals daily, and I eat well. Except for the occasional Pop-Tart."

I laugh because it's true. You'd think Chloe was an Olympic athlete the way she's been taking care of her body throughout this pregnancy. Not even I have that kind of willpower. But my girl will still manage to devour a box of Pop-Tarts a week. At least.

"Well, I think we can let the Pop-Tarts slide. Ah . . ." The doctor switches tones, and I guess it has something to do with the baby. "There's that little heartbeat. Do you hear it?"

At first all I hear is a whooshing sound coming from the speakers plugged into the machine, but then I hear it. A fast-pumping but consistent *whoosh-whoosh-whoosh-whoosh.* "I hear it," I say, amazed.

"I hear it too!" Chloe says with a radiant smile, and I know she's about to cry. Or maybe that's me. "Wow, it's getting faster."

I look at the monitor because the doctor isn't talking anymore. She's moving her device around on Chloe's belly as if she's looking for something. The pounding in my chest intensifies as I ready myself to hear the news. *Boy or girl.* "Well, that's interesting."

"It's a boy!" I shout, because obviously the doctor just saw his junk.

The whooshing has definitely doubled, and the doctor seems to be hovering over something. "Well, now that's a surprise . . ." the doctor responds, and her eyes dart between Chloe and mine. "And you're right, it is a boy."

"It's a boy!" Chloe's squeezes my hand and I lean over to kiss her, but something about the doctor's expression has me distracted.

"What is it, doctor?" My heart is louder than our baby's double-heartbeat pumping through the speaker, and I think I already know why. Chloe seems to catch on too.

"Doctor?" she asks nervously.

Dr. Langley points to the screen. "Well, usually we can tell as early as your first appointment, but it's definitely clear here . . . See that? Two amniotic sacs. One placenta. Congratulations, Mr. and Mrs. Rhodes. You're having identical twins."

Chloe and I exchange panicked glances. "Gav," she says, her voice low with warning.

I lean in and place a kiss on her temple. "I'm right there with you, babe."

While there's no question of our excitement, there's only one thing crossing our minds at this very moment. There is no way in hell our boys will be going anywhere near that treehouse.

Thank you so much for reading Chloe and Gavin's story! Want more stories from the BelleCurve world? Check out the entire series here —> www.kkallen.com/bellecurveseries. And keep flipping the pages for a special preview of the next book in the series, Under the Bleachers *(www.smarturl.it/underthebleachers).*

Want a FREE BOOK? Subscribe to my newsletter (smarturl.it/ GravityFreePrequel) and receive *Falling From Gravity*, a short story in the Gravity Romance world.

Under The Bleachers

Excerpt

Prologue

My lungs put up a fight as the burn intensifies with each sip of air. Adrenaline overrides every ache, pumping through me as my feet pound unforgivingly against the pavement.

Just another hundred yards.

I'm not sure why I decided to come. It was a last-minute decision, one I had talked myself out of before. To love someone despite their inability to love us back may be selfless, but it also leaves us vulnerable. Defenseless.

For two years I thought cutting ties would eventually numb the pain, but I'm starting to forget him ... and that just might be worse.

Rounding the corner, I see the bright lights of the high school stadium. They shine down like heaven to reveal one hundred twenty yards of lush greenery glistening from the dewy grass. Even from this distance, everything is in focus.

Players huddle near the sidelines as their quarterback's booming voice leads a chant that is echoed by his team. With a synchronized clap of their hands, it's like a bomb has just dropped at their feet. They fly apart like shrapnel, heading to their respective positions on the field. Their coach, average height with dark and thick stubble barely disguising the nervous tick of his jaw, hangs back, pacing and rubbing his palms against his outer thighs in anticipation.

And then comes the snap.

A boy wearing red and black grips the pigskin as his feet dance inside the pocket. They call him the Rocket because when he lets go of the ball, you can practically see the smoke trailing behind its spiral. But his arm isn't what makes him a star. It's when he moves outside of the pocket that the real show begins.

Speed carries him like he's the chariot of the sky, an unstoppable force. No one knows what he'll do next, but it doesn't matter. The field is his. His movements are so quick that he barely touches the ground, dodging one sack after another until he's lunging downfield in search of his next target.

I'm not nearly as fast, but a burst of energy tears through me as I skip the main entrance of the stadium and circle the perimeter. The disguised opening in the fence was created six years ago. I know, because it was my father's shears that cut into the steel.

When I press into the barrier it lifts easily from its pole, and I slip through.

Trespassing. Totally worth it to avoid a possible confrontation.

Before the loose fence slaps back against the post with a thwack, I take off again, my body cloaked in the shadows of the stands. For tonight, I'll let the bleachers be my mask.

I weave around the support beams, slinging myself forward like they're vertical monkey bars and this is my personal playground. Using the last beam to steady myself, I scan the slits between the stairs to find the best view of the game.

I can see at once that the boy has found his target. He rears back, preparing for launch while offense works like a well-oiled machine around him. His grace, unbridled. His timing, flawless.

And then, in the most perfect arc I've ever seen, the ball sails through the air and straight to the end zone, dropping easily into the arms of the receiver. Impeccable execution.

The crowd's roar is deafening as six points light up the jumbotron. A glorious rush surges through me as the spectators in the stands erupt into cheers and a thunderous beating of feet to wood surrounds me, making my nerves jump like Pop Rocks in my chest.

I adjust my blue and gray cap to ensure protection from the random articles that inevitably fall during every game as dirt and mold swirl through the air. All around me, food droppings, loose change, and God knows what else hit the gravel.

As much as I'd rather be in the stands with everyone else, stomping my feet and screaming until I'm hoarse, being part of the crowd is too risky.

Curiosity won. I'm here to see him ... but I'm not ready for him to see me.

The wounds are fresh. We're all still bleeding. But I'm not the victim in this story ... and I sure as hell am not the enemy.

CHAPTER 1 - CHOCOLATE COVERED EVERYTHING

Where's a buttery nipple shot when a girl needs one? *This* girl needs one. All this effort put into my Superwoman outfit, but not one hero or villain has asked me to dance tonight. Am I losing my touch?

It's not like my options are plentiful, anyway. The limited number of hot guys at this event are either off-limits or paid to be here and otherwise occupied with photo ops for the majority of the night.

BelleCurve, the creative agency I work for in Bellevue, Washington, has long been known for their work with nonprofits, but this event is far more impressive than any campaign I've seen.

Heroes and Legends, the theme of the evening, is an awareness event that recognizes kids who have lived through bullying. The room we've secured at Melrose Market in Seattle is alive with laughter and chatter, and comic sketches decorate pop art backdrops on every wall to match the theme.

But as great as tonight has been, with just an hour left of the event, I'm ready to hang my heels.

Like the resourceful chick I am, I've managed to make do riding the buzz of flirtation to get me through this night. And I've done so void of the same fairytale expectations most girls have. My heart isn't set on finding Prince Charming among these superheroes in tights. Tights are hot and all, but let's face it: Prince Charming is as real as those pretty packages nestled snug between those muscular legs. Every time I see a costumed man with that ridiculous bulge I want to grab hold of the decorative swell, give my potential prince a seductive smile, and whisper—*we all know it's a sock.*

I laugh, shifting my focus to a plate of goodies being carried by a passing Wonder Woman. Taking in the sweet scent as it floats by, my mouth immediately waters. Now *there's* a pick-me-up. There's no better distraction than this beautiful arrangement of white and dark chocolate, melted and hardened upon the most perfect set of strawberries.

I think I'm in love.

I track Wonder Woman to the dessert table on the other side of the room where a chocolate fountain draws a small crowd. Why didn't I see this earlier? Because there it is: the only thing sure to turn this night around for me. I snake my way through the crowd and toward my own personal heaven.

Chocolate. The food of the gods, as my grandma used to call it. And I totally agree. It's the answer to prayers. Emotional relief. A form of currency. An aphrodisiac. Raw and dark. White and saccharine. Milky sweet. Mouthwatering. It's all good; I don't discriminate.

My mom, my sister, and I moved in with my grandmother a

year after my parents' divorce. I was thirteen and having the most awkward year of my life. Newly separated parents, new school, new home—and a sister who was in every way, shape, and form perfection. My grandmother, who had taken a turn for the worse after a broken hip, spent most of her days reading the newspaper, watching CNN, and mumbling to herself or to anyone who would listen. Usually, that anyone was me.

She had spent most of her adult life working as a tour guide at the chocolate museum in Cologne, Germany. She reveled in the history of the Mayas and the Spaniards and the cacao trees that produce fruits the size and shape of a football. Every now and then she'd get extra sentimental, and we would watch *Willy Wonka* with a box of assorted chocolate she'd sneak into the house. My mom would have murdered us if she had known. It would have been worth it. I'll never forget the sound of Grandma giggling when Augustus Gloop fell into the chocolate river.

Sorting through the memories of that time in my life is never fun, as it's mostly filled with confusion and false hope. But I can always rely on the moments of comfort with my grandmother and chocolate to bring a smile to my face. Like now, as I'm weaving through a thinning crowd to get to the dessert table.

When the waitress I've been stalking steps away, I swoop in, snatching a strawberry from the collection and planting it between my lips. Closing my eyes, I sink my teeth into the sweet fruit and rich chocolate, swallowing with a deep moan.

Holy mother of flying bananas, that's good. I go for another bite, this time closer to the stem, the berry filling more of my mouth as I bite down.

Someone clears their throat behind me in an obvious attempt to get my attention. I ignore it.

Seriously? Worst timing ever. I'm a little busy here.

"Glad I stuck around for this."

Panic shoots through me the instant I hear his voice. That subtle Texas drawl that takes me back to my life before moving to Washington. A drawl that he probably doesn't even realize he still has after living in Seattle for three years. Over the two years I've known him, it's certainly faded.

Swiveling around, I lock eyes with the host of tonight's event. *Zachary Ryan.*

Otherwise known as the sexiest man to walk planet Earth. That's my definition of him, anyway. He's more commonly known as Zachary Ryan: NFL quarterback, Super Bowl champion, and Washington's most eligible bachelor (according to Seattle Magazine). And now he's watching me go to town on a chocolate covered strawberry like I'm in bed with it.

Zach suppresses a smile beneath his unshaven stubble as I nearly gag on my dessert. Please tell me this is not happening right now.

He's a mesmerizing sight with ocean-filled eyes that stare back at me from under the curve of his brow. And his light brown hair, closely shaven at the sides, is long enough on top to style with his signature lift.

Giving him an awkward, crinkly-eyed smile, I hold up my hand in a gesture for him to wait. I grab a Batman cup from the table, spit into it, and toss it into the nearest trashcan.

What a waste of a perfectly good strawberry. Then again, if Zach is my consolation prize, I'll take it.

After using my tongue to swipe my teeth clean, I look up to find Zachary, who's given up the fight to hold back his amusement. His laugh is deep and rumbly and all sexy man. It's a sound I've quickly become familiar with since he seems to always be laughing at me.

Who does he think he is?

I tilt my head and glare at him. "Can't a girl eat some dessert without getting interrupted? I could have choked to death."

His laugh settles into a teasing smile. "Good thing for you I know CPR."

Now that wouldn't have been so bad.

Zachary's lips curl and he nods to the plate of desserts. "*That,* Monica Stevens, was the best entertainment I've had all night."

Now it's me trying to hold back a grin. First, why does he feel the need to always address me so formally? *Ugh.* Politeness is a weakness of mine; I'll admit it. And Zachary Ryan is the epitome of polite. And charming. And handsome. Unfortunately, the list of positives is far too long to go over in this moment. The man can't be perfect, but I've yet to find a single flaw.

Second, the fact that he even knows my full name ... six points to him. But I won't let him have the extra point.

"Not saying much about yourself, since you're the entertainment and all."

His eyes narrow, but he never loses his smug expression. "I'm just the host. I wasn't entertaining anyone tonight."

"I think if you're hosting an event, you're considered part of the entertainment. Besides, your profession *is* broadcast to millions, which means you *are* an entertainer. No getting out of this one, Zachary Ryan." I throw his full name at him like he did mine, but it doesn't have the same effect. I don't know why, but I feel like this puts me at a disadvantage. I don't like that. In fact, I don't like that Zachary might always have the advantage over me. His charm is like a stun gun to my wit.

He chuckles, low and husky. My eyes track him as he steps forward, closing in until we're almost touching. In a momentary state of paralysis, I just stand there, leaving little room for him to reach around my body to the dessert table. I might even breathe him in as he passes. But to my defense, who wouldn't want to sniff the NFL's hottest new quarterback if given the opportunity? It would be silly not to.

My lungs expand, pulling in the crisp, woodsy scent that wafts off his body. If heaven had a scent, this would be it. Whatever it is contrasts with the strong citrus blend coming from his carefully styled hair, bleeding seduction. Heaven and seduction. A potent combination. A dangerous elixir to my already raging hormones.

He rights himself to standing, still in front of me, this time grinning with a chocolate covered strawberry teasing his lips. I swallow and he winks, acknowledging my reaction.

When he bites into the chocolate, I have to steady myself on the table at the sight of his strong jaw and beautiful lips in action. Zachary closes his eyes as he chews, a smile lifting his cheeks once again.

By the time he tosses the stem into the trash, I'm hot everywhere and glaring at him. He's an evil man. And now he's doing that thing where he smiles playfully and rests his teeth on his tongue.

"Was that as good for you as it was for me?"

I really do try to hold back the laughter climbing up my throat, but the way he's waiting for my reaction—he's too good.

"I think you should stick to football."

With a wink, I start to move past him. His hand, calloused and strong, catches mine, halting my steps. Everything seems to fall still except the beating of my heart, which is now thundering in my chest.

"Where do you think you're going? You owe me a dance."

Letting out a breath of air, I scold my heart for quickening its rhythm without the support of the rest of the band. It just takes off at its own pace like it thinks it's earned a solo.

"I don't recall owing you anything. In fact, I think you're the one who owes me for interrupting my meal."

"Your meal?"

"Dessert," I deadpan.

"I hate to break it to you, but dessert isn't a meal. It's a snack that comes after dinner."

My mouth hangs open. Did he just call dessert a *snack*? My grandma's probably rolling over in her grave right now. If she were here, she would set him straight.

"Okay," I say with a forced smile. "It's obvious we're not going to agree on this one, so I'm going to be the bigger person and let you change the subject."

Zachary's eyes twinkle as he tugs on the hand he's already holding. I should probably take that away from him...

"Deal," he says. "Since I owe *you*, I'll do you the honor of dancing with you." This time a full smile lights up his face, and his white, straight teeth practically blind me. "Don't break my heart. Dance with me, Monica Stevens."

"Tell you what." I start with a challenge, as if I really have to bargain with the man to give him what he wants. *What I want.* "You can stop addressing me by my full name. Then I'll dance with you." He starts to agree; I see his head lift in a half-nod when I realize I'm making this too easy on him. "Just one dance."

With a pinch of his lips, he tells me he wants to argue, but he won't. Still, satisfaction relaxes the lines on his forehead once we fall into step on our way to the dance floor. He's respectfully silent as he guides me, as if worried a single word could blow his entire game plan.

His grip on my hand is impressive. Engulfing even—and I like it. For a fleeting moment, I imagine this is what Belle must feel like when she dances with the Beast. Small, yet important. Strong, yet vulnerable. Afraid, yet too proud to show it. And protected— not that I need protection. Though it should be noted that Zachary Ryan is a far cry from anything beastly, unless you're referring to his physique.

I glance down at the fingers threaded through mine, considering their magnitude. My friend Chloe has a theory about hands, one that I can't seem to stop thinking about now...

"What are you gawking at?"

I look up and shake my head, feigning complete innocence. "Nothing."

When we reach an empty space on the dance floor, he turns and pulls me close to his body. If I weren't so distracted by everything Zachary Ryan, I would attempt to resist him—or at least cross my arms across my chest and make him apologize for laughing at me earlier.

But who am I kidding? I'm partially to blame for this. For the past month, we flirt, we laugh, we poke fun at each other, and then when he has me all flustered, we part ways. So far it's been frustrating, but safe.

I'm not sure what's changed.

One Month Earlier

"Well, look who's making a statement. Fashionably early suits you, Zachary Ryan. But I'm afraid your fanfare hasn't arrived yet." I give him a dramatic bat of my lashes. "Your appointment with Chloe isn't until eleven."

Forming an overly exaggerated pout, I attempt to distract him from my efforts of blindly clicking the mouse, fumbling to minimize the open window of my computer screen.

He isn't fooled. I swear he hasn't taken his eyes off me since he walked through BelleCurve's main doors, but his expression wears all the conviction he needs to torment me. He already saw.

"Plants vs. Zombies, huh?" He struts closer, straightens his arms, and wraps his thick fingers over the edge of the counter. "The water levels are the hardest."

I clear my throat, fighting a blush while darting a look at my screen where my favorite game is prominently displayed. There's no point in hiding it now. The executives are at a conference in New York and everyone else who matters is already in meetings. Zach wasn't supposed to arrive for another thirty minutes.

I quickly tap on the computer's sleep icon anyway, fighting the heat that rushed through my body the moment his tall and wide frame pushed through the glass doors. Am I embarrassed to be caught messing around on the job? Sure. But more than anything, I'm thinking Zachary Ryan should come with an alert signal so everyone can prepare for his arrival. Or maybe he should carry a fire extinguisher to blast away the heat he leaves behind his every move.

Yeah. That.

His looks are off the Richter scale, but it's those big, blue eyes that speak directly to my ovaries and capture my attention whenever he's near.

Folding my arms on the desk, I try to pretend I'm not affected by the hard lines of his jaw shielded by a layer of closely shaven stubble or the light brown of his hair that's begging for a rough comb-through of my fingers.

"I'm on a cigarette break."

His face twists with disappointment. "Monica Stevens smokes?"

"Of course not, but good to know that would have been a problem for you." The corners of my mouth turn up into a full-blown smile.

Ignoring my insinuation, he leans into the reception counter. "Funny girl. Humor me. Why do you need a smoke break if you don't smoke?"

I shrug as if the answer is obvious. "Smokers are rewarded with breaks throughout the day. That's discrimination to nonsmokers. Nonsmokers must demand equal rights."

A throaty chuckle passes his lips, making it hard to not stare directly at them and imagine how well they'd fit with mine. "I'm sure your fellow nonsmokers would be proud of your advocacy."

"Oh, they would be. Aren't you?" My cheeks lift before I can stop them.

"Am I proud of you?" There's a twitch of his lips before he speaks again. "That depends."

Tilting my head, I have to bite my bottom lip to keep the ridiculous smile on my face from gaining wattage. "Depends on what?"

He nods to my computer screen. "Show me your strategy."

My jaw drops in mock horror. "You can't have my secrets. We barely know each other."

With eyes locked on me, he stares a little too long. "If you won't give me your secrets, I'll find them out, Monica Stevens. Trust me." And then he stealthily moves around the counter.

Something stirs in my belly, but I push the feeling aside. He's on my side of the desk before I can come up with a retort, but he doesn't attack me for my computer like I expect. Instead, he pulls up the stool in the corner of my workstation and sits beside me.

"C'mon, let's see this. I've got"—he glances at his watch—"twenty-five minutes to kill before my meeting. If you can't impress me with your zombie killing skills, I might have to file a formal complaint with your manager."

"My manager?" I level him with my eyes. "I work for the CEO, and she loves me."

"She loves me more."

Caught in the undertow of his crystal blue eyes, I don't doubt it. Tearing my gaze away, I swallow and wake up the monitor. "Sandra isn't here this week, so that will be a challenge for another day."

The corner of his mouth tips up. "Looking forward to it."

PRESENT DAY

I lose my train of thought when Zach's free palm grips my waist and gently guides me toward him until I'm mere inches from his body. He's watching me intently, like I'm the football he's in possession of tonight. Never taking his eyes off the ball. I guess I don't mind. Zachary is passionate in every sense of the word. He's someone who means every gesture, every look, every syllable—and right now, he's studying me as if he's mapping out his next play.

As he moves us around the floor with progressively advanced steps, I'm both impressed and amused. He's observing me, waiting for me to break, for me to miss a step. But I don't. I won't.

Zachary Ryan doesn't know it yet, but he's just met his match on the dance floor. Just because I don't carry a deep southern drawl doesn't mean I didn't put in my time. I know every line dance, I can manage a horse with ease, and I sure as hell know my way around a shooting range. Looking at and listening to me, you wouldn't guess I'm a country girl at heart. I've learned to hide it well since leaving Rockwall, Texas, and my love for stilettos trumps my love for my embroidered leather cowboy boots. Most days.

I'm thoroughly disappointed when the song transitions to a slow one, and it's not because of the tempo change. I was just starting to enjoy this.

One dance. My words. Is it too late to take them back?

He must be thinking the same thing because both of his hands are on my hips now, and his grip only tightens, but not in a way that hurts. It feels ... *good* to be possessed like this.

"That wasn't a full song. I get another one." His voice is low but commanding, forcing me to pretend that his grin doesn't ignite the wick below my waist.

I should say no.

"That's only fair."

My arms slide up his navy blue suit jacket and over his shoulders until I'm clasping my fingers behind his neck, my eyes never leaving his. Zachary is nearly a foot taller than me, and I like that I feel small in his massive arms.

Who would want to let this man out of their sight? A true southern boy living in the Emerald City is a rare find. You don't find charm like this everywhere you go. But he fits in well here, better than most, blending in easily with the city slickers in their flashy suits and designer denim.

Hell, I fit in well too, but every now and then I'll hear something in Zach's tone that brings me back to my life growing up in Texas, and I'm not sure how I feel about it. There's a reason I moved away from the small-town life and found my home in the city of Bellevue, just across the lake from Seattle. And it's not something I like to think about.

"You can dance." Surprise is evident in his voice, and the crinkle between his brow tells me he just might be impressed too.

"You're an excellent lead." It's the truth, and it earns me a smile as his hands move from my waist to the small of my back. After many months of greeting Zach when he'd arrive at Belle-Curve, showing him from one room to the other, serving him cold waters, buying his catering, and booking his appointments with our staff, it's a little hard to believe that I'm in his arms now. "You're not the only one with some country in this joint, you know?"

His eyes widen at my confession. I hadn't planned on telling him about my roots. It's not something I talk about, so people just assume I'm from around here. "Rockwall, Texas," I answer before he can even ask.

"No way. Did you drop your twang on your way to the city?"

I laugh. "You're one to talk."

His smile grows bright. "My momma told me I'd lose it the moment I stepped foot over here. It didn't happen that quickly, but being surrounded by a bunch of Neanderthals did the trick eventually." He winks.

"Mine wasn't hard to drop once I moved here." Especially since I *tried* to drop it, leaving everything I possibly could behind me.

"Well, look at that. I feel right at home now. I guess I saved the best for last." He presses his lips together as his eyes lock on mine. It takes me a minute to realize he's referring to me being his dance partner.

"Not how I look at it," I say, shaking my head. "It doesn't feel so good to always be the last one picked for a team. Not that you would know the feeling."

"Oh, I know the feeling. Did you miss my speech?"

I shiver in response, because his speech tonight brought everyone to tears. I don't think I'll ever forget his experiences with bullying.

"All right, then." I shake off the distraction, putting my challenge face back on. Because this is what we do well. We spar. We flirt. We laugh. "Don't think I haven't seen you dance with every other girl in here tonight."

His chest expands, and he seems to grow taller. "So, you've been watching me."

I shake my head. "It's kind of hard to miss a two-hundred-thirty pound, six-foot-three NFL player and a giggling, doe-eyed girl twirling across the dance floor."

"Tell me, why aren't *you* all giggly and doe-eyed? You've obviously got my trading card memorized." He suctions me in, the small gap between us vanishing as I'm now pressed flush against his chest.

It takes a second to adapt to the hard body melded with my soft one.

Deep breaths, Monica. Hold it together.

"I suppose those girls felt special that you asked them to dance."

His lip curls. "And you?"

"Don't."

His smirk grows into a full-blown smile. "Hmm. Well, you should. Just to set the record straight, the music only started thirty minutes ago, and you're the only one I've asked to dance. Those other girls asked me. It would have been rude for me to say no."

Oh. "Is that right?"

"It is. I've had my eye on you."

Unease creeps through my veins. This was supposed to be a fun exchange of innocent flirtation. Why does it feel like something else?

"I'm calling your bluff," I try again. "We both know your eyes have been elsewhere."

This time I'm serious and referencing my friend and coworker, Chloe Rivers, who Zach was crushing on when they first started working together. Nothing ever happened between her and Zach, but that doesn't change the fact that he asked her out—twice. Talk about a blow to my ego.

"Ouch." He frowns. "I'll give you that one, but that's not really fair. I thought you were dating that comic artist guy, Gavin. But I figured it out about a month ago. He's really turned out to be a problem for me, and I don't even know him beyond the conference room."

I laugh, knowing how right he is. Gavin and I started working for BelleCurve around the same time two years ago, and there was an immediate attraction between us. I'd only met Zach twice the entire first year of working there. He didn't start frequenting the office until one year ago, and that's when Gavin and I ... well. We were something, but we were never official. Deep down I always knew his heart belonged to someone else, and since I wasn't looking for anything serious, it worked for us both.

"So then you finally saw the shining light that had been standing in front of you for two whole years." I sigh, removing a hand from his to fan myself dramatically.

He grabs my hand back as his lips curl up slowly. "As a matter of fact, it was just like that. You were sneaking a piece of cake from the catering station outside the conference room when someone flicked on the entry light. Prettiest damn deer I ever saw. Wide-eyed and so guilty."

His laughter is infectious, but I roll my eyes, hoping to hide the fact that his honesty throws me off balance. He's playing my game, and he might be doing it better than me. There's a reason Zachary Ryan needs to be kept at a distance. I just need to remember what that reason is.

"You going to come out to any of our games this season?"

There it is. That's the reason right there: football. Not my thing.

At any other sporting event, consuming copious amounts of booze, squeezing into a youth-sized jersey, and losing my voice in the crowd would be an exceptional time for me. But not football.

"Chloe mentioned getting tickets to a game. You never know." I bat my eyes up at him. He'll get no promises from me.

There's a lift of the side of his mouth. "Ah, I can't take the anticipation. How about I leave you tickets for our first home game?"

"Really?"

He eyes me suspiciously. "I guess it depends on who you bring. Chloe, sure. A guy, no."

His directness is so surprising, I laugh. "Why not? Guys are into football, aren't they?"

Narrowed eyes glare back at me in a challenge. "Well, that's kind of the problem. We have a female fan presence quota we need to meet. If I give you these tickets, it's a girls-only deal." He shrugs in mock helplessness.

"No promises, Zach."

"Have you been to a Seattle game before?"

I wrinkle my nose. "No."

"Then you need to come. You won't regret it. The energy in that stadium is insane."

The hope in his expression lights me up just enough to ignore the warning signs, and I give him an overly dramatic eye flutter. "You mean I have a choice?"

I should remember, Zachary is competitive. If I'm going to throw sarcasm and wit his way, I should expect he'll be ready with a response. What I'm not expecting is for him to lean down and press his full lips to my ear. A breath escapes before he speaks, and it dances across my skin, raising the hairs on my arms and neck. *Ah.*

"You always have a choice with me, Monica." He doesn't pull away, and I feel my body tense in his arms, waiting for what comes next. "But just so you know, I can be very convincing when I want something."

It definitely doesn't sound like we're talking about football anymore. He leans back to study me as I swallow the ball of nerves in my throat.

"No response?" he challenges. "That might be a first."

Heat creeps up my neck as I struggle to find words. Any words will do. "I wouldn't want to distract you from the game."

He winks. "Not a chance, Cakes. And I promise not to blame you if we lose."

Cakes?

An eyebrow raise is enough of a question to get him laughing again before answering. "What? You have a problem with that name too? You're the one who made me promise not to call you by your full name." He shakes his head. "No take-backs. This one's sticking. Cakes it is, for more reasons than one."

I'm not even going to ask. There's silence between us, just as my eyes catch sight of two familiar faces heading eagerly for the door. I sneak a look at the retreating figures of Chloe and my ex-fling buddy, Gavin.

It's not weird, really, and I would never call him my *ex-fling buddy* out loud. I've been rooting for them to hook up since Gavin confessed their history to me over lunch one day. Chloe had just started working as creative writer at BelleCurve, and he was not handling it well. Turns out there was a treehouse full of issues they had to overcome. Their history is deep and complex, but it's beautiful. I'm just hopeful them leaving together now means they've finally learned how to communicate.

I'm so lost in thought that I don't notice the hand lift from my waist and turn my chin, commanding my attention. When I stare back into Zachary's eyes, my heart does a chaotic dance of its own. He's a beautiful man, with kind, blue eyes that transport me to the Caribbean. His brows, slightly downturned toward his nose, give away his permanently curious nature. But my favorite feature is his aquiline nose that speaks to his strength and dominance. It sits perfectly above those full lips—lips that turn up into perfect curves and widen into the most teasing and beautiful smile—a smile that makes it impossible not to grow taller in his arms, as if he's the sun and I'm powerless without his light.

It's at this moment that I need to remind myself that no man is perfect. Not even Zachary Ryan. I admire him for what he stands for, for his charm and playfulness. I like him, even. But I know guys like him too well, and while I'm more than happy to partake in some mutual flirtation, he isn't fooling me.

For the past month, the back-and-forth banter has been steady but fleeting. Every time he comes to BelleCurve, he stops by my desk without fail. We banter and flirt until it's time for him to run off to practice, or to a press conference, or wherever the heck it is he goes. It's never been a big deal. Besides, flirting comes as second nature to me. It's how I communicate with guys, ensuring I always maintain the upper hand.

It's good to feel wanted, but it bothers me that there's more effort involved than usual in maintaining the upper hand with Zach. It makes me uneasy. Something tells me this man could crush me if given the chance.

In arms that feel far too good—too addictive—I recognize this for what it is, what it should be ... and what it cannot be.

Zachary Ryan is a fairytale. And I don't believe in those.

Keep reading Zach and Monica's story Here —> www. smarturl.it/underthebleachers

DEAR READER,

I hope you enjoyed Chloe and Gavin's story! If you have a few minutes to spare, please consider leaving a review on your preferred retailer. Reviews and sharing your love for our stories mean the world to an author. Just a few lines goes a long way!

I love connecting with my readers! Here's where you can find me.

Get Weekly Updates + a FREE Book:
smarturl.it/KK_MailList
Instagram:
Instagram.com/KKAllen_Author
Facebook:
Facebook.com/AuthorKKAllen
TikTok:
Tiktok.com/@k.k.allen
Website:
www.KKAllen.com

Join Forever Young

Want to join my Facebook group?

Enjoy special sneak peeks of upcoming releases, exclusive giveaways, LIVE events, enter to win ARCs, and chat it up with K.K.

Facebook.com/groups/foreveryoungwithkk

ACKNOWLEDGMENTS

If you've gotten this far then I want to thank YOU, the reader, first and foremost for taking this journey with me. *Up in the Tree-house* was inspired by a scene from *The Descendants* (now titled *Taken, Enchanted Gods Book 3*) and I'm ecstatic with how the story turned out. But it would have never gotten to this point without some very special people—friends and family who have been nothing but supportive along the way.

To Jagger, my son, my number one. Never lose your innocence. To T.R., for creating a monster (me). Two years ago, you pushed me to do something so far out of my comfort zone, I changed my name and swore I never would tell a soul I published a book. And then . . . well, six books later, I just thank you for always encouraging me to keep going. To my parents, especially my mom, who is always one of the first to read my novels!

Shauna Ward. I'm forever grateful to Lilo for introducing us. You are, in all aspects, a fantastic editor. I can't wait to see where your career takes you. Another book down, another million more to go. Thank you for your honesty and always pushing me to take my writing to the next level. Monica and Zachary are waiting for us.

Richard Duerden. You know I adore you and your peer editing madness. I don't know how I lucked out in finding you but I'm so grateful. I trust you to read anything! Always my first reader, editor, and enthusiast of my work.

My Beta readers! Where my ladies at? I will come up with a name for you. Something Diva'ish. All three of you are some of my favorite people ever and helped *Up in the Treehouse* become what it is today. I mean it. Joy Eileen, not only are you a kick ass writer and Beta reader, but you allowed me to steal your Jackholes for a scene. Baha, does that mean Kill is mine now? Cause I'm not giving him back. Suzanne Merrick-Zewan, you, my friend, are fantastic. I cannot wait until you publish your first novel. Getting to talk backstory and character intricacies with you is now one of my favorite things ever (preferably over a glass or five of wine). Thank you for the insightful and invaluable feedback. Stephanie Kneese, another amazing writer. You've been one of my biggest cheerleaders since the day we met (and even before that!). I'm always so appreciative of your support. Can't wait to see you next year!

After all the hard work that went into putting this novel together, I had to have the BEST cover, and that's what I got. Sarah Hansen of Okay Creations, your talent blows my mind. I can't wait to work with you for Monica and Zachary's story.

To every book blogger who accepted a review copy of *Up in the Treehouse*. I am so appreciative of your time and support. A special thanks to Derna, Michaela and the rest of the ladies at New Adult Book Club of Goodreads! You're an amazing group and I can't wait to work with you again in the future. Another special thanks to Sandy Lu from (YouTube's @SandyReadsaLot). I met you two years ago through #IndieBooksBeSeen but you've continued to read and support my novels and that means the world to me.

Last but not least, I want to give a special shout out to my social media family! Facebook, Twitter, Instagram—You all make this journey so much fun! Let's never stop sharing success stories, opportunities, and each other's work.

To everyone. Keep reading. Keep reviewing. Keep spreading the love. Until the next time.

Much Love,
K.K. Allen

K.K. ALLEN NOVELS

Up in the Treehouse
Haunted by the past, Chloe and Gavin are forced to come to terms with all that has transpired to find the peace they deserve. Except they can't seem to get near each other without combatting an intense emotional connection that brings them right back to where it all started... their childhood treehouse.

Under the Bleachers
Fun and flirty Monica Stevens lives for food, fashion, and boys... in that order. The last thing she wants to take seriously is dating. When a night of flirty banter with Seattle's hottest NFL quarterback turns passionate, her care-free life could be at risk.

Through the Lens
When Maggie moves to Seattle for a fresh start, she's presented with an unavoidable obstacle—namely, the cocky chef with a talent for photography and getting under her skin. Can they learn to get along for the sake of the ones they love?

Over the Moon

Silver Livingston has spent the past eight years hiding from her past when the NFL God, Kingston Scott, steps off the bus to mentor a football camp for kids. Kingston wants to be anywhere but at Camp Dakota... until he sees her. The intoxicating woman with the silver moon eyes, the reserved smile, and the past she's determined to keep hidden.

Dangerous Hearts (A Stolen Melody, #1)
Lyric Cassidy knows a thing or two about bad boy rock stars with raspy vocals. In fact, her heart was just played by one. So when she takes an assignment as road manager for the world famous rock star, Wolf, she's prepared to take him on, full suit of heart-armor intact.

Destined Hearts (A Stolen Melody, #2)
With stolen dreams, betrayals, and terrifying threats--no one's heart is safe. Not even the ones that may be destined to be together.

British Bachelor
Runaway British Bachelor contestant, Liam Colborn, is on the run from the media. When he gets to Providence to stay with his late brother's best friend, all he wants is a little time to regroup from his time on a failed reality show. That is, until he meets the redheaded bombshell nanny who lives in the pool house.

Waterfall Effect
Lost in the shadows of a tragedy that stripped Aurora of everything she once loved, she's back in the small town of Balsam Grove, ready to face all she's kept locked away for seven years. Or so she thinks.

A Bridge Between Us
With a century-old feud between neighboring families with only a

bridge to separate them, Camila and Ridge find themselves wanting to rewrite the future. It all starts with an innocent friendship and quickly builds to so much more in this epic second chance coming of age romance.

Center of Gravity (Gravity, #1)

Lex was athleticism and grace, precision and passion, and she had a stage presence Theo couldn't tear my eyes from. He wanted her...on his team, in his bed. There was only one problem... He couldn't have both.

Falling From Gravity (Gravity, #1.5)

Amelia was nothing like Tobias had expected. Even after all the years—of living so close to her, of listening to her giggle with his sister in the bedroom next to his—he hadn't given much thought to his sister's best friend, until a secret spring break trip to Big Sur changed everything.

Defying Gravity (Gravity, #2)

The ball is in Amelia's court, but Tobias isn't below stealing—her power, her resolve, her heart. When he wants a second chance to reignite their connection, the answer is simple. They can't. Not unless they defy the rules their dreams were built on and risk everything.

The Trouble With Gravity (Gravity #3)

When Sebastian makes Kai an offer she can't afford to refuse, she learns taking the job will mean facing the tragedy she's worked so hard to shut out. He says she can trust him to keep her safe, but is her heart safe too?

Enchanted Gods

As powerful forces threaten the lives in Apollo Beach, Katrina can't escape the evocative world of mythological enchantment and evil prophecies that lurk around every corner. If only she wasn't cursed.

Find them all here: www.kkallen.com

ABOUT K.K. ALLEN

 K.K. Allen is a *USA Today* best-selling and award-winning author who writes heartfelt and inspirational contemporary romance stories. K.K. is a native Hawaiian who graduated from the University of Washington with an Interdisciplinary Arts and Sciences degree and currently resides in central Florida with her ridiculously handsome little dude who owns her heart.

K.K.'s publishing journey began in June 2014 with a young adult contemporary fantasy trilogy. In 2016, she published her first contemporary romance, *Up in the Treehouse*, which went on to win the Romantic Times 2016 Reviewers' Choice Award for Best New Adult Book of the Year.

With K.K.'s love for inspirational and coming of age stories involving heartfelt narratives and honest emotions, you can be assured to always be surprised by what K.K. releases next.

Printed in Great Britain
by Amazon

78037731R00230